Detective Inspector Jack Dawes Mystery Book 2

THE
BLUEBELL
KILLER

An enthralling British murder mystery with a twist

FRANCES LLOYD

D1262918

JOFFE
BOOKS

Revised edition 2019
Joffe Books, London

Please join our mailing list for free Kindle books and new releases.

www.joffebooks.com

ISBN 978-1-78931-227-0

CHAPTER ONE

WEEK ONE — SUNDAY

The early-morning sunlight glinted on the rippling water, breaking through the mist that hovered, wraithlike, over the surface. A mute swan, neck erect and wings folded, paddled serenely down river, glancing only briefly at the two figures on the bank. Detective Sergeant Malone and Detective Constable Pinkney stood under the overhanging willows, watching the swan's wake lap gently around the naked body caught up in a clump of reed irises. It was floating face down — or it would have been, except the body had no head.

The 999 call had come in at 6 a.m. and the stricken police constable who attended the scene had immediately radioed Control. They, in turn, performed a rapid finger-tip pass to the Murder Investigation Team. DC Pinkney arrived first, scrubbed and shaved and wearing his best suit. Pinkney had recently joined MIT as a fast-track graduate and couldn't wait to get his white and perfectly even teeth into his first murder investigation. His unbridled enthusiasm and eagerness to impress were beginning to make DS Malone's crooked, nicotine-stained teeth start to ache. He'd already warned the lad never to wear anything to a murder scene that he wouldn't want to see covered in blood, guts and vomit, yet here he was, at sparrow's cough, done up like a double glazing salesman.

'Shouldn't the SOCO team be here by now, Sergeant?' Pinkney checked his watch for the eighth time.

Detective Sergeant Malone, short, fat and balding with two days' growth of beard, swallowed the last of the elderly pork pie he had snatched hastily from his malodorous fridge before he left home. 'Give 'em a chance, son. It's still only half past six and it is Sunday.' He licked his fingers and wiped them down his trousers. 'Blimey, Pinkney, what's that pong?' Malone sniffed the air like the veteran bloodhound that he was.

Pinkney blushed. 'It's me, Sergeant. New cologne. "Stud in Action". My girlfriend bought it. It's a bit powerful first thing in the morning. Sorry.'

Malone wrinkled his nose. '"Stud in Action", eh? Well, I suppose it smells better than "corpse in river" but not much.'

Some five minutes later, the SOCO transit van nosed its way into the narrow lay-by that was little more than a foot-path running parallel to the river. Suddenly it was well-ordered chaos with police tape around all the trees, securing the area from unauthorized personnel such as the press or just the morbidly curious. Scenes of Crime Officers in wellingtons and white coveralls picked their way along the river bank, measuring, photographing, examining, searching and bagging anything that might turn out to be evidence. Malone and Pinkney were shepherded politely out of the way. They ambled across to the roadside to wait for Detective Inspector Jack Dawes, the senior investigating officer assigned to the case.

DS Malone, unkempt and largely unwashed, rubbed his grizzled chin and yawned. 'The guv'nor should be here soon. He radioed to say he was on his way.'

'What's Inspector Dawes like to work for?' DC Pinkney had met the boss only briefly and was keen to make a good impression on his first murder investigation.

Malone was unequivocal. 'Straight as a die. Everything by the book. No knee-jerk hunches, no short cuts and no sloppy ground work. If you cock something up accidentally, he won't be pleased but he'll back you. If you cut corners or bend the rules, he'll nail your bollocks to the station notice board.'

* * *

Kings Richington was a green and leafy town nestling beside a quiet stretch of the Thames. It was sufficiently distant from the more urbanized developments of Hampton and Teddington to have become the favourite retreat of the rich and famous. Here were the luxury homes of High Court judges, cabinet ministers, Harley Street surgeons and premiership football stars.

Detective Inspector Jack Dawes parked his car beside a row of pollarded lime trees, standing like sentries along the well-kept avenue. Gracefully for a big man, he uncoiled his wiry, six-foot-three frame from the driver's seat. A crooked nose, jug-ears and off-centre grin were evidence that his features had undergone considerable repositioning during his rugby-playing days but, nevertheless, he presented a formidable and imposing figure to police colleagues and villains alike. He locked his car, mildly observing that car crime seemed highly unlikely in such peaceful and affluent surroundings. But then, so did murder.

'Morning all.' DI Dawes nodded to Malone and Pinkney who had stepped smartly across to meet him. 'What have we got, Bugsy?'

DS Malone had joined the police service as a constable in 1976 when the popular musical, with its eponymous 'gangster', was first released. Inevitably, Malone had acquired the nickname 'Bugsy' and now there were very few coppers still in the job who knew his real name was Michael. It was doubtful whether he could remember himself. The reason he had risen only to Detective Sergeant after so many years in the service had more to do with attitude than ability. Malone, laconic and cynical, didn't believe in overdoing it. At the same time, he had scant regard for the shiny-arsed uniform-dummies who directed operations from the safety of their offices, where they spent their time scrutinizing overtime claims and constructing itemized timetables. But he liked and respected Jack Dawes. Jack was a hands-on copper. He got results by getting out on the streets and nicking villains and he wasn't afraid of getting his hands dirty. Malone gave him what little information they had.

'Pretty gruesome one this time, guv. It's a bloke but the body's been hacked about a bit.'

'I only get the gruesome ones,' said Jack, ruefully. He glanced at his new DC. 'Are you all right with this, Pinkney?'

DC Pinkney was eager to get started. 'Oh absolutely, sir. No problem at all, sir.'

'OK. Let's take a look at him.'

They strode back down the avenue and along the narrow path to the river bank where the once tranquil crime scene was now heaving with 'experts'.

'Who found the body?' Jack asked, checking out the multimillion-pound, mock-Tudor mansions with their cabin cruisers moored along the riverfront. 'Don't tell me — it was a gorgeous foreign au pair, taking the borzois for their early-morning walk.'

Malone grinned. 'Unfortunately not, guv. A big hairy lorry driver spotted it from his cab. He's long distance so he'd parked up by the river to take his break and eat his breakfast.'

'Where is he now?'

Malone pointed. 'Over there in the bushes, fetching it back up again.' He craned his neck to see. 'Looks like it was a bacon roll. Terrible waste.'

Jack sympathized. His own stomach was prone to queasiness when faced with mutilated cadavers first thing in the morning. His wife, Corrie, professional caterer and successful proprietor of 'Coriander's Cuisine', was always telling him he should eat breakfast before he went out on a case. No doubt she was right but he hadn't yet decided which was more unpleasant — throwing up because his stomach was full or passing out because it was empty.

'Has the pathologist arrived yet, Bugsy?'

'Yep.' Malone jabbed his thumb at a battered Land Rover tucked in behind the SOCO van. 'It's Big Ron.'

Jack whistled softly. 'Blimey. Keep your heads down, lads.'

'Who's Big Ron?' asked DC Pinkney, innocently.

Malone wagged a warning finger. 'She's Doctor Veronica Hardacre to you, son, and don't give 'er any back-answers. She's the best in the business and she bites the heads off tender young coppers like you.' He ran a finger around the inside of his collar. 'Come to think of it, she's 'ad a pretty good chomp at some of us old 'uns.'

The body had now been taken from the water and laid out on the bank, still face down. Ideally, SOCO would have erected a canvas tent over it, but its proximity to the river's edge and the overhanging willows made that impractical. The moist, clammy skin was pale and dimpled like a dead chicken. Torn sinews and shattered bone fragments protruded from the stumps where the head and both hands had been hacked off. DI Dawes's first thought was that it was going to make identification a bit tricky. His second thought was that he was glad he'd skipped breakfast.

Doctor Hardacre was on her hands and knees, poking the sodden corpse with a podgy, latex-clad finger. She was a big-boned woman, strong and muscular, with bristling black eyebrows and a moustache to match. Her biceps bulged as she lifted the torso to examine the severed end of the neck.

'Morning, Doc. I take it suicide's out of the question?' quipped Malone, cheerfully. He was rewarded with an icy glare.

'I can do without comedians first thing on a Sunday morning, Sergeant.'

Big Ron returned to her preliminary examination and the three detectives watched in respectful silence until she carefully eased the body over onto its back. Jack Dawes's eyebrows shot up, Pinkney swallowed hard and Malone instinctively clapped a protective hand over his crotch. Whoever had removed the victim's head and hands had also sliced off his genitals.

Doctor Hardacre did not react except to say, calmly, 'Well, somebody certainly had it in for the poor devil.'

'Any thoughts on the cause of death, Doctor?' Jack asked, eventually.

'How the hell should I know?' she snapped. 'Lack of a head can sometimes do it! On the other hand, he may have had his skull bashed in first or half a dozen bullets through his brain. I don't suppose you've found the head? No, I didn't think so.'

Jack trod carefully, conscious of Big Ron's well-documented lack of regard for senior police officers who considered themselves more important than the due process of science. 'Sorry if I'm pushing you, Doctor, but Chief Superintendent Garwood was notified of the incident early this morning and apparently he's a bit twitchy about this one. He says the commander spends a great deal of time with friends who live in the area — dinner parties, golf, the yacht club, that type of thing. The esteemed residents of Kings Richington aren't accustomed to crime in their midst and they're expecting the commander to ensure it's cleared up as quickly as possible before the press get hold of it.'

Big Ron sniffed, confirming her supreme indifference to the Chief Superintendent's twitchy nerves or the commander's potential social embarrassment. She continued lifting and prodding.

DC Pinkney edged closer, feeling brave. 'Can we learn anything about the murderer from the way the head and so on were removed, Doctor Hardacre? Might he have been a surgeon or a butcher, for example?'

Big Ron glanced at him and sighed, pityingly. 'That kind of convenient forensic evidence, young man, occurs only in television dramas to provide clues for an incompetent detective who otherwise wouldn't be able to detect his arse with both hands.' She addressed DI Dawes. 'My initial opinion is that this man's head, hands and genitalia were amputated very soon *after* death and in a hasty, clumsy way, probably by someone with an axe. Or even a very large knife. Anyone could have done it, with no kind of professional expertise at all. He didn't die here so it's probable he was dismembered where he was killed, then transported to the river for disposal.'

'So the rest of him could be in another part of the river or somewhere else entirely?' commented Jack, gloomily.

'Indeed. And don't assume yet that the perpetrator was a man or even that it was murder. I have no preliminary thoughts regarding the cause of death. I'll know more after the autopsy.'

'Is there anything else that might help us?'

She pointed to the legs. 'You will observe that although the deceased was, in the main, flabby and out of condition, he had quite well-toned calf and thigh muscles.'

'Why is that?' asked Malone.

'I don't know, Sergeant. Maybe he had a bike.' She struggled to her feet, wheezing. 'One thing is certain, though. Whoever mutilated him and dumped him in the river didn't want you lot to find out who he was, did they?'

'How long has he been in the water, Doc?' asked Malone.

'Best guess based on what I can see at present, I'd say not long — less than six hours. I'll be more specific after the autopsy.'

Jack chanced his arm. 'Any likelihood of an early one, Doctor Hardacre? Only, as I say, the Chief Super is expecting MIT to come up with a quick result.'

'I'll sprint back to the mortuary and do it straight away, shall I?' she said, sweetly.

'Could you?'

'No, I bloody couldn't! I've got three stiffs waiting on my slab already, each with a full set of body parts. Your jigsaw puzzle will have to wait until tomorrow. Who knows? You might have found a bit more of him by then.' She stuffed all her paraphernalia back into her bag and motioned to the mortuary men, hovering like vultures. 'All right, gentlemen, you can take him, now.' She turned to DI Dawes. 'Post-mortem tomorrow. Eight o'clock sharp. Don't be late. I'm off to get some breakfast.' She stumped away towards her battered Land Rover, her sturdy legs encased so tightly in brown surgical stockings that Malone's rumbling stomach was irresistibly reminded of two sizzling sausages, about to burst their skins.

* * *

Saturday night had been moonless and cloudy with misty rain just beginning to fall. The woman pulled up the hood of the pram to keep its precious contents dry, then the hood of her coat, to protect her hair. She had arranged it very carefully in an elaborate bun on top of her head. Her appearance was important to her and she spent a great deal of time ensuring it gave the right impression. But, of course, looks were not as important as good breeding.

She liked to walk along the Old Richington Road, especially at night. Even though it was poorly lit and shadowy, the lights were nearly always on in the houses. Nice people lived here, respectable people from good families like herself. Other people's homes fascinated her. They looked so safe and protected. She liked to look in the windows as she passed. Sometimes, she could see their furniture and what kind of carpet they had. It was ten o'clock and the nice people in their immaculate houses were settling down to watch the news on TV or read the paper. In one house, it looked like they were having a party. She could see people with glasses of wine in their hands, chatting and laughing. She hadn't been to a party for a very long time.

The woman didn't hear the car. She was halfway across the road with the pram when the blinding glare of its head-lights transfixed her through the drizzle. It was a big, powerful car, moving fast. Like a wild animal, the vehicle suddenly reared up and leapt at her, tearing the pram from her grasp and sending it high in the air. Then a terrible crunching blow, screaming pain and finally she was sucked down into a merciful pit of black oblivion.

* * *

The area car discovered her body around midnight, lying on the pavement in a crumpled heap. They slid to a halt alongside her, just managing to avoid the pool of blood and shards of broken glass. The police officers covered her with blankets and retrieved her pram from the front garden of a nearby house while they waited for the ambulance.

At precisely 6 a.m. on Sunday, just as the early-morning sun was glinting on a headless corpse, floating in the rippling river at Kings Richington, the hospital doctor pronounced the woman dead. There were no witnesses to the hit-and-run. None of the respectable people in the nice houses had seen or heard anything.

CHAPTER TWO

Monday morning. Seven-thirty. Half an hour to spare before the autopsy on Mr X, as they had now labelled the headless corpse. DS Malone and DC Pinkney were sitting round Jack's desk, mulling over what they knew about the murder victim so far, which was very little.

'I suppose, as he was found in the river, we shouldn't automatically rule out death by drowning,' offered DC Pinkney.

Malone looked scathing. 'Why would someone drown him, pull him out, chop off a few bits, then sling him back in again? It don't make sense.' Incredibly, he pulled a greasy hot dog out of his pocket, unwrapped it and clamped his jaws around it. The smell of fried onions pervaded the room, as fried onions tend to do.

Jack wrinkled his nose. 'Dear God, Bugsy, how many of those have you eaten this morning?'

'Only three, guv. I suffer from fluctuating blood sugar; it's up and down like a whore's drawers. The quack reckons I'm borderline carbohydrate dependent. If I don't keep eating, me brain shuts down.'

'God help us if the canteen ever shuts down. We'll have to install a fast-food van in the car park just to keep you warm and breathing.'

'I can see why the murderer might cut off a man's head and hands to hinder identification,' said Pinkney, thoughtfully. 'But why his wedding tackle? You could hardly identify a bloke from that.'

'Don't you believe it, son,' mumbled Malone, through a mouthful of hot sausage and even hotter mustard. 'There are toms up west who could identify their regular punters blindfold, just by the feel of their — '

'Thank you, Sergeant,' interrupted Jack, hastily. 'Spare us the benefit of your misspent youth in Vice Squad. But you're right, Pinkney, it's a particularly vicious thing to do. If it hadn't been Kings Richington, I'd have said it was a gangland killing carried out by the type of sadistic thugs who aren't averse to nailing you to a garage door, just as an example to other thugs.'

'You mean it could be some kind of grudge execution, sir? A city drug baron eliminating the competition in a turf war?'

'Possibly, Pinkney. But where's the logic of transporting the body all the way out to the country in order to dump it in the Thames? You could do that equally well on some anonymous bit of waterfront in the city with much less risk of being seen. No. In the absence of any evidence to the contrary, I reckon we have to treat Mr X as relatively local to Kings Richington, where he was found. Whoever bumped him off, chopped him up and chucked him in did it in a hurry. Mind you, they probably hoped he'd be carried a lot further down river before he was found, rather than become caught up in the reeds.'

'My guess,' said Malone, 'is that he either had a ten-foot dick, or maybe his name tattooed on it, and it was sliced off by a woman with a score to settle. She did him in, then took the carving knife to him in a fit of jealous rage. Big Ron said it could have been done by a woman and those rich, classy birds can be bloody vindictive.'

'All we know so far, until after the autopsy,' said Jack, 'is that he was already dead when he was mutilated and he'd only been in the river about six hours. Not much to go on, is it?'

'Don't forget his well-toned calf and thigh muscles, sir,' added Pinkney.

Malone grinned. 'Big Ron reckoned he had a bike.'

'I doubt if anyone in Kings Richington would be seen dead on a bike,' said Jack.

'He wasn't seen dead on it, was he?' said Malone, dead-pan. 'He got off it once he was dead. Probably found he couldn't steer properly. I expect we'll find it in the river. You can always dredge up a bike from the bottom of the Thames, even in the posh areas.'

'Maybe he was a politician who went about on a bicycle to demonstrate he was reducing his carbon footprint,' offered Pinkney, deadly serious.

Malone snorted. 'They only do it in front of the cameras. That wouldn't be enough to build up his leg muscles.'

'Perhaps he jogged or rode a horse. Polo's quite popular among the upper classes.'

'Come on, Pinkney.' Jack stood up. 'Enough spurious speculation. You and I are going to attend the autopsy. When we know the cause of death, we might get a few more clues to his identity. In the meantime, Bugsy, I want you to organize a house-to-house in the area around the crime scene. There's no CCTV on the river bank to help us so we'll have to do it the old-fashioned way by knocking on doors. Find out if anyone saw anything or whether anyone's been reported missing. But go careful and be polite. We don't want complaints from any of the commander's dinner party chums.' He grinned. 'It could be severely career limiting, especially for Chief Superintendent Garwood.'

* * *

DI Dawes and DC Pinkney, suitably masked and gowned, stood a respectful distance from Doctor Hardacre in the icy-cold chill of her white-tiled autopsy room, where an acrid, antiseptic smell left a lingering aftertaste of something unpleasant.

Doctor Hardacre was, as always, brisk and matter-of-fact. 'Age around forty-five, I'd say. Well nourished. A bit too well nourished, actually. Very flabby around the stomach but as I mentioned before, quite well-toned calf and thigh muscles. No birthmarks, scars or tattoos.' She lifted the arms and examined the stump ends. 'That subcutaneous bruising around the wrists could be ante-mortem, indicating that he'd been bound prior to death, but it might also be the result of the hands being hacked off in a brutal manner, either by someone in a rage or someone in a panic.' She pointed to the feet. 'There's similar bruising around his ankles so he may well have been tied up or perhaps he simply wore exceptionally tight bicycle clips.' This was as close as the pathologist ever got to humour.

Doctor Hardacre picked up her scalpel and with surprising delicacy for such a substantial woman, made a Y-incision from either shoulder to the lower end of the breast bone and then downwards in a straight line over the abdomen to where the genitalia would have been. Then she plunged in both hands and removed all the main organs in one dripping, armful of offal, as was her custom. It was at this point, recalled Jack, that rookie DCs turned green and keeled over. Pinkney showed no such tendency, even stepping closer for a better view. It was Jack who felt the waves of nausea wash over him. He'd lost count of the number of autopsies he'd attended but it happened every time. He reckoned it was the smell as much as anything. He mopped his cold, clammy brow and went to lean against the mortuary fridge for a bit.

'Would you care to examine the contents of the stomach, Detective Inspector Dawes?' Doctor Hardacre thrust a stainless steel bowl under his nose. 'In this case, they're a possible confirmation of the time of death and might even assist with identification.'

'No thanks,' said Jack, queasily waving the white flag, 'I'll take your word for it.'

'Please yourself. The body was discovered at six o'clock on Sunday morning after about five or six hours in the water. The corpse was mutilated and chucked in the river very soon after death, which means he died sometime between midnight on Saturday and one a.m. on Sunday.' She turned to DC Pinkney who was clearly enthralled, even behind his mask. 'The physiological time of death, young man, is the point at which the deceased's body, including vital organs, ceased to function. The food in the deceased's stomach had hardly broken down at all, so chances are, his last meal was his dinner, eaten around eight or nine o'clock on Saturday evening. No obvious sign of any drugs or toxins, incidentally, but I'll do a full analysis later.'

She poked about amongst the partially digested food in the bowl. DC Pinkney moved in closer to look over her shoulder. DI Dawes remained where he was, leaning against the fridge. Doctor Hardacre tutted. 'This man bolted his food appallingly — not properly masticated at all.'

'I reckon indigestion was the last thing on his mind,' said Jack, trying not to look at the empty space where the deceased's mind should have been.

'The meal,' continued Big Ron, 'consisted of meat pâté, white fish, roast poultry and some sort of chocolate muck.'

'Isn't that a piece of potato and an asparagus tip?' asked Pinkney.

'Well done, Detective Constable. And our man finished off with big chunks of Stilton, swallowed almost whole. It's all sloshing about in a large quantity of red wine . . .' she stuck her nose in the bowl and sniffed hard,'. . . possibly a Burgundy.'

'Any idea of the vintage?' muttered Jack.

It was then that Big Ron delivered her *coup de grâce*, as she so liked to do at the end of an autopsy. 'The deceased was in poor physical shape. If he was in the habit of wolfing down several courses of rich, fatty food and the best part of a bottle of wine for his dinner, it's little wonder he died of a heart attack.'

'What?' exclaimed DC Pinkney, bitterly disappointed. 'You mean Mr X wasn't murdered after all?'

'As a pathologist, DC Pinkney, I'm required to consider four categories of death when determining how a person died. Natural causes, homicide, accidental death and suicide. This man died from acute myocardial infarction due to occlusion of his coronary artery. In my book, that's natural causes and I'll provide the full report later in the week. However, the fact that someone saw fit to conceal his identity by stripping him naked, mutilating his body and chucking him in the Thames may lead DI Dawes to conclude that there are other considerations to be investigated, not least unlawful disposal of a body that shows possible indications of having been bound prior to death.'

'But if he wasn't murdered, why go to all that trouble?' Jack wanted to know.

She shrugged. 'You're the detective, DI Dawes. I just run the abattoir.'

* * *

Coriander Dawes sliced the liver and kidneys into a colander and washed them under the tap. Blood ran in scarlet rivulets down the drain, like the consequence of some unspeakable act of carnage. Mixed grill was Jack's favourite and after an early-morning autopsy and a long day trying to get a lead on this latest case, he'd be in urgent need of a good dinner and a glass or two of wine. She'd heard all about the mutilated corpse they'd found in the Thames at Kings Richington from Cynthia Garwood, the Chief Superintendent's wife and one of Corrie's old school chums, but she wouldn't mention it unless Jack did.

Unlike most husbands who will happily go into hours of boring detail about widgets and statistics and balance sheets at every opportunity, Jack wouldn't talk about his work at home. Whenever she asked the smallest, most innocent question, just to show interest, he'd give her a long lecture about how he was unable to discuss any details of his murder cases. They were always hush-hush and could only be disclosed to specific individuals on a need-to-know basis because leaked information jeopardized convictions, etc., etc. It was the usual load of policemen's balls. But it didn't stop him from using her to keep an eye on people and listen for information when it suited him and without giving her the smallest clue why she was doing it. It was hardly surprising that she usually ended up having to work things out for herself, and naturally the law of averages decreed that occasionally — just occasionally, mind you — she got it a bit wrong.

Jack worried that her track record of interfering in dangerous criminal situations would eventually get her badly hurt; she'd already had a couple of near misses. And police work, he declared, was none of her business so the less she knew about it, the better. She said that was totally unfair because without her masterly intuition and tireless assistance, he would never have cracked so many crimes or rounded up some of the nastier members of the underworld. There was no denying it; she had a talent for detection. She was convinced that it was thanks to her he had been promoted to DI and transferred to the Murder Investigation Team, but you'd never get him to admit it.

Mind you, she didn't have much time to help him with his detection work these days. Her reputation as a top-class caterer had spread and business was booming. Most of the senior police officers' wives hired 'Coriander's Cuisine' for their cocktail and dinner parties. So did the wives of many other public figures in the affluent area into which they had moved after Jack's promotion. They had married late in life, Corrie having been married once before, briefly and disastrously, and Jack having worked so hard to reach DI that he had never managed to sustain a relationship without getting called away during crucial moments of it. But having stumbled across each other, they somehow managed to fit their busy lives together to their mutual and continuing satisfaction and were, when they stopped to think about it, very happy.

Jack would have been surprised to learn how much Corrie knew about the influential people in the neighbourhood. But the integrity of her business depended on her ability to keep information to herself, unless, of course, it turned out to be vital evidence in solving a murder.

She heard Jack's key in the door and uncorked a bottle of Bordeaux. He wandered into the kitchen and bent to kiss her, something of a stoop as she was only five feet tall to his six-foot-three.

'Have you had a good day, darling?' She poured him a glass of claret of a capacity that the self-appointed wine police and other killjoys strongly advised against.

'Not really.' He perched on one of the kitchen stools and passed a weary hand across his brow. 'Bit of a blighter, this current case. I think it's going to take a while to crack and Garwood's leaning on me because Sir Barnaby is leaning on him.'

'I think Sir Barnaby is a real sweetie,' declared Corrie.

'Oh, do you?' said Jack, surprised. 'And when have you rubbed shoulders with our revered commander?'

Corrie smirked smugly. 'Last Saturday night. He was at a *very* distinguished dinner party that I catered in Kings Richington and he was kind enough to say my roast guinea fowl was the best he'd ever tasted.'

'Good for you.' Jack sipped his wine absent-mindedly, trying to think of some inspired way of determining the identity of his corpse. There had been no local reports of anyone missing and so far neither the autopsy results nor the house-to-house questioning had produced anything meaningful. DNA sampling, while an undoubted boon that had revolutionized detective work, was little use with identification unless you had something to match it against. If only they could find the rest of him. And given that Big Ron had confirmed the bloke died naturally, he did wonder whether it was still an appropriate case for MIT anyway.

Corrie glanced sideways at him while continuing to slice onions with a professional dexterity and speed that made Jack anxious for her fingers. 'Still no joy with Mr X, then? Bad enough to drop dead of a heart attack, but to be dumped in the river with your bits chopped off, instead of being returned, intact, to your loved ones — that's just awful. Have you tried Missing Persons? He's been dead two days. You'd think someone would have noticed he'd gone.'

Jack groaned. 'Thank you for that, sweetheart. I'd never have thought of it on my own. Have you considered that it might have been his "loved ones" who chopped him up and dumped him, rather than fork out for a funeral. How come you know so much about it, anyway?'

'Cynthia Garwood. We were talking about it when she called to confirm the buffet menu for her next "At Home".'

'How bloody pretentious! And she had no business discussing an ongoing case.'

Corrie grinned. 'She was always a terrible gossip at school, couldn't keep anything to herself. But we weren't discussing the case as such. She just happened to mention that according to the autopsy report, poor Mr X at least died with a full stomach.'

Jack nodded, surprised that Chief Superintendent Garwood let his wife read confidential police documents over his shoulder. 'That's right. Wherever he ate his last meal on Saturday night, he went right through the menu. His stomach contents were a gourmet's delight.'

'What had he eaten, just out of interest?' Corrie was curious about all things culinary.

Reluctantly, Jack cast his mind back to when Doctor Hardacre and Pinkney were poking through the remains of Mr X's undigested dinner in a steel bowl.

'Pâté, white fish . . . er . . . roast poultry with potatoes and asparagus and some sort of "chocolate muck", according to Doctor Hardacre. And he finished off with — '

'Stilton?' suggested Corrie.

'Yes, that's right.'

'And the wine was red Burgundy?'

'That's what Big Ron said but I'm not sure her knowledge of red wine is as comprehensive as her knowledge of red blood.'

Corrie was becoming increasingly animated — always a dangerous sign, thought Jack. He braced himself to rein her in.

'Now, isn't that the strangest coincidence? The menu for that *very* distinguished dinner party that I catered on Saturday night was Ardennes pâté, fillet of sea bass, and roast guinea fowl with new potatoes and asparagus. The "chocolate muck" could have been my three-chocolate truffle pie. Flippin' cheek! Mind you, it probably wouldn't look too appetizing after a couple of hours in someone's stomach. Then I served Stilton with the port.'

Jack thought about it. As coincidences go, it was such a long shot it was almost out of sight, but it was the best lead he'd had so far. It was the *only* lead he'd had so far. He supposed it was always possible that Mr X had been one of Corrie's dinner party guests. The time and location would have been right.

'Can you remember who was at this very distinguished dinner party?'

''Course I can. It was the twentieth wedding anniversary of Sebastian and Annabelle Whittington. You must know Sebastian: he's that famous prosecution QC, practically a celebrity. Whenever you open *The Times*, there are pictures of him being handsome and histrionic on the steps of the Old Bailey. He's enormously successful; they reckon he'll be made a judge very soon. The Whittingtons own that amazing, stone-fronted country house overlooking the river, with split level decking and an eighty-foot mooring at the end of the garden. It's got six en suite bedrooms, an enormous open plan drawing room and independently controlled under-floor heating. Not that I paid much attention, you understand. I was there to prepare a dinner party.'

Jack smiled. 'Of course you were, darling. Who else was there?'

Corrie closed her eyes and pursed her lips, mentally working her way around the Whittingtons' very expensive, antique oak dining table.

'Annabelle's mother and father — Lord and Lady Eustace Henley-Ffoulkes. He's a High Court judge and absolutely loaded, so I reckon it's Annabelle's father's money and influence that have pushed Sebastian to the top of the legal profession so quickly. Then there was Sebastian's Head of Chambers, a bit of an old bore who smokes those fat, smelly cigars at the end of a meal. His wife came wearing a long velvet cloak, like Madam Arcate in Blithe Spirit.' Corrie paused, thinking hard. 'Oh yes, Martin Laidlaw, the MP, was next. Completely out of his depth in that company, I'd say, but at least he had the good sense not to peddle his dreary Marxist views about distribution of wealth and the power of the proletariat. His wife, Jennifer, is very attractive if you fancy a neurotic, simpering Barbie doll with a tattoo and a personality bypass. She came in her own car, a bloomin' great Chelsea tractor, then left half way through the main course with a migraine. I don't think she should have been driving at all, after all the champagne she put away. If you ask me, Jennifer Laidlaw needs a good slap. Next to her, was the dear old bishop, bless him. He's a distant cousin of Lord Eustace, Annabelle's father, and he has a very healthy appetite for a man of the cloth. On his right, there was a Harley Street surgeon from Dubai, simply gorgeous looking, he does cosmetic work for ageing but wealthy women with more money than sense. I believe he did Annabelle's last face lift and tummy tuck.' Corrie counted on her fingers. That's only ten; there were twelve around the table. Oh yes, of course. Sir Barnaby, your commander, and his wife. Nasty blouse. Her neck's too short for a mandarin collar and she doesn't suit mauve.'

Corrie looked triumphant but if she thought that the recital of this all-star cast would impress her down-to-earth husband, she was disappointed. Jack had whipped out his notebook, a constant companion, and was writing down the basic facts without the embellishments, although he had to admit that Corrie would make a marvellous witness. Nothing seemed to escape her.

'What time did you leave?'

'It would have been about midnight by the time I'd cleared up and packed everything away. Everyone had gone by then.'

'Right.'

'Aren't you going to ask me if I noticed anything unusual?'

'Well, did you?'

Corrie became conspiratorial. She looked from left to right as if checking for eavesdroppers then lowered her voice, even though there was no one to hear besides Jack. 'While I was in the kitchen, collecting my serving dishes, I heard Sebastian and Annabelle arguing in the dining room — quite loudly, actually. I wasn't eavesdropping with my ear to the door or anything. He was saying something about having to go to his chambers to do some urgent work.'

'What — at midnight?'

'That's exactly what Annabelle said. She asked him why it couldn't wait. She said she had never, ever, complained about him going out late at night so he could at least have the decency to stay with her on their anniversary. I heard her say, "You promised me you wouldn't, Sebastian. Not tonight." in a hoarse, angry whisper.'

'And what did Whittington say?'

'He said it was important to him and he'd only be gone an hour or so. Then the door slammed and I saw him leave in a cab.'

'Hasn't he got a Roller?'

'Yes, but he'd had too much to drink to drive it anywhere.'

Corrie capered about excitedly, quite certain this was the breakthrough Jack needed in identifying his corpse. 'Mr X was one of the men round the table, wasn't he? He was at the Whittingtons' dinner party!' Corrie grabbed the phone, full of confidence in her snap judgement, as always. 'Shall I ring Annabelle?'

'What, and ask if any of her male guests dropped dead on Saturday night after eating your food? I don't think so, do you?'

Corrie put the phone down and chewed her lip. 'Mm. I see what you mean. But it's worth following up, isn't it?'

'It might be. Leave it to me, please.'

Corrie sidled up to him and sat on his lap. 'You know, you're very masterful when you're questioning witnesses.'

Jack grinned. 'I know. What's for supper?'

'I've made you your favourite. Mixed grill with the liver and kidneys smothered in a thick, glossy, red wine sauce, just as you like it.'

Jack gulped as waves of mortuary nausea returned. 'Autopsies tend to take away my appetite, sweetheart.'

She ruffled his hair. 'Poor darling. Shall we just have a sandwich and an early night?'

Jack looked hopeful. 'Does that mean we're going to make love?'

'No, it means we're going to make a sandwich.'

CHAPTER THREE

On Monday evening, while Corrie Dawes was pouring Jack his restorative glass of wine, Jennifer Laidlaw, wife of Martin Laidlaw MP, was pouring herself another large gin. She knew she was very drunk even though it was still only seven o'clock. Happy hour, she thought, and laughed bitterly. She hadn't been happy for a whole hour since she moved into this bloody awful, hideous little house. In fact, there was very little about her life that was remotely happy. She reached for the tonic to add to her gin then changed her mind. Tonight, most especially tonight, she needed it neat. Her nerves, always taut to breaking point, were screaming in her head, threatening to split it in two.

At the age of thirty-one, Jenny should have been supremely content. A privileged, only child of wealthy, doting parents, she had grown up with the expectation that life would provide everything she wanted without any effort on her part. The most expensive public school education had been followed by two years at an exclusive college in Switzerland, then her own apartment in town, sleeping until noon then shopping until cocktail time. And at night, the endless clubs and parties.

It was at one such party that she met Martin Laidlaw. At first, she found his raw, uncompromising ambition exciting. He was, he told her, the last of the working-class rebels. Unlike the other young men she knew who drove her about in Porsches and BMWs, he ripped up the town on a powerful Harley Davidson, jet black from fender to fender. His plebeian attitude to women — especially women like her — was dismissive, almost rude and she regarded it as a challenge. She didn't begin to understand his entrenched, socialist principles so she simply ignored them. Martin, despite himself, was captivated by Jennifer's perfect body, her wild recklessness and the fact that her fatuous, extravagant lifestyle was the very antithesis of everything he believed in. One day, he promised her, he would be a cabinet minister, maybe even prime minister. Then he would bring down the despised 'old school tie' regime and evict the ruling-class elite who still controlled the Establishment, with their bloated snouts firmly in the trough. There would be no such things as 'old money', nepotism or preservation of an unelected upper house. Like many such politicians, Martin Laidlaw's socialist ideals did not, apparently, preclude him from seeking ultimate power and control for himself under the pretext of ensuring freedom from such power and control for the oppressed 'workers'.

Being a shallow, foolish woman, Jennifer believed all his impossible claims and to everyone's complete amazement, they were married three months after they met. Nine months after that, she gave birth to their son, Timothy.

But that had been seven years ago and the promised power and status had not materialized quickly enough for Jennifer. She became bored with being an inconsequential MP's wife, tired of having to pretend she cared about the community, and sick of living in a plain, unremarkable little house at the unfashionable end of Kings Richington, instead of the elegant, luxury home on the river that her parents had wanted to buy them. Martin had said it would send the wrong message to his constituents.

Laidlaw had, by now, developed an outsized chip on his shoulder. He was an embittered, resentful man, convinced that he was unfairly handicapped by his north country accent and obvious lack of breeding. He believed his beloved Party had taken a wrong turn and it was now demonstrating many of the behaviours that he had pledged to eradicate. What he completely failed to see was that his immature, extremist posturing was no longer fashionable and modern government had moved on, while he had not. Finally, he adopted the stance of poacher turned gamekeeper, union leader turned managing director. His new strategy was that if you can't beat them, join them, if that's what it took to win their endorsement. He began to seek out the company of the affluent and influential whom he had once claimed to despise. Meanwhile, Jennifer looked for solace in a gin bottle.

Tonight, she was exhausted. She hadn't been able to sleep since Saturday, even after taking her strongest pills. She couldn't even close her eyes without enduring yet another horrific replay of the woman pushing the pram along the pavement. It had been the night of the Whittingtons' anniversary dinner party. Jenny was in the habit of taking her own car to these endlessly dreary functions so she could fake a migraine and leave early. She knew Martin would stay right to the bitter end. These people were important, he'd said. Useful to his career. His bloody pointless, pathetic, stupid, going-nowhere career.

Jenny had bailed out halfway through the roast guinea fowl, saying that the headache had become so bad it was making her nauseous. She had not been insensitive to the look Martin gave her as she told him that, of course, he must stay and enjoy himself. What the hell. She didn't care what he thought any longer. She apologized, briefly, to her hostess, grabbed her wrap and made for the door rather more hastily than the etiquette she had been so expensively taught dictated. By ten o'clock, she was speeding down the Old Richington Road, heading out of town towards the small, anonymous hotel where she had arranged to meet Jas, the man she adored. The whole purpose of her futile existence now centred around the blissful, precious hours she spent in bed with him whenever she could. Jas understood her needs, calmed her perpetual fretfulness but, at the same time, made every nerve in her body throb. Anticipation made her drive fast, oblivious to the built-up area and the drizzling rain.

Without any warning, the woman had started to push the pram across the road. Jenny tried to brake but somehow the message from her brain had taken too long to reach her feet. Suddenly the woman was somersaulting off the bonnet of the car and bouncing hideously along the pavement. The pram shot up into the air and over the hedge into someone's garden.

Thinking about it now, Jennifer pouted sulkily. She hadn't been drunk — not really — although the police would have said she was. So would Annabelle Whittington. The dried-up, supercilious cow had glared at her every time she helped herself to more champagne. That's why she hadn't dared stop after the accident. In any case, there was no point. She was certain she'd killed the woman and probably the baby in the pram, too. Well, she couldn't possibly stop after that, could she? They could send her to prison and that was unthinkable. She'd never stand it. Vaguely, she'd realized it would also finish Martin's career, such as it was. Even a mediocre politician couldn't survive the disgrace of a wife convicted of death by dangerous driving with God knows how much excess alcohol in her blood. So she'd rammed the car into gear, gunned the engine and raced back home where she locked it away in the garage and hid the key. There was only room in their miserable little garage for one decent car and Martin's was old, so he always parked it in the drive. Then she'd had a long, hot shower, several large brandies and a handful of sleeping pills. By the time Martin finally returned from the Whittingtons' dinner party around half past midnight, she was in bed, out cold.

Now she paced the expensive Persian carpet, a present from her adoring parents. She was desperate to find a way out of the ghastly mess she was in. If only she could turn back the clock. The woman shouldn't have been out with a baby at that time of night. It was her own fault. Terrifying possibilities plagued Jenny. What if there had been a witness, some nosy old pensioner who sat peering out of the window half the night? But it had been dark and drizzly and the car had tinted windows. She would simply swear it wasn't her driving. But could the police find some way of tracking her down from the broken glass she left behind?

She had to do something about the car. The front headlamp and several other bits were badly damaged and some paint was missing from the wing. What if there was blood on it, too? She hadn't been able to bring herself to look too closely. Her nerves wouldn't stand it. She suffered terribly with her nerves.

Her first thought had been to abandon the car somewhere, then report it stolen. Or better still, take it to some sort of breaker's yard and pay for it to be crushed. But questions would be asked and the police involved. She didn't think her nerves would stand up to police questioning. And how would she explain to her parents that she no longer had the brand new Range Rover Cosworth they had bought for her birthday, only a month ago?

She drained her glass and was pouring another when there was a tap on the door and Debbie came in with Timothy, warm and comfy in his Spiderman pyjamas. He let go the nanny's hand and ran to his mother.

'Hello, Mummy. Are you feeling better tonight? Can I have a bedtime story?' He sniffed her breath. 'You smell funny. You always smell funny.' Timothy climbed on her knee and she kissed his shining hair. He was the only clean, decent thing in her life. The only person she cared about almost as much as herself.

'He's all ready for bed, Mrs Laidlaw. I'm just off, now, if that's all right.' She's drunk again, thought Debbie, disgusted. She wondered if it was safe to leave Timmy with her.

'Debbie's boyfriend is taking her to see a film,' piped Timothy.

It was then, through the mists of alcohol, that Jenny had the brainwave. You could always find a solution to your problems in a gin bottle. It was just a case of drinking a sufficient amount to generate ideas.

'Debbie, what's the name of that handsome young man of yours?'

'Graham, Mrs Laidlaw.'

'That's right, I remember you telling me.' Her speech was slurred. 'Doesn't he work in a garage somewhere?'

'Yes, Mrs Laidlaw. On the east side of the city. He does repair work mostly.'

'Excellent. You see, I had a teensy-weensy little accident in my new car. I swerved to avoid a cat, but hit it, unfortunately.' That would explain any blood, she thought, pleased at her ingenuity. 'Then I skidded on the wet road and ran into a tree. As you can imagine, I don't want to worry Mr Laidlaw with it. He has enough on his mind at the moment and there's really no need for him to know. I wonder, would you take it to Graham's garage for me, instead of the big one in town that we usually use? I'd prefer to get it fixed privately. I'd be so grateful.' Jenny grabbed her bag and pulled out the car key from its hiding place together with fifty pounds from her purse. 'This is for your trouble, Debbie, dear. Just take it away and let me know how much Graham wants when he's done the job. It won't be a problem. Thank you so much.'

When Debbie saw the damage to the car, she decided it must have been a bloody big cat. Bloody big tree, too. Being a smart girl with an instinct for self-preservation and private enterprise, she took some photos of the damage with her phone before driving it away to be discreetly repaired.

CHAPTER FOUR

Nine o'clock on a dreary Tuesday morning. Progress was slow in the incident room. Everything they had so far was negative. The rain on Saturday night had effectively washed away any footprints there might have been on the river bank, there were no tyre tracks and none of the evidence bagged up by SOCO appeared to have any relevance to the corpse or the people who dumped him.

Malone mooched in, rubbing sleep from his eyes with one hand and scratching his behind with the other. DC Pinkney, freshly shaven, highly polished and immaculately dressed in yet another new suit and crisp white shirt, looked like he'd been there since dawn. He'd set up an incident board with photographs of Mr X taken from various different angles and was now sticking coloured pins in a detailed map he'd drawn of the area around Kings Richington. The pins marked the sites where the body might have been thrown into the river in order for it to have fetched up where it did, within the time available. Alongside were columns of complicated calculations and equations in black felt tip to demonstrate the possible distances covered, estimated time taken and analysed influence of the tide. He turned round as Malone ambled across to look.

'What do you think, Sergeant?' He stood back, proudly.

'Very good, son. Just shows what a university education does for you. Only one snag.'

'What's that, Sergeant?'

'Your map's arse about face. According to this, Mr X swam up river against the tide as far as Teddington, jumped out to operate the lock, then dived back in, leaping over the weir as he went, and paddled the last hundred yards upstream to Kings Richington. It's a corpse, son, not a bloody salmon.'

'Bugger,' said Pinkney, who never swore.

'Tell you what. Nip down to the canteen and get us a couple of cups of tea and a few doughnuts and we'll have another crack at it.' He spotted DI Dawes through the window, parking his car. 'Better make that three cups of tea. Here comes the DI.'

Jack strode in just as Pinkney hurried out. 'Where's Pinkney off to? Have we got a lead?'

'No, guv.' Malone looked apologetic. 'I've sent him for tea and doughnuts.'

'Well, I hope he's bringing some for me. I only had a sandwich for supper last night.'

'Missus on strike?'

'No. She was giving me what might turn out to be some useful information about the guests at a dinner party she catered last Saturday night. Bloody funny coincidence, I know, but one of them might just be our . . .'

He paused as Chief Superintendent Garwood's melancholy features appeared in the doorway. 'Can I have a word, Inspector?' He turned on his heel and strode back to his office.

'I expect he wants a report on the progress we haven't made,' said Malone. 'Barnaby must be putting the screws on again.'

Jack pulled a face. 'In that case, I'll be back very soon. Don't eat my doughnut.' He turned and followed the Chief Super down the corridor to his office.

The Murder Investigation Team was one of the specialized homicide squads of the London Metropolitan Police

Service and formed part of Scotland Yard's Serious Crime Group. The commands were split geographically, each unit being led by a Detective Chief Superintendent. DCS Garwood was a career man, determined to rise to the top of his chosen profession. He considered that his flair for leadership and organization, which he had taken pains to bring to the right people's attention, had been instrumental in gaining his promotion to Chief Superintendent and subsequently the command of MIT. But this was only a stepping stone. Garwood planned to be the next Assistant Commissioner and he was only too well aware how easy it was to slip from grace if those same 'right people', the ones with influence, were in any way inconvenienced or embarrassed. One wrong move and the proverbial could hit the fan in a big way. He had seen it happen to other senior policemen, but it was not going to happen to him.

'Come in and sit down, Jack.' Garwood settled himself on the throne-like chair behind his oversized, status symbol of a desk. His oak-panelled office was immoderately well appointed and contrasted with the rest of the building like a tiara on a tart. He regularly commandeered the cleaners so that the furniture always gleamed and reeked of polish. Down one end were two easy chairs and a coffee table where he entertained Sir Barnaby with a glass or two of single malt, when he arrived for his deceptively casual updates. It was in preparation for the next of these that he now needed to speak to DI Dawes.

'How are we doing with the unidentified corpse, Jack?'

Jack frowned. 'Not too well, I'm afraid, sir. We don't have much of any substance to go on at the moment.'

'Well, speed things up a bit, can't you? This kind of incident can cause a lot of unease in a place like Kings Richington. The residents don't like anonymous, mutilated stiffs turning up in their nice clean river. One or two of them have communicated their concern to the commander in no uncertain terms. Somehow, they've got wind of the police enquiry and they're naturally worried about any leaks to the press, never mind the possible effect it might have on the value of their properties. Discretion, Jack, that's the watchword. Discretion.'

Jack smiled to himself. Malone's door-to-door enquiries must have ruffled a few exotic feathers. It was probably the only contact some of them had ever had with the police other than on the golf course or when some smart burglar managed to blag his way past their elaborate and highly expensive alarm systems. Garwood leaned forward, propped his elbows on the desk and steepled his fingers. Jack recognized this as a sign that he was about to impart something profound.

'The reason I called you in, however, is about another matter entirely. I've just had a telephone call from the commander. Now, I want you to understand, Inspector, that this is a very delicate issue and at this point I think circulation should be on a need-to-know basis only.'

'As you wish, sir.' Jack crossed his legs. Get on with it, you pompous old windbag.

'Sir Barnaby had a telephone call last evening from Mrs Annabelle Whittington. I expect you're aware that she's the wife of Sebastian Whittington, the distinguished QC and a leading figure in the legal profession. She's also the daughter of Lord Eustace Henley-Ffoulkes, the High Court judge.'

Jack nodded.

'Sir Barnaby and the Whittingtons interact socially and she therefore felt able to speak to him directly.'

'What's the problem, sir?' Jack was pretty sure he knew what was coming.

'It was the Whittingtons' wedding anniversary last Saturday and they celebrated with a dinner party which was attended by, among others, Sir Barnaby himself. It seems that afterwards Sebastian Whittington told his wife he needed to visit his chambers to catch up on some urgent business and he left the house around midnight.' He paused for dramatic effect. 'Mrs Whittington says he never returned. At first, she wasn't unduly concerned because apparently it's not unusual for him to stay at his club in town for a night or two when he's extremely busy. But when he hadn't returned by Monday evening, she contacted Sir Barnaby to report her husband missing.'

Bells and whistles were sounding in Jack's head but he decided to tread carefully. Garwood was always banging on about budget constraints and not taking responsibility for anything that wasn't appropriate to his command. Jack adopted a suitable air of puzzled incomprehension.

'I'm not quite sure where the Murder Investigation Team fits in, here, sir. We have a corpse who we now know died from natural causes, not murder, and now a MISPER enquiry. I don't believe either is within the team's financial remit.'

Garwood blustered. 'Use your common sense, man. This isn't an ordinary missing persons enquiry. We're dealing with very influential people here. If Sebastian Whittington really has gone missing, the gutter press will have a field day, speculating on what he may have done and where he may have gone. Sir Barnaby insists we avoid that at all costs. I want you to stay with this one, Jack, until you find him. Sir Barnaby is fully prepared to underwrite the budget.' Garwood paused, staring hard at his blotter, then he adjusted it half an inch to the left. 'And for the same reasons of tact and diplomacy, I'm instructing you to continue investigating the body in the river until the whole business has been cleared up discreetly and to the commander's and the local residents' satisfaction. Let me know the minute you have any information.'

Jack stroked his chin. 'As it happens, sir, we do have just one, tenuous lead that I was about to follow up when you called me in. The Whittingtons' dinner party was catered by my wife, Corrie. I believe Mrs Garwood uses Coriander's Cuisine for your own social gatherings.'

'Yes, indeed. Cynthia has been very impressed by the quality of her food. But I don't see how that is relevant.'

'The five-course menu that my wife served around nine o'clock on Saturday evening at the Whittingtons' dinner party matched, almost exactly, the stomach contents of our headless corpse, which you will recall from the autopsy report, were consumed by the deceased, also at around nine o'clock on Saturday evening. Now it appears that Sebastian Whittington has gone missing.' Jack couldn't spell it out any plainer. 'Of course, it could just be a coincidence.' He waited while the dozy old sod worked it out.

Garwood stared at him for some moments without speaking. Then he said, 'Oh my God' and got up and paced about the room. 'Bloody hell, Jack! So what you're saying is . . . the body in the river and Sebastian Whittington could be one and the same?'

The eagle had crash landed. 'All I'm saying at this stage, sir, is that it's one line of enquiry that I believe is worth following up.'

Visibly agitated, Garwood sat down again and fidgeted with the papers on his desk. Then he pulled the cap off his fountain pen and put it back again a couple of times. 'Now, we need to be very careful, here. Maximum security on this one, Jack. After all, it might not be Whittington at all. It may just be a coincidence, as you say. There could be a number of other reasons why he might not have returned home or contacted his wife.'

'Like what, sir?'

Garwood floundered. 'I don't know . . . use your imagination, man. Maybe he's taken his mistress away for a long weekend.'

'Has he got one?'

'I've no idea. In any event, we can hardly ask Mrs Whittington to positively identify a headless, handless corpse with no distinguishing marks as her husband. We need proper evidence, positive proof that it's him, before we put her through such an ordeal.' He eyeballed Jack. 'Now listen. I've told the commander that I'm sending a DI round to Mrs Whittington's home to take all the details and launch a full missing person enquiry — no resource spared. Go careful with her. Barnaby says she's a good friend but she could also be a very bad enemy. Let her know we're keeping her name quiet. It could make things go a lot smoother in any later dealings. Above all, she mustn't have any idea about your corpse and its stomach contents until we have more information. Mustn't set hares running, must we? And for God's sake, pull out all the stops to locate the rest of the body. Obviously something untoward has occurred but the press mustn't get wind of it. We particularly don't want details leaked about the corpse's missing . . .' he coughed uncomfortably, '. . . er . . . genitals. Just the sort of thing they'd seize upon and turn into the worst kind of sleaze. Is all that clear, Inspector? I'll leave it to you. Keep me informed at all stages.' He picked up the phone and pressed the direct hotline button to Sir Barnaby, clearly a sign that Jack was dismissed.

Jack returned to his office and sat down at his desk. His tea was cold and there wouldn't be any doughnuts left by now. Bugsy's fluctuating blood sugar would have taken care of that. Then he suddenly remembered something Corrie had given him that morning to make up for his lack of supper. He reached into his briefcase and lifted out a large, foil-wrapped Bakewell tart.

'Is that a Bakewell tart, guv?' It was Malone, homing in like a sugarseeking missile.

'Yes, it's one of Corrie's specialities. Help yourself to a slice. I can't afford to have your brain shutting down on me now.' Jack looked unusually excited. 'You're not going to believe this, Bugsy, but Mrs Annabelle Whittington, wife of Sebastian, has reported her husband missing.'

'What. . . Sebastian Archibald Whittington, the superstar barrister with the flameproof arse? Blimey!'

'Apparently, he left home on Saturday around midnight, after their anniversary dinner party and she hasn't seen him since. Now here's the interesting part. Corrie catered that dinner and the menu she served is virtually identical to what Big Ron found in Mr X's stomach.'

Malone, being only a DS, latched on much quicker than the Chief Superintendent. 'So you reckon our Mr X could be Whittington, then?'

'Well, none of the other blokes at the dinner party has been reported missing. The chances are at least odds-on in our favour. And Corrie also heard them having a row before he left, which was in a taxi, incidentally, not his Roller.'

'Right. What's our next move, guv?' Malone stood up and rubbed his hands together, glad of something positive to work on at last.

'First off, we go and interview the wife. Get all the guff she can give us.'

'Such as whether or not her old man suffered from a dodgy "strawberry".'

'Exactly. Find out which of his regular haunts she's contacted already and tell Pinkney to try everywhere else — hospitals, clubs, etcetera. Get him to ring round all the local taxi firms, find out who Whittington used that night and whether they took him to his chambers or somewhere else. Somebody's bound to remember having Sebastian Whittington in the back of his cab. Barnaby is putting both his money and his mouth behind this one, no overtime expense spared.'

'Makes you wonder,' said Malone, 'whether he'd have been as big-hearted if the poor sod had been a bricklayer or a road sweeper.'

'I very much doubt it, but now we have a possible ID, we should be able to clear it up pretty quickly. After we've questioned the wife, we ask her for a sample of Whittington's DNA. Discreetly, mind you. We don't want her suspecting we've already got a body. Just tell her it would help with our enquiries. Then we get the lab to compare it with a sample from the corpse, which should prove conclusive, one way or the other. With any luck at all, the rest of the body parts will turn up in the meantime. Then Big Ron will suture him back together using her best daisy stitch and we ask Mrs Whittington to identify him. All we have to do then is find out where he went last Saturday night and why somebody decided to dissect him and dump him in the Thames, when all he died of was, as you say, a dodgy "strawberry". Piece of cake.'

'Don't mind if I do, guv.' Malone picked up Jack's paperknife and chiselled himself another generous slice of Corrie's Bakewell tart.

CHAPTER FIVE

Jack could see that Corrie hadn't been exaggerating when she described the magnificence of the Whittingtons' house. If anything, she'd missed a few small details such as the four balconies and the striking side window which ran the full height of the three-storey corner bay. Malone discreetly abandoned his elderly Volvo under some trees in a secluded corner of the drive, well away from the silver Rolls Royce and top-of-the-range Mercedes that were parked out front. The two detectives climbed out and crossed the paved drive, expensively imprinted to look like old English cobbles. Malone rang the bell several times and finally, a plump, comfortable-looking woman in an apron opened the double-fronted, triple-glazed doors.

'Mrs Whittington?' enquired Bugsy. Frankly, he had expected someone better dressed and with more class.

The woman shook her head and her mouth formed an intractable, lipless line.

'Mrs Whittington is resting. Please make an appointment.' She would have closed the door again except for Bugsy's size ten boot, wedged firmly in the gap. He took out his warrant card and held it up.

'I'm Detective Sergeant Malone and this is Detective Inspector Dawes. I think you will find Mrs Whittington is expecting us.'

Her sour expression didn't soften and a sharp sniff indicated exactly what she thought of them, barging in and disturbing Mrs Whittington, but she stood aside and let them pass. 'Please wait in the drawing room.' She looked disdainfully at Bugsy's boots. 'And wipe your feet.'

While they waited, Bugsy strolled around the opulent room, fingering the rich velvet curtains and picking up some valuable pieces of Sèvres porcelain to examine the double-L marking on the bottom. Not that it meant anything to him, but he'd seen the experts do it on the telly. He whistled softly.

'Last time I visited a place like this, I had to pay to go in. Whittington must be earning a good screw.'

Jack thought he recognized some important twentieth-century paintings and, if he was not much mistaken, some fine French furniture.

'According to my wife, it's Mrs Whittington who holds the major purse strings. Her father's Lord Eustace Henley-Ffoulkes, the High Court judge. I reckon old money paid for this lot.'

The door opened and an elegant woman in her early forties swept in. She was wearing an afternoon dress in muted shades of mink with an apricot silk scarf draped tastefully around her shoulders. It was fastened on one side with a gold and emerald brooch. Her ash-blonde hair was arranged in a shining pleat and her make-up was subtle and immaculate. She strode confidently across the room to Jack and held out a cool right hand. This lady, thought Jack, is a thoroughbred. Aristocratic, haughty and proud. He wondered how much she knew and how much she would be prepared to divulge.

'Detective Inspector Dawes. Detective Sergeant Malone. I'm Annabelle Whittington. Thank you for coming so promptly. Let me get you some tea.'

She walked across to the marble fireplace, an original Georgian antique with carved columns and corbels, and pressed the inlaid bell push. The tight-lipped woman who let them in must have been hovering outside the door because she appeared immediately.

'Madam?'

'Will you bring us some tea and cakes please, Mrs Mackay?'

Mrs Mackay regarded the two detectives with the same distasteful expression she bestowed upon the fur balls that the Whittingtons' Persian cat brought up on her nice clean rugs. 'Certainly, madam.'

'Please sit down,' Annabelle Whittington indicated a large brocade sofa and Jack and Bugsy sat obediently, while she arranged herself in the matching armchair opposite. 'Sir Barnaby told me you'd be coming, Inspector. I imagine you'll want to ask a number of questions.' She smiled graciously, waiting for him to begin.

Malone wondered how gracious she would be if the mutilated body they had in the mortuary really did turn out to be her missing husband.

'Before I ask any questions, Mrs Whittington,' said Jack, 'I wonder if you'd mind repeating what you told Sir Barnaby last night, just so we can be certain we're all starting with the same level of information.'

'Of course. As you're no doubt aware, my husband and I celebrated our twentieth wedding anniversary last Saturday.'

'China,' muttered Bugsy, scribbling in his notebook.

'I beg your pardon, Sergeant?'

Malone looked up. 'I believe the traditional present is china, madam.'

Mrs Whittington inclined her head, surprised. 'That is quite correct. But one doesn't always have to adhere strictly to tradition. The modern gift for a twentieth wedding anniversary is platinum.' She extended a slim, beautifully manicured hand. 'Sebastian gave me this ring.' Jack and Bugsy looked at her middle finger on which sat an enormous diamond set in platinum.

'Very nice, madam,' said Bugsy, plainly unimpressed. 'And you gave a dinner party for your friends?'

'Yes.' She smiled at Jack. 'I can, if you wish, provide a list of the guests who attended but I imagine, Inspector, that your wife has already done that. Mrs Dawes did an excellent job with the catering and Sebastian and I will certainly be using Coriander's Cuisine again. The food was superb.'

'Thank you. I'll tell her. What happened next, Mrs Whittington?'

'After everyone had left, my husband told me he needed to visit his chambers to catch up on some urgent business and he left the house around midnight. As yet, he hasn't returned, nor has he been in touch.' She settled back in her chair, indicating that as far as she was concerned, that was all the information about her husband that it was necessary to provide and they should now run along and find him.

'He didn't take his own car?' Jack asked.

'Oh, no, Inspector. Sebastian would never drink and drive. He took a taxi.'

'Do you know which taxi company he used?'

'No, I'm afraid not.' Her disdainful expression clearly said: *Do I look like the kind of woman who would recall anything as mundane as a taxi logo?*

'I notice you have a security camera on the corner of your house. Do you think we might see what's on it for Saturday night?' With any luck, thought Jack, it would have picked up the taxi's registration.

Mrs Whittington smiled apologetically. 'I'm afraid you can't, Inspector. Sebastian had the engineers set it up to record and delete every twenty-four hours' so it will have only Monday evening on it by now.'

'Does Mr Whittington often go away at night without telling you how long he'll be gone, madam? It must be very worrying for you.' Malone never beat about the bush no matter how esteemed the witness.

She flashed him an angry glance, her lips aching from the effort of maintaining the false smile. 'One doesn't panic for no reason, Sergeant. It's not unusual for Sebastian to stay over at his club when he's extremely busy, so I wasn't unduly concerned at first. But when he hadn't returned by last evening, I thought it prudent to contact Sir Barnaby, in case my husband had met with some kind of an accident. I imagine if he sustained a head injury there is also the possibility that he may have temporary amnesia.'

There was a light tap on the door and Mrs Mackay wheeled in a tea trolley bearing a Georgian silver tea service, a delicate china cup and saucer for Mrs Whittington and two utilitarian looking mugs for the policemen which the housekeeper obviously reserved for the use of 'trades people'. Dainty slices of fruit cake, Victoria sponge and chocolate gateaux were arranged on a three-tiered cake plate.

'Would you like me to serve, madam?'

'No thank you, Doreen. I can manage.'

Malone noted that she pronounced it 'D-reen' rather than 'Daw-reen' as any normal person would. Typical upper-class plum in her mouth!

Mrs Whittington smiled at the housekeeper who nodded and withdrew, somewhat reluctantly, Jack thought. They were silent while she deftly poured the tea and proffered slices of cake which Jack politely declined. Bugsy helped himself to a slice of all three.

'I believe my wife served five courses at dinner. Can you remember if Mr Whittington ate some of everything?'

'Oh yes.' She smiled wryly. 'Sebastian enjoys his food. Probably a little too much. I keep telling him he needs to lose a little weight. But I'm sure he didn't eat so much that it made him ill.' She became concerned. 'You don't think he has collapsed somewhere and is lying in pain, do you?'

'No,' said Jack, cautiously. 'I think it's safe to assume he isn't in any pain.'

'Did you have an argument before he left?' enquired Bugsy through a mouthful of Victoria sponge. He had jammed his notebook between his knees so he could eat with one hand and write with the other.

Mrs Whittington regarded him coldly. 'My husband and I never argue, Sergeant Malone.' She made it sound as though arguing was a disgusting aberration indulged in only by the kind of mutants who lived on council estates.

But Corrie said they *had* argued, and quite vociferously, Jack recalled, and he knew who he'd rather believe. Why had Mrs Whittington lied? Was it out of conceited embarrassment or was there a deeper motive?

'I am quite accustomed to Sebastian going to his chambers late at night to prepare for the next day. It's not unusual and I have never objected. Normally, he returns after an hour or two.' She became a little flushed. 'The main reason that I became worried and consulted your commander was because when I telephoned the Head of Chambers next day, he questioned his clerk and discovered that Sebastian never arrived there on Saturday night. He could apparently tell from the way the alarm system had been set.' She paused and sipped her tea.

'I have to ask you for some personal information, I'm afraid, Mrs Whittington. It's standard procedure in the case of a missing person.'

'I understand, Inspector. I shall, of course, tell you what I can.' Her uncompromising expression indicated that she would tell them exactly what she thought appropriate and no more.

Malone looked up from his notebook. 'Could your husband have gone to stay with friends or relatives?'

'Not without telling me, Sergeant. In any event, I've spoken with our closest friends, in confidence you understand, and they know nothing. I've also contacted our children. Neither has seen or heard from him. Obviously one can't question them too closely for fear of alarming them.'

'Don't your kids live at home, then?' asked Malone, puzzled.

She gave him a patronizing look. 'Toby is reading law at Oxford. Camilla is only seventeen and is studying music and drama at Roedean. That's a girls' boarding school in East Sussex, Sergeant.'

Jack smiled privately at Bugsy's deliberately dumb expression. 'Does Mr Whittington suffer from any health problems or medical conditions? A weak heart, for instance?'

'Not at all. It's true he isn't in peak physical condition. He's a little overweight and is unable to find time for regular exercise due to the exacting demands of his profession. But he's never had difficulties with his heart to my knowledge.'

'Financial problems?' asked Malone, looking around him. It must cost a bomb to live like this and if the geezer was a heavy gambler, for instance, he might have got into debt with some heavies that he didn't want his snooty missus and her dad to find out about. Bugsy knew a few villains who wouldn't think twice about chopping bits off you if you didn't come up with the readies.

'Definitely not.' Mrs Whittington's expression brooked no argument. 'Money is not something we ever felt the need to discuss.'

'Could you let us have a recent photograph of your husband, please?' asked Jack.

'Why? My husband's picture appears quite regularly in the more superior newspapers. Could you not ask them for one?'

'We could, madam, but press pictures are not always of the best quality for police purposes.' Jack could imagine the hue and cry that would ensue if the police approached *any* newspaper and asked for a photo of Sebastian Whittington. Garwood would wet himself.

'Very well.' Annabelle Whittington sighed, got up from her chair and moved smoothly across to the fireplace. She took down a heavy, ornate silver frame from the mantelpiece and handed it over. It was a photograph of Whittington in his wig and gown, gesturing extravagantly with a dramatic, theatrical hand. Jack removed the photo and handed back the frame.

'Might there be someone outside your immediate circle of friends who could be linked to your husband's disappearance?' asked Bugsy, scribbling furiously.

She took a deep breath, clearly having trouble controlling her irritation with this short, fat, scruffy oaf of a policeman. 'If that is an oblique way of asking if he has a mistress, Sergeant, I can tell you most emphatically that he has not. We've been married for twenty years. I'm his wife — I'd be the first to know.'

No you wouldn't, love, thought Bugsy privately. Not in my experience.

'I wonder,' began Jack carefully, 'do you think we might possibly borrow his hair brush or perhaps a toothbrush?'

She arched perfectly shaped eyebrows in surprise. 'Whatever for?'

'It would help if we had a sample of Mr Whittington's DNA.'

Her eyes saucered. 'Does that mean you think he's dead?'

'Not at all,' Jack said quickly. 'It might help to speed up our enquiries, that's all.'

She looked doubtful but summoned the fearsome Mrs Mackay who left the room briefly and returned with an expensive, silver-backed hairbrush which she handed to her employer. Then she withdrew after giving both men a withering glare.

'Will this do, Inspector?' Mrs Whittington handed it over.

'That's perfect, madam. Thank you very much.' Jack passed it to Bugsy who whipped a large sample bag from his inside pocket and dropped the hairbrush in. Then he licked the end of his pencil and continued scribbling. 'Are there any places he's known to visit on a regular basis?'

'Sebastian is a member of several clubs, including one exclusively for members of the Bar, but enquiries have been made and he hasn't been to any of them since he disappeared.'

'Has he behaved out of character or done anything unusual recently?' asked Jack.

She hesitated, glancing at Malone. 'I wonder, Inspector, if I might speak to you in private?'

Jack nodded at Bugsy who got up and shambled towards the door, helping himself to another slice of cake as he passed the tea trolley.

Once she could see Malone through the window, leaning against the bonnet of the Mercedes to make a roll-up, Annabelle Whittington lowered her voice and inclined her head slightly closer to Jack. 'I'm sure this isn't at all relevant but I suppose I must mention it as you will no doubt find out during the course of your enquiries. Sebastian and I attend the De Vere Académie every Tuesday and have done so for the last five or six months.'

Jack's face was deliberately expressionless. 'What kind of academy would that be, madam?' After the hushed tones she had used, he was expecting her to say it was a crack house or at the very least a nudist club. He wondered why he'd never come across it.

'It's an Académie de Danse, Inspector. Sebastian feels that one is obliged to acquire all the social skills necessary in order to function successfully in what is a very competitive profession. We have strictly private lessons, naturally, and Madame Gloria De Vere, the principal, is a very cultured woman, highly qualified and classically trained in Paris. She is refined and very discreet. Nobody else must know about this, you understand.'

Jack found himself temporarily without speech. Ballroom dancing? Sebastian Whittington QC? Mind you, if the corpse *was* Whittington, it might explain why his calf and thigh muscles were toned while the rest of him was flabby. They'd considered a bike and jogging and horse riding but even Malone's irreverent flights of fancy wouldn't have come up with ballroom dancing. Jack could imagine how Bugsy would react when he told him.

'May I ask why Mr Whittington decided to learn to dance at this particular time?' he asked, as straight-faced as he could manage.

Mrs Whittington bridled. 'I can tell from the barely disguised derision on your face, Inspector, that, like many men, you regard ballroom dancing as effeminate and ridiculous. Well, allow me to correct your prejudiced misconception. The ability to dance competently with one's wife, and indeed the wives of other important dignitaries, is still mandatory at prestigious evening functions which are attended by some very important people including the Metropolitan Police Commissioner himself. The requirement will become even more crucial when Sebastian is made a judge.' She poured herself another cup of tea while her palpable annoyance subsided. 'But obviously,' she said, more calmly, 'Sebastian and I attend the Académie together, as a couple. He would have no reason to go there alone. There'd be no point. He's very sensitive about it, Inspector, for reasons of the blinkered ridicule that you have already displayed. He doesn't wish his professional colleagues to know that he never learned this particular social etiquette in his youth so I should be obliged if you would keep the information private.'

'If it isn't relevant to his disappearance, Mrs Whittington, I see no reason for anyone to find out.' What a fuss about nothing, thought Jack, who had been hoping for a shocking revelation that would prove to be the solution to why his corpse was dismembered. All the same, it might be a good idea to check out this Académie de Danse. He wondered how many other public figures went there on the quiet. He couldn't see what help it would be, though. Not a dancing school.

'Thank you.' She smiled, well-bred serenity restored but determined that things be run her way. 'What happens now, Inspector?'

'Now that we have an official report from you, madam, immediate enquiries will be undertaken by my team to try to find Mr Whittington as soon as possible.'

He didn't tell her it was normal procedure to circulate her husband as 'missing' on the police national computer so any police officer nationally or internationally could contact the team to get more details. Nor did he say they would usually search the home address to establish any further leads such as whether she owned an axe or if there was forensic evidence that she'd chopped him up in the bath. And as for using the media to appeal for information about his last movements, that was a complete non-starter in this case. The commander had ordered that everything should be kept strictly under wraps, so Jack was leading this investigation with one eye closed and his arm up his back. He thanked her for her cooperation and she summoned Mrs Mackay to show him out. Later, she heard the loud guffaws of laughter from outside as Jack started to update Malone on the latest development.

'Ballroom dancing, guv? You're having a laugh.' They climbed back into the clapped-out Volvo and Malone coaxed it down the drive and through the heavy wrought-iron gates into the peaceful, tree-lined avenue.

'That's what she wanted me to believe. But I doubt very much if it's got anything to do with Whittington's disappearance.'

'Unless he quickstepped himself to death,' chortled Bugsy.

'No, I think the wealthy and highly respectable Mrs Annabelle Whittington is putting up a smokescreen to confuse us. She knows more than she's telling. I sensed an inner tension under that cool exterior and, if I were a betting man, I'd stake next month's salary on Mr X being Sebastian Archibald Whittington. Get that hairbrush to the lab as soon as you can, Bugsy. The sooner we can prove it's him, the sooner we can start asking some really tough questions.'

CHAPTER SIX

Friday morning. Nearly a week since Sebastian Whittington's disappearance. Sergeant Malone put the phone down, leant back in his chair and scratched his crotch thoughtfully. Progress at last. He'd better tell the DI. He scrunched up his empty crisp bag, chucked it into the air and headed it against the wall. Then he lumbered down the corridor to Jack's office.

DI Dawes was examining the predictably fruitless results of Pinkney's intensive MISPER enquiries of the last few days. As expected, Sebastian Whittington had not turned up anywhere. Jack was now ninety-nine per cent sure that this was because his body, minus a few vital bits, was in a drawer in the fridge down in the mortuary. But just because you had a missing person and a body that matched his description right down to the stomach contents, you couldn't simply put the two together and assume it was the same bloke. Whittington's hair brush had gone off to the lab together with samples from Mr X for an urgent DNA comparison. Until he had the results from that analysis, Jack was playing safe. He'd seen the devastation that an incorrect identification of a cadaver could cause. The really bad bit of luck was that none of the many registered taxi firms that Pinkney contacted had any record of being hired by Whittington on Saturday night. As Pinkney reluctantly concluded, 'It must have been a private minicab, moonlighting. Could've been anyone, sir. They're impossible to trace.'

Some of Jack's critics, and that occasionally included his impetuous wife, Corrie, considered his methodical and cautious approach to detection work somewhat unimaginative, not to say frustrating. But his success rate and sound record of convictions were undoubtedly due to his attention to detail. Unlike one or two of his more flamboyant colleagues, he never went off at half-cock, cut corners, or made risky assumptions resulting in a prosecution case that some smart barrister such as Sebastian Archibald Whittington, could demolish in ten minutes. The main principle of detection work was to keep asking why — and that's what he was doing now. Why had Annabelle Whittington lied about the argument she'd had with her husband the night he disappeared? Why had she tried to take Jack's eye off the ball with all that nonsense about ballroom dancing? Why had Whittington insisted on going to his chambers at midnight but never arrived there? And why was the corpse chopped up and chucked in the Thames when death had been from natural causes? What he needed was some hard evidence. If only they could find Mr X's missing parts.

Malone knocked on the door, ambled in and flopped heavily on the chair opposite his boss.

'I've just had "uniform" on the blower, guv. D'you want the good news or the bad news?'

'Might as well give me the bad news first,' said Jack, philosophically. 'Then I can add it to all the other bad news I've accumulated today.'

'Old Smelly Nellie, the bag lady, was killed in a traffic accident on Saturday night.'

Jack frowned. 'That really is bad news. I'm sorry.'

Nellie was well known in that part of the manor, wheeling her pram full of rags and old newspapers up and down the Old Richington Road. Despite her filthy appearance, she was very well spoken, always claiming she could trace her family right back as far as the Elizabethan nobility. Accordingly, she preferred to frequent the more affluent areas of the neighbourhood but the toffee-nosed residents weren't too pleased to see her. One or two had even complained to the police that she peered in through their windows and they demanded that she be told to confine herself to a more 'appropriate' area if she must wander the streets at night. Jack considered her a local character and, although she was dirty and tattered now, he reckoned she must have been quite a beauty in her day. He'd often wondered what trauma in her life had caused such physical and mental decline. Too late to find out now.

'How did it happen, Bugsy?'

'Hit-and-run.'

'Any witnesses?'

Malone shook his head. 'The traffic lads are investigating but visibility was poor that night, dark and drizzling with rain. And you know what they're like in that part of town. Wise bloody monkeys. They don't hear anything except the chink of money. Traffic are appealing for information but they don't hold out much hope unless someone spots the vehicle and comes forward. They reckon it must be badly dented, probably with blood on it. There were traces of silver paint on the pram and there was broken glass from the headlamp of something big, they reckon, like one of the more powerful four-by-fours.'

Jack scowled. 'Probably already repaired and pristine by now, no questions asked.'

'Yeah,' grunted Malone. 'Bastards.'

'So what's the good news?'

Bugsy grinned. 'It looks like they've found Whittington's dick.'

* * *

'Another ten minutes, Inspector, and it would have been buried in cement.' The site foreman was clearly shocked, sweating profusely under the conventional donkey jacket, but otherwise reasonably coherent.

They were in the extensive and elaborately landscaped grounds of a grand country house, an early example of popular, twentieth-century 'Tudorbethan' architecture with herringbone brickwork and tall, mullioned windows. The house was on the outskirts of Richington Magna, a tiny village roughly half a mile down river from the quiet stretch of the Thames where the headless body had been found floating.

The crime scene, an excavation destined to be a swimming pool, had been duly taped off by uniform branch who had been first to respond to the foreman's insistent phone call. The SOCO team were already down in the hole, taking photographs, bagging up samples of earth and rubbish and searching for any significant footprints. They were, in Bugsy's view, pissing in the wind, since the entire team of builders had been plodding about in it for the last week and, thanks to the rain, it was now the consistency of a swamp.

'I probably wouldn't have bothered with it, if it hadn't been for the eye.' The foreman swallowed hard. 'I don't suppose anyone's got a fag, have they?'

'How long have you been working here, sir?' DI Dawes steered the foreman by the elbow and sat him down on a nearby garden seat. DS Malone gave him a cigarette and DC Pinkney whipped out his notebook.

'Six weeks. Me and my lads were hired to put in a swimming pool. That and a gazebo.'

'Where are the owners?' asked Bugsy.

'Barbados. Been gone a month. Away for another three. They want it all finished by the time they get back. We're a bit behind schedule because of the rain.'

'Can you describe exactly what you found, please?'

'Well, we'd excavated and prepared the cavity and were all set to pour in the cement when I spotted a lump of black plastic like a bin bag, sticking out of the ground in that far corner.' He pointed to where the SOCO team were most active.

Why is it always a sodding bin bag? wondered Malone. What had villains done with their nastier bits of garbage before bin bags were invented?

'Normally,' continued the foreman, 'it wouldn't have mattered too much on a construction job like this but I'm a tidy sort of bloke and I thought someone had dumped their rubbish on the site. It wouldn't be the first time. In any event, I knew it hadn't been there when we dug the hole so I jumped down and went across to get rid of it.' He paused and dragged on his fag. 'I scraped back the earth and pulled hard at the plastic bag and that was when it split open and I saw this eye looking out at me. Gave me a proper turn, I can tell you.'

'Did you pull the bag and its contents right out of the ground?' Jack asked.

'No, I bloody well didn't! After it split open, I could see a hand and something shrivelled that looked like . . . well . . . private parts. That was enough for me. I told the lads not to go near it and rang you people. What is it? Some sort of black magic ritual? A human sacrifice? Wouldn't surprise me. There are some right funny buggers living round here.'

Up at the house, a battered Land Rover scrunched to a halt in the drive and a stout, familiar figure climbed out. She opened the boot and took out a large medical bag.

Malone jabbed a thumb over his shoulder. 'Big Ron's here, guv.'

DI Dawes turned to the foreman. 'Thanks for your time, sir. DC Pinkney will take full details from you. We'll need the names and addresses of your men and anyone else who might have had access to the area.'

Jack and Bugsy went to meet Doctor Hardacre. She stumped towards them in coveralls and gumboots.

'They tell me the rest of your cadaver has turned up at last, Inspector.'

'Looks like it. Obviously whoever buried the bits reckoned on them being set in concrete under a swimming pool by now, so we'd never have found them. How long do you reckon it will take to establish a formal ID, now we've got the head and hands?'

'No time at all.' She handed him a brown envelope. 'It's the results of the DNA scan between the body samples and the hair in the hairbrush. It's your man, all right. Sebastian Archibald Whittington QC.'

* * *

'Poor Annabelle. Bad enough to be told your husband's dead without having him delivered back to you as a construction kit.' It was Friday evening and Corrie Dawes was cutting cherry tomatoes into rose shapes for a big buffet luncheon party she was catering next day.

Jack raised a surprised eyebrow. 'And how, precisely, did you find out we've confirmed the identity of Mr X as Sebastian Whittington?'

'Cynthia Garwood told me.'

'Well, the body won't be given to his wife in pieces. Big Ron will cobble him back together first.' Jack liked to be in the warm kitchen with Corrie when she was cooking. It felt domesticated and almost normal compared to what he'd been doing all week. He poured them both another glass of wine. 'Mind you, the body won't be released for burial just yet. Whittington may not have been murdered but we've still got to find out who chopped him up and why. Disposal of a body outside the law is a crime. Big Ron is analysing the severed parts to see if there's any kind of a lead.'

'Who got the job of breaking the news to Annabelle?'

'The commander did it personally. Spent most of the day with her.'

'It's just as well she's got Doreen. She'll need some support.'

'Would that be Doreen as in Mrs Mackay, the grim housekeeper?'

'That's right. Been with her for years. She reminds me of Mrs Danvers in *Rebecca*. Did Sir Barnaby tell Annabelle they found Sebastian in instalments?'

'Had to, didn't he? We may need to question her again about who she thinks might be responsible for carving him up, although I doubt she'll tell us even if she knows. She wants the whole thing hushed up. Barnaby has promised her that any publicity about the death, obituary and so forth, will only say Whittington died of heart failure. She's terrified of the merest hint of scandal.'

'Well, she has Toby and Camilla to consider. It would be horrible if they found out.'

'What about her father, Lord Eustace? He's a High Court judge, isn't he? Wouldn't do for people to know his Lordship's son-in-law, the rich, successful Old Bailey barrister, ended his career partly in the Thames and partly in a bin bag. People would suspect all kinds of skulduggery.'

Corrie looked up from her growing pile of tomato roses. 'And what about you? Do you think Sebastian was up to something dodgy?'

Jack thought about it. 'Yes, on balance, I think I do. If only because, otherwise, the whole thing is so implausible. On the face of it, the man was squeaky clean. No speck of dirt on his character at all. But he was an eloquent and ruthless advocate which may have made him enemies — or even worse, friends — amongst the criminal fraternity.'

Corrie put down her knife. 'What about this for a theory, then. Sebastian leaves after the dinner party to go to his chambers to do some urgent work, like he said. He didn't take the Roller, he went in a cab, because he'd been drinking and, as you say, he had to be squeaky clean.'

'Did you catch the name or the logo of the taxi firm?' asked Jack, wondering why he hadn't thought to ask her before.

'It didn't have one. It was an ordinary car. A minicab, I expect.'

'What make was it?'

'How should I know? It was dark and I only glanced out of the window briefly when I heard it pull away. It was just a car.' Corrie was impatient to continue with her inspired reconstruction. 'Now we know, don't we, that he never arrived at his office that night? Suppose a villain ambushed him after he got out of the cab, someone he'd put away years ago but who's recently been released. He's holding this great big knife . . . ' she picked up her vegetable knife and brandished it over her head like a pirate's cutlass, ' . . . and he says something like *I've come to settle a score, Whittington, you dirty rat!*'

Jack grinned. 'I thought James Cagney was dead.'

Corrie ignored him. 'The ex-con strikes at Sebastian like this.' She executed a lunge and recovery with the vegetable knife. 'But before he can stab him, the QC dies of a heart attack brought on by fright.'

'Well, it's a very lurid hypothesis, but why chop him up? Why not just leave him lying in the road?'

'Because he's frightened him to death with the threat of violence, hasn't he? That's murder — or unlawful killing at the very least. He has to get rid of the body and conceal the victim's identity because, as a newly released prisoner, prosecuted by Sebastian, he'd be an obvious suspect. Maybe he had grabbed his hand and he was afraid he'd left some of his DNA.'

'Did he grab his todger as well?'

'No, of course not. That was removed just to put you off the scent.'

Jack laughed. 'It's an interesting theory. And you may have a point about the DNA. They couldn't find anything on the torso after it had been in the river but I'll ask Big Ron if she found anything interesting on the rest of his bits.'

Corrie was worryingly keen. 'Shall I ring Annabelle tomorrow? I could question her without her realizing it. Find out whether Sebastian had ever successfully prosecuted an axe-murderer.'

'No, Corrie. Definitely not.' Jack was emphatic. 'You're not supposed to know anything about this case and you're not to interfere. The official line is that he simply died of a heart attack.'

She went quiet for a bit then she glanced sideways at him, slyly. 'Did you know Annabelle and Sebastian used to have private ballroom dancing lessons?'

Jack was amazed, not for the first time, at how his wife managed to acquire classified information that she wasn't supposed to have. Sometimes it was information that would have taken the police weeks to get hold of.

'Yes, I did know. Mrs Whittington told me in the strictest confidence. She said Whittington wanted it kept top secret for some rather vain, spurious reason. I didn't believe her, to tell you the truth. How on earth did you find out?'

'Doreen Mackay told me when I was over there, catering the anniversary dinner party.' Corrie opened another bottle of wine, thinking what a boon screw caps were when it came to maximizing drinking time. 'Sebastian was extremely keen, apparently, but wasn't picking it up as quickly as Annabelle, so he started to go for extra lessons on his own.'

Jack frowned. 'Did he, indeed?' That didn't tie in with what the wife had said. She reckoned they only ever went there as a couple. Maybe this Académie was indeed worth a visit, although it was hard to visualize anything criminal taking place in a dancing school. It was all sequins, foxtrots and blokes in spandex leotards, wasn't it? Nowhere to hide a whacking great knife in one of those.

Corrie warmed to her subject. 'It's a huge building, the De Vere Académie de Danse, and very posh. Thick carpets and chandeliers everywhere. There are lots of individual private studios but the main ballroom is magnificent, with a sprung maple floor and mirrors all around the walls. You can have a shower and a massage after your lesson and there are glitzy bars where you can eat chic little snacks and drink champagne. They've even got a gym, a whirlpool bath and a sauna. More like an upmarket health club, really, and they employ an awful lot of qualified staff, personal trainers and beauticians as well as dance teachers. All the gentry go there, it's the latest, fashionable place to be seen. It was recommended to the Whittingtons by Sebastian's Head of Chambers. He and his wife learned to dance the tango there.'

'How come you know so much about it? You haven't been having private lessons yourself, have you?'

'What, me?' She laughed. 'Good Lord, no. I could never afford the astronomical membership fees. And I've got the proverbial two left feet. Besides . . . ' she indicated her cuddly proportions, ' . . . I'm not built for Terpsichore, I'm built for haute cuisine. That's how I know all about it. I'm the one who provides the chic little snacks. I was shown around when I went to discuss the catering contract, which, I'm happy to say, is a very lucrative one. Mind you, they can afford it. Doreen Mackay says they charge a fortune for an hour's tuition, especially if you're taught by one of the principals.'

'And how does she know that?'

'She used to open Sebastian's post every morning and put it on his desk. She noticed, purely by accident of course, that he had an account with the De Vere Académie de Danse and the monthly direct debit charges were huge.'

Jack was beginning to think that if he was going to find out what had really happened to Sebastian Whittington, he could do worse than go back to the Whittingtons' house and this time interrogate the housekeeper. Then perhaps he'd go and talk to Gloria De Vere.

Corrie chewed her lip thoughtfully. 'I can't quite put my finger on it but my intuition tells me that despite what you see on the surface, there's something not quite right about Madame De Vere's Académie.'

'Do you mean it makes you feel uncomfortable? Spooky?'

'Oh no, nothing like that. The ambience is all very opulent and relaxed.' She frowned, trying to work it out. 'It's the dimensions that puzzle me; like the Tardis only the other way around. I can't really explain. I think you should go and see for yourself, Jack.'

'Yes, darling. I think it might be simpler. Just you leave it to me.' He bent over to kiss the top of Corrie's head and she popped a tomato rose into his mouth.

CHAPTER SEVEN

WEEK TWO-MONDAY

It was eight o'clock on a chilly, dismal Monday morning with the sky black and heavy with rain. Jack parked his car and hurried across the station car park, his shoulders hunched against the penetrating drizzle, his collar turned up around his face to blunt the teeth of the wind. Once in the warmth of his office, he sat at his desk looking gloomily at the mountain of paperwork that was piling up. He had reports on all the previous week's enquiries made by the MIT, the 'uniform' lads and the forensic experts into the grisly and unlawful disposal of Sebastian Whittington, and there wasn't a shred of useful evidence in any of it.

Chief Superintendent Garwood had made it very clear that both he and the commander thought it was high time the MIT had it all tied up and had made some appropriate, discreet arrests. What on earth had they been playing at for the last week? This was a nasty business, involving important figures in the community. If they didn't get some serious results soon, promotions would be at stake, pensions even. They weren't at all impressed that MIT had found the MISPER and identified the anonymous corpse at a single stroke. They didn't even seem particularly concerned that Whittington was dead. What had really made them jittery was the dubious and gruesome manner of his disposal and the scandal that would almost certainly attach to it if it were leaked.

The phone rang. Jack picked it up.

'DI Dawes? This is Veronica Hardacre. I've finished analysing the body parts of your distinguished silk.'

'Did you discover anything that might help us find out who took him apart and why?' asked Jack, more in hope than expectation.

'Not much, I'm afraid. The hands were soft, smooth and expertly manicured as you'd expect.'

'Yes, I remember how he used to like to wave them about expressively when he was demolishing my police statements in court.'

She sniffed, 'I imagine there will be more than a few humiliated expert witnesses who won't be sorry to see the back of him. There was nothing about the head that you wouldn't guess. Excellent dentistry, must have cost him a fortune, and he'd had a hair transplant at some time recently. Worried about going bald, I imagine. The procedure was done extremely well, I have to say. Rather better than some I've seen before. Probably carried out by a cosmetic surgeon from outside the UK. All in all, Whittington was a somewhat vain, self-indulgent man. But then, you knew that already. There is one thing that you might find interesting, though. I made a very thorough examination of his penis.'

'That must have been nice for you.' Jack fidgeted at the very idea.

'It wasn't a problem, Inspector. It's only you men who squirm at that kind of thing. As far as I'm concerned, when you've seen one, you've seen them all, attached or otherwise. And believe me, they all shrink in formaldehyde. However, there is something worthy of comment regarding Whittington's genitalia. I made a note, when I first examined the body, that there was an excessive amount of bruising in the groin area, even taking account of the fact that he had been mutilated soon after death. But his penis and scrotum were quite badly scarred, consistent with systematic assault with a sharp or rough object, possibly even having been placed in some kind of vice or clamp.'

Jack winced. 'Dear God! Are you saying there's evidence he'd been tortured?'

'I couldn't possibly speculate, Inspector. That's your job. But whatever happened, he would have bled quite a bit and it would have been extremely painful.'

'Painful enough for the fear to have brought on heart failure?'

'Quite possibly. I'll let you have the full report.'

'Thanks very much, Doctor Hardacre.' Jack put the phone down. So it may still be murder. Evidence, at last, that Whittington had been involved in something dubious with some very unpleasant characters. This would put the wind up Garwood and the commander. When they said they wanted results, what they really meant was they wanted the right kind of results. Some comfortable explanation that would show Whittington and all his illustrious friends and relatives to be whiter than white, totally uncontaminated by anything remotely disreputable. Somehow, Jack didn't think that was going to happen and he had no intention of tarting up the facts in fancy clothes. He was scribbling notes on his jotter when Bugsy sloped in carrying a mug of tea and a corned beef sandwich from the canteen. The sandwich also had cold baked beans in it . . . and ketchup.

'You look pleased, guv,' said Malone. 'Don't tell me; Mr Garwood has gone down with something nasty and will be off sick for a couple of months.'

Jack grinned. 'It's better than that.'

Malone perched on the edge of the desk. 'Nothing could be better than that. What have we got, then?' He sank his teeth into his sandwich. Some beans escaped and dripped down his tie, which already looked like a canteen menu.

'Big Ron tells me that just before he died, someone had been systematically torturing our Mr Whittington.'

'But I thought she said he wasn't mutilated until *after* his death. Other than that, there wasn't a mark on him. Not even a bruise, except those doubtful ones around his wrists and ankles.'

'Forget about his torso. Where would you torture a bloke so it was most effective? Think of all those SAS thrillers you read when you're supposed to be on obbo.'

Bugsy washed down a mouthful of sandwich with a swig of tea while he thought. Then a sickening suspicion slowly dawned on him. 'You don't mean they had a go at his privates?'

'Oh yes they did. You don't want to know the details but Big Ron reckoned it included sticking them in some sort of vice. I reckon that's what gave him the heart attack.'

'It'd bloody give me one,' agreed Malone, shuddering. 'What kind of sadistic bastards was the bloke mixed up with?'

'Some pretty ruthless ones, apparently.' Jack stroked his chin. 'Has Mrs Whittington formally identified the body, yet?'

Malone shook his head. 'No. Big Ron only finished sewing him back together this morning.'

'Can you arrange it, then, Bugsy? Get her in, let her have a good look at him and then we'll question her again. I think she's been selective about what she's condescended to tell us so far. I want some honest answers this time. We'll rattle her cage a bit. Sod her influential connections. Speaking of which, it's time we spoke to her dinner party guests, see if they remember anything unusual about Whittington's behaviour that Saturday night and whether they knew something about his private life that would assist with our enquiries. Especially the MP's wife who left early. What was that all about? You could let Pinkney loose on Jennifer Laidlaw. See what he comes up with. And we'll lean on the housekeeper, Mrs Mackay. I reckon she knows more than she's letting on.'

'Blimey, Jack. We're sticking our necks out a bit, aren't we? Mr Garwood will do his nut if we start giving the commander's chums a tug.'

'In light of this new evidence, I'm treating this as a murder investigation, Bugsy. Chief Superintendent Garwood's decisions and actions are taken solely in the light of what's best for his career. Happily, I'm not similarly constrained so we go ahead with our enquiries just as we would if the suspects were normal punters and not beautiful people who think they're above the law. But keep schtum about it being a murder case for now. We'll let the villains think they've got away with it.'

Bugsy gave a mock salute. 'Whatever you say, guv.'

After Malone had gone, Jack sat and thought hard for a while. He wasn't prone to hunches and Corrie reckoned he'd been off school the day they gave out intuition but she had tons of the stuff. He remembered what she'd said about the De Vere Académie and her odd feeling about the place. He picked up the phone again and dialled his opposite number in uniform branch. There might be some local knowledge about Gloria De Vere and her stable of hoofers. After all, she was the only lead he had, however tenuous. If he was really lucky, she might even have some form. The response was disappointing.

'There's never been any suspicion of trouble with the De Vere Académie. All the appropriate licences are in place. Inspections are carried out regularly, according to the book. All very respectable. She's a very imposing lady, Madame De Vere. Have you met her?'

'No, can't say I have.'

'Incredible woman. Over six feet tall, still glamorous with a back as straight as a ramrod, although she must be in her sixties. She was born in England but studied ballet in Paris. Used to be a Bluebell Girl, they reckon, till she got too old for it, then she taught ballet. Finally, she came back here with her son — he's got some sort of French name as far as I recall — and they set up the dance school in town. She contacted some of the young men and women she used to teach in Paris and invited them to come over and work for her as assistants. They took Kings Richington by storm, I can tell you. Anyway, the Académie is extraordinarily successful by all accounts, and expensive, of course. Only the well-heeled can afford it. Why are you asking, Jack? Have you got something on her?'

'Not, yet,' said Jack. 'Just preliminary enquiries at this stage.'

'I'd tread a bit careful, if I were you, mate. Gloria De Vere has friends in high enough places that they can give even Sir Barnaby his orders. I suppose you know he and his missus go to drinks parties at her dance studio?'

'No, I didn't know that. Thanks for the tip off.' Jack put the phone down. That explained a lot of things, including the surprisingly nifty samba performed by Sir Barnaby and his wife at the last Metropolitan Police Charity Ball. But it seemed he had reached a dead end with that particular line of enquiry, despite Corrie's intuition. He wasn't surprised. He'd never seriously considered a school of dancing to be a likely source of any criminal activity unless you counted gross humiliation and taking money under false pretences.

* * *

Seated comfortably in her private drawing room in the penthouse suite of the De Vere Académie de Danse, Gloria De Vere read the announcement in the Monday morning paper with mild astonishment.

Sebastian Archibald Whittington QC, the charismatic and hugely successful barrister, has died suddenly and peacefully at home from heart disease, a condition he had borne bravely and privately for some years. His death is a great loss to the legal profession. Mr Whittington, who was only forty-five, was tipped to become a judge in the very near future. He leaves a wife and two children.

It was accompanied by a picture of him in his wig and robes with the caption, *A debonair and dashing figure in action at the Old Bailey.*

Gloria smiled philosophically and pulled her peignoir closer about her still shapely shoulders, sending the pale pink marabou fluttering gently about her throat. Well, well. It just goes to show, you couldn't believe everything you read in the newspapers. She put the paper down, poured herself an Armagnac and sipped it slowly. Vintage Armagnac was a taste she had acquired many years ago in Paris and she indulged whenever life bowled her an unexpected googly. She wondered what stance the police were taking, for they must surely have adopted one, now that Whittington's body had been identified. So far, luck had indeed been on their side. She sighed. What a dreadful week. When death comes, it comes not in single spies but in battalions, to paraphrase the Bard.

The door opened quietly behind her.

'I've brought you some coffee and brioche, Mother. I see you've already poured your Armagnac.'

'Yes thank you, Lucien. Come and give me a kiss, darling.'

Lucien De Vere was handsome, intelligent and, in both formal and colloquial parlance, very fit. At thirty-three, he had matured into a powerful and spectacular dancer. Like his mother some years before, he had been classically trained at one of the top *Conservatoires de Musique et de Danse* in Paris.

He fell in love with ballet as a boy and his ambition had always been to dance *Premier Danseur Noble*, Principal Dancer, in the classical theatres and companies around the world. But regrettably, he had stopped growing at five-feet-three and, because of his diminutive stature, directors were reluctant to cast him in the traditional male lead roles. Ironically, his mother, at just over six feet, had been too tall and powerfully built to become a slender, graceful prima ballerina. Pragmatically, Lucien decided to switch disciplines and, together, mother and son studied modern dance instead. When they eventually moved to England, they discovered that ballroom dancing in all its exotic forms was enjoying a strong resurgence of popularity. While the genre would inevitably lack the compelling passion both the De Veres felt for the ballet, they found it provided them with a great deal of respect in the community and, accordingly, a very comfortable living. They were continually amazed at the overwhelming response from affluent couples prepared to spend a fortune treading on each other's toes and arguing about whose fault it was.

Gloria had a poise and dignity that reminded people of Fonteyn, and Lucien turned out to be a very astute businessman. He also had that indefinable Gallic charm. Bucket loads of it. Ladies of all ages found him sensitive, talented and incredibly sexy despite his lack of height. Born and brought up in Paris, the husky French accent that he could assume at will made everything he said sound seductive and irresistible. When he asked a lady to come closer and place her thigh between his, the better to accomplish a pivot turn in the tango, she would jump to it with enthusiasm, willingly and without demur. At the same time, he could teach men to lead and dance in a masculine way that removed the debilitating burden of self-consciousness and embarrassment, which they inevitably dragged behind them when they first came through the door. The success of mother and son was apparent to anyone who took a step inside their lavishly appointed Académie.

'Have you seen the newspaper today, Lucien?'

He was sombre. 'Yes, Mother. Such a terrible waste. What a dreadful end to a brilliant career. And Mr Whittington so enjoyed his lessons here. I believe he was even beginning to show some improvement.'

Gloria sipped her Armagnac. 'Indeed he was. That was thanks to you, Lucien. You have an amazing talent for knowing what people need, darling. I know it isn't how you saw your future and it's certainly not what I had planned for you. You had the ability to be a wonderful, charismatic dancer. The finest in the world.'

'If only I'd grown a few more inches. I'm sorry, Mother.'

'Don't be — it isn't your fault. Your father's to blame. Short and stocky. Not a dancer's physique at all.' She ran her fingers through her son's thick, curly hair. 'I was right to name you Lucien, though. It suits you. Lucien Petipa was my inspiration for you. He was responsible for so many of the principal male roles during the Romantic era. I should have loved to see you dance as Albert in *Giselle*.'

'Don't be disappointed, *Maman*. I'm not. Not any longer. We have a wonderful life here and we're making shed-loads of money. And we should at least thank my father for that. The money he gave you when we left Paris was enough to set us up. He may be the wrong shape for a dancer but, on the other hand, Papa is a rich, handsome, successful business man, isn't he? You've always said so. I wish I could meet him.'

'You know that isn't possible, my darling. He has discreet family and business commitments in Paris. But you're a credit to him. I don't know what I should do without you.' She hesitated. 'But I know I shall have to — one day — when you take a wife. There are lovely girls falling over themselves to marry you. I've seen them following you about with adoring eyes. You just need to choose the right one.'

Lucien laughed and gave her a hug. 'And no doubt the right one would be a teacher in the Académie since the girls are all beautiful and most are six feet tall, like you. Then there would be a chance our children just might grow to be the right height for the ballet.'

'I didn't say that,' she protested.

'You didn't have to. No, I shan't marry, *Maman*. I'm much too busy enjoying myself and making money.'

Framed on the far wall of Gloria's drawing room, there was a colourful poster of a dance troupe which had once been displayed outside the Lido nightclub on the Champs-Elysées. Lucien went across to admire the glamorous star taking centre stage, something he had loved to do since he was a boy. It was Gloria, twenty years old, and decked out in a sensational costume of pink feathers, silver G-string, high heels and very little else. Lofty, proud and stunningly beautiful, she had performed with the well-drilled Bluebell dancers.

'You were so beautiful and talented, Mother. Women nowadays are ugly by comparison, both in appearance and nature. There's nothing they won't do for money. How should I ever find anyone like you?'

Gloria De Vere smiled fondly at him. 'In those days, my darling, there was never any confusion between a Bluebell Girl and a stripper or lap-dancer. It was a celebration of the female body and we never strayed beyond that. For a man, securing a Bluebell Girl for a wife had a social cachet.' She sighed. Now, the only blue things she had were her striking cobalt eyes, the subtle rinse through her greying hair and the first traces of veins in her still spectacular legs. She became serious. 'What about poor Mr Whittington, Lucien? Will it be all right, do you think?'

'Of course it will, dear. Trust me.' He poured some strong black coffee into a French bowl, picked up a brioche and dipped it in. 'After all, he had only himself to blame.'

* * *

Now they had confirmed the identity of the body beyond any doubt, Malone agreed with Jack. There was no reason why Annabelle Whittington shouldn't be asked to formally identify her husband. Nor was there any basis for holding back on questioning the guests at the dinner party. It was, after all, standard procedure, being the last time anyone other than the anonymous minicab driver and the murderer had seen Whittington alive. He went across to DC Pinkney, who was painstakingly sifting through all the taxi firms he'd contacted in case he'd missed one.

'Got a job for you, son.' Malone handed over a file. 'The guv'nor wants you to question this lady.' He stabbed a grubby forefinger at Jennifer Laidlaw's photograph, taken alongside her husband at the opening of a community centre. She looked very glamorous but utterly bored. 'She was one of the guests at the Whittingtons' bun fight. Find out how well she knew Whittington, whether she noticed anything unusual about him and why she pushed off early. She claims she had a migraine but the inspector's doubtful. Those posh tarts usually hang about at a smart nosh right up until the national anthem.'

Pinkney leapt up, full of enthusiasm at the prospect of some action instead of paperwork. 'Yes, Sarge. Leave it to me. I'll get the truth out of her.' He almost snatched the file.

Malone patted his shoulder. 'All right, son, don't wet your knickers over it. Just ask the nice lady some polite questions and write down the answers. But don't let on it's a murder enquiry. The official line is still that Whittington snuffed it naturally from a dicky ticker. We don't want to put the nasty killers on their guard, do we?'

'No, Sarge. You can trust me. I'm on my way.'

*

Whittington's body had been cleaned up as much as possible and carefully sutured together by Big Ron herself, a not inconsiderable task accompanied by much stentorious breathing and all fourteen movements of Mozart's *Requiem in D Minor*.

Bugsy telephoned the grieving widow. It took ten minutes to get past Mrs Mackay but finally Mrs Whittington agreed to speak to him. Her tone was weary and patronizing.

'Is this intrusion really necessary, Detective Sergeant? My children have come home to be with me for a while and I really need to spend my time comforting them. As you can imagine, they are very shocked by their father's sudden fatal heart attack, as of course, am I.'

'I appreciate that, madam, and I'm very sorry to have to bother you.' His tone was suitably deferential. 'It's just a formality, obviously, but we'd be very grateful if you'd come down to the mortuary and identify your husband's body.'

'I would find that extremely distressing, Sergeant. Especially in view of Sebastian's horrific . . . well, his final physical condition. Couldn't somebody else do it?'

Malone coughed deprecatingly. 'Well, of course, madam, if you prefer it, we could ask one of your children — '

'No!' she almost shouted. 'No, certainly not. I couldn't possibly permit that. They have no idea that their father experienced anything untoward, other than a heart attack.'

'I think Detective Inspector Dawes was rather expecting that you would *want* to see your husband's body, madam. I can assure you that his condition has been appropriately . . . restored.'

She hesitated, her attitude suddenly more acquiescent. 'Yes, of course. Thank Inspector Dawes for his consideration. Obviously, I should like to see my husband one last time. To say goodbye.'

Malone sent a car for her and, when she arrived, he escorted her to the mortuary. She wore black, of course, a beautifully tailored suit and a tasteful little designer hat with a veil. Having descended from a long line of sturdy, stiff-upper-lip stock, she didn't cry in front of the mortuary staff. She gazed for some minutes at her dead husband, covered to his chin in a white sheet, in stoic silence. Then she quietly confirmed his identity and asked if she might spend some time alone with him. When Malone went to fetch her half an hour later, her eyes were very red but she was once more in full control of herself.

He brought her back to Jack's office as instructed. Then he spooned sugar into a cup of the canteen's hot, strong tea and placed it in front of her. The cup clattered in the saucer as her shaking hands raised it to her mouth. She seemed not to be taking in what the inspector was saying.

'I know this has all been a terrible shock, madam, but if you could answer one or two questions.'

The cup rattled against her teeth as she took a sip then she lowered it back to the saucer and pushed it away. 'Yes, of course, Inspector. I'll try . . . if it's absolutely necessary.'

'Where did your husband *actually* go after the anniversary party? It wasn't to his chambers, was it?'

She stared at him, shocked by the unexpected bluntness of the question.

'Must you be so brutal, Inspector?'

Jack stared back. 'If I'm pleasant, people lie to me.'

'Well, I've already told you, Inspector. As far as I knew, that's where he went but he never arrived. At some point, he died of a sudden and massive heart attack and then somebody did those vile things to his body.' Her eyes filled with tears and Malone pushed a box of tissues towards her but she took an old-fashioned, lace-edged handkerchief from her bag and dabbed her eyes.

'Who was it, Mrs Whittington?' asked Bugsy. 'Who sliced him up and chucked him in the river to conceal his identity?'

She looked away, screwing up her face. 'You're quite disgusting, Sergeant.'

'Well, you're his wife. You said you knew everything about him. So was it you?' Malone snarled, aggressively.

She lost control now and shrieked at them. 'Of course not! How dare you? I loved my husband. I've no idea who did it. It was clearly some kind of psychopathic maniac. Why aren't you out there looking for him instead of insulting me?'

'Were you aware that Mr Whittington had been seriously assaulted before he died?' asked Malone, with only the merest hint of dumb insolence.

She managed to look wary yet unaware at the same time. 'Assaulted? I don't know what you mean. In what way was he assaulted?'

Jack took a deep breath and watched her face closely for a reaction. 'According to the pathologist, he had suffered severe pain from a form of torture, deliberately and systematically applied to his genitals.'

She screamed and leapt to her feet. 'No! I won't listen. You're lying. That's a foul and loathsome thing to say.' She picked up her bag and made for the door. 'I demand to be taken home immediately. I won't answer any more of your despicable questions.' She turned to face Jack when she reached the door, her face drained but defiant. Her eyes blazed fire. 'You are aware, of course, that Sir Barnaby is a personal friend of mine? I shall ensure he is made fully aware of your inexcusable conduct. And if one word of your filthy allegation becomes public, I shall sue everyone from the Home Secretary down.'

Jack nodded to Bugsy who opened the door for her and escorted her down to the car pool. He returned ten minutes later with two cups of tea and half a dozen sticky buns. He passed one to Jack.

'What d'you reckon, Bugsy?

'I reckon this time next week, we'll be down the shopping centre in tall hats telling tourists the time, guv,' said Bugsy, unperturbed.

Jack grinned. 'No, I mean what did you make of the virtuous Mrs Whittington?'

'I think she's so far up herself, she could clean her teeth from the inside.'

Jack laughed. 'Yes, but does she know what happened to her husband?'

'Yes and no. I think she suspected he was involved in something nasty but being the toffee-nosed daughter of a lord, she preferred not to know the details.'

CHAPTER EIGHT

Jennifer Laidlaw was sprawled on the sofa in the despised little drawing room of her despised little house. Legs curled beneath her, she was thumbing through a fashion magazine, admiring the designer clothes that she knew Martin wouldn't buy for her. Daddy would, though. She needed to ask him to increase her clothing allowance. Everything was so expensive these days and she had to look her best for Jas. He had such exquisite taste and would know immediately if her clothes, her lingerie, her shoes were anything other than haute couture. She couldn't bear it if he were disappointed with her appearance and stopped fancying her. She sighed. It would be another two whole days and nights before she could be with him again, lie naked in his arms, feeling his hands bring her neglected body slowly back to life. And then there was the present Jas always brought her. Life would be unbearable without her nose candy.

Bored, she glanced at her watch. Half past one — time for lunch. She got up and went across to the drinks cabinet where she took out a glass and filled it three-quarters full with gin. No need for the subterfuge of colouring it with orange juice, she would be completely alone until evening. Timothy was at school, and after that Debbie would fetch him and take care of him until bedtime. Martin was running one of his tedious surgeries for old people. She used to go with him when they were first married. Endless queues of shabby, smelly pensioners, shuffling through the door to whine about their fuel bills and the cost of their nasty food. It was simply too ghastly for words and now she refused to go anywhere near them. She fully intended to kill herself before she got old, that's if the gin and the cocaine didn't do it for her. She wondered how much more of her life she'd have to spend with Martin. How long it would be before she could run away with her true love and leave this awful squalid existence behind. He'd promised to take her away with him as soon as he was free.

When she heard the car pull up outside, she thought it might be Martin, back early from ministering to his ugly, crusty wrinklies. She waited for his key in the door, but the doorbell rang instead. She ignored it. Nobody exciting was likely to be visiting at this time of day. The bell rang twice more, insistently. She uncurled her legs and went out into the hall to see who it was. How very bourgeois having to answer your own front door. Mummy and Daddy had staff who would swiftly dismiss anyone you didn't want to see. She could just make out the outline of a young man in a suit, through the vulgar, coloured leaded lights in the glass panel. Probably selling something. Intrigued and bored, she opened the door.

Pinkney held out his warrant card. 'Mrs Jennifer Laidlaw? I'm Detective Constable Pinkney. I'd like to ask you a few questions, if it's convenient.' This was just for civility's sake because he intended to interrogate her whether it was convenient or not. Her skin was free of make-up and her blonde hair was pulled off her face and tied with a narrow, black ribbon. He thought she looked much younger than the thirty-one years recorded in her file, until he got closer and saw the premature lines of dissipation, the eyes puffy from too much gin and the discontented mouth, turned down at the corners.

Jennifer Laidlaw nearly cried out with shock and horror. *Christ, it was the police! How had they found out?* She'd conveniently forgotten all about the woman that she'd mown down that Saturday night in the rain. It was over a week now and she'd heard nothing, so she thought it was safe to assume the police had forgotten about it too. Debbie had returned her car to the garage days ago, perfectly repaired, without a mark on it. It had cost her a fortune but it was worth it. Nobody would ever be able to tell the Range Rover had been in an accident. So how had the law managed to hunt her down? How had they found out that it was she who had killed the stupid woman and her baby in the shoddy, dirty pram? She froze, unable to move. She stared at Pinkney like a petrified rabbit confronted by a fox, her glass clutched so tightly in her hand that it was in danger of shattering. He smiled politely.

'May I come in please, madam?'

Jennifer felt physically sick but years of social conditioning came to her rescue, enabling her to cling on to a modicum of control, conceal her terror. This frightful little oik in his cheap, shiny suit actually expected to be invited in so he could bully her in her own home. Make her confess. Her nerves screamed in her head and she put a hand to her temple. It was not to be tolerated.

'No, you most certainly can't come in! It isn't convenient. And in any case, I don't speak to constables. Get your superior officer to ring and make an appointment.' She made to slam the door but Pinkney remembered Malone's maxim always to have your boot ready. He jammed it against the door frame.

'I'm sorry, madam, but it doesn't work like that.'

'What do you mean?' She didn't like the attitude of this nondescript little pip-squeak.

This is a murder investigation. If you don't cooperate, then I shall have to take you down to the station and question you there.'

Pinkney waited for the usual load of bollocks that snobs who thought they were above the law tried to give him, but surprisingly, she turned and led him meekly through to the drawing room. Her buttocks, gyrating under a short, tight skirt, aroused an unexpected sexual response in him which he rapidly quelled.

She went straight to the drinks cabinet, topped up her glass with trembling hands and gulped half of it. So they were treating the hit-and-run as murder. They couldn't do that, could they? Murder had to be premeditated and she certainly hadn't gone out that night intending to kill anyone. It was a wretched accident, that was all. The woman should never have been there in the first place. She paced fractiously about the room, wondering whether to call the family solicitor. Maybe she should refuse to say anything more until Martin was present. But what if this jumped-up little shit actually tried to arrest her and take her to the police station?

Pinkney took out his notebook. 'I believe you and Mr Laidlaw were guests at Mr and Mrs Whittington's anniversary party last week?'

Here it comes, she thought. The questions about her drive home afterwards. Did she see anybody? Did she hit anybody? May he take a look at her car, please?

'Yes. My husband and I were invited.'

'I expect you will have heard of Mr Whittington's unfortunate and untimely death.'

'Yes, we heard. And, of course, it was in all the newspapers. A terrible loss. I sent Annabelle a note of condolence.' She was confused now. What had this to do with the hit-and-run? Was he trying to put her off guard, trick her into saying something incriminating?

'How well did you know Mr Whittington?'

'Not very well at all. My husband knew him better than I did. I believe they played golf at the same club, once or twice.' What she actually meant was that Martin considered Sebastian to be one of the powerful people whose approbation he needed in order to get on, so he brown-nosed quite nauseatingly whenever Sebastian was around. She remembered how pathetically pleased he'd been when they'd been invited to the anniversary party.

'You left the dinner early, Mrs Laidlaw. Why was that?'

'I had a terrible migraine. I get them quite often, especially at social functions. That's why I take my own car, so I can go home alone without spoiling my husband's evening.'

'I understand.' He did. Pinkney suffered from migraines himself and had every sympathy with her. What could be worse than a sick headache at a party where you were surrounded by a crowd of braying stuffed-shirts? 'I wonder, do you remember anything unusual about Mr Whittington's behaviour that Saturday night? Did he seem ill or anxious at all?'

'Not while I was there, Detective Constable. He was the life and soul of the party. Wolfed down the food, drank several glasses of wine and told us amusing stories about his appearances in court. Of course, I can't comment on how he behaved after I left. You'd have to ask my husband, or one of the other guests.' So that was it! The police were simply making enquiries about the death of the awful, pretentious Seb Whittington who had groped her shamelessly whenever Martin wasn't looking. But why? The papers said he died naturally of a heart attack but this idiot constable had said it was a murder investigation. Maybe they suspected his beastly, stuck-up bitch of a wife had bumped him off. What a laugh! Good riddance, as far as Jenny was concerned. Relief flooded through her, much like the spectacular effects of the cocaine she snorted with Jas.

She stopped pacing and dropped down on the sofa, patting the cushion for Pinkney to sit next to her. It was a smallish sofa and they were so close he could feel the animal heat of her body. She smiled flirtatiously. It was the kind of smile that crept inside his shirt and made its way slowly down into his trousers. He scribbled frantically in his notebook.

Now, Jennifer thought, it was her turn to question him. 'I can't go on calling you Detective Constable, can I? What's your first name?' She leaned towards him so that he could see her breasts jiggling under her T-shirt and spilling out of the top in a deep, inviting cleavage. It was obvious she wasn't wearing a bra. Her perfume, heady and erotic, overpowered the stale gin fumes.

He blushed. 'It's Jonathan.' His voice sounded a trifle high-pitched, so he cleared his throat and tried again. 'My name's Jonathan.'

'Well, Jonathan, I'm afraid I'm not much help to you, am I?' She brushed back a straying wisp of hair. 'I didn't notice anything out of the ordinary at all. My head was splitting and I just wanted to go home to bed.' She rose to her feet and went to top up her glass again. 'Can I get you a drink?' Pinkney wondered how she managed to stay upright after all that gin. He prevented himself very firmly from picturing her flat on her back.

'No, thank you, madam.'

'Of course,' she smiled and sat even closer to him with her legs apart, offering him a lingering view of her black, lacy crotch before he tore his eyes away. 'Not while you're on duty. I understand. So are the police speaking to everyone who was at the dinner party?'

'Oh yes, madam. In the case of a suspicious death, we need to get as full a picture as possible of the deceased's last hours.' As soon as he said it, Pinkney realized his crucial mistake. Nobody was supposed to know Whittington died of anything other than natural causes and right at the outset of the interview, when she was being uncooperative, he remembered telling her he was conducting a murder investigation. Sergeant Malone had been emphatic that the inspector wanted it kept quiet. He tried to recover the situation but knew it was too late. His only hope was that she was so drunk she wouldn't remember anything about it the following day. 'However, at present, Mrs Laidlaw, we are treating his death as natural causes from heart failure. As you can appreciate, it would severely jeopardize our enquiries if anything else became public at this time.'

The room was hot. Pinkney could feel the sweat forming in beads on his forehead then running down his neck inside his shirt. Jennifer Laidlaw's T-shirt had ridden up revealing her naked, creamy midriff. The butterfly tattooed above her navel fluttered invitingly. She smiled and patted his knee, then slowly slid her hand up his thigh. 'It's all right, Jonathan. I won't tell anyone. Your secret's safe with me.'

Pinkney wanted to put his arms around her — and not just out of gratitude.

After he'd left some time later, Jennifer Laidlaw sat wondering how best to use the juicy snippet of information she had acquired. So the police want to hush up their suspicions that Whittington had been murdered. Well, she'd go along with that . . . as long as it suited her. She poured more gin and put on some music — loud and raunchy — and began to salsa around the room. Life had suddenly taken a turn for the better. Nobody was interested in the hit-and-run any longer and she had a spicy piece of gossip that she could use to smack that snotty cow Annabelle Whittington in the eye. She couldn't wait to tell Jas.

* * *

It was 11.00 p.m. and most of the MIT had gone home long since. DC Pinkney and DS Malone had stayed behind in Jack's office to sort through the files for any detail they may have missed.

'You did *what*, Detective Constable Pinkney?' Sergeant Malone put down his chicken tikka takeaway and smote his forehead in despair.

'I may have let slip to Jennifer Laidlaw that we were conducting a murder investigation into Whittington's death.' Pinkney knew it was better to own up straight away rather than let the boss find out for himself.

'You didn't slip her anything else, did you? Please tell me you didn't give her one while the balance of your mind was disturbed by her jiggling tits.'

Pinkney was indignant. 'Course I didn't, Sarge. And I think it'll be all right. By the time I left, she was plastered to the hairline. Completely wrecked. I doubt she'll even remember I was there by the morning.'

'You'd better hope not, son. Her MP husband's a pinko, lefty bed-wetter who believes in making everyone's life equally miserable. When he was first elected, he wanted to purge Kings Richington of capitalist scum like the Whittingtons, so he'll pounce on anything to discredit the nobs. Mind you, rumour has it Mrs Jennifer Jiggle-Tits doesn't talk to her husband much, so keep your head down and maybe we'll get away with it.'

'Get away with what, Bugsy?' DI Dawes plodded in carrying a sheaf of neatly typed reports which he dealt out to them like playing cards. He dropped wearily into his chair and ring-pulled the lager Malone passed him.

Malone winked at Pinkney. 'Nothing important, guv. Just a small ricket, not worth bothering you with.' He picked up one of the reports. 'What are these?'

'They're statements from the other dinner party guests. Sir Barnaby took them personally — over the phone — and it's taken his secretary until now to send them over.'

'So they're not signed?'

'No need, according to Garwood. Word of mouth is perfectly adequate in the case of witnesses of this calibre . . . and I quote.'

'Anything useful in 'em?'

'What do you think, Bugsy? The whole thing's stitched up tighter than a nun's knickers. Identical story from each of them — Lord and Lady Henley-Ffoulkes, Sebastian's Head of Chambers and his wife, the bishop, the Harley Street surgeon and, of course, Sir Barnaby himself. It was a very pleasant evening. Excellent food and wine. Sebastian and Annabelle were happy, enjoying their anniversary celebration with friends and relatives. Of course, everyone was shocked and upset when they found out later that Whittington had died of a heart attack. Not surprised, mind you. The man worked much too hard and was out of condition. They were regarding it as a warning. Could happen to any of them.'

'There's confirmation here from Whittington's Head of Chambers that he never arrived at his office that night, but we already knew that,' said Pinkney, shuffling through the papers.

'You won't find anything there from the Laidlaws,' said Jack. 'I'm assuming that's because Sir Barnaby doesn't consider them sufficiently important to warrant his personal attention. I think most of the other guests were surprised to see them there at all. Out of their social comfort zone, according to my wife. What did you make of Jennifer Laidlaw, Pinkney?'

'She can drink an awesome amount of gin without falling over and suffers badly from migraines.'

'Is that it?'

'More or less, sir. My report of the interview is in your tray. She was a little hostile at first, but I managed to persuade her it was in her best interests to cooperate. She didn't notice anything unusual about Mr Whittington and had to leave early because her head was splitting and she wanted to go to bed.'

'I wonder who with,' muttered Malone, cynically.

Pinkney rushed to her defence. 'Oh, I don't think it was anything of that nature, Sarge. Seems like a genuine lady to me. Probably drinks out of boredom. Who wouldn't, married to an intellectual midget like Martin Laidlaw?'

'OK. So we haven't learned anything useful from any of the other guests,' concluded Jack.

No, thought Malone, but one of 'em may have learned something useful from us if she was in any state to remember it. He hoped not, for the lad's sake.

Jack yawned. 'Come on, it's late. Let's go home and get some kip. We'll have another crack at it tomorrow.'

* * *

Corrie was in the kitchen, stirring something green and sloppy in a plastic bucket when Jack arrived home. It was well past midnight and he was in dire need of food, sleep and some uxorial comfort. From the expression on his wife's face, it didn't look as though the comfort would be forthcoming.

She stopped stirring and confronted him, hands on hips. 'What the devil have you been up to today, Jack?'

'Me? Oh, nothing much, my little food processor. Just getting another bollocking from Garwood, being threatened with an official complaint and possible litigation and discovering my chief suspect — my *only* suspect — is ring-fenced by top brass and therefore untouchable. Otherwise, I've been sitting idly twiddling my thumbs and reading the paper all day.' He picked up a grissini, poked it into the bucketful of sludge and crunched off the end. 'What's this?'

'You can see very well what it is. It's my avocado, carrot and sweet corn dip. I made a bucketful last year for your Great Auntie Beryl's birthday buffet.'

'Oh yes, I remember. She drank too much Dubonnet and was sick in it and everyone said it didn't look any different.'

Corrie snatched the half eaten grissini from his fingers. 'Never mind that! You're treating Sebastian's death as murder, aren't you? Some ghastly story about someone torturing his sensitive bits until he had a heart attack. And if that wasn't bad enough, you dragged poor Annabelle into the police station and accused her of chopping him up.'

'How the blazes do you know all that?' Once more, Jack was astounded at the speed and ease of Corrie's access to privileged information.

'Annabelle phoned me this evening. She's cancelled a very large order for the catering I was to do at Sebastian's funeral — over two hundred mourners. That's assuming you ever get around to releasing his body. She said she felt it would be inappropriate for me to handle it while my husband was intent on creating a scandal and destroying her family's good name.'

'Did *she* tell you about the torture?'

'No, of course not. It's the very last thing she'd want made public. Cynthia Garwood told me, in the strictest confidence. She says George is absolutely furious. Apparently, Annabelle has been on to Sir Barnaby making all kinds of threats and Sir Barnaby has told George it'll be his neck on the block if she sues.'

Jack calmly dipped another grissini. 'I doubt if she'll risk suing anyone. Once you start lifting stones, all sorts of nasty things come crawling out. And methinks the lady doth protest too much. I'm sure she knows Whittington was up to something dodgy and she's desperate to keep it quiet.'

Corrie frowned. 'Actually, I think you're right. She sounded almost hysterical today, like she was losing her iron control. Obviously, I didn't let on that I knew anything beyond what everyone else knows — that Sebastian died peacefully of heart failure at home in his bed, like it said in the papers and on TV.'

'I should hope you didn't. That Cynthia Garwood's a loose cannon. Makes you wonder who else she's gossiped to.'

'All the same, I'm a bit miffed about losing the Whittington's order.'

'Sorry, sweetheart, but you know me. A copper's got to do what a copper's got to do, and if that puts a few aristocratic noses out of joint, that's too bad.'

Corrie stood on tiptoe and kissed him. 'I know. I shouldn't expect anything less.' She looked doubtfully at the bucket of dip. 'Does it really look like sick?'

'Yes dear, but not as sick as I suspect Garwood will look tomorrow morning when he gives me yet another bollocking.'

CHAPTER NINE

Nine-thirty on Tuesday morning. Police Chief Superintendent Garwood stamped down the corridor to DI Dawes' office. He was angry. Last night, his sleep had been continually disturbed by calls from the media and then from the Chief Press Officer demanding his comments on the untimely death of the famous Sebastian Archibald Whittington QC. The tabloid press, its celebrity antennae twitching, had already got wind of some kind of cover-up and was baying for a juicy story.

Then Sir Barnaby had been on, asking why the whole thing hadn't been cleared up after over a week and the huge amount of overtime budget that had been spent. And as far as he could see, he'd done most of the interrogation work himself! Why the hell, he'd bellowed down the phone, had Annabelle Whittington been pulled in and questioned like a common criminal? Hadn't the poor woman been traumatized enough having to identify her husband's body, sewn together like a patchwork quilt? She had complained to him at great length, threatening legal action of immense and damaging proportions, and she had the necessary influence to do it. Had Garwood no control over his officers at all?

Garwood flung open Jack's door. His nose twitched. There was a sour, rancid odour of old curry and stale lager.

With impressive sleight of hand, Sergeant Malone picked up a crime file and placed it strategically over some foil containers at one end of the desk, evidence of last night's takeaway when the three policemen had worked late. At the same time, he nudged the waste paper basket out of sight under the desk with his foot. Its cargo of empty lager cans clinked gently.

'Good morning, Mr Garwood,' said Jack, pleasantly. 'What can we do for you?'

Garwood eyeballed Pinkney. 'Carry on, Detective Constable.' The lad was clearly dismissed from whatever was about to take place.

'Sir.' Pinkney stood up smartly and left the room.

Ignoring Malone, Garwood turned on Jack, eyes blazing. 'What the hell are you playing at, Dawes?'

'I'm sorry, sir?' asked Jack innocently.

'Last night I was woken from sleep no fewer than five times!'

'Mrs Garwood's night starvation playing her up again, sir?' asked Bugsy, deadpan. 'They say Horlicks works quite well. Failing that, you could try giving her a good — '

Garwood glared him to silence and resumed his tirade.

'First it was the press, demanding a statement for the early editions then Sir Barnaby called me. Twice. He'd had Whittington's widow on the phone, making a serious complaint about the way you're handling the case. What's all this about questioning her as if she were guilty of some complicity in her husband's death?'

'We don't know she isn't guilty yet, sir. And I think she may be holding back some vital information about — '

'The commander says you told her Whittington had been tortured before he died. That's an appalling thing to tell a grieving widow. Do you have any proof? Solid evidence about where it took place and who was responsible?'

'Well, not exactly, sir. But the pathologist's report indicates that — '

'In that case, you had no business upsetting the poor woman. For God's sake, Dawes, the pathologist's report confirmed that the man died of heart failure. Just find out who dumped the body, charge them quickly with unlawful disposal or whatever, and then Sir Barnaby wants us to drop it. He's sure Mrs Whittington isn't involved in anything criminal. Dammit, she's a family friend of his! I've told you several times that this case demands the utmost discretion. It's imperative that we keep the whole nasty business quiet. The press has already been tipped off that something's going on and we need to put a stop to any unsavoury conjecture before it begins. Do you hear me?'

'Forgive me, sir,' said Jack, pretending to look puzzled, 'but is this a bit of PACE that I've missed? That we mustn't question any suspect who happens to be a friend of the commander?'

Garwood leaned towards him, his face creased with anger. 'You know damn well that's not what I mean.'

'In that case, I can't believe the widow would want us to ignore the expert's report and perhaps allow her husband's murderers to go free. But if that's what the commander wants, I think I'd like the order in writing. Just in case something serious surfaces at a later date and Sir Barnaby wants to know why MIT didn't act on information already held.'

The Chief Superintendent took a deep breath, ever mindful of his high blood pressure and his pulse, pounding on the back of his eyeballs. 'Of course I'm not suggesting we should hush anything up, Inspector. If there has been foul play, then obviously it has to be properly investigated. All I'm saying is, don't make a meal of it and don't insult any more of Sir Barnaby's friends. You've got their statements. That should be enough for you to go on. And always remember, Dawes, if this goes tits-up, I'll come down on you like a ton of bricks.'

' . . . a good shot of whisky, sir,' continued Malone, innocently.

Garwood glared at him. 'What?'

'Try giving Mrs Garwood a good shot of whisky. For her night starvation.'

The Chief Super gave Malone a searching look, trying to decide if he was being insolent. 'For pity's sake, open a window, man. This office stinks like a Saturday night booze-up down the Taj Mahal.' He turned on his heel and strode out, spurred on his way with a 'V' sign behind his back from Bugsy.

'Well, I reckon that clinches it, guv.' Malone took the folder off the foil trays and absently speared some cold gobbets of leftover chicken tikka masala with a plastic fork. 'The Whittington woman's got the wind up good and proper. I reckon we should lean on her a bit more till she cracks.'

Jack pondered. 'Somehow, Bugsy, I don't think that'll be necessary. If I know her sort, all pursed lips and padlocked knickers, she's very close to cracking on her own. Sooner or later, something will push her over the edge.'

* * *

On Tuesday afternoon, the bouquet of roses arrived. There were at least three dozen of them, crimson and velvety, elaborately wrapped in cellophane with a large bow of dark red ribbon around the stems. Must have cost someone a pretty penny, thought Doreen Mackay as she took them from the florist's delivery boy. She carried them straight in to Mrs Whittington, who was taking her afternoon tea in the drawing room. The poor soul could do with cheering up a bit.

Annabelle Whittington was very pale and seemed to have lost much of her proud bearing over the last few days. The shock of losing her husband and the manner of his discovery had taken its toll. But she was from sound breeding stock and presented a plucky countenance to the world — if only for the sake of her children, who were home now until after their father's funeral. They had adored and looked up to him and were devastated by his death. Obviously, they had been told nothing about his mutilated corpse.

Like a number of wives in her social position, Annabelle had deliberately avoided delving too deeply in her husband's activities outside of those in which she was publicly involved.

Issues that remained unacknowledged did not have to be addressed. Therefore, when she had told those dreadful policemen that she had no idea who would want to dismember her husband's body or why, she had been speaking the truth. But she was not a stupid woman and, in her bleaker moments, she believed she knew exactly what Sebastian had been up to. She hadn't been married to him for twenty years without discovering some of the darker aspects of his personality. But now it was all over and she simply refused to allow any part of it to be substantiated, especially by the police, whose brutal insinuations she couldn't bear even to contemplate.

'How kind.' She buried her face in the musky, fragrant blooms. 'Probably from Mummy and Daddy or one of our close friends. Maybe even Sir Barnaby. Was there a card, Doreen?'

Mrs Mackay pulled a small white envelope from among the roses and handed it to her. Then she took the flowers away to arrange in the pair of matching Georgian silver rose bowls that were set aside for superior floral tributes.

There was a note inside the envelope rather than a card. It was typed in a plain, smallish font on a square of white computer paper which had been neatly folded in four. Annabelle took out her spectacles and settled down to read it, a sad but grateful smile on her lips. Seconds later the smile had faded.

Dear Mrs Whittington. Please accept my condolences on the untimely death of your husband. I have some photographs of his last moments that I think it would be wise for you to purchase, if you wish to preserve the reputation of your smug, self-satisfied family. For example, what would happen to Lord Eustace's privileged position on the bench if the tabloid press published pictures of his late son-in-law, indulging in his depraved proclivities? What memories would Toby and Camilla have of their precious father if they learned of his disgusting appetites from the sensationalist newspapers?

Predictably, the note went on to assure Mrs Whittington that none of this need happen if she did exactly as instructed. She was to put a large sum of money — it was written in words and figures so there could be no misunderstanding — in a chain store carrier bag. They should be used notes, small denomination and non-sequential. Then she must go to the ladies' public convenience in the High Street and leave the money in the sanitary bin in the second cubicle. She should do it at some time during the following Saturday morning, this should give her ample time to get the cash. The photographs would then be posted to her in a plain, brown envelope. The police were not to be involved under any circumstances nor was there to be any kind of surveillance.

Annabelle Whittington feared she was about to faint. This was her worst nightmare come true. While she had deliberately made no effort to find out the details of her husband's clandestine activities, she was nevertheless in no doubt that they would prove sufficiently sordid and shocking to gratify his enemies and destroy his family. And whoever he had been involved with obviously saw this as a golden opportunity to make some money after his death. She sat, still and cold, silent tears running down her cheeks.

Mrs Mackay returned with the roses in their bowls to find her employer and friend of many years very far from 'cheered up a bit' by the flowers.

'Whatever's the matter, dear? Is it all starting to get to you?' She sat down beside Annabelle and put an arm around her. 'I'm not surprised. Mr W's death was a terrible blow to us all and you've borne up wonderfully well, so far. I expect you're suffering from delayed shock. Shall I get you a couple of the pills the doctor prescribed?'

Wordlessly, Annabelle handed her the note, which Doreen read in silence. Then her hand flew to her mouth.

'Ooh, my Gawd! Whatever are you going to do?'

Annabelle looked defeated. 'Pay up. What else can I do? If I don't, this will destroy us all . . . reputation, careers, our standing in the community, the children's futures, everything. I couldn't bear the disgrace.'

Doreen moved briskly to the drinks cabinet, poured them both a brandy then sat beside Annabelle on the sofa and took her hand firmly. 'I know you're desperate and horrified right now, but don't be too hasty about parting with your money.

Photos these days are usually stored on a computer and they can print any number. This is blackmail and we need to think it through or you could go on paying for ever. Do you have any idea what the "depraved proclivities" were that the note says Mr W was indulging in? If we knew that, it might help us to work out who could be doing such a wicked thing?'

'None at all. I know only what Sebastian saw fit to tell me. I never questioned where he went or what he did. I simply didn't want to know. I thought his career and status were everything to him. I trusted him not to bring shame and scandal on the family but it seems he let me down badly.'

'Well, it's too late for recriminations, dear. We've got to decide how best to handle things. I know it's awful, but common sense says you should tell the police immediately. Couldn't you speak to your friend, Sir Barnaby? He'd be very discreet, I'm sure.'

Annabelle blanched. 'No, Doreen, I couldn't possibly. It's because he's a family friend that I couldn't discuss it with him. It was quite bad enough that he knew Sebastian was found mutilated, but this . . . ' She took a couple of stiff gulps of her brandy and gagged slightly.

'Well, if you don't want to involve the police, why don't you let Nat help? See what he can dig up.'

Nat Fiddler was Doreen Mackay's younger brother. He had been a policeman once, not a very good one. There had been rumours at the time that he was taking backhanders from petty crooks, including stolen goods when it suited him, but nothing was ever proved. He left the force before he was sacked and set himself up as a private investigator, grubbing a living by taking the jobs that other PIs turned down. He was scruffy, smelled of booze and chain smoked. Nevertheless, he was a potential port in a very turbulent storm.

Annabelle was frantic but doubtful. 'Doreen, I've no idea how dreadful this will turn out to be, what Nat might find. Would he be discreet?'

'Course he would. Discretion's a major part of his job. He'd be a sight more careful than some of those clod-hopping coppers who've been snooping around, I can tell you. And he's my kid brother — he'll do what I tell him.'

'The blackmailer sounds pretty ruthless. I shouldn't want your brother to get hurt. Look what they did to Sebastian.'

Doreen shook her head. 'Nat can look after himself. Besides, it's got to be a woman at the back of it, hasn't it?'

'Why?'

'Well, it stands to reason that the blackmailer has to be the person that Mr W was . . . er . . . involved with, doesn't it?' She coughed, embarrassed. 'I'm assuming he didn't bat for the other side?'

'Pardon?' Annabelle was flummoxed. What had cricket to do with anything?

Doreen sighed impatiently. 'His preferences . . . they were for women?'

'I think so.' Annabelle looked blank, realizing she didn't really know for certain. One of her mother's friends had only recently discovered her husband was gay when he invited his boyfriend to their golden wedding party, so anything was possible.

'And anyway,' continued Mrs Mackay, 'look at where she wants the money left. A man couldn't risk going into a ladies' loo without being noticed, could he? Especially on a Saturday morning when the town's busiest. If all else fails and you decide to pay, we could leave the money, like she wants, then Nat could keep watch outside and jump on her when she comes out carrying the bag. Then we hand her over to your friend, the commander, and he'll confiscate her computer or whatever. Nobody else need know anything about it. She'll get a long stretch for blackmail. But I don't think you should be in too much of a hurry. Once you give in, it's usually the thin end of a very nasty wedge. She'll bleed you dry. We've got until Saturday. I'll speak to Nat and get him to do a bit of snooping. Put his ear to the ground amongst his underworld contacts and see what he can find out.'

'All right, Doreen, if you really think that's the best thing.'

'I do. I'll go and see him tomorrow in his office.'

CHAPTER TEN

Jennifer Laidlaw spread-eagled herself in the middle of the bed. It was Wednesday afternoon and she had managed to sneak away to what was actually quite a good hotel. A bit basic but anonymous. They couldn't go anywhere smart where she might be recognized, could they? As the local MP's wife, she was often called upon to carry out public engagements, with and without Martin. Here, in the unfashionable part of town, they didn't know her from Adam, or should it be Eve? She had a vague recollection of going with Martin to open some crappy little supermarket somewhere near here, but that was yonks ago, just after he was elected.

Martin was in Westminster all day for Question Time. As a government backbencher, he was a 'patsie', a minister's poodle who asked pre-set questions that usually started '*Could the Minister discuss the benefits of the government's initiative on . . . ?*' which then allowed the minister in question to discuss the virtues of government policy, or to attack the opposition. How sad was that? She could no longer remember why she'd married Martin. He was a common, flat-cap northerner with chips on both shoulders and a bad case of adenoids. Talk about stereotypes! His father still lived in Lancashire in a terraced house with a pigeon loft. And he actually kept a whippet in the back yard, for God's sake. And yet Martin still had delusions of a place in the cabinet. In his dreams. Not in hers, though.

She'd been lying there beneath the sheets for half an hour. She liked to be early. Anticipation was half the pleasure. Jas would be here soon, the love of her life. Even his name . . . Jas . . . sounded sexy, although she knew it wasn't his real name. He didn't like her to use his real name and she was forbidden to phone him. He always contacted her to arrange their assignations. She sat up and poured herself another glass of champagne, glancing in the mirror to make sure she looked her best. The oyster silk underwear was expensively subtle, his favourite. Jas preferred her to wear a bra and knickers, at least to start with. He said it was less primitive than total nakedness. She'd once asked Martin how he liked her to look in bed and he'd said 'without a glass in your hand'. Pathetic!

She was proud of how quickly she'd recovered from the unpleasantness with the woman wheeling the pram, especially as she suffered so dreadfully with her nerves whenever there was an inconvenience of any kind in her life. Debbie's boyfriend had repaired the car beautifully before anyone saw the damage and, apart from the initial shock when that stupid little constable had turned up, she hadn't heard anything at all from the police. She had never attempted to find out who the woman was or whether the baby had survived. The less she knew about it, the sooner she could forget it. There was no way they could trace it to her now. As long as she kept her mouth shut. She heard footsteps outside in the corridor, then the door handle started to turn. She squirmed with eager anticipation.

* * *

Nat Fiddler's office was small, seedy and noisome, like the man who worked in it. The door to the street was warped and splintered from years of slamming by disgruntled clients and small-time crooks. Above the door, a battered metal sign creaked and groaned as the biting wind swung it to and fro on its hinges. Through the rust, it was just possible to make out the words painted on it.

FIDDLER INVESTIGATION SERVICES.

Matrimonial — Surveillance — Undercover Operations
Discreet and Professional Services — Ex-police officer
No job too big or too small

Inside the office, a portable gas heater in one corner ensured a permanent fug of stale tobacco, dirty raincoat and fast food of dubious content, emanating from the back street kebab-house next door. Papers were strewn across the rickety desk, along with an overflowing ashtray and the remains of what was once a cheese sandwich but now resembled a developing penicillin culture.

Doreen Mackay perched on a wonky chair and wrinkled her nose.

Fiddler glanced at her. 'Excuse the mess, the butler's on holiday.'

'Nat, you really ought to clean this place up a bit. It stinks. And there's nowhere for clients to sit comfortably.'

Fiddler was in the corner making two mugs of tea on a stained, plastic table. He was in his late fifties, short and sharp-featured with a sallow, unhealthy complexion. He dropped the tea bags in the mugs and poured boiling water on them from a lethal-looking electric kettle, its bare wires held in the socket with spent matches. Then, to Doreen's distaste, he added evaporated milk from a tin and copious quantities of sugar which he then stirred up with a pencil. He handed her a mug without removing the tea bag.

'People don't come here to sit comfortably, Reen, they come to hire my services. Usually because they've got themselves into some kind of mucky scrape that they don't want anyone respectable to find out about. Like your Mrs Whittington. So they can't afford to be too picky, can they?'

'I've just told you, Nat, it isn't her fault. It was that arrogant, self-centred husband of hers. Typical middle-aged man. If he'd kept his trousers zipped, he'd still be alive and his poor widow wouldn't be in this awful mess.'

'Don't be daft. If he was still alive, she wouldn't be his widow, would she?' He took out a battered tin and offered his sister an elderly digestive biscuit which she declined on account of what looked like mouse droppings. Fiddler frowned. 'I'm not sure about this one, Reen. I don't normally touch blackmail. It's a nasty business and the blokes that do take it on often end up dead or badly damaged.'

Doreen took a sip of the mud-coloured tea and grimaced. She made a space on the corner of the cluttered desk and abandoned her mug there. 'This blackmailer's a woman. I've already told you. Surely you can handle a woman?'

'Yeah, but if she's a tart, she's probably working for someone — her pimp. He could be a six-foot Rasta with a pathological grudge against small PIs in raincoats.'

'We'll worry about that after you've caught the girl. Now listen to me. There were a few things I noticed about Mr W's behaviour over the last few months that I never mentioned to Mrs W. It wasn't my place and I didn't want to upset her. And I hope I know how to hold my tongue when it comes to my employer's private affairs. But now he's dead and he's left her with a right old muddle to sort out. She couldn't be any more upset than she is right now so I may as well tell you. It might give you a lead.' She leaned forward and spoke in hushed tones. 'It's my belief that Sebastian Whittington was involved in M&S.'

Fiddler was puzzled. 'Marks and Spencer?'

'No, course not!' Doreen frowned. 'Maybe I mean S&M. It's when you pay someone to inflict pain on you.'

Fiddler shrugged. 'I know some gorillas down the pub who'd do it for nothing. How d'you know that was what Whittington was up to?'

'I used to do his washing, didn't I? When he came back from his so-called late-night work in chambers, he used to put his clothes straight in the laundry basket. But never his underwear, which I thought was a bit odd. Then, one day, I was putting out the rubbish and purely by accident, I found a pair of his expensive silk boxer shorts, the ones he used to order a dozen at a time from a shop in Savile Row. He'd wrapped them in a plastic bag and put them in the wheelie bin outside so nobody would see them. They were stained with blood. Quite a lot of blood, actually. Now what else can that mean other than he was up to something nasty involving his privates?'

Fiddler looked doubtful. 'You sure he didn't just have a bad case of "farmers"? They can bleed something terrible. I should know. Like whacking great, throbbing bunches of grapes.' He slurped his tea. 'After all, you never knew much about the state of Whittington's health, did you? You never even knew he had a dodgy heart.' He shook his head. 'No, I think you've got it wrong, Reen. I mean, surely his missus would have noticed something was amiss with his equipment when he was . . . you know . . . in bed with her, having his matrimonials?'

Doreen was resolute. 'No, she wouldn't. They had separate bedrooms. And from what I can gather, Mrs Whittington finished with all that nonsense after the children were born. Not having sex is quite normal among the aristocracy.' She rummaged in her handbag. 'All right, Nat. If you don't believe my explanation, what about this?' She handed Fiddler a business card. 'After Mr W died, Mrs W asked me to sort through his clothes for the charity shop. I found it hidden in the inside pocket of one of his suits. I haven't shown it to anyone else, not even her.'

Fiddler reached in his pocket and fished out a pair of bent spectacles, held together on both hinges with dirty sticking plaster. He peered at the card. It had the De Vere Académie de Danse logo and the single name 'Sadie' artistically entwined with a bluebell.

'Course,' continued Mrs Mackay, arms folded firmly across her bosom and mouth in a disapproving line, 'This Sadie person might just be his dancing teacher, but I doubt it, don't you? Not for the sort of money he'd been handing over. You could make a start with her.'

Fiddler trousered the card. 'OK, I'll see what I can find out. Tell your Mrs W that I'll take the case.' Even as he said it, an alternative and much more lucrative agenda was already forming in his irredeemably corrupt brain.

* * *

Jennifer Laidlaw took a fifty-pound note from her bag, rolled it up and snorted one of the long lines of cocaine that Jas had divided up on the bedside table. She sighed and lay back against the pillows, waiting for the incredible high to wash over her. Coke made her feel confident, wide awake and on top of the world. She felt hot and her heart began to beat faster. The powerful effects would peak soon and, with luck, last at least half an hour — long enough for her to shag Jas out of his mind. She knew she was hooked but so what? Without Jas and her nose candy, her life would be intolerably grim and cheerless. Her dependence was more psychological than physical, and the low moods that followed these sessions simply tempted her to want more. The fifty-pound note they used was hers but Jas always put it discreetly in his own pocket after they were finished. He also left her to pay for the hotel room and the bottles of champagne. She didn't care. What was money compared to the ecstasy he gave her? She had long ago discovered that you only get what you pay for in this world. She poured more champagne and handed him a glass.

Propped up on the pillows beside her, he dipped a finger in the chilled golden liquid and traced it lazily round her taut nipples, making her shiver. 'So tell me, Jenny, why did you stand me up last week? I thought we had arranged to meet on Saturday night.'

The combined effects of champagne and cocaine released her inhibitions and likewise her tongue, making her careless. 'I was on my way but then I had to go home.' Her speech was becoming slurred, her brain over-active and wild. She knelt up on the bed and straddled him, lowering her breasts to his lips so he could suck at her nipples.

'And why was that, my darling?'

'Hit someone in my car. Stupid woman with a pram. Dead, probably.' Her hands began to crawl down over him, exploring, caressing, lightly scratching his lower stomach with long, elegant fingernails. Burning with pent-up need, she kissed her way down to his groin, tickling his navel with the tip of her tongue then biting, licking and moaning. Gently but firmly, he grasped her by the shoulders and flipped her over on to her back.

'Do the police know about it, my angel?'

Frustrated, she struggled to get up, eager to mount him again. 'What? No, course not. A dopey constable came but he was only interested in Sebastian.'

Jas held her down. 'Sebastian Whittington? What about him?'

She squirmed and giggled helplessly. 'They think he was murdered. Isn't it a hoot?'

'Do they indeed?' He picked up the bottle of champagne and dribbled some over her stomach and between her parted thighs. Then he bent his head and very slowly and deliberately began to lick it off.

CHAPTER ELEVEN

On Thursday morning, the unseasonably cold spring weather had mellowed slightly. By eight o'clock, weak sunshine was already fingering its way through the leaden clouds. Nat Fiddler, looking gritty and crumpled, unlocked his warped office door and shouldered it open. He picked up his meagre post — mostly bills — from the mat and without taking off his raincoat, went across to put on the kettle. Today, he planned to make an early start on the Whittington case by snooping around De Vere's poncey Académie de Danse. He'd find this 'Sadie' tart that the visiting card belonged to, and ask her a few pointed questions. He was used to dealing with toms. Much of his work came from suspicious wives wanting to know if their husbands were 'picking up trade' on their way home. If this girl knew anything, he'd soon get it out of her. But he couldn't do anything until he'd got outside of a good strong cup of coffee and a fag. Yawning, he salvaged a decent-sized dog-end from the overflowing ashtray and lit up.

Of course, he had to keep in mind that his sister, Reen, could be completely mistaken. In Fiddler's experience, women often got hold of the wrong end of the stick, especially where sex was involved. Even with his ear very firmly to the ground, he'd never heard a whisper against De Vere's or the people who ran it, and to be honest, he'd be surprised if it had anything to do with Whittington's kinky sex games. Nat knew lots of establishments where you could get that kind of thing and for much less cash than Reen said Whittington had been forking out every month. Chances were that 'Sadie' was just a nice girl who'd taught him to do the hokey cokey or something similar, a perfectly innocent reason for her business card to have turned up in his pocket. On the other hand, she could be in it right up to her neck and De Vere's could be a hotbed of vice and corruption. It was his job to find out and, if he played it clever, maybe line his own pocket at the same time. He rummaged amongst the papers on his desk until he found a stub of pencil and an empty fag packet. He flattened it out and scribbled a reminder to himself. *Ask Keen which florist delivered Mrs W's roses. Get description of who ordered them. Did they pay by credit card?*

Once he'd drunk his coffee, he went across and locked the outside door. Then he retrieved a key from the unsavoury depths of his trouser pocket and unlocked a small metal box that he kept out of sight in the desk drawer. Inside, draped in a soft cloth, was a Walther P22 pistol. He carefully unwrapped the gun and caressed it lovingly, feeling the black polymer grip snug in his hand. Nice and compact. It weighed less than a pound and was only six inches long, small enough to fit comfortably in the pocket of his raincoat without an obvious bulge, but it was man enough, with ten rounds in the mag, to do the business if he needed it. As he told his sister, blackmailers could be dangerous animals and he was taking no chances.

He'd had some experience with firearms during his days in the police force but he'd bought this illicit one from a nervous bloke in the pub who'd been anxious to get rid of it. When guns were outlawed and you could get banged up for just having one, they became as freely available in pubs as packets of crisps. Fiddler gave the barrel a final polish with the cloth and slipped the pistol in his pocket along with

Sadie's business card and his camera phone. Then he ground out his fag, slurped the last dregs of his coffee and slammed the door on his way out, rattling the rusty sign.

* * *

Outside the Académie, Fiddler paused and grudgingly admired the ritzy frontage. It looked more like the entrance to a luxury hotel. The only thing that identified it as an Académie de Danse was a glass display case containing some tasteful photographs of smiling people, in elegant clothes, dancing around a huge, chandelier-hung ballroom. Nat pushed through the revolving doors into the plush foyer and was immediately confronted by a couple of gorillas in security uniforms.

'Can I help you, sir?' It was the gorilla on his left, six feet tall with a shaved head and bowling-ball muscles that threatened to burst through his green uniform if he got angry. He peered down his flattened nose at Fiddler as if he was a dollop of something smelly that had been carried in on someone's shoe.

'I've come to see Sadie,' said Fiddler, ever the optimist. He hadn't expected security guards. He thought he'd just be able to sneak in and snoop around a bit until someone pointed out the girl. It was how he usually worked in pubs and clubs.

'Do you have an appointment, sir?' growled the gorilla on his right.

Nat improvised. 'Not exactly. She said she might be able to fit me in if I came early.'

The guard moved towards him, threateningly. 'I'm afraid that won't be possible, sir. You'll have to ring and book . . . '

'Is there a problem, Wayne?'

Nat jumped abruptly as a good-looking young man in an immaculate suit suddenly emerged from a door behind him. He'd obviously been spotted by the manager on CCTV cameras. Both security men became deferential.

'No problem, Mr De Vere. This "gentleman" wants to see Sadie. I've told him he'll have to make an appointment first.'

Nat chanced his arm. 'But she's expecting me. I'm a paying customer. Look, she gave me her business card.' He reached in his pocket and pulled out the card with Sadie's name entwined with a bluebell, now grubby and creased due to its proximity to a Walther P22.

Lucien De Vere looked first at the card and then at Fiddler. Several conflicting thoughts were going through his head. Finally, he made a decision. 'It is customary to book a lesson in advance, Mr . . . er . . . ?'

'Johnson,' said Fiddler.

' . . . Mr Johnson, but since you're here, I'll see if Sadie is available.' He snapped his fingers at one of the heavies who immediately lumbered off to find her.

Lucien turned to the other man. 'Wayne, would you show Mr Johnson into Studio Three, please?'

Nat put the card back in his pocket and followed Wayne down a thickly carpeted corridor where he was shown into a room with a highly polished dance floor, elaborate sound equipment and mirrors all around the walls. The guard glared at him then left, closing the door carefully behind him. Fiddler sat down on a plush-covered seat that ran the length of one wall. He wasn't sure what to make of all this but his gut instinct told him to play it careful. The place just might be legit — if you didn't count the rip-off element. He'd seen the tariff of exorbitant fees in the foyer.

When Sadie came in and undulated elegantly across to him like a model on the catwalk, he seriously wondered if Reen had indeed got it wrong. This girl didn't look like a tom with a vicious sideline in blackmail. She was early twenties, he reckoned, very tall (mostly legs), delicately slim and stunningly beautiful with an ethereal, angel's face. Her poise and muscle tone indicated even to Nat, who was ignorant in these matters, that she'd been properly ballet trained. She smiled and held out a small, pale hand.

'Mr Johnson? Have I taught you before? Monsieur De Vere says you have my card but I'm afraid I don't remember giving it to you. What kind of lessons are you looking for?'

Was this really the tart who was putting the squeeze on Annabelle Whittington? Fiddler reckoned he'd blag for a bit, see what occurred. If she *was* a tart, she was a very high-class one and he'd never met one of those in his line of business. He'd test her out. What had he got to lose?

'Don't give me that!' he said, sleazing up to her. 'I know what game you're playing, love.' He showed her the card. 'I happen to know you gave this to Sebastian Whittington. He was one of your kinky clients and he paid big money for your "special services", didn't he? Now he's dead and the income's dried up, you're trying to screw money out of his widow.'

'What?' Sadie went white, apparently genuinely shocked. 'I don't know what you mean. I taught Mr Whittington to dance, nothing else. The poor man died in his bed of a heart attack. I don't know anything about any money.'

Fiddler ignored her protests. 'Tell you what, sweetheart, I'll do a deal with you. I'll persuade the grieving widow to pay up and leave the cash in the ladies' lavatory, like your note said. Then I'll keep watch outside but I'll tell Mrs Whittington you got away. You pick up the money and we split it between us. Everyone's a winner — except Mrs W, of course, but she can afford it. Come on, love. What d'you reckon? Have we got a deal?' He put his arm around her and gave her a squeeze. She struggled free.

'What note? I don't understand. Who are you?' She was becoming hysterical and ran to the door, flung it open and rushed down the corridor.

Gloria De Vere was on the way up to her penthouse for her morning coffee, croissants and Armagnac when Sadie, in a panic, cannoned straight into her.

'Sadie, dear, a dancer never runs, at least, not like that. Whatever's the matter?'

Sadie pointed at Fiddler who was slinking down the corridor, his head constantly jerking from side to side like a terrier looking for a rat. He was starting to believe there really was something dodgy going on after all and was hoping to snoop into some of the other rooms. Sadie gulped, still horrified. 'It's that man . . . Mr Johnson! He's been saying terrible things, Madame De Vere.' Her voice dropped to a whisper. 'I think he knows something about poor Mr Whittington.'

Gloria drew herself up to her full six feet plus four-inch heels. 'Off you go and have some coffee, dear. I'll deal with this.' She strode up to Fiddler.

'I'm Gloria De Vere, principal of this Académie. What is it that you want, Mr Johnson?'

At five feet four, Fiddler had to crane his neck to look at her. No point blagging any more — he'd let this scrawny old bird have it straight. 'The name's Nathaniel Fiddler and I'm a private investigator. I've been hired to look into the racket you're running here.'

'I beg your pardon?' replied Gloria, coldly. 'This is, and always has been, a respectable Académie de Danse with the very best, classically trained teachers and some very esteemed members. I can't imagine why anyone would want to hire you . . .' she looked down at him with haughty contempt, ' . . . because there is no "racket" as you delicately put it.'

Fiddler snorted. 'Bollocks! I know what this place is, it's a glorified knocking shop and now you're branching out into a spot of blackmail.' He pursed his lips and tutted. 'Naughty, naughty. Course, if you cut me in, I might turn a blind eye and no one will be any the wiser. If not, I'll be obliged to go to the cops and tell them what I know.'

'Mr Fiddler,' replied Gloria, with great aplomb. 'I don't know what you're talking about or what it is you think you know, but I can tell you that many high-ranking police officers are members here. If you don't leave immediately, I shall contact one of them and have you arrested.' She pressed an alarm button concealed in the ornamental dado that ran the length of the corridor. The two uniformed guards materialized from nowhere like genies from a lamp. 'Mr Fiddler is leaving,' instructed Gloria, calmly.

The guards each took an arm and frogmarched Fiddler, legs dangling, to the foyer where they spun him through the revolving doors and catapulted him out into the street.

Lucien appeared at Gloria's elbow. 'I've been speaking to Sadie. She's very upset. Is everything all right, Mother?'

'Fine, thank you darling.'

'I understand Mr Johnson didn't want a dancing lesson after all.'

Gloria smiled wryly. 'His name's Nathaniel Fiddler and he's a crooked little private eye, poking about trying to stir up trouble and extort money from us. I don't believe he knows anything at all. He was just bluffing.'

'Do you want me to follow him and speak to him?'

'No need, thank you, darling. I can deal with this on my own.'

'You won't do anything . . . extravagant, will you, dear?'

She kissed his cheek. 'Of course not, Lucien. Trust me.'

* * *

That same evening, at about 9 p.m., a vegetable preparation assistant at the Kings Richington Hotel took a break from peeling potatoes and went outside to get a breath of air. The kitchen was like a furnace when they were fully booked for dinner and they'd already served forty covers. It was cool in the alley round the back of the hotel, where the bins were kept, and he sat on the stone steps, drinking spring water from a bottle. Glancing up, he noticed a piece of dirty brown material sticking out of the large bin set aside for recycling. Who put that in there? That bin was only meant to hold food waste. He put down his water, went across and lifted the lid to pull it out. Then he leapt back several paces.

There had been no elaborate attempt to conceal the body or its identity. Nathaniel Arthur Fiddler had been dumped face down in a large dollop of what had once been expensive sherry trifle. His short legs were buckled beneath him and he had been crammed in unceremoniously, so that his bum and the flap of his raincoat were left sticking out from under the lid.

CHAPTER TWELVE

Thursday evening. The large and industrious police presence outside the Kings Richington Hotel at nearly ten o'clock did little to encourage late-night supper customers. It was just as well since the back alley where the bins were kept, the hotel kitchen and some of the restaurant had all been designated no-go areas and duly taped off. The alley, normally dark and deserted at this time of night, was dazzlingly illuminated and heaving with figures in white coveralls and high-viz jackets. Uniformed police, who were first on the scene, had erected emergency flood lights so that the SOCO team and the pathologist could see what they were doing. The SOCO photographer, draped with an array of cameras and lenses in leather cases, was blazing away around the corpse which remained *in situ*, head first in the waste food container. Members of the forensic team crawled about on their hands and knees and the fingerprint man flicked busily away with his little brush at the multiplicity of prints on the bin.

The hotel manager, pacing up and down outside the cordoned crime scene, was muttering anxiously into a mobile phone. He wasn't paid to deal with dead bodies and, despite the late hour, he felt it was only right that the hotel management company should take over responsibility. When he finally succeeded in locating somebody, it was not reassuring. The woman at the other end of the phone was, at first, sceptical, as if he had imagined the whole thing, then her voice rose to a pitch even more agitated than his own. Her main concern was what the press would make of it and how a body in one of the bins might harm the reputation of the hotel chain. She forbade him to speak to any journalists then cut him off in order to contact her own boss and alert the company's publicity office. He glanced impatiently down the alley. Why the hell didn't the police just pull the body out of the bin and take it away? The poor devil might have been in there for hours. After all, the staff were not expected to make regular checks for abandoned corpses as part of their job. This was a superior, two-star hotel, for goodness sake, not Fawlty Towers. He shuddered. The dead body might already have attracted rats, bluebottles, maggots, anything. And if they got into the kitchen . . .

The passageway was narrow and swarming with experts so Inspector Dawes had to almost fight his way through to the corpse. Jack had been sharing a companionable late supper of *lasagne al forno* and a rather good Montepulciano d'Abruzzo with Corrie when the emergency call came and the area car pulled up outside to fetch him. Another corpse was just what MIT didn't need while Garwood was still leaning on him to come up with a 'satisfactory' result to the Whittington murder. His team, including the office staff, was small by Met standards and fully stretched. Resources would be even tighter now he had been assigned to head up this new case.

Malone and Pinkney, already in attendance, were pulling on latex gloves. Bugsy was typically dishevelled, having spent the earlier part of the evening sprawled on the couch watching football on the box and eating a vast pepperoni pizza, the last slice of which was now congealing in his pocket. Pinkney, sharp and alert, displayed his usual sartorial elegance except for a smudge of lipstick on his shirt, an indication of how his evening had also been abruptly cut short. They stood a safe distance from Big Ron who was directing the photographer to snap specific aspects that she wanted on record. She looked up as Jack arrived.

'Well, well, Inspector. Two suspicious deaths in less than two weeks. Must be a record for the decent, upright citizens of Kings Richington. One more cadaver and I shall start to think you have a serial killer on the loose.' She turned and bellowed at the SOCO team. 'Has everyone got what they want? Right. Let's get him out, then.'

They hauled the body out of the bin and laid it out on the ground for a closer look. The photographer moved in again and Doctor Hardacre pointed.

'Can you take a couple of shots of his neck, please? And someone scrape that trifle off his face and bag it.'

'How long has he been dead, Doctor?' asked Jack.

She prodded the face and neck. 'Less than four hours I'd say. Rigor occurs in these smaller muscles first and works its way down through the body as the muscles become larger. The process normally begins roughly two hours after death. He hasn't been dead long, because the killer was able to bend him double to get him in the bin.'

Pinkney consulted his notebook. 'I questioned the potato peeler, sir. He says he came out here to throw vege-table scraps in the bin at around seven o'clock and the body wasn't here then.'

'Any CCTV?'

'Yes, all over the hotel, sir, but unfortunately not in this back alley. The manager says a camera wasn't considered nec-essary as people don't normally try to nick the rubbish. No point in asking if anyone saw anything, either. It's a blind alley with just pedestrian access and there are no windows, so it isn't overlooked.'

Malone jabbed a finger at the filthy, Columbo-style raincoat the corpse was wearing. 'OK if we go through his pockets, Doc?'

'Please do, Sergeant. We've got half a chance of finding some kind of identification on this one.'

Malone rummaged in one side and Pinkney in the other. They fished out a squashed pack of cigarettes, a box of matches, some loose change and a cheap camera phone. Then Pinkney produced half a dozen grubby business cards from one trouser pocket and Malone, a private investigator's licence and ID from the other.

'It says Nathaniel Arthur Fiddler on his business cards,' said Pinkney. 'The address is down the lower end of Kings Richington High Street. Not very salubrious. Mostly fast-food shops, dodgy pubs and turf accountants, as far as I recall.'

Malone was peering closely at the ID card. 'Here, guv, I think I know this geezer. I didn't recognize him with his face covered in trifle. He used to be in the police force — sorry, service — a while ago. I wasn't a detective then but I could spot a bent copper when I saw one. Up to all sorts of scams, he was. I remember they were on the point of chucking him out when he resigned to become a private dick. Reckoned he could make pots of money.' He looked down at the skinny corpse in scruffy clothes and down-at-heel shoes. 'Looks like he got it wrong.'

'He certainly did, Bugsy. Rotten way to finish up, though. We'll need to inform his next of kin. Did he have a wife?'

'Not when I knew him. I seem to recall there was a widowed sister but I never met her and I can't remember her name. I'll get someone to check the records and go round there, guv.'

'Yes, do that.'

Pinkney took Fiddler's mobile phone between gloved finger and thumb and flipped it open, carefully. 'A private detective, eh? I wonder what he was investigating.'

Malone shrugged. 'Maybe he wasn't investigating any-thing. I reckon he just got on the wrong side of his dodgy, criminal mates and one of 'em bumped him off.'

'What do you make of these pictures, sir?' Pinkney held the camera phone in front of DI Dawes and scrolled through the photos. There were only four on the memory, all badly out of focus, and showed skewed aspects of an elaborately decorated foyer with Greek columns, deep carpets and cut-glass chandeliers. They had apparently been taken under duress as though the PI had been moving at some speed with the camera held lopsided. Pinkney rotated it to get some perspective. 'Looks like the lobby of a very expensive hotel.'

Jack looked. 'In that case, it definitely isn't this one.' He indicated the Kings Richington Hotel in whose grimy back alley they were presently grovelling.

Pinkney examined the photos closely before slipping the phone into an evidence bag. 'I wonder what he was doing in a place like that?'

'Getting chucked out, I expect. Go through his call register when you get back to the station, Pinkney. Make a list of everyone he's been talking to.' Dawes turned his attention to Big Ron who was intensely absorbed with the dead man's neck. 'Cause of death, Doctor?' he asked, optimistically. 'Was it violent, like Sergeant Malone suspects?'

'Well, he didn't dive head first into a bin full of trifle and drown himself in custard, if that's what you mean. Off the cuff, I'd say manual strangulation. There's a blunt force injury of the tissues of the neck that's distinctive for strangulation.' She pointed. 'See those patterned contusions and abrasions? Caused by fingernails and finger pads. Sometimes they don't show up until much later but they're quite clear here.'

'So they belong to the murderer,' assumed Pinkney.

'Not entirely, young man.' She beamed at him. 'Fingernail marks are rarely associated with the assailant's hands. More commonly they are made by the victim's own fingers, as he struggles to pry the assailant's grasp off his neck. But those finger pad contusions were certainly caused by the killer's grasp, especially that single thumb impression. The thumb generates more pressure than the other fingers and, from the shape, I would guess that he wore gloves.' She took out an old-fashioned magnifying glass, like Sherlock Holmes, and looked into Fiddler's unseeing eyes. 'Yes, I thought so. In addition to the blunt force injuries of the neck, strangulation produces evidence of asphyxiation, recognized as red pinpoint haemorrhages in the conjunctiva of the eyes. They're called *petechiae*. See there?' She handed the mirror to Pinkney who squatted down beside her and examined keenly.

'So the murderer was a strong man, then.'

She shook her head. 'Not necessarily. It would take strength but not inordinate strength.'

'Could a woman have been strong enough to strangle him?' Jack's mind had gone off at a tangent. A very unlikely one, but as Doctor Hardacre had implied, with two suspicious deaths in as many weeks in a place like Kings Richington, it was not unreasonable to suspect they might be connected in some way and he already had a private theory about the first one.

'Quite easily. The actual force you'd need to apply to the neck is not a meaningful guide. It can vary tremendously from one person to the next depending on development of neck musculature. Furthermore, if even a small force is applied in just the right anatomical area, like so . . . ' She grasped Pinkney around the neck with her large, beefy hands and squeezed just enough to cause his eyes to bulge, ' . . . it would be enough to kill him.'

'Ergo a small woman could easily strangle a large man,' concluded Jack.

Big Ron nodded. 'Correct. And this man wasn't large. He was a scrawny little bloke with a scrawny little neck.' She pointed behind her. 'If you look at those empty vegetable boxes over there, they've been piled up neatly in the corner, but over here, they're scattered all over the place, indicating a fairly violent scuffle. My initial opinion is that he was strangled here sometime between 7 p.m. and 9 p.m. Forensics will tell us more.'

'So the murderer met him in this dark alley, maybe even by appointment, killed him, then stuffed him in the nearest bin,' suggested Malone.

'Would a woman be strong enough to do that?' asked Jack.

'Why not?' Big Ron flexed her own impressive biceps.

'Bit risky,' said Jack. 'What if one of the kitchen staff had popped out and caught her?'

'I doubt if much forward planning went into it, Inspector. I imagine the murderer was in something of a hurry to dispose of the throttled Mr Fiddler and the bins were simply serendipitous.' She glanced at Bugsy's blank face. 'Opportune, Sergeant.' She gathered up her equipment and returned it to her case. 'I'll give you more accurate evidence after the post-mortem when I've had a chance to dissect his neck.'

'May I come and observe please, Doctor?' croaked Pinkney, still coughing slightly.

'By all means, young man.' She turned to Jack. 'Smart officer, that. Don't let too much of Malone rub off on him.' She turned on her heel, motioning to the mortuary men to follow with the body.

'What did she mean by that?' asked Bugsy, offended.

'I couldn't begin to guess,' replied Jack, pokerfaced.

'Sir, look at this.' Pinkney had been sifting through the business cards he'd taken from Fiddler's pocket and had found an odd one among them. He held it out. It was the card with the De Vere Académie de Danse logo and the name 'Sadie' entwined with a bluebell.

Jack cursed under his breath. 'It's Gloria blasted De Vere's dance school again. It keeps coming back to haunt me, like yesterday's kippers. There's a connection, I know there is, but I'm blowed if I can see it.'

'What possible business can a low-life like Fiddler have had with a posh establishment like Madame De Vere's?' queried Malone. 'It's the favourite playground of all the local nobs, including our own dear commander. No, I think you must have it wrong this time, guv.'

'OK, so what have we got? Two murders. One was a top barrister who we know went to De Vere's for dancing lessons, both with his wife and more recently, on his own. His body is found tortured and dismembered then chucked in the Thames with the rest of his bits buried in a bin bag. He'd come straight from a dinner party where at least four of the guests were personal friends of Gloria De Vere and regular visitors to her posh club. The second murder is a scruffy, crooked ex-copper, now a PI down on his luck, who ends up strangled and shoved head first in a wheelie bin with one of De Vere's business cards in his pocket. And unless I'm well off target, I bet we'll find that those photos on his phone were taken inside the hallowed halls of the Académie de Danse. Our two victims are at opposite ends of the social spectrum. So come on, guys, where's the link?'

'Maybe Fiddler was having dancing lessons, too?' offered Pinkney.

Malone snorted. 'With those flat feet? No chance. This man wouldn't know a quickstep from a doorstep. In any case, he couldn't have afforded it. I reckon he must have been investigating someone who goes there or maybe someone who works there.'

'Which means someone else hired him — for money. He wouldn't be doing it for nothing, would he?' Jack scratched his head. 'But who? And why?'

'When we know that,' said Bugsy, 'we'll have cracked it.'

'They told us at Hendon that the last person to see the victim alive is usually the murderer,' said Pinkney helpfully.

Malone put an arm around his shoulders. 'Pinkney, son, in a case of strangulation, the last person to see the victim alive is *always* the murderer. Think about it.' He looked at his watch. 'The pubs are still open. Anyone fancy a pie and a pint?'

CHAPTER THIRTEEN

On Friday mornings, it was Lucien De Vere's custom to visit the town's wine warehouse. It sold good-quality wines including excellent champagne at competitive prices and was the first choice of most of Kings Richington's wine cognoscenti when it came to restocking their cellars. He could quite easily have delegated the job to his bar manager, but the wine merchant had become a personal friend of Lucien's and frequently invited him to private tastings in the exclusive, climate-controlled wine room in the cellars of the warehouse. De Vere was a good customer and although an undoubted iconoclast in the prosperous but conventional community, he was also admired as something of a minor celebrity. He possessed the vibrant, extrovert personality of a professional dancer with the concomitant charm needed for seducing a succession of beautiful women and keeping them all happy in the process. For his part, Lucien liked to keep up these weekly meetings because the wine merchant gave him a significant discount but, more importantly, he was an inveterate gossip, a constant and reliable font of knowledge about what was going on among the town's rich and respected community. This included the more salacious and entertaining activities that they often let slip after a very heavy wine-tasting session.

On this particular Friday, Lucien needed another case of vintage Armagnac for his mother and fresh supplies for the De Vere Académie's exclusive Cuban Rum-Bar. There was also a Café Cha-Cha where the more abstemious members could choose from fourteen different kinds of tea. Gloria, the purist, considered the names vulgar but Lucien, the businessman, realized that where advertising was concerned, tacky invariably attracted more attention than tasteful. He had left his beloved Porsche at home and now eased one of the Académie's liveried vans slowly through the traffic in the main street, observing the large number of police cars still double parked outside the Kings Richington Hotel. A small crowd of curious onlookers was being pushed away from the entrance by a uniformed constable.

Lucien turned left into King's Square, parked in the warehouse car park, and strolled into the cool, airy show-room. The young woman on the front desk recognized him immediately. His smile, direct and intimate, made her feel like the only girl on the planet. She smiled back as seductively as she could, admiring the tailored suede jacket, watered-silk shirt and Italian handmade shoes. He moved like a cat, supple and agile, his steps soft but self-assured. She sighed inwardly, wishing she could afford dancing lessons, then picked up the phone to summon the manager, who always insisted on dealing with Mr De Vere personally. After an hour, she was asked to provide coffee, the sales meeting having lasted rather longer than usual. There had been much of interest to discuss.

* * *

When he got back to the Académie, Lucien left the bar staff to unload the supplies and went straight up to the penthouse to see Gloria. She was relaxing on her chaise longue with her legs up, to give them support. Despite her age, she was fit and very strong and, as a lifelong dancer, she took care of her legs, which she still considered her greatest asset. Lucien went across to kiss her and she took his arm, pulling him down to sit beside her.

'How was your friend at the wine warehouse, darling?'

'Generous with both discount and gossip, as usual. The man's a mine of information:

'Anything interesting that I should know?'

'*Mais bien sur*. The Metropolitan Police were swarming all over the Kings Richington Hotel. It seems they found a dead man in their wheelie bin yesterday evening.'

'Goodness me! Not another of our paying customers, I hope. I haven't fully recovered from poor Mr Whittington yet. You don't expect such dreadful things to happen in a decent, highly regarded community. The reason we chose to set up business here in Kings Richington was so that we would attract wholesome clientele from the upper classes; rich people in good health with a more than even chance of living long enough to master a decent quickstep.'

'It's all right, Mother, he wasn't a client, but I believe he may have been here. According to the manager's description, it sounded a lot like that squalid little man you threw out yesterday morning. The one who said he was a private investigator and upset Sadie.'

'Really.' Gloria became pensive. 'How do they think he died?'

'Strangled, apparently.'

She was unperturbed. 'Well, violent death is always terrible, of course, but I can't say I'm surprised. He was just the type to poke his nose into places where curiosity would turn out to be dangerous. He obviously went too far and seriously annoyed someone so they simply put a stop to him.'

'Obviously.' Lucien looked thoughtful. 'He had Sadie's bluebell card but she says he didn't get it from her. It was the one she gave to Sebastian. Fiddler showed it to her then put it back in his pocket. Did you take it off him before you threw him out, dear?'

She bit her lip. 'No, I didn't. That was very remiss of me, wasn't it?'

'That means it was probably on him when the police searched his body.'

She nodded. 'In that case, I suppose we should expect a visit. I'm surprised we haven't had one already. Although I'm sure dear Sir Barnaby will prevent any intrusive pestering by the police.'

Lucien stood up. 'All the same, I think we may have to be particularly vigilant for a while, Mother. I understand the good old plodding gendarmes are treating Sebastian Whittington's death as murder.'

'What?' Gloria paled. 'But that's not true. He died of a heart attack.'

'I know, but I think they're beginning to suspect it wasn't triggered entirely by overwork. And now they have another murdered man with one of our cards in his pocket.'

'You're right, Lucien. From now on, we need to be especially cautious.' She frowned. 'What appalling luck we're having. Will you please pour me an Armagnac, my darling? A large one.'

* * *

On that same Friday, in the afternoon, Mrs Whittington and Mrs Mackay sat close together on the French brocade sofa in Annabelle's drawing room. Doreen had been crying and this time it was Annabelle's turn to provide a sympathetic shoulder.

'It must have been a dreadful shock for you, Doreen.'

'It was. The police were very kind. They traced me from Nat's old police records.' Doreen smoothed out the damp tissue clutched in her hand and blew her nose on it. 'Two uniformed officers came to my house early this morning and broke the news. One of them was just a young girl and she tried to be comforting but it's just so awful. Poor Nat. He was my little brother. What a terrible way to end his life — choked to death and dumped in a wheelie bin, like a piece of old rubbish.'

Annabelle sighed with feeling. 'I know.'

Doreen put a hand on her arm. 'Course you do, dear. I'm so sorry, I wasn't thinking. It's only a fortnight since they found poor Mr Whittington and some of him was in a bin bag, wasn't it?'

'What's happening to us, Doreen? This is Kings Richington, a peaceful, cultured town with refined people who just want to lead quiet, civilized lives. Suddenly, there are ugly, sordid things going on all around us.' She put her arm around Doreen's shoulders. 'You don't think your brother was murdered because of something he'd found out about Sebastian, do you? I'd never forgive myself if he'd died as a result of taking on my blackmail case. I feel I'm responsible in some way.'

'Well, you mustn't, dear. Nat had to deal with a lot of nasty thugs in his line of business. It was an occupational hazard. I'm sure he had several other unpleasant cases on the go as well as yours. And anyway, I only briefed him on Wednesday. Knowing the speed that Nat worked, I doubt he'd even started on it yet, so you're not to blame yourself.'

Annabelle was unconvinced. 'It's a strange coincidence, though, isn't it?'

Doreen shook her head. 'It's a dangerous job being a PI and Nat knew that. He must have got too close to nailing one of the other vicious brutes he was investigating. I expect the police will want to get into his office and look through his files to see what he was working on. They'll be lucky if they find anything useful. Nat wasn't a very tidy person and paperwork wasn't top of his priorities. He hardly ever wrote anything down. It was all in his head, you see. The young lady police officer said plain-clothes detectives are going to question me when I'm feeling better, in case I have any information that might help them catch his killer, but don't worry, I won't mention anything about Mr Whittington. But it still leaves you with your dilemma, doesn't it? What are you going to do about the blackmail demand? The money has to be left in the public lavatory tomorrow morning and we haven't got Nat to help us, now.'

Annabelle was fearful but feisty. 'I've thought about it a great deal, Doreen, and I've decided I'm not going to do what the blackmailer wants. It could just be a despicable bluff, an attempt to extort money from me while I'm vulnerable and distracted with grief. After all, we don't have any proof that Sebastian was involved in anything shameful or that this woman has incriminating photos, do we? No, there's been enough violence already, first Sebastian and now Nat, and I want to put an end to it, once and for all, for the sake of the children. I shall do nothing and if the blackmailer tries again, I shall demand to meet the woman so I can look at the photographs myself.'

* * *

On Friday evening, the weather worsened and torrential rain hammered down from a menacing sky. Martin Laidlaw was driving home after a long, irksome week working with his belligerent, complaining constituents. He didn't mind the storm clouds; they matched his mood. He was tired, depressed and in need of a stiff drink — maybe several. That's if Jennifer had left him any. He wondered if he should call at the off licence. Probably the Chinese takeaway as well. It was rare for Jenny to be sober enough on Friday nights to cook him a meal.

He clogged the accelerator and the ageing engine coughed and protested before lurching forward. How was he ever going to be accepted by the class-conscious fat-cats while he had to drive around in this old heap? What he'd really like was a Jaguar, preferably an XK convertible in racing green. Fat chance. There was his wife, swanning around in a brand new Range Rover Cosworth, paid for by her obscenely minted mummy and daddy, while he was stuck with this old banger. He wouldn't care but Jennifer was a godawful driver.

She was always having accidents. It was a miracle she hadn't killed somebody.

He was obsessed with a nagging suspicion that the people he wanted to get close to were starting to avoid him. He could tell by their cool, dismissive attitude when he tried to approach them. Even his ungrateful constituents thought he was inferior, not up to the job. He had expected that as an MP he would command respect. It was an important role and he'd been voted into it, for God's sake. Granted it had been something of a rush job after the last incumbent was forced to resign. His wife had caught him in bed with his researcher and, being a vindictive woman, she told everyone she knew, including the press. He might just have fronted it out if the researcher hadn't been a beautiful young Asian man. Even then, Martin had only just got in and the by-election had clashed with Royal Ascot so it had been a minimal turn out from the people who really mattered. He got the impression they didn't much care who their MP was anyway. They were sufficiently powerful to get what they wanted under their own steam, without seeking the dubious backing of a common, working-class socialist whom they wouldn't have voted for anyway.

He blamed his background for his failure to reach the top of the political ladder. It was his lack of a public school accent, his lack of breeding and family money, his under-privileged upbringing in a socially deprived environment — but most of all, he blamed Jennifer. His initial lust for her had worn off very quickly, but he'd married her because she came from a rich, socially elevated family and he thought she'd help to rocket his career rapidly upwards. In fact, she hadn't wanted to support him at all and that was before she became a drunk. She kept saying she was bored. God knows what she did with herself all day apart from drink and put it about, neither activity being remotely helpful to him, that was certain. The nanny looked after Timothy and the only thing Jenny was good at while in an upright position was clothes shopping. Even when they were invited to important social occasions with influential people that he needed to impress, she invariably got drunk and came on to every man in the room, like a bitch on heat. Look at the Whittington's anniversary party. They'd been very honoured to be invited at all. She'd only stayed long enough to drink Christ knows how much champagne and flirt with that oily Arab surgeon, then she'd got bored, driven herself home and started straight in on the brandy and pills. She'd been completely trashed by the time he got home.

It was a queer business, Whittington suddenly dying of heart failure like that. Probably overwork. He'd have to watch himself. Granted he was ten years younger than Sebastian and in much better physical condition, but all the same. His tyres crunched up the untidy but suitably cheap gravel drive and he parked outside the single garage, which was only just big enough to house Jenny's stonking great car. He let himself in the front door and called out that he was home, just in case anyone cared. Debbie appeared with Timothy, who squealed 'Daddy' and hurled himself at Martin for a hug. Martin held the boy close. His son was the only worthwhile consequence of his bleak, joyless union with Jennifer. The only thing she had ever done that wasn't totally self-centred.

'I'm just about to bath Timmy and give him his tea, Mr Laidlaw.'

'OK, Debbie.' Martin handed the boy back, ruffling his curly hair. 'I'll come and see you before you go to bed, mate.' He sighed wearily, throwing off his jacket and loosening his tie. 'God, I'm bushed. I need a drink and some food.'

Debbie looked uncomfortable. 'Erm . . . I think you should go and see Mrs Laidlaw, first. She isn't very well.'

He groaned heavily. 'Drunk again, I suppose.'

'Well, yes, but I think it's more than that, this time. She's really upset about something. You need to speak to her.' Debbie made a hasty, diplomatic retreat, towing Timothy.

Laidlaw could hear Jennifer's hysterical sobbing before he opened the front room door. He insisted on calling it the 'front room' instead of the drawing room, just to annoy her.

He took a deep breath and braced himself for the insane, screaming row they always had when she was drunk and more than usually irrational. Jenny was slumped on the floor surrounded by dozens of ravaged, crimson roses, their blooms ripped apart and flung around the room. Crushed, velvety petals had been shredded and strewn about, their fragrance heady and sickly sweet. Jennifer was clutching a gin bottle and howling like a banshee. Mascara coursed in ugly black streaks down her cheeks and her hair had come loose and was matted and tangled. As soon as she saw Martin, she cried out and stumbled clumsily to her feet. She staggered to him, dropping the gin bottle which spun around, sending a stream of gin all over the expensive carpet.

'Martin, thank God you're home! You have to help me. I don't want to go to prison.' She clung to him, desperately.

Disgusted, he wrenched her arms from around his neck and pushed her away. 'What is it this time? You haven't been pinching things, have you? I'm sick of having to use my influence to get you out of trouble.'

She shivered and shuddered in real terror, her voice thick from the effects of the gin. 'No, no. It's much worse than that. I didn't think anyone knew. Didn't think they would ever trace it to me.'

'Trace what to you? What are you talking about?'

She handed him the note that had been delivered with the bouquet of roses. It was word processed in a small, plain font on a square of white computer paper which had been carefully folded in four.

Dear Mrs Laidlaw. You're a drunk and a murderer. When the police find out you ran down that woman and failed to stop, you will go to prison and your husband will have to resign his seat. And when Mr Laidlaw discovers you are also a cocaine-snorting slag who screws around, he will divorce you while you are in jail and you will never see your son again.

There followed details of the amount of money the blackmailer was demanding and where she should leave it — in the sanitary bin in the ladies' room of Kings Richington's chic department store. No police must be involved. She was not to look back. She was to drive straight home. When Martin had finished reading, he looked at her with such loathing she felt herself literally shrivel into something dried up and defiled.

'Is this true?' he said coldly. 'I don't mean the part that says you're a drunken, cocaine-snorting slag who screws around. I already knew that. Did you really run someone down?'

She gabbled incoherently. 'It wasn't my fault, honestly, darling. You must believe me. It was an accident, just a stupid accident. It was last Saturday night after the Whittington's party. You remember I felt a terrible migraine coming on and I was driving home in agony when I knocked down a woman with a pram and killed her . . . and her baby.'

'You did what?' He was horrified, hoping desperately she was babbling rubbish as she often did when she was drunk. He grasped her by the shoulders. 'What woman? Who was she?'

'I don't know. Just a woman with a pram. It wasn't my fault,' she said again. 'It was dark and raining and I couldn't see properly because of the migraine. She walked right out in front of me. I didn't stand a chance.' She bawled deafeningly and clung to him. Then he remembered. The hit-and-run incident had been reported in the local paper. The press had sent the details to his constituency office as it was of community concern and the police were appealing for witnesses. He grabbed his wife roughly and hurled her on to the sofa.

'There was no baby, you stupid cow. The woman was a bag lady wheeling a pram full of rags.'

She stopped howling then and breathed a deep, shuddering sigh of relief. 'Oh, thank heavens. Nobody will care about a bag lady. Probably be glad to get her off the streets. They won't waste public money investigating, will they? I dented my new car a bit but I've had it repaired and now you can't tell it's ever been in an accident. They can't prove a thing, so it's all right, isn't it?' She reached for the half empty bottle of gin still lying on the carpet, but he knocked it out of her hand, sending it crashing into her favourite Hockney print, smashing the frame.

'Of course it isn't all right, you callous bitch. You killed a human being and you didn't even stop to help or check if she was dead.'

'But I couldn't, Martin. I'd had all that champagne at the party. They would have said I was over the limit and arrested me. I couldn't let that happen, could I? I was thinking of you. Your career.' She got up and tried to put her arms around him again. 'I did it for you, darling.'

He shoved her away, his mind racing. 'Who else knows about this?'

'Nobody. I told you. Nobody knows. I told the garage I hit a cat, to explain the blood, and that I skidded and ran into a tree.'

He waved the note at her. 'Well, somebody knows, don't they? Think, woman. Who else have you told?'

He grabbed her and shook her, hard. Her head rocked backwards and forwards like a rag doll. She screamed and covered her face with her hands. 'Stop it! I don't know. I can't remember. It's my nerves. I sometimes say things when my nerves are bad.'

'When you're rat-arsed and out of your skull on cocaine, you mean! Do you think I'm stupid? Do you think I don't know what you've been up to and who with? I bet I know exactly who you told.' He stuffed the blackmail demand in his pocket and glared at her, white with fury. 'You bloody stupid fucking bitch! Have you any idea what you've done? Stay here, and for Christ's sake, stop drinking.'

Moments later, she heard the door slam and his tyres spin and scrunch away through the gravel. She dropped to her knees, choking and sobbing, then threw up over the Afghan Killim rug.

CHAPTER FOURTEEN

Saturday morning. Nine o'clock. The windows of the incident room were beginning to steam up. Jack had pulled in the entire Murder Investigation Team, plus some keen officers he'd borrowed from uniform. There were always plenty of volunteers to work with DI Dawes. His reputation for scrupulous policing, giving credit where it was due and not ducking when the chocolate hit the fan had earned him widespread respect and cooperation.

The coppers had been told to bring 'civvies' and to expect to work the whole weekend. A couple of them had been sent to turn over Fiddler's office and had found the usual accoutrements of a private eye: field glasses, telephoto lenses and concealed microphones; as one constable put it, 'the complete nosy bastard's kit'. Two more men were searching his high-rise flat and another had obtained his phone records from the mobile company and was ringing the list of contacts, but without much success. They were mostly blokes demanding money he owed them or adulterous husbands threatening to knock his block off if he didn't stop following them. All the outgoing calls seemed to be to his bookmaker. Not impossible candidates for committing murder but highly unlikely.

Sir Barnaby was now breathing fire up Chief Superintendent Garwood's trouser leg and Garwood, sensing that the high regard he had so painstakingly fostered with the commander was rapidly diminishing, had ordered DI Dawes to 'stop buggering about and pull his finger out'; a mixed metaphor the execution of which defied even Bugsy's fertile imagination. It was now two weeks since Whittington had died and when Jack had briefed the DCS at midnight on Thursday about the second killing, Garwood had reacted as if the MIT had arranged it on purpose, just to jeopardize his next promotion and push up the overtime.

'Another murder?' he'd barked, making it sound like he blamed Dawes personally. 'Well, sort it out, man. A quick result, that's what I want. Something that's been sadly lacking so far. And do you know why? Sloppiness and gross inefficiency, that's why.'

'I'm sure you're doing your best, sir,' said Jack, innocently.

The Chief Superintendent snorted with rage. 'Get yourself organized, Detective Inspector! Allocate tasks and resources to the best advantage instead of sodding about. And stop wasting time and money harassing perfectly innocent members of the public.' Just before Garwood slammed down the phone, Jack overhead Cynthia Garwood mutter sleepily, 'Stop shouting, George, you'll wake the goldfish.'

As Fiddler had merely been a corrupt, inconsequential PI and not a celebrated QC and son-in-law of a lord, there were no inhibiting embargoes on the investigation of his murder. More significantly, there were no classified security restrictions on the people that MIT were permitted to lean on and who they must leave alone, so it was no holds barred and activity was feverish. Phones were ringing non-stop in response to enquiries about the deceased's last movements and although none of the leads seemed very hopeful, all had to be followed up.

For the time being, Jack had decided to restrict knowledge of the De Vere business card with 'Sadie' on it that was found in Fiddler's pocket. Similarly, the photos on his phone that just might be the entrance lobby of the Académie de Danse. He proposed to check those out personally before too many people knew about them. He was still convinced there was a link between the murders but the evidence was shaky at best, and if Garwood got wind of it, he'd spontaneously combust. Of course, such a conflagration may prove unavoidable if, as Jack suspected, he would eventually have to apply for a warrant to search the De Vere premises. But before that happened, he needed to be on much firmer ground.

* * *

Saturday. Twenty past twelve. Malone's stomach growled in protest as it realized he was walking past the canteen where the enticing aromas of succulent steak and kidney pudding and jam roly-poly were drifting down the corridor. But the wall clock told him he had another forty minutes to go before his lunch break and he needed to take the autopsy report on Fiddler to the DI.

'Tell me again, guv. Why are we working on a Saturday when it's the big match this afternoon? I wouldn't care, but Nat Fiddler was a lying, cheating, slimy little sod.'

'I agree, but now he's been murdered, that makes him *our* lying, cheating, slimy little sod and it's our job to find and arrest whoever did it.'

Malone sighed, reluctant but resigned. 'Yes, guv. I knew that. I just needed someone to remind me.' He handed over the report which consisted of twelve, closely typed foolscap pages of Big Ron's thorough but deeply scientific jargon. Jack tossed it to Pinkney.

'You were present at the post-mortem yesterday, Pinkney. Give us the quick, easy version in simple words that even dim sods like me and Bugsy can understand.'

Pinkney bustled to the front of the room, pleased to have the chance to shine before his boss and the rest of the team. He opened the file. 'The deceased was a man in his late fifties, five feet four inches tall, 135 pounds and poorly nourished.

Lungs and liver in the early stages of necrosis. Estimated time of death was between seven and nine on Thursday evening. Stomach contents indicated his last meal consisted of beer and kebabs eaten at lunchtime. He appeared to survive on junk food, alcohol and cigarettes.'

'What's wrong with that?' asked someone to a chorus of titters.

'Cause of death,' continued Pinkney, undeterred, 'was pressure obstruction of carotid arteries and larynx preventing blood flow to the brain and air flow to the lungs. Doctor Hardacre's diagnosis is homicidal strangulation — no ligature abrasions so the murderer used his hands. A thorough examination revealed superficial and deep injuries fitting a pattern that supports her diagnosis. The autopsy included complete dissection of Fiddler's neck with removal of the larynx, including the hyoid bone, unbroken, and with the tongue attached.' There were groans of revulsion which Pinkney mistook for dissent. 'Actually, fracture of the hyoid bone is only found in a minority of all fatal strangulations, probably less than a third.'

Malone stood up and put an arm around his shoulders. 'Pinkney, you're a very disturbed young man and I worry about you. It must be all that university swotting. It stunts a growing lad's natural development, which is why you're not sensitive and emotional, like me.' Laughter crackled around the room. Malone winked encouragingly and whispered, 'Carry on, son. You're doing fine.'

'Sometimes it's possible to actually recover the assailant's skin cells from the victim's injured neck, then you can DNA-match them to the suspect.'

The coppers perked up, ever hopeful.

'But not in this case, unfortunately.' More groans. 'Doctor Hardacre's opinion is that the strangler wore gloves; soft ones, possibly kid leather or calf, so they could belong to a woman. Now, this bit is very interesting. The lab found evidence that shortly before his death, Fiddler had held a gun in his right hand and before that, he had carried it in his raincoat pocket. Needless to say, he didn't have a licence and owned it illegally. We didn't find a gun at the scene, nor was it found when his flat and office were searched this morning, but they did find the container it had been kept in and a cloth he used to clean it.' He looked straight at DI Dawes. 'That means he either ditched it just before he was killed, sir, or the more probable scenario — the murderer took it.'

* * *

Sunday morning. The mood in the incident room was one of quiet desperation. Phones had stopped ringing, all lines of enquiry had been followed up and discarded and the few leads that they did have had been tested to destruction. Fiddler's workload had been sparse and poorly documented, mainly because most of it was unlawful. He seemed to specialize in invasive matrimonial surveillance, debt collecting that amounted to demanding money with menaces, and tracing missing persons who didn't want to be found. Such of his contacts that the team had been able to speak to either had watertight alibis for Thursday evening (two were in prison and another was in hospital with a ruptured spleen and his ribs kicked in), or they were going through an expensive divorce 'thanks to that interfering little sod, Fiddler. Bloody good riddance if you ask me!' and therefore not overly enthusiastic to rack their brains for any information that might help catch his killer.

DI Dawes noticed a few barely stifled yawns and told Pinkney to open the window. Never one to do things by halves, he flung it open to its fullest extent, letting in a blast of cold air. The door was suddenly kicked open and Malone entered backwards, balancing a plate of bacon rolls on two mugs of tea. Under his arm was a bundle of crinkly newspaper that looked like it had been out in the rain, then dried off again. He deposited his load in front of Jack.

'Three interesting bits of information for you, guv.' He shivered. 'Blimey. Bit nippy in here, isn't it?' He slammed shut the gaping window and flopped into a chair. 'First off, it looks like old Smelly Nellie wasn't kidding when she said she was descended from the nobility.' Bugsy passed Jack a piece of yellowing, crumpled newsprint from the bundle. Jack studied it, nonplussed.

'It says here that Prime Minister Harold Macmillan is planning to end National Service.'

'Sorry, guv. Wrong article.' Bugsy fished out another page that had once been an illustrated article, cut from a 1958 copy of Vogue magazine.

'Uniform found this and a lot of similar stuff in the bottom of her pram under the rags. You always reckoned she was class once, didn't you?'

Jack looked at the faded image which was unmistakeably Nellie, aged about 17 or 18, being presented at court to a young Queen Elizabeth II. The caption was *One of the Last Debutantes*. Her real name, it seemed, was Helena (Nell) Devereux, and according to the magazine article, she was descended from Robert Devereux, second Earl of Essex and favourite of the first Queen Elizabeth around 1587. Jack looked at it with sadness. Young Nell had indeed been an outstanding beauty in her day. How heart-breaking that a once vibrant young woman should plummet into a life of such personal neglect. And what a wretched death at the end of it. Whoever ran her down and left her there to die in a pool of blood was guilty as sin but had got away scot-free. He wondered how they could live with themselves. Bugsy's cheery voice nudged Jack out of his abstraction.

'Now this second piece of info is *really* interesting.' The sergeant bolted the last mouthful of his bacon roll, wiped his fingers down his tie, then pulled a flattened cigarette packet from his pocket and dropped it on Jack's desk.

Jack looked down at it for a while. 'All right. I give up. What's interesting about an empty fag packet with bacon grease on it, Bugsy?'

'Sorry, guv.' Malone flipped it over. 'Read the writing on it.'

Jack read it aloud. '*Ask Reen which florist delivered Mrs W's roses. Get description of who ordered them. Did they pay by credit card?*'

'The lads found it when they searched Fiddler's office this morning. It was on his desk amongst a heap of other rubbish and it's the only thing they found of any relevance. They compared it to some other stuff and it's definitely his writing. Looks like he left a reminder to himself. I wonder if he lived long enough to follow it up. In any event, I think *we* should — P.D.Q.'

'Who's Mrs W, Sarge?' asked Pinkney, still puzzled.

'Annabelle Whittington, who else?' bragged Bugsy, as though it should be obvious to anyone with half a detective's mind. 'It supports your theory that the two murders may be connected in some way, guv.'

'Yes, but who's Reen?' Jack wondered.

Malone grinned broadly. 'Ah, now *that* brings me to the third interesting bit of info. I've just been speaking to the uniform constables who broke the news to Fiddler's next of kin. He's only got one surviving relative and you're never going to believe who it is.'

'Go on. Surprise us.'

'It's his widowed sister, one Doreen Mackay, a.k.a. Reen, for short.' He watched with satisfaction as DI Dawes and DC Pinkney chewed this over.

'What, the same Mrs Mackay who works as a housekeeper for Annabelle Whittington?

'The very same, which is how I worked out who Mrs W was. Reckon we should pay the crabby old bat a visit? Offer our condolences?'

'Too right, Bugsy. They're all tied up in this together, somehow. Too many similarities to be a coincidence this time.'

'I wonder what the roses have to do with it?' said Pinkney, thoughtfully. 'Can't be for Whittington's funeral; we haven't released the body, yet. And why did Fiddler want to know who sent them?'

'I expect the sister will be able to tell us that. We'll get straight over there and — '

The phone interrupted, loud and insistent. It was the Chief Super. Jack sat to attention and saluted so the others would guess who it was.

'Good afternoon, sir. Yes, I've pulled in the whole team. Where? Who? Could you slow down a bit, sir? For a moment there, I thought you said something about another dead body. Right. I understand. We're on our way.'

He put the phone down, his expression a mixture of frustration and disbelief. Malone and Pinkney looked at him expectantly.

'Mrs Mackay will have to wait. We've got another stiff . . . a bloke. Found this morning by a retired brigadier in a rubbish skip outside his house in Richington Parva.'

'You're joking, guv.'

Dawes pulled a wry face. 'Am I laughing? And the Chief Super sounds like he's having apoplexy. I could hear him shaking tablets out of a bottle even while he was shouting at me.'

'Christ Almighty!' groaned Bugsy. 'Well, I'm warning you now, if the deceased is wearing sequinned spandex and dance shoes and has one of De Vere's business cards in his pocket, I'm going to pack it in and become a traffic warden.'

CHAPTER FIFTEEN

Big Ron was crawling about in a very large skip when they got there. There wasn't room in it for the SOCO team as well, so they were waiting patiently for her to finish before they started their inspection, evidence bags at the ready. Her head popped up briefly while she studied a rectal thermometer, gave it a shake, then wiped it clean and replaced it in her bag. Her lips moved as she did the mental calculation. Spotting DI Dawes and his two henchmen, she glared at them over the side.

'Could you try to confine this systematic extermination of all the males in Richington to weekdays, Inspector? Some of us have a life beyond grovelling in skips with dead bodies on Sundays. I'm supposed to be on the golf course.'

Jack smiled apologetically. 'Sorry, Doctor. Do we know who it is?'

'I should think so. It's our red but very dead MP, Martin Laidlaw.'

'Bloody hell,' said Malone. 'Bit young to die, wasn't he? Either one of his crumbly constituents turned a bit nasty and welted him with her zimmerframe or Jennifer Jiggle-Tits shagged him to death. Any ideas as to the cause, yet, Doc?'

'Ideas, Malone? I'm just a pathologist. Unlike detective sergeants, I'm not allowed to have salacious ideas.'

'Your professional opinion would be greatly valued, Doctor Hardacre,' said Jack politely.

'Well, I shouldn't want to make any wild guesses at this stage, Inspector, but the bullet hole between his eyes could have had something to do with it.' She ducked down into the skip, and they could hear her scrabbling about, then she bobbed up again. 'There's no exit wound so the bullet's still lodged in his skull somewhere. I'll winkle it out at the autopsy.'

'Maybe it was suicide,' suggested Malone, innocently. 'MPs are under a lot of pressure these days, what with furnishing their second homes and filling in their expense forms smart enough for no one to understand 'em.'

'It would take a very smart MP to shoot himself between the eyes, dispose of the weapon, then jump into a skip, Sergeant. Estimated time of death around 36 hours ago, some time on Friday night. There's no blood in the skip or the surrounding area so, in my opinion, he was shot elsewhere, kept cool for 24 hours, then brought here and dumped in the skip last night.' She disappeared again then popped up holding an ugly African totem, a naked female with exaggerated breasts, protruding tongue and bulging eyes. Shuddering, she passed it over the side of the skip to Pinkney. 'Can you get rid of that for me please, Jonathan, it was wedged under the cadaver and it's giving me the creeps.'

'Jonathan?' mouthed Bugsy to Jack, grinning. 'The lads back at the station are going to love that.'

Blushing, Pinkney took the totem and handed it carefully to a member of the SOCO team who immediately placed it in a bag.

'Sorry about that. Hideous, isn't it?' The retired brigadier, whose skip it was, tottered down the path followed by his wife, carrying a tray of cups and a plate of biscuits. They stayed obediently on their own side of the police tape. 'Given to me by a Dinka chief in the Sudan. Apparently, if you lie with her at night, she brings you luck next day.'

'Didn't bring Laidlaw much luck, did she?' observed Bugsy.

'We're having a clear out,' explained the wife. 'Downsizing to a bungalow on the Isle of Wight. That's why the skip's here. You've never seen so much accumulated rubbish. Decades of it.'

'I realize neighbours tend to dump their own junk in your skip once it gets dark,' said the brigadier, 'but I never expected to find a body in it this morning, let alone the body of our MP. Recognized him straight off. I mean to say, I don't agree with his politics, either, but topping him's a bit strong, what?'

Big Ron climbed down out of the skip, courteously assisted by Pinkney. Malone, fascinated as always by her bulging, brown, surgical stockings, had a sudden craving for bangers and mash and remembered that he still hadn't had his lunch. Doctor Hardacre motioned for the body to be taken away to join Whittington, Fiddler and Nell Devereux in a rapidly filling mortuary refrigerator. Then she bore down on Jack and jabbed him painfully in the chest with a stubby finger. 'If anyone else gets himself murdered this weekend, I shall consider you personally negligent, DI Dawes!'

'Doctor, I'm deeply wounded,' he said. 'After all, I'm your best customer.'

She snapped her hag shut and stomped away to her car.

A young man in shiny corduroy trousers and a scruffy sports jacket pushed his way through the gathering bystanders and shoved a digital voice recorder in Jack's face. '*Kings Richington Herald*, Inspector. Can you confirm that it's Martin Laidlaw, the MP, who's been shot?' He was accompanied by a photographer who was snapping away at everyone and everything. 'Have you any leads? What about the gun? Have you found it yet? Is it a political or domestic murder? Have you ruled out terrorism?'

Malone shoved his bulk between Jack and the reporter. 'Piss off! You'll get a statement when we're ready and that won't be until after the next of kin has been informed.'

The journalist laughed. 'You're too late, chum. The beautiful but sadly sozzled Jenny Laidlaw already knows about the untimely demise of her boring old man. We've got a reporter in her house right now, feeding her gin and getting an exclusive. Would you like me to send an early edition round to the station?' Grinning, the photographer clicked off several shots of Bugsy waving his fist and looking aggressive. Jack could imagine Monday's headlines.

'How the hell did they get here so fast? It's Sunday, for Christ's sake.'

Malone scowled. 'Some idiot must have tipped 'em off.'

The detectives left SOCOs to swarm all over the skip like an army of white ants and accompanied the brigadier and his wife into their home.

'I wonder if you would mind answering a few questions, Brigadier? I'm DI Dawes and this is DS Malone and DC Pinkney.'

The brigadier invited them to sit. 'Not at all, Inspector. Pleased to help if I can.' He looked sheepish. 'Incidentally, I'm sorry about the newspaper johnnie. Think that may have been my fault. The editor of the *Kings Richington Herald* is a neighbour, do you see? Friend of ours. Dinner parties, charity do's, that kind of thing. He came across to see what was going on this morning, when the hullabaloo first kicked off, and naturally, I told him I'd found a dead MP in my skip. Never gave it a thought. He must have phoned his paper and got the reporters down here.'

Jack breathed deeply and counted to ten. Wonderful. Bloody wonderful. He'd crossed swords with this particular editor on several occasions since joining the Met. There had never been any attempt to cooperate with the police or to delay publication of information that might jeopardize an investigation. Jack had no doubt that by now the whole story would have been fed nationwide to both the broadsheets and the tabloids. A murdered MP was a juicy scoop and they'd inflate it into a massive one, even if it wasn't. And goodness only knew what Jennifer Laidlaw had told them. Wait till Garwood sees tomorrow's papers.

'Never mind, Brigadier. It can't be helped now. Our Press Office will try to do some damage limitation. Tell me, did either you or your wife see or hear anything unusual during the night?'

The brigadier shook his head. 'Not me. I sleep like the dead. Oh, sorry. Bad taste. But the wife did, didn't you Elfrida? She's a very light sleeper and a terrible fidget at night, always hopping out of bed to wash her socks or bath the cat.'

'What exactly did you see, madam?'

'Nothing exciting, I'm afraid. It's just that I woke about two and remembered I hadn't given General Gordon his nightcap.' She went across and offered a nut to a mangy African Grey parrot, sitting on a perch in the corner. The old bird was moth-eaten and scabby with rancorous, red-veined eyes. It snatched the nut and rolled it around with a black, bulbous tongue, muttering psittacine oaths under its breath. Elfrida stroked its balding head, lovingly. 'Anyway, I got up and went down to the kitchen to warm his whisky and ginger and I happened to glance out of the window. Someone was walking towards a car on the other side of the lane. I wouldn't have thought much about it except it's unusual to see anybody about at that time of night. Richington Parva is a very quiet neighbourhood. Mostly retired people like us.'

Pinkney whipped out his notebook. 'Can you describe the man, madam?'

'Oh it wasn't a man, officer. It was a woman. Slim and smartly dressed. A coat with a fur collar, long blonde hair and very high heels. Beautifully made up, I could see as she passed under the street lamp. Then she got into the car and drove away.'

'Did you get the registration at all,' asked Jack, fingers crossed.

'No, I'm afraid not. I'd have needed my glasses for that.'

'What kind of car was it, madam?' asked Pinkney, scribbling furiously. She shrugged apologetically. 'Smallish.

Possibly grey or maybe light blue? Old I think, because the engine was fairly noisy when she pulled away.'

'Any idea of the make?' Bugsy was clutching at straws.

The brigadier laughed. 'I'm afraid my wife wouldn't know a Porsche from a Punto, Sergeant. Never driven a car, you see. Now, put her on a camel and it would be a completely different matter, wouldn't it, old gel?'

'Was she tall, this woman?' asked Jack, feeling his will to live ebbing slowly away.

'Depends what you mean by tall,' said Elfrida doubtfully.

'Well, around six feet, say? Like me?'

'Goodness no, Inspector. She was nearer my height, maybe a little taller.'

Jack looked. About five-six. Not Gloria De Vere, then. His opposite number in uniform had said she was at least six feet tall. Was he becoming obsessed with this woman whom he hadn't even met but who seemed to hover, phantom-like, in the background of every case? No, he didn't seriously believe it could be her. In fact, he doubted that the person in the lane had any connection with the body at all. A woman like that could hardly heave a man's corpse out of her car boot and up into a skip. She was obviously just a harmless lady passing through who had maybe stopped to check the lights on her car, especially if it was an old one, like the witness said. It might still be worth trying to trace her, though, in case she saw something useful. But what might have been their first lead to a suspect had petered out like all the others. They thanked the brigadier and his wife and told them someone would be round later to take statements. Then they shambled silently back to the car, minds focused on the profile of their killer.

'Tell you what, guv,' said Bugsy. 'This geezer is getting too bloody cocky, dumping bodies all over Kings Richington. He's really taking the piss out of us now, and he's doing it too bloody often. And we're no nearer to catching him than we were at the start.'

'Cocky often means desperate and therefore careless, Bugsy. If someone else had looked out of their window at a different time, they might very well have seen the murderer. Get the team to start knocking on doors. Ask everyone if they saw anything suspicious.'

'Like what, guv?'

Jack was edgy. 'Anything. I don't care how trivial. Even if they only saw someone dragging a dead MP out of the back of a van and happened to take down the registration number. It's little things like that that could help us.'

Bugsy grinned. 'OK, guv, but it's a bit of a long shot. Look at the houses.'

Jack looked. With the exception of the brigadier's house, which was enclosed by a white, pseudo-African palisade, all the occupants of Richington Parva, with the typical privacy paranoia of their class, had surrounding themselves with leylandii hedges and tall fences, which effectively prevented people from looking in but also blocked any view they might have had of the world outside.

* * *

Some hours later at the station, Jack and the team were attempting to make sense of an increasingly senseless situation. They had no hard evidence that the De Vere Académie of Dance was criminally linked to any of the murders but the circumstantial evidence was beginning to build up and couldn't be ignored. Unfortunately, it wasn't enough to justify a warrant and top brass had virtually forbidden Jack to question Gloria or her staff on a voluntary basis. To focus their minds, Pinkney started to make a list of the basic facts on the incident room whiteboard.

'First off, Whittington, the QC, is found floating in the river, tortured and dismembered. Then Fiddler, the PI, is found strangled in a wheelie bin. Now Laidlaw, the MP, is found shot and dumped in a skip.'

Malone grunted. 'It's gettin' like bleedin' Cluedo. We're only short of Colonel Mustard in the library with a rope.'

'Or how about Miss Sadie Scarlett in the ballroom with a gun, sir?' suggested Pinkney.

Jack was impressed. 'A distinct possibility, Pinkney. Now what, if anything, did the victims have in common? Whittington used to go to Gloria De Vere's on his own for extra dance lessons. Fiddler, brother of Mrs Mackay, the Whittingtons' housekeeper, is found with the business card of one of De Vere's dancing instructors in his pocket. Laidlaw is an acquaintance of the Whittingtons and, by association, maybe also one of De Vere's elite crowd.'

Pinkney wrote fast, adding names and drawing lines and arrows that linked and doubled back until it looked like a spider's web with Gloria De Vere at the centre.

'Just as a starting point,' offered Jack, 'let's work on a simplistic assumption that whoever tortured Whittington to death also strangled Fiddler, then took his gun and used it to shoot Laidlaw. And according to Big Ron, the murderer could quite easily be a woman.'

'No, I can't buy that, Jack,' objected Malone. 'I can see where you're going but where's your motive? And I'm still not convinced it was a woman. Are you sure you're not getting too hung up on the ballroom connection? I mean, however bad Whittington's dancing was, I can't believe they kicked him in the nuts whenever he got the steps wrong. And Fiddler didn't strike me as the kind of bloke who'd pay good beer money for foxtrot lessons, so we have to assume that if he went to De Vere's it was to snoop around. Who was he looking for? Probably just an unfaithful husband who was playing around with one of the girls. And we don't have any-thing at all to connect Marxist Martin with De Vere's, apart from the fact that the Laidlaws were at the Whittingtons' anniversary nosh. I'd have said Comrade Laidlaw was the last geezer to go to a posers' palace and part with a fortune just to trip the light fantastic and rub shoulders with the nobs. He was a fully paid up, 24 carat, doom-peddling lefty.' The sergeant paused briefly to pull a cold, congealing burger from his pocket and sink his teeth into it. It was a good sign when Bugsy turbo-charged his blood sugar. He wiped ketchup off his chin with the back of his hand and continued. 'How about this, guv? All three of the deceased came in contact with villains and ex-cons as part of their job. Whittington prosecuted 'em, Fiddler tracked 'em down and double-crossed 'em and Laidlaw met the ones who regularly complain about police brutality, prison conditions and their human rights. It could be one killer with a grudge against all three of 'em. Or even three completely different killers, although I agree that's unlikely.'

Jack smiled to himself. At this rate, they were in danger of going full circle and returning to Corrie's ambush theory — melodramatic but, as with all Corrie's theories, not totally unfeasible. 'You're right, Bugsy, we ought to consider other possibilities but the bodies are starting to pile up and it's one hell of a coincidence if there's no link between them at all. We've got one aggravated heart attack, one hit-and-run, one strangulation and a shooting. All within the space of two weeks. It may be normal for Midsomer but it's a bit excessive for affluent, crime-free Kings Richington, and so far the murders are all unsolved, as I have no doubt the editor of the *Herald* will waste no time in pointing out.'

'Too bloody right it's excessive,' grumbled Malone. 'When I applied for this job, they said don't worry, Bugsy, nothing naughty ever happens in that part of the manor.'

Everything they had pointed to a common denominator and Jack's flat and crooked nose still told him it was De Vere's. But the more he thought about it rationally, the less probable it seemed. And they didn't have a motive for any of the murders unless Gloria De Vere turned out to be a closet psychopath who had taken a sudden dislike to men. Jack leaned back in his chair, hands linked behind his head, and looked up at the ceiling for inspiration. The urge to castigate himself for his lack of progress was overwhelming.

'Who was it who said, "If you stare into the abyss long enough, the abyss stares right back at you"?'

'Friedrich Nietzsche, sir,' said Pinkney, without looking up. 'German philosopher, existentialist, postmodernist and psychoanalyst. Went round the bend and snuffed it in

1900. Me displayed a fondness for aphorisms, hence your quotation. And given our progress to date, very apt, if I may say so, sir.'

'That lad's too smart by half,' muttered Jack.

'That's why he makes such a good cup of tea,' said Malone. 'Go on, son, the canteen closed hours ago so you'll have to put the kettle on. And see if there are any chocolate digestives left in PC Molesworth's drawers.'

* * *

By the time Jack got home, late on Sunday night, Corrie was in bed. Exhausted but ravenous, he demolished the slice of chicken and ham pie and potato salad she had left out for him. He'd have liked a glass of wine with it and he was sure there was a bottle of cabernet sauvignon around somewhere but he couldn't find it so he crept upstairs, undressed in the dark, and slid into bed beside Corrie. She wasn't asleep.

'Jack, is it true Martin Laidlaw's been shot?'

Sensing a prolonged and gruelling interrogation, he sat up and put on the bedside light, wishing even more that he had a glass of wine. 'Blimey, bad news certainly travels fast around here and it hasn't even hit the headlines, yet. Don't tell me — Cynthia Garwood.'

'Yes. And she said that the grimy little PI you pulled out of the hotel wheelie bin on Thursday night was Doreen Mackay's brother, Nat.'

'My word, she really is a mine of information, isn't she?'

'So it's true. Jack, that's terrible. Poor Doreen. Poor Jennifer. Poor Annabelle.'

'What about poor me?' complained Jack, desperate for sleep. 'Three murders in two weeks and not a bloody clue who the killer is or why. Garwood's doing his nut.'

'Does that mean you think the same killer murdered all three?'

'I've no idea. Don't you have any theories, Miss Marple? You usually do.'

Corrie sat up and produced the elusive bottle of cabernet sauvignon and two glasses from under the bed with the artistry of a magician plucking a rabbit from a hat. Wine helped her think. She poured them each a glass and settled back to work it out.

'Well, I think we're both agreed that Sebastian Whittington became involved with some very dangerous characters who tied him up and tried to torture something out of him but they went too far. When he died suddenly, his tormentors panicked and chopped him up so he wouldn't be identified. Find out where he went that Saturday night and what nasty business he was mixed up in and you'll find his killers.'

'Should I be writing all this down?' asked Jack, deadpan.

'Don't be silly. Now, as far as Nat Fiddler's concerned, he was Doreen's brother, so naturally, she loved him and believed he was honourable and law-abiding, but forensics said he'd carried a gun, didn't they? I shouldn't be surprised if most of his activities involved swindles, scams and racketeering with villains at the bottom of the criminal food chain. It's a PI's job to integrate with thugs and thieves, isn't it?'

'Well, it certainly seemed to be Fiddler's.'

'I expect he swindled one of them and they started threatening him, which is why he felt it necessary to carry the gun — for his own protection.' Corrie was making it up as she went along, something she was good at, except her scenarios were always lurid and rarely close to the truth. 'What about this.' She put down her wine glass and pushed up the sleeves of her pyjamas, ready to demonstrate. 'The thug is lying in wait down that dark alley outside the hotel. As Nat walks past on his way home, the thug calls out his name, softly. Nat thinks it's one of his crooked chums wanting to do a deal, creeps down the alley to meet him and wallop! The thug pounces!' She grabbed Jack around the throat just as he was swallowing a mouthful of wine, causing him to gag in a most realistic manner. 'Yes, that's it,' said Corrie, appreciatively. 'He starts to choke, just like that, and drops the gun in the struggle. Then, the very next day, someone else finds it and uses it to shoot Martin Laidlaw.'

'Why? And if Fiddler dropped the gun, how come Big Ron and her team didn't find it on Thursday night?'

'Well, I don't know, do I? I can't do all the work for you.'

'How d'you know it was the same gun?'

'It has to be. Too much of a coincidence, otherwise. After all, this isn't Dodge City. There can't be that many illegal firearms knocking about in Kings Richington, can there?'

Jack refilled their glasses. 'What about Jennifer Laidlaw as a suspect? A surprisingly high percentage of murder victims are done in by their spouses.'

Corrie crossed her arms and pursed her lips virtuously. 'Now, you know me, Jack, I'm not one to make snap judgements and I'd be the last person to offer anyone marriage guidance, but we all know that when something goes wrong between a couple, it's nearly always the husband's fault.'

'Is that a fact?' said Jack, amused.

'Oh, yes. Scientific research has shown that when discord breaks out in the home and the air is thick with harsh words, recriminations and, in Jennifer Laidlaw's case, flying gin bottles, the wife is hardly ever to blame. However . . . ' she held up a finger, ' . . . in the case of the Laidlaws, I think it far more likely that Martin would have been driven to top Jennifer rather than the other way around. I'm sorry she's been widowed, especially with that little boy to bring up, but she's a truly awful woman. Spoiled, unprincipled and totally self-centred.'

'So what you're saying is that Whittington was tortured to death by black-hearted villains from the underworld, Fiddler was strangled by a common thug that he'd swindled and Laidlaw was shot by someone who conveniently happened to find a gun and decided it was time for a by-election?'

'Something like that, yes. Of course, it needs a little fine tuning.'

'And where does Madame De Vere's Académie with its mysterious dimensions fit into all this?'

Corrie looked blank. 'It doesn't.'

Jack climbed out of bed and put on his dressing gown.

'Where are you going?'

'Well, since you have effectively shot all my best theories up the fundamental orifice, I thought I'd go down and get myself another slice of pie.'

'Greedy pig!' Corrie shouted after him. 'Will you bring me a piece, please?'

CHAPTER SIXTEEN

WEEK THREE-MONDAY

Monday morning, eight o'clock. The team was subdued, hard at work but keeping their heads down. The incident room was littered with newspapers wallowing in a media feeding frenzy. KILLER LOOSE IN KINGS RICHINGTON screamed the *Guardian*'s headline. 'Police are baffled by the recent spate of unexplained murders.' As Jack feared, the story had been taken up by the nationals, hugely magnified and distorted, and most papers carried a variation on the theme from MP GUNNED DOWN IN COLD BLOOD to CRIME WAVE IN LEAFY SUBURB. Pinkney had spread them round the room so the team could get up to speed on what intelligence, if it could be called that, was now in the public domain. Each paper ran a different account of the same events, depending on their political bias and the perceived reading ability of their distribution, many of whom considered the *Sun* too intellectual.

Malone picked up the *Kings Richington Herald* and snorted his contempt. 'Have you seen this, guv?'

POLICE DRAGGING HEELS IN SEARCH FOR KINGS RICHINGTON KILLER, CLAIMS WEEPING

WIDOW. A tearful Jennifer Laidlaw gazed groggily from the front page, white-faced, and bleary-eyed. One hand was clutching Timothy, who looked confused and seemed to be struggling to get off her lap. The other hand held a glass that was only half out of shot. The caption under the picture read, 'Grief-stricken widow of popular MP, Martin Laidlaw, with their seven-year-old son, Timothy. Police are caught napping but *Herald* reporters act promptly to break the tragic news and offer support.' The article continued, 'Attractive blonde, Jennifer Laidlaw, 31, told *Herald* reporters, "I'm devastated. Martin was a devoted husband and father and an exceptional politician with a brilliant career ahead of him. Everyone loved and respected him, he had no enemies. Who would want to do this terrible thing? My heart is broken but I shall continue to devote my life to the community work that was so important to Martin and caring for our beloved son, Timothy."' Beside her was a smaller picture of the brigadier and his wife outside their house, beaming vacantly and pointing at the skip.

'I don't soddin' well believe it!' Malone spluttered. 'We all know what Jennifer Jiggle-Tits has devoted her life to and it doesn't have anything to do with social work, unless you count servicing as many blokes as possible and keeping the gin manufacturers in business. And as for grief-stricken, give her a week and she'll be posing half naked in the celebrity magazines.'

'Oh, I say, Sarge. I think you're being unnecessarily hard on her,' protested Pinkney.

Jack picked up one of the nationals and read aloud: '"Gun crime hits leafy suburb, Kings Richington. What are our police doing to stop it?" There's a statement from Sir Barnaby's Press Officer assuring the public that the Met is hot on the trail and the commander expects several arrests very soon. I wish I shared his confidence.'

'Many of the papers have picked up on the Nat Fiddler murder, as well as our other unsolved cases, sir,' said Pinkney. 'Most of it is more imaginative than accurate and conveniently ignores the fact that Fiddler was a disgraced ex-copper. This one says, "PEACEFUL TOWN STALKED BY KILLER. Police are bewildered as one of their colleagues is strangled and dumped in a rubbish bin by the Kings Richington Killer. The murder of detective Nathaniel Arthur Fiddler, 58, is yet another in the spate of mysterious deaths that has struck this select, affluent community. Only recently, a woman was knocked down and killed in a callous hit-and-run incident while walking along the Old Richington Road, and the driver has not, as yet, been apprehended. And mystery still surrounds the death of Sebastian Whittington, who died prematurely and unexpectedly from a heart attack just two weeks ago, in his luxury, multimillion-pound mansion in this pleasant town. Now local MP Martin Laidlaw has been shot and killed in an apparently motiveless crime. This makes four suspicious deaths in a fortnight. Is this just a tragic coincidence or is there a dangerous killer at large? Police are under pressure to act before another murder is committed.'"

'Did you hear that noise, guv?' asked Bugsy.

'What noise?'

'The sound of property prices dropping like a stone all over Kings Richington.'

'Indeed they are, Malone.' Chief Superintendent Garwood stood in the doorway, gnashing his teeth like a rogue Rottweiler, uncertain whose throat to tear out first. Jack groaned audibly and Bugsy stared at the ceiling and swore, softly, as Garwood marched in and stood at the front of the incident room where the silence had now reached pin-dropping level. A pulse throbbed in his temple, indicating that his temper was only barely under control and his blood pressure was threatening to blow like a Texas oil gusher. 'First of all,' he said coldly, 'I'm sure I don't need to tell you that Sir Barnaby is very unhappy. He has been summoned by the Assistant Commissioner, who will expect answers to a number of crucial questions. So would someone like to explain how the press got to Mrs Laidlaw before us? And who gave the papers the information about our ex-colleague,

Fiddler, whose fifteen minutes of fame we could well have done without? And how come we suddenly have an armed serial killer in our midst, about whom we apparently know nothing? Finally, ladies and gentlemen, is there a small possibility, however remote and unlikely, that we may be able to solve any of the killings that the papers have so helpfully drawn to our attention?' Jack opened his mouth to reply but Garwood cut him off with a peremptory wave of his hand. 'No, Inspector Dawes, don't tell me now, it'll spoil the surprise. I shall expect a detailed and comprehensive report on my desk by close of play.' He glowered about him to show he meant business then strode out.

'Better get typing, Pinkney,' suggested Malone. 'This could take some time.'

Pinkney's face was a picture of frustration and disillusionment. He had expected a job on the murder squad to be exciting — car chases and breaking down doors and shouting 'you're nicked'. So far, all he'd done was draw charts, write endless reports and interview people who didn't know anything — or if they did, they weren't about to tell him. And in his spare time he was keeper of the Home Office statistics. As far as he could see, the team was no closer to solving anything than they had been a fortnight ago.

Hearing his deep sigh, Jack went over to Pinkney's desk. He knew exactly how the lad was feeling because he'd experienced the same impatience and disappointment when he had been a DC, some twenty years ago, and little had changed in terms of expectations compared with reality.

'You're doing a good job, Jonathan, a crucial job. I know it doesn't feel like it to you but honest groundwork is vital, particularly when a case comes to court. Genuine police detectives don't have a wow factor like the ones on TV who strut about giving orders but never do any real work. And lucky breaks that solve the whole mystery rarely come out of the blue without effort. People like Garwood are entirely political. They have knee-jerk responses to bad press and angry phone calls from the Home Office. But ordinary coppers like us have to play the long game. It's sheer dull application that finds your villain. You have to persist, miss nothing and always keep your chin up. Understand?'

'Yes, sir. Thank you, sir.'

'What the guv'nor really means, son,' said Bugsy grinning, 'is that the better you do your job, the more likely you are to be shot, injured, complained about, sued, investigated, or subpoenaed on your day off. It isn't criminal law — it's sod's law.'

Pinkney grinned back.

* * *

Doreen Mackay, lost in childhood memories of her murdered younger brother, was carefully dusting a collection of very valuable Meissen figurines arranged tastefully along Annabelle Whittington's magnificent mantelpiece. She glanced briefly out of the window just in time to see something that caused her almost to condemn the cupid she was holding to a shattering demise on the marble hearth below. A vehicle was pulling into the drive. It was a florist's van, the same one that had delivered the fateful bouquet of blackmailer's roses the previous Tuesday. Despite the warmth of the room, Doreen shivered as the delivery boy pulled open the doors in the back of the van and lifted out another, identical bunch of crimson roses. She hurried to open the front door before his ring disturbed Mrs Whittington, who was resting in her bedroom. She had read about Martin Laidlaw's death in the paper together with the snide insinuations about Sebastian's unexpected death and she had taken it badly.

'Morning, missus. Someone must love you,' said the boy, a chirpy youngster with green hair, a ring through everything and barbed wire tattooed round his neck. He handed over the flowers. 'That's two bunches I've delivered here in two weeks.'

Doreen took the bouquet which all but filled her arms. 'You don't happen to know who's sending these, do you?'

The lad indicated a white envelope tucked into the ribbons. 'It'll say on the card, I expect. They're only usually anonymous on Valentine's Day.'

'And if they are anonymous, would you be able to tell me who sent them?'

The boy sucked air through his teeth. 'Not me, love. I only deliver 'em. You'd have to ask the boss who runs the shop. He takes the orders and the money. He might remember, as it was an expensive order. He may even be able to trace it in his book. Depends how the bloke paid.'

'It was definitely a man who ordered them, then?'

'Dunno, do I? I was just thinking that women don't often send romantic red roses to other women, do they? Have a nice day.' He plugged his ear phones back in and strolled back to his van, whistling and chewing gum simultaneously.

Doreen carried the blooms inside with the white envelope protruding menacingly from the red ribbons. She stood in the entrance hall, staring at the bouquet and dreading the moment when she would have to give it to Mrs Whittington, but Annabelle was already halfway down the grand staircase. She was calm and in perfect control of her emotions.

'It's all right, Doreen, I saw the van arrive from my window. Just give me the envelope and put the roses in the rubbish bin.'

Doreen pulled out the envelope and handed it over. Only the slight tremble in Annabelle's fingers betrayed her inner trepidation. The housekeeper bore the flowers away to the wheelie bin outside, their beauty tainted by the evil message that accompanied them. She would make Mrs W a nice cup of coffee with lots of sugar. She was going to need it.

Annabelle went into the drawing room, where the rich brocade furnishings never failed to soothe and comfort her, and settled herself in her favourite chair. Bravely she tore open the envelope, somewhat larger than the first, and braced herself for the second blackmail demand. No doubt the amount they wanted would also be somewhat larger. But even a lady of Annabelle's mettle could not have been prepared for what she saw. The photograph had been printed on computer paper but the definition was sharp and Annabelle recognized her husband immediately, as would anyone else, including the press. Sebastian was naked and tied by his wrists and ankles to a modern version of the medieval rack. Without his elegant clothes, his body looked bloated and flabby with pallid rolls of fat around his chest and stomach. Annabelle's eyes moved reluctantly downwards. His groin was spattered with blood and a spiked metal instrument had been clamped around his penis and scrotum. The hand of someone out of shot was gripping the instrument, twisting it tighter, so that the spikes bit cruelly into his flesh. Whittington's eyes were shut tight, his face contorted with agony and his mouth wide open in a Munch-like scream of excruciating pain. The image was obscene and sickening, more than Annabelle could bear. She crushed the print and let out a cry of pure anguish that brought Doreen running from the kitchen.

'What is it, dear? What are they threatening to do now?'

'They have sent a photograph.' Annabelle whispered it, unable to breathe.

Doreen hesitated. 'Do you want me to look?'

'No!' she shouted. 'No.' This time more quietly, her face drained of colour. 'I don't want anyone to see it — ever. Oh Doreen, I think I'm going to be sick.'

Coffee was no use in a situation like this, Doreen decided. This called for a double brandy. She went to the drinks cabinet and poured it. 'Here, dear. Sip this, it'll settle your tummy. Have you read the note?'

Annabelle sipped, grateful for the warmth flowing through her cold, numb insides. 'No. Will you read it to me, please?'

Doreen took the note and trawled up her spectacles on the chain around her neck.

Dear Mrs Whittington. Are you so arrogant that you believed you could simply ignore me and I would go away? Perhaps you doubted that your late husband could behave in this way. Maybe you did not believe that the photographs really existed. Well, here's the proof. Not one for the family album, is it? This is your last chance. The cost has doubled. You have until Saturday morning to get the cash. Leave it in the ladies' public convenience as before. And this time, don't involve anyone else. You saw what happened to your snooping private detective.

Mrs Mackay looked up from the note, hands shaking, her eyes full of tears.

Annabelle was devastated. 'Oh my God, Doreen. Your brother really was killed because of me. I'm so sorry.' She braced herself, drawing on every moral fibre she possessed. 'I have to put a stop to this woman, whoever she is.' She picked up the phone. 'I'm going to telephone Coriander Dawes.'

Doreen gulped back the tears. 'Corrie? Why? I thought you'd cancelled the funeral catering. How can she help?'

'She can't, not personally . . . but I think she might persuade her husband to help us. It's time I told the police about this but I can't face Sir Barnaby; it would be too painful, too awful, and I don't want my parents to find out which is why I can't ring the police station. Despite our contretemps the last time we met, if I'm honest, Inspector Dawes seemed like a fair, decent man who was simply trying to get to the truth about Sebastian's death. I'll ask Corrie if he would consider coming here on his own, to talk to us again. This time, we'll tell him everything that's happened, everything we know. Then, of course, we must accept whatever action he decides to take.'

* * *

Jack was in his office when Corrie rang so Pinkney took the call. He shouted through. 'Call for you, sir. It's Mrs Dawes. She wants to speak to you urgently. Shall I put her through?'

'Yes, please, Pinkney.' Jack raised an eyebrow, slightly concerned. It was most unusual for Corrie to ring him at the station. In fact, they had an unspoken agreement that neither would interrupt the other at work unless it was really important. Clearly, this was really important. 'Hello, Corrie. Are you OK? Is there a problem?'

'Hello, darling. Not a problem exactly, but I think you might want to do something about it straight away. I've just had Annabelle Whittington on the phone.'

'Really? I thought she wasn't speaking to either of us ever again.'

'So did I, but she sounded different, Jack. Like she was at her wits' end and almost . . . well, scared.'

'What about?'

'She didn't tell me. She asked if I thought you would consider going back to talk to her again. She has some information for you. She said she was prepared to come to the station but she'd much prefer it if you would be good enough to go to her home. Those were her exact words.'

'Blimey. Doesn't sound like the snooty Mrs Whittington. I wonder what's rattled her cage. When does she want to see me?'

'As soon as possible. And she wants you to go alone, Jack. No back-up.'

'OK. I'm on my way. See you tonight, if she hasn't eaten me alive.'

* * *

The atmosphere in the Whittingtons' house had changed radically since Jack's last visit with Sergeant Malone. Mrs Mackay greeted him almost cordially, opening the door before he knocked and showing him straight through to the drawing room where Annabelle paced up and down, pale and nervous.

'Please sit down, Inspector Dawes, and thank you so much for coming.' She sat herself then and nodded to Doreen who went off to make tea.

'Not at all, Mrs Whittington. My wife said you had some important information for me and it was a matter of urgency. But I think I should stress that if the information proves relevant to an ongoing murder investigation, I have no option but to act upon it. Obviously I shall try to be as discreet as possible.'

'Yes, I appreciate your position, Mr Dawes, and thank you for your candour.' Annabelle hesitated, swallowed hard then plunged straight in at the deep end. 'I'm being blackmailed. The first demand arrived last Tuesday. It was delivered by the local florist in a bouquet of roses. The black-mailer is threatening to publicize certain information about Sebastian that would totally destroy me and my family. I'm afraid I burned the note and ignored the demand.'

'Last Tuesday?' said Jack, appalled. 'Why didn't you get in touch with the police straight away, madam? If not my team, then I'm sure Sir Barnaby would have been anxious to help.'

She gulped. 'I couldn't, Inspector. You have to under-stand, I simply couldn't. After what you said about my hus-band being assaulted before he died, I just couldn't face it. But it seems you were right. He was cruelly tortured to death and as if that wasn't bad enough, they mutilated him after-wards. Today, the blackmailer sent me another demand and a photograph of the abuse actually taking place. Can you imagine that? It was . . . revolting. Simply vile.' She paused, looked down at her lap and took long shuddering breaths.

Jack concealed his surprise. Whatever he'd been expect-ing, it wasn't blackmail. On the other hand, people like the Whittingtons, who set themselves up as paragons of respectability, were always going to be an easy target when they slipped from their pedestals. 'Take your time, Mrs Whittington. I can see this is difficult for you.'

Her voice was very quiet, not at all like her usual, auto-cratic delivery. 'The blackmail note implied that Sebastian had voluntarily indulged in some lewd, depraved activities but I don't believe that for a moment. All the same, the woman has threatened to send the photographs to the press if I don't give her a very large sum of money and I'm quite sure the press will believe anything they choose.'

'How do you know the blackmailer is a woman?'

'Got to be, hasn't it?' answered Mrs Mackay, wheeling in the tea trolley. This time Jack noticed he had been given a china cup and saucer instead of a mug. 'She wants the cash left in a ladies' convenience. It'll be the same mercenary, vicious little cow who lured poor Mr W into all this wickedness in the first place.'

Jack wondered how much of that was fact and how much loyal but sheer speculation.

'Do you still have the photograph, Mrs Whittington?'

She shook her head. 'No, Inspector. I'm afraid I destroyed it. I had to. It was too awful. I couldn't bear to have it in my house. It wouldn't have been any use to you because only the hand of Sebastian's tormentor was visible.' She pulled a piece of paper from the pocket of her elegant jacket. 'But I do still have the note that came with it.'

Jack took the note from her by the merest corner, pulled out a transparent evidence envelope and slipped it in.

'Who else has handled this apart from you and Mrs Mackay?'

'No one. It's not the kind of thing you pass around at a coffee morning, is it?'

'I'll send an officer to take your finger prints so that we can eliminate them.' They might be lucky and lift the blackmailer's prints from the note but he doubted it. The two women remained silent and solemn while he read it.

'The private detective that's mentioned was my brother, Nat Fiddler.' Mrs Mackay fished a hankie out of her apron. 'I asked him if he'd investigate on behalf of Mrs Whittington after she received the first demand last week. He said he'd try to find out who was behind it. The bastards strangled him and dumped him in a rubbish bin. But of course you know all about that. It was your people who came and told me.'

We certainly *didn't* know all about it, thought Jack, scribbling furiously in his omnipresent notebook. This was the connection between Whittington and Fiddler that they'd been looking for but had thought highly improbable. At least now they had a motive for Fiddler's murder. He had got too close to the blackmailer, probably more by luck than judgement, knowing how inept the poor bloke was. But where, if at all, did Laidlaw fit in?

'And now poor Martin Laidlaw has been shot,' said Annabelle, as if reading his thoughts. 'That's why I had to speak to you. It's all so sudden and tragic. Do you think the deaths might be connected in some way, like the papers are saying?'

'We really don't know at this stage.' Jack was positive that they were but this was not the time to express opinions. 'How well did you know the Laidlaws?' he asked.

'Not at all well, really. He was our MP but naturally Sebastian and I didn't vote for him. His politics were completely anathema to us. The Laidlaws weren't really our kind of people, Inspector, although Jennifer came from a good family, I believe. Our anniversary dinner party was the first time we had invited them to our home. It was Sebastian's idea. I think he felt sorry for Jennifer, trapped in an impossible marriage with that tedious prole, but it was clearly a mistake. Martin was completely out of his depth socially and visibly awkward in sophisticated company. Jennifer drank a good deal of champagne, behaved appallingly and left early. But I shouldn't speak ill of her. The poor woman's a widow now, like me.'

'Do you know if they were members of the De Vere club that you and Mr Whittington attended?'

Annabelle looked bewildered. 'What has De Vere's got to do with it?'

'Probably nothing, madam. I'm just trying to cover every possible angle.'

'I see. Well, I'm pretty sure the Laidlaw's weren't members. It wasn't Martin's kind of place at all.' She frowned, trying to recall. 'But now you mention it, I have seen Jennifer Laidlaw there once or twice. Drinking in the bar, though, not dancing or exercising in the gym. I suppose she might have been a member.'

Bingo, thought Jack. At last a link of sorts between all three dead men and Gloria De Vere's benighted club. Surely now he'd got enough to apply for a warrant and turn the place over? But until he identified the photos on Fiddler's phone, there was still no proof that either he or Laidlaw had been near the place. Fiddler could have picked up the business card anywhere. And why would the murderer pinch his gun and shoot Laidlaw with it? He turned his attention to the housekeeper. 'Do you know if your brother owned a gun, Mrs Mackay?'

She looked shocked. 'Not since he left the police service. Nat didn't like guns, and anyway, it's illegal now, isn't it? Nat would never have done anything illegal.'

Jack questioned the two women for an hour and this time he was as sure as he could be that they had told him everything they knew. Plus a lot of things that they only half suspected. Mindful of Fiddler's note on the back of the fag packet, Jack also obtained the address of the florist who took the orders so they could check who sent the roses. That was a job he'd give Pinkney when he got back to the station.

Deep in thought, Jack strode back across the expensively phoney cobbles to his car.

'Inspector Dawes, just a minute.' Doreen Mackay came scurrying after him, looking furtively behind her to ensure Annabelle Whittington wasn't watching from the window. 'There's something else. Something I couldn't tell you inside because it would only distress Mrs W and she has enough on her plate already.' She beckoned him to stoop then put her mouth close to his ear, as if afraid the copper beeches might be bugged. 'One morning, after one of Mr W's so-called late nights working in his chambers, I was putting out the rubbish, and I found a pair of his silk boxer shorts in the wheelie bin. He'd wrapped them in a plastic bag so no one would see them. They were stained with blood.'

'Really? Do you have any ideas about where Mr Whittington actually went on these alleged working nights?' Back aching, Jack attempted to straighten up but she grabbed his tie and pulled him down again.

'No, I don't, but after he died, Mrs W asked me to sort through his clothes for the charity shop and I found a business card. Obviously, Mr Whittington was given business cards by all sorts of people. He kept them in a pot on his desk or threw them away. But he'd hidden this one in a small inside pocket of one of his jackets. That's what made me suspicious. I mean, why would he do that if it wasn't dodgy?'

Jack crossed his fingers. 'Do you remember what was on the card, Mrs Mackay?'

'I'll never forget, sir. It's been etched on my memory ever since. You see, it was the only bit of a clue we had — that and the bloody pants — so I gave it to my poor Nat last Wednesday afternoon to assist with his enquiries. And by Thursday night, he was dead.' She lifted the corner of her apron and dabbed her eyes with it.

'I know. I'm very sorry for your loss.' Jack kept his voice as steady as possible. 'What was on the card, Mrs Mackay?'

'It had De Vere Académie de Danse printed on it and the name Sadie. Oh and there was a flower. A bluebell, I think. Yes, that was it. A bluebell.'

So that, thought Jack, was how it came to be in Fiddler's pocket. Mrs Mackay had no way of knowing that the card was still on her brother when they found him. And there was every probability that he started off by snooping around De Vere's in search of Sadie. 'Thank you very much, Mrs Mackay. You've been very helpful.' It was all Jack could do not to kiss her.

'You will catch them, won't you, sir? The people who strangled my brother.'

'Oh yes, Mrs Mackay. I think I can safely say you've given us some very useful leads.'

* * *

When Jack got home that evening, Corrie was naturally bursting with curiosity.

'So what was it that put the wind up Annabelle Whittington so badly that she deigned to ring and ask for your help?'

Jack's face was serious. 'If I tell you, you have to promise not to tell a living soul, especially not Cynthia Garwood.'

'As if I would.'

'Mrs Whittington's been receiving blackmail demands.'

'What?' Corrie eyes widened with disbelief. 'But she's a paragon of virtue, an example to the community: charity fund raiser, chair of the Women's Guild, president of the Ladies' Christian Society and she's adopted one of every endangered species on the planet, never mind funding clean water projects in the Third World and retirement homes for knackered donkeys. What skeleton could a woman like that possibly have in her closet?' She thought for a moment and the penny dropped. 'It's to do with Sebastian, isn't it? The blackmailers are the same people who tortured him and chopped him up. What on earth had he been up to?'

'If the note they sent is to be believed, he'd been paying prostitutes for kinky sex.'

'What . . . spanking, stuff like that?' She frowned. 'Funny, isn't it, how the sexual appetites of men like Sebastian are often triggered by their early experiences in the nursery with nanny?'

'I'm afraid it was rather more hard core than a bare-arsed romp with Mary Poppins. Apparently, the last demand included a photo of how he got those injuries to his wedding tackle.'

'Ugh,' shuddered Corrie. 'How very nasty. No wonder Annabelle wants it kept quiet.'

'She says she doesn't believe Sebastian would voluntarily indulge in what she called "lewd, depraved activities" but I don't think she's being totally honest. As long as she keeps denying it, she can pretend it isn't true. But if it gets into the press, they won't let the truth spoil a sensational revelation about a well-known celebrity. And Mrs Mackay told me he used to hide his bloodstained pants afterwards, which doesn't sound like the behaviour of an innocent victim.'

'Dear God, Jack, it could bring down the whole family, Lord and Lady Henley-Ffoulkes too.'

'Which is why Annabelle doesn't want her parents to know.'

'Yes, I can understand that. But what is she expecting you to do?'

'She says she must accept whatever action I decide to take in order to put a stop to it but she can't face talking to Sir Barnaby, what with him being a family friend. And I certainly don't want Garwood to know. Not until I've had a chance to investigate, anyway. He'd go off at half-cock in the interests of his career and soon the whole station would know. I've promised her I'll be as discreet as possible for as long as possible.'

'Yes, I see.' Corrie chewed her lip thoughtfully.

'On the plus side — if there is a plus side to this nauseating business — I know now how the De Vere business card with "Sadie" on it came to be in Fiddler's pocket when we fished him out of the bin. Doreen Mackay found it in one of Whittington's jackets and gave it to her brother the previous day, thinking it might assist with his enquiries.'

'What enquiries?'

'Annabelle Whittington hired him to trap the blackmailer, and the second note implied that was why he was bumped off and told her she wasn't to get anyone else involved.'

'Blimey, no wonder she's scared. But as for the card, you surely don't think Sebastian's dancing teacher had anything to do with it? Why shouldn't he keep her card in his pocket? He went to De Vere's regularly for lessons and I expect he found he made the best progress with this Sadie so he wanted to be sure to get her the next time.'

'What if Fiddler believed Sadie was giving Whittington a different kind of lesson — of the strict, disciplinary variety? It's how his seedy little mind would work. He might start off by going to De Vere's to try and speak to her, bully her into admitting it.'

Corrie shook her head. 'That's because he believed everyone was as corrupt as he was. A moment's thought

161

— or two moments in Nat's case as he obviously wasn't too quick on the uptake — would have revealed the flaws in his hypothesis. He'd have realized that Gloria would never allow anything like that to take place in her respectable, high-class Académie, especially with all those senior policemen and judges coming and going. It's far more likely Sebastian had a dominatrix in Soho somewhere. Fiddler probably had dealings with most of them and the pimps who managed them. What if he demanded they cut him in or he'd blow the whistle? They'd simply get rid of him.'

Jack frowned. 'Maybe you're right. And I accept that Martin Laidlaw doesn't seem to fit in anywhere. His only link with De Vere's is that his wife was seen drinking there sometimes.'

Corrie sniffed. 'That doesn't mean a thing. Jennifer Laidlaw can be seen drinking anywhere that sells booze, including straight out of the bottle in Tesco's.' Corrie grimaced. 'This is going to be a tough one to crack, Jack.'

'Tell me something I don't know. But I'm certain there's some kind of link with Gloria De Vere's Palais de Danse and I'm still going to turn it over — just to eliminate her from my enquiries.'

CHAPTER SEVENTEEN

Tuesday morning. The Chief Superintendent was flapping about in a state of high agitation. As Dawes entered the station, Garwood grabbed him and hustled him into his office.

'What's this?' He waved a piece of paper in the inspector's face. Garwood was almost foaming at the mouth.

Jack remained calm. Garwood knew exactly what it was, but if he wanted it spelled out, that was fine. 'It's an application to a justice of the peace to authorize entry and search of the De Vere Académie premises, sir. While I'm there, I'd also like to question the staff and obtain a comprehensive list of all the members, which I believe will be quite revealing. Then I propose to question them, too.'

'Definitely not, Inspector. Not as long as I'm in charge here.' The Chief Superintendent sat down behind his desk after hitching his trouser legs to preserve the razor edge of their creases. He flicked a curt wrist towards the chair opposite. Jack sat and Garwood treated him to a long, hard stare. 'I'm sure,' he said at last, 'that you don't need me to remind you that the issue of a search warrant is a very serious interference with the liberty of the subject, and a step which should only be taken after the most mature, careful consideration of all the facts of the case.'

'With respect, sir, that's exactly what I've done. Until a fortnight ago, there had only been two murders in Kings Richington in the last fifteen years. Both were domestics and both arrests were made within the first half hour. In just over two weeks, we've had two murders, a hit-and-run and one suspicious death with unlawful disposal of the body. I doubt if the hit-and-run is connected in any way. Uniform think it was probably some drunk in a big car he couldn't handle. But I'm convinced there's a link between the other three and all the evidence suggests that we'll find that link somewhere in De Vere's Académie.'

Garwood took off his glasses and polished them at some length. Then he gave Jack the carefully practised glare that meant he would brook no argument. 'Gloria De Vere is a highly respected figure in this community. She sits on several charity committees, makes large donations to laudable causes, including our own Police Orphans Fund and she runs free dance and exercise classes for the disabled. That son of hers sponsors dancing scholarships for youngsters from deprived areas and holds tea dances for the elderly. How will it appear if the police treat them like criminals on the flimsiest of justification that eventually turns out to be totally spurious, as I'm sure it will? You're clutching at straws, Inspector. Trying to manipulate meagre evidence to fit your chosen suspect instead of searching for other possibilities. And as for questioning all the club members, have you taken leave of your senses, man? Very important dignitaries go there. Even some minor royals. They won't tolerate the police plodding all over their private entertainment. Why are you so certain there's a connection, anyway? You've no hard evidence that I've seen.'

'That's precisely why I need the warrant. If we turn the place over, my gut feeling is that we'll find all the evidence we need.'

'Well, I'm afraid your gut feeling isn't good enough, Inspector. One of your unsolved murders is Martin Laidlaw, shot, you say, by a gun previously owned by Fiddler. But you've no proof it was the same gun, have you? And you surely can't think the Laidlaws were members of De Vere's? The man was a bona fide product of his politics. Prided himself on never abandoning his grass-roots principles. Saw himself as a champion of the common man. If he'd been associating with the De Vere set, he would have felt he'd sold out to the exploiting capitalists. And his wife has a reputation for knocking back the sauce and knocking off his friends. An unkind person would say she couldn't get off her back long enough to dance. No, I can't see any sort of connection there at all. And as for Fiddler. He started out as a bent copper and finished up as an equally bent private eye, choked, in all probability, by one of his equally criminal associates during a drunken brawl. Just because he had a De Vere card in his pocket doesn't mean he ever went there or had any connection with Gloria De Vere. He could very well have stolen it or picked it up in a pub. Must be plenty of them about. Madame De Vere has at least twenty teachers working for her, mostly young French men and women, all highly respectable and classically qualified. Whittington and his missus had a perfectly legitimate reason for going to De Vere's for lessons; they were taking some exercise, probably for the benefit of his weak heart. Then the poor devil went and died anyway. Exhausted from overworking, like me, I daresay. You've no proof whatsoever that the Académie had any involvement in mutilating and illegally disposing of his remains.' He shuddered. 'Ghastly business and you still haven't a clue who's responsible or why. And as for your torture theory, the pathologist's report proved nothing, just that the man had sustained some nasty injuries to his genitals at some point in his life. Not the sort of thing he'd have made public, is it? No, Jack. I want you to investigate each of these crimes separately. Just because the gutter tabloids would prefer it to be a serial killer, it doesn't mean we go along with it. You're wasting a lot of time and a good deal of taxpayers' money grubbing about for a reason to link everything to Gloria De Vere. It's turning into an obsession. And the press are already making fools of us. What do you suppose the headline will be if I allow you to continue with this vendetta? BAFFLED POLICE VICTIMIZE LOCAL CHARITY PATRONS. That's all we need.'

At this point, Jack opened his mouth to tell Garwood about his interview with Annabelle Whittington and Doreen Mackay the previous afternoon. Then he closed it again. The evidence he now had of blackmail, torture and the deceased Fiddler's role in it might have gone some way to convincing the Chief Super that the crimes *were* linked and he had enough ammunition to apply for a warrant. But he knew exactly how Garwood would react. The funny-handshake Mafia would close ranks and there would be an immediate call on the hotline to Sir Barnaby who would first contact the Assistant Commissioner, then Mrs Whittington's father, Lord Eustace, then Sebastian's Head of Chambers and finally, in all probability, he would speak to Annabelle as well to offer his personal support. This was to say nothing of the potential leak of information via the garrulous Mrs Garwood. Jack had promised Annabelle Whittington discretion, at least until he had had time to investigate further. To share the information with Garwood now would ensure that he got no further cooperation from her, her housekeeper or anyone else.

'I want the investigations into these murders carried out exactly according to the book.' Garwood took off his glasses and leaned across his desk, menacingly. 'And believe me, Inspector, I know the book inside out. I assume you're reasonably familiar with the Police and Criminal Evidence Act 1984.' This was Garwood's party piece and he stood up and began to stride about the office. 'In order to issue a search warrant, the JP must be satisfied that there are reasonable grounds for believing that a serious arrestable offence has been committed, *and* . . . ' Garwood paused, rolled his eyes to the ceiling and held up a finger, ' . . . that there is material on the specified premises which is likely to be of substantial value to the investigation of that offence, *and* . . . ' another raised finger, ' . . . that the material is likely to be relevant evidence.

166

I don't believe you can assure me on any of those grounds, Inspector Dawes. If it should become necessary to speak to Madame De Vere in the course of these investigations — and I don't believe for one moment that it will — then the interview will be carried out by Sir Barnaby or myself, having made an appropriate appointment first. The important thing is to prove her innocence so conclusively that we can scotch any rumours before they have a chance to spread.'

'PACE also states,' persisted Jack, 'that a warrant may be issued if any of the conditions specified in subsection (3) applies. For example, if the purpose of a search may be frustrated or seriously prejudiced unless police arriving at the premises can secure immediate entry to them. Sir, if we give the De Veres advance warning, I guarantee there will be nothing to find when we search.'

The vein in Garwood's forehead began to throb. 'But we are not going to search, are we, Inspector? Do I make myself clear?'

'Sir.' Jack stood up and made for the door. Damn, damn and bloody double damn! His only ace trumped. He was still convinced he was right but to prove it he needed a good look around inside De Vere's and if he couldn't do it 'according to the book', he'd have to find another way.

* * *

Tuesday afternoon. Jack picked up the phone and speed dialled his colleague, the uniform Inspector. He answered straight away.

'Hello, Jack. I was just about to call you. I've got a couple of things I think you ought to know. But you first — what can I do for you?'

'Has Gloria De Vere ever applied for a firearms licence? You know, as a member of a gun club or something. Can she handle a gun, do you know?'

The inspector laughed. 'I shouldn't think so. Why would she? Do you reckon she teaches her students at gunpoint?

Fires bullets at their feet to make them dance like John Wayne in the old-fashioned westerns? I'll check the records, Jack, but I doubt if I'll find anything.'

'Yeah, thanks. I expect you're right. It was just a thought. What were you going to tell me?'

'The traffic lads have found Laidlaw's car abandoned in Richington Woods.'

Jack perked up. 'Any forensic?'

''Fraid not. It was burned out. I mean really incinerated. Just a blackened shell. They only identified it from the chassis number. It was just about readable.'

Jack groaned. 'Nothing to tell us who was in it or where it went, then. You said there were a couple of things. What's the other one?'

'Guess who has come forward to claim the body of old Smelly Nellie, the hit-and-run victim?'

'Surprise me.'

'Gloria De Vere. She's going to pay for the funeral.'

That woman again. Haunting his every move. Turning up when he least expected.

'Why?'

'No idea. We didn't ask. After we released the body for burial, she just sent the funeral blokes round to take it away.'

'What car does she drive? Is it a big one?'

'Dunno. Not sure she drives at all. I think she gets chauffeured by a member of her staff when she wants to go anywhere. From what I can gather, she spends most of her time in the penthouse of that whacking great dance palace — rarely leaves it these days. I can check if she's got a current driving licence, if you like.'

'Would you?'

'Are you thinking she might have been the hit-and-run driver? Taking responsibility out of guilt?'

'Stranger things have happened.'

'Yes, I know, but it's a bit obvious, isn't it? Drawing attention to herself like that. I think you're on the wrong track, Jack.'

'Probably, but thanks anyway.' He put the phone down, leaned back in his chair, closed his eyes and began to think very hard, so when DC Pinkney put his head round the door he thought at first that the inspector had dozed off.

'Yes, Pinkney, what have you got for me?' Jack spoke without opening his eyes, recognizing the DC by the pungent cologne given to him, no doubt, by an adoring girlfriend.

'I've interviewed the florist who took the orders for the roses, sir. Evelyn's Eden is a very upmarket establishment at the posh end of Kings Richington Boulevard specializing in elaborate floral arrangements for the rich and famous.'

'And what could she tell us, this Evelyn?'

'It isn't a "she", sir. Evelyn is a "he" as in "Waugh".'

'Which war?' asked Jack, bemused.

'Er . . . never mind, sir.' Pinkney ploughed on, reading from his notebook. Two of their superior-quality bouquets of roses were delivered to Mrs Whittington, each bouquet containing three dozen large, deep-crimson blooms tied with red ribbon. The first was ordered and delivered last Tuesday morning and the second yesterday. They were really expensive, which is why they stuck in the florist's mind.'

Jack sat up and paid attention. 'And could he describe the bloke who placed the orders?'

'Yes, in some detail. Except it wasn't a "he" — it was a "she".'

'Pinkney, you just said the florist was a man who'd been in the war.' Jack's head was still throbbing from his frustrating and futile exchange with Garwood earlier in the day.

'Sorry, sir. I'm confusing you. The florist is a man but the person who ordered the flowers was a woman.' Pinkney consulted his notebook. 'About five feet four, short black hair, wearing a track suit, trainers and dark glasses. Late twenties, early thirties, he reckoned, sporty-looking but attractive with a nice figure. She brought her own note to go with the flowers on both occasions and sealed it up in the envelope the florist provided. No noticeable accent, just an ordinary, pleasant voice, he said. Oh and she paid in cash.'

Most definitely not Madame De Vere, thought Jack, ruefully, although she could have paid one of her staff to do it. No, too risky. They might have been curious and read the note. It also ruled out the woman that the brigadier's wife saw outside in the lane the night Laidlaw was dumped in the skip. She had been rather taller, slimmer and more conventionally glamorous, with long blonde hair, lots of make-up and high heels. Not that Jack had ever seriously considered she was involved; he would just have liked to question her in case she had seen something suspicious. But so far, they hadn't been able to trace her.

'Would the florist know this woman again?'

'He says it's doubtful, on account of the dark glasses. And before you ask, sir, she didn't come in a car — she jogged.'

'OK. Well done, Pinkney. Keep at it. We have to find her and fast. She's our blackmailer, all right, and possibly even a murderer as well, although I suspect she has an accomplice for the heavy stuff. I don't suppose we've found the gun yet or the knife they used to hack off Whittington's extremities? If we're no further forwards by Saturday, we may have to put Sergeant Malone in a skirt and sit him in a cubicle in the Kings Richington ladies' convenience.'

Right on cue, Bugsy appeared in the doorway. 'I hope you're joking, guv. My best frock's at the cleaner's.' He held up a report. 'Forensics have found a couple of good dabs on that blackmail note that don't belong to Mrs Whittington or Mrs Mackay.'

'Terrific! Our first break. Have we got a match?'

'Er . . . no, guv. Nothing on record. Our blackmailer doesn't have any previous. But at least when we catch the bugger, we'll have some hard evidence to tie him or her to the note.'

'Sir, there's something else.' Pinkney was clearly bursting to tell them. 'Evelyn, that's the florist, said that a third, identical bouquet of roses was ordered by the same woman and delivered last Friday. Brought her own note and paid in cash like before.'

Jack frowned. 'That's very odd. Why didn't Annabelle Whittington mention a third bouquet when I spoke to her yesterday?'

'Because it wasn't delivered to her, sir. It was delivered to Jennifer Laidlaw.'

* * *

Malone interviewed Mrs Laidlaw in the drawing room of her parents' house. With her husband now permanently out of the way, she had immediately closed up the despised little house, squalidly close to the perimeter of Kings Richington's council estate and FOR SALE notices had quickly sprouted in the dismal front garden. She had taken her son, Timothy, and moved in with her parents in their elegant mansion on the river, now confident that the blackmailer, whoever it was, wouldn't dare to try to contact her there. In any case, they couldn't threaten her now that Martin was dead because there was no longer any money in trying to trash his career and there was little point in them going to the police because they had no proof she had committed any crime.

She was drunk, Malone observed, but not paralytic, so he considered it within acceptable police guidelines to go ahead and question her. For her part, safe in her secure childhood environment where she was ring-fenced by both domestic staff and protective and influential parents, she could enjoy being rude and dismissive to this fat, scruffy policeman whose clothes stank of fried food and cigarettes. She confirmed that her husband had returned from his constituency on Friday evening and had immediately gone out again in his car. She never saw him again until she identified his body at the morgue. No, they hadn't argued and no, she had no idea where he went or who he met. She didn't know why anyone would want to kill him. They couldn't speak to the nanny, Debbie, because she was no longer needed to look after Timothy and had already left the UK to take an au pair job abroad. She didn't know where but thought it was one of those ghastly Balkan countries where the women wear headscarves and make cabbage soup. She had already told all this to the police once; why did she have to repeat everything over again? Weren't they supposed to keep notes or were they just too thick to remember anything for longer than ten minutes?

When Malone asked her about the bouquet of roses she had received on that same Friday, she became instantly vague and defensive. If any flowers had been sent to her, she said, she didn't remember them and no, she didn't know anything about a note. There must be some mistake. She suffered badly from migraines and spent a good deal of time under strong sedation which affected her memory. In addition, she had been through a lot of trauma since then and couldn't be expected to remember silly things like bunches of flowers. And now, if there was nothing more, she would like to go and lie down. She was still shocked and distraught following her husband's murder and she insisted she was not to be harassed by the police again; they should speak only to the family solicitor. She rang for the housekeeper who showed Malone out but not before he had seen the look of animal cunning that had flickered across Mrs Laidlaw's puffy, gin-soaked features. Oh yes, Jennifer Jiggle-Tits knew exactly what he was talking about and he'd bet his pension that right now she'd be wondering how the hell the police had found out. But what dirt, he wondered, did the black-mailer have on her that wasn't already common knowledge? That was the question. Surely not her infidelities. Her husband may have been a gloomy git with all the political sub-tlety of a Siberian labour camp but he wasn't totally stupid. He must surely have known she was screwing around. Pretty well everyone else in Kings Richington did and it hadn't done anything to affect his limp reputation as an MP, one way or the other, so it was hardly ammunition for blackmail. No, Malone reckoned, it must have been something else, something much more incriminating and it just might have led to Laidlaw getting a bullet through his brain. They were getting closer.

* * *

After Malone had left, Jennifer went up to her bathroom, locked the door and turned on the power shower. Suitably sound-proofed from her interfering, overattentive parents, she took out her mobile phone and dialled. It was a short conversation.

'Jas? Hello, my darling. Yes, I know I'm not supposed to ring you but you must have heard the wonderful news; it's been in all the papers. Martin's been shot dead and I'm free at last. We can go away together like you promised.' There was a pause. 'What? No, of course I don't know who shot him. One of his loony anarchist friends, I expect. It doesn't matter, does it? The important thing is that we can be together. And I've an even more exciting piece of news. I did a pregnancy test this morning and guess what? You're going to be a father, my darling . . . hello . . . Jas, are you there? . . . hello.'

Damn! These blasted mobile phones. Always losing the signal when you most needed them. Never mind. He was bound to call back. And what did she care if the stupid plod had found out about the ghastly roses? They obviously didn't know what she'd done — what had been in the blackmail demand — or all hell would have broken loose by now. They would have arrested her, impounded her car for examination and kicked up the most frightful fuss, all over some dreary old bag lady. In any case, she'd be abroad soon with her lover and they couldn't touch her then. She and Jas would take her parents' cabin cruiser and be across to the Continent in no time. She had it all planned. She took a glass, a bottle of gin and a packet of white powder from her wardrobe and, unmindful of the vulnerable new life now growing inside her, she poured herself a comforting slug and snorted a line of coke. Then she undressed and stepped into the shower.

* * *

'You can leave those potatoes now, Jack.' Corrie glanced at the chip mountain building up on the worktop. 'Get that blow-torch thingy and caramelize the crème brulee for me. And try not to singe the curtains this time.'

Jack had been chopping away absently. Helping Corrie in the kitchen after a hectic day at work was a kind of therapy, a way of clearing his head so he could think logically, rather like Morse listening to Wagner. He took a large glug of merlot and slowly swilled it around his mouth to savour the full depth of the grape.

'You know, Corrie, every ounce of intuition I possess tells me I'd find clues to all three murders and the blackmail in Madame De Vere's poxy palais de danse if only I could get in there.' Jack had long since abandoned any unease he felt about discussing the case with Corrie because she got all the guff from her school chum, Cynthia Garwood, anyway.

'Darling, you know very well that you don't *have* an ounce of intuition. You don't have even a nanogram of the stuff. Your consistent and undeniably impressive success rate is based on facts, evidence and good sound policing.' She leaned across and put a blob of whipped cream on the end of his nose.

'I wish you wouldn't do that.' He wiped it off with his sleeve. 'I can't help thinking my success rate is going to take a steep and unimpressive nose dive if we don't get a result on this one soon. I'm sure we're close but it's like trying to negotiate your way through smoke and mirrors.'

'Because George Garwood won't let you apply for a search warrant?'

He opened his mouth in surprise but she forestalled him. 'Cynthia told me. To be fair, he doesn't know about the blackmail notes, does he? Or that Doreen Mackay had given her brother Sadie's card and asked him to investigate just the day before he was found murdered?'

'No, and I don't want him to know yet, so no blabbing to Mrs Supergrass Garwood. OK?'

Corrie's tone was scathing. 'Don't be silly, Jack. Cynthia and I may have gossiped away seven years of our lives at St Agnes's Academy for Gobby Girls but nowadays the flow of information between us is strictly one way.'

'It would help,' said Jack, 'if I could just look around inside De Vere's and try to match something to those wonky pics we found on Fiddler's phone. They were all dated so at the very least I could prove he was there on the Thursday he was killed.'

Corrie put down her whisk and removed the blow-torch from Jack's dangerously gesticulating hand. She wore that devious expression that usually meant she was hatching one of her more radical plots. 'I can see that you won't move on until you've satisfied yourself that Gloria De Vere isn't involved in any skulduggery. Suppose you could get in to the Académie and look around legitimately — without a warrant?'

'How?' Jack was nervous, knowing that Corrie's attitude to police investigation was 'who dares wins'.

'We could book a dancing lesson.'

'What? Oh no, I don't think so, sweetheart. Garwood would never buy that.'

'Why not? Sir Barnaby and his wife go there, why shouldn't we? It's a free country — just about. There's no reason why a humble DI shouldn't learn to dance, too.'

Jack shook his head. 'Without a warrant, any evidence I found wouldn't be admissible in court anyway.'

'Maybe not, but at least you'd know whether you were on the right track, and you'd know exactly where to look if you went back later with your warrant.'

Jack scratched his head. Like a lot of Corrie's half-baked schemes, it was risky but tempting — very tempting — and time was running out. It was over two weeks since they'd found Whittington's mutilated body, five days since they'd pulled Fiddler out of the wheelie bin and four days since Laidlaw had copped a bullet between the eyes. In Jack's experience, the first twenty-four hours after a murder were crucial; after that, the trail began to go cold, evidence became contaminated, witnesses lost their memories and it became less and less likely that the villain would be caught.

'Even if I agree, we could never afford to join De Vere's club. The membership fees are colossal and I couldn't claim it on expenses.'

Corrie looked smug. 'What if we got a concession? A one-off trial lesson, just to see if we're suitable?'

'Can you do that?'

'I already have. You forget that I hold the catering contract at De Vere's. I provide all the chic little snacks that Gloria sells, no doubt at a huge profit, and when I phoned her, she said she'd be delighted to accommodate us. We're booked in for a private ballroom lesson with Madame De Vere herself, would you believe? Seven o'clock tomorrow night, so don't be late home.' She looked down at his policeman's feet, clad in slippers the size of two small sofas. 'And you'd better get yourself some dancing shoes. Shiny black patent ones, like they wear on TV. I don't want you treading on me in your great big policeman's boots.'

CHAPTER EIGHTEEN

Wednesday morning. In the incident room, Pinkney was hunched over his laptop. He had found the website of the De Vere Académie de Danse which, as he suspected, was lavish and extravagant with lots of glitzy photographs of the Grand Ballroom and other luxury facilities which were available to the rich and famous. There were online membership forms that could be completed discreetly with the minimum of fuss or publicity. But his interest was in a picture he had found of the elegant entrance lobby and he was attempting to digitally enhance the fuzzy images he had pulled off Fiddler's phone to see if they matched.

Jack had come out of his office and was prowling restlessly up and down, wracking his brain for any piece of intelligence they might have missed; the logical link that would pull all the crimes together. His copper's nose knew there must be such a link but, all the same, he still felt he was chasing what Corrie called 'chimeras' — wild and impossible ideas. He fetched up behind Pinkney's chair.

'Any luck, Pinkney?'

Pinkney took off the glasses he wore for computer work and rubbed the indent on the bridge of his nose. 'Well, sir, I'm pretty certain in my own mind that the photos match but

I'm afraid I can't find anything definite that would hold up as evidence. I could send them off to the boffins in the Digital Forensics Unit and see if they can come up with anything.'

Jack shrugged. 'OK, but I won't hold my breath. Print me off some copies of Fiddler's snaps. They might come in useful.' Particularly, he thought, at seven o'clock tonight when he would actually get to see inside the place.

'There's one funny thing about this website, though?'

Jack raised an enquiring eyebrow.

'There are no pictures of any of the personnel. Not even Madame De Vere and her son. I find that a bit odd, don't you? It's a flash business, dancing. The sort of occupation that would lend itself to lively, colourful advertising. For example, why don't they have pictures of the girls wearing those skimpy Latin dresses with their names underneath so the punters could choose one they fancy. It would be great for business.'

'That's exactly why they don't,' said Bugsy, joining them. 'De Vere's promotes itself as a respectable dancing school and health club. They don't want dirty old men like me, or even dirty young ones, like you, Pinkney, using it as an escort agency.' He handed Jack a report. 'My interview with Jennifer Jiggle-Tits, guv.'

'Gimme the gist, Bugsy.'

'She's holed up in her parents' house, one of those mansions on the river. It's like a bleedin' great fortress, all tight-arsed servants and her doctor hovering in the background in case I made her nerves bad, but I eventually got a statement out of her. Pack of lies, of course. Reckons her old man came home that Friday night then went straight back out and she never saw him again. No row, no idea where he went or why anyone would want to shoot him.'

'Any witnesses?'

'I suppose the little lad could have overheard something but I doubt it, and anyway, he's only seven. His nanny might have had some information to give us but they packed her off double quick to a convenient job in the Balkans, apparently.'

'What about the roses and the blackmail note?'

'Said she couldn't remember any flowers and she never got a note.'

'And what is the famous Malone gut feeling?'

'Well, she was pissed as a mattress, of course, but she knew exactly what I was talking about. Didn't strike me as particularly grief-stricken, her face was inch thick in make-up, so it's my guess that whatever the blackmailer was threatening, it involved telling Martin Laidlaw and maybe even losing her kiddie. But now Laidlaw's dead, she's in the clear.'

'I'm sure a charming, well-bred lady like that couldn't possibly have done anything bad enough to warrant blackmail,' said Pinkney. 'Maybe she just fibbed about her income tax or overspent on her credit card and she didn't want her husband to find out? He might well have had a violent temper. Those sort of chaps often do, you know.'

Grinning, Bugsy put an avuncular hand on the lad's shoulder. 'Oh, Jonathan, Jonathan. So much to learn and so little time before you're next in line for Commissioner. I'll be amazed if Mrs Jiggle-Tits isn't up to every kind of illicit act in the book, some of which would make an innocent lad like you blush. The only question in my mind is whether she was an accessory to her old man's murder.'

' . . . because it suits her to have him out of the way,' finished Jack. 'You don't reckon she could have shot him herself?'

Malone shook his head. 'Doubt it. You need a steady hand to plug someone straight between the eyes, even at close range. She hasn't had a steady hand for years — too bladdered. Besides, how would she have got hold of the gun — assuming it was Fiddler's?'

Jack's eyes narrowed. 'How indeed? Maybe someone gave it to her.'

* * *

Wednesday afternoon. Sadie had finished her last lesson of the morning session and was now free until late evening when three of her regular clients were booked in. She stood in front of the mirror in Studio 3 and did ballet exercises at the *barre* to unwind and relax her muscles. Despite Madame's reassurance, she was still very worried about the accusations that the grubby little man in the raincoat had hurled at her. Fiddler was his name — a private investigator — she'd read about him in the newspaper because now, of course, he was dead, which made her even more anxious. She hadn't known what he was talking about. She'd never written any notes or made any demands for money from poor Mr Whittington's widow. Why would she? She had liked Sebastian. He always thanked her profusely after his lessons and his tips were more than generous. If she'd known about his weak heart, she would never have allowed it to happen. She felt personally responsible. It had been a terrible experience, the worst of her life. If only he'd said it — the safe word — bluebell. She shuddered. It was wrong, what they did to him.

When she heard that Martin Laidlaw had been shot, she had been shocked, naturally. Shootings simply didn't happen in Kings Richington. But it hadn't upset her half as much as the other two deaths because unlike Mr Whittington and Mr Fiddler, she'd never met Laidlaw, so he wasn't a real person to her, just an MP, a political figurehead. But after she'd brooded on it, seriously thought it through, she became really frightened. She had seen his wife, Jennifer Laidlaw, quite often, drinking in the Cuban Rum-Bar. To Sadie, ingenuous but not without intelligence, it was beginning to look as though three people, all with some kind of connection to De Vere's Académie de Danse, had died very recently and in suspicious circumstances. She needed to discuss her unease with someone. Not Madame, she decided. She didn't want to bother her. Madame had been so very good to her, giving her a job, finding her somewhere to live after she had fled Paris only hours ahead of the *gendarmerie*. She would speak to Monsieur De Vere. Perhaps he could put her mind at rest.

Lucien was kind and comforting. She should forget all about it, he said. There was nothing at all to worry about. He sat her down, patted her arm and poured her a small glass of Gloria's Armagnac. The death of Mr Whittington had been tragic, he agreed, but nobody could have predicted it and it was certainly not her fault. And as for Fiddler, he was simply a sleazy, small-time crook who had tried, unsuccessfully, to extort money out of De Vere's under false pretences. It was what the odious little man did, how he made his sordid living. Clearly, he had attempted the same outrageous threat on someone less honourable than Madame and they had put an end to him, once and for all. Legally or not, he had been executed for his shabby crimes. She should think of it like that.

As for Martin Laidlaw, as far as Lucien knew, the man had never been near the Académie so he failed to see why Sadie thought there might be a connection. Laidlaw had been a Member of Parliament and while Lucien confessed he was not entirely *au fait* with the methods of the British Government, there might be a number of political reasons for someone wanting him out of the way, none of them remotely to do with De Vere's. It was up to the police to find out who shot him. Mrs Jennifer Laidlaw? No, he hadn't realized she visited the club to drink in the bar. He had seen her picture in the newspapers a few times but he doubted he would recognize the lady even if he saw her and he was certain she wasn't a member. Maybe she had accompanied someone as a guest — he would investigate. Now, he told Sadie, she should go home and rest so she would be fresh for her evening lessons. She thanked him and left, feeling better. Monsieur De Vere was so considerate, so caring, and she must accept what he said. But deep down, she was still not wholly convinced.

Lucien returned to his office and stood before the huge picture window, deep in thought. His steely eyes gazed out over the sparkling Thames, offering glint for glint. Watching Sadie gliding down the street on her graceful, ballerina's legs, he sincerely hoped he had allayed her fears because she was one of the Académie's most popular operatives. However, if she persisted with this hysterical nonsense it could reach the ears of the press, possibly even the police, and that would severely damage their business. He may, reluctantly, find it necessary to speak to his mother about getting rid of the girl.

Wednesday evening, 7 p.m. Jack parked the car in the spacious car park provided for patrons of the De Vere Académie de Danse. It had, he observed, not only security lights and CCTV but a uniformed guard patrolling the perimeter with a big, hairy Alsatian. No expense spared, but he couldn't help wondering why someone felt a dance school needed such extreme precautions. They would no doubt say it was for the protection and privacy of the important public figures and minor royals who regularly used the club. It could even have been Sir Barnaby's security team who had advised them about what equipment to put in place.

Fearing he may yet change his mind, Corrie put her arm firmly through Jack's as they climbed the steps to the hallowed halls of dance. 'How are you feeling about your first dancing lesson, darling?'

'Nervous as a novice in a knocking shop.' It was intended as a joke but privately, Jack wondered if it might turn out to be uncomfortably close to the truth. 'But remember, we're here primarily to have a good snoop around.'

'What are we looking for?'

'Anything and everything that will prove Gloria De Vere is a blackmailer and killer or at least that she's the architect.'

'Pardon?'

'The draftsman, the mastermind behind it. For a copper's wife, you don't know much criminal slang, do you?'

Corrie spoke with caution. 'Are you sure you're not getting too fixated on this particular suspect, Jack? I mean, wait until you meet Gloria. You may change your mind about her.'

'OK, so I'll keep an open mind on Madame De Vere . . . for now. But I'm sure the answer's in there somewhere.'

Jack followed Corrie through the revolving doors into the foyer where they were confronted by Wayne, the belligerent, bullet-headed guard in his smart green uniform with his name and 'De Vere Académie de Danse' tastefully embroidered on the pocket. Bugger, thought Jack. He wouldn't be able to do much snooping with security guards following him everywhere. Wayne grunted something and held out his hand. Jack's command of simian was scant but he assumed the gorilla wanted his raincoat, so he handed it over, first making sure there was nothing of interest in the pockets.

'See?' he whispered to Corrie. 'Security is so easy, even a monkey can do it.' She glared at him.

A surreptitious glance around the foyer confirmed it could well be the one on Fiddler's phone like Pinkney said, but Jack knew the images were too blurred to justify a warrant, nor would they stand alone as evidence that Fiddler was there the day he was killed. He needed much more.

The guard motioned them to follow him and they trudged silently down a long corridor, their footfall muffled by the deep pile carpet. The walls were punctuated every few metres by soundproof doors bearing studio numbers. Around the final bend, the corridor widened into a lofty hall with a sweeping oak staircase carpeted in dark crimson with Hanover brass rods. Corrie was just as impressed as when Gloria showed her around on her first visit. Nowadays, when she delivered her snacks, she rarely strayed beyond the kitchens which were, themselves, an exposition in culinary excellence. But now she was getting that baffled feeling again, when what she was seeing didn't quite add up. Unlike Jack, she found it impossible to believe that Gloria was a villain, but she still felt the Académie wasn't entirely what it seemed. It was something to do with walls in the wrong place and the sheer, over-the-top lavishness of it all. Could it really be a cover for something altogether different and less wholesome? No. She immediately dismissed the idea. It wasn't possible.

At the top of the stairs, they approached the Grand Ballroom where the burnished, automatic doors parted like an obliging Red Sea. And there, waiting for them, was the almost legendary Madame De Vere. Despite what he'd been told, Jack had a mental image of a crabby old ballet teacher in a long skirt and shawl carrying a stick to support her knackered hips and knees and to bash on the floor in time to the music. What he saw was a slim, vibrant lady who he knew was over sixty but could have been anything from forty-five to fifty-five. Toned and upright, she wore close-fitting, blue silk trousers, softly flared from the knee, and a matching tunic that emphasized her shapely figure as she moved. Corrie looked enviously at Gloria's high-heeled Latin sandals. Twinkling with crystals, they were buckled firmly around trim, well-formed ankles and strong arches. Arms extended in a warm welcome, she bore down on them like a galleon in full sail.

'Corrie . . . my most excellent caterer who makes the best canapés outside of Paris,' she stooped and kissed her on both cheeks, ' . . . and Detective Inspector Dawes.' She shook his hand and her grip was firm and warm. 'I'm delighted to meet you. May I call you Jack?'

CHAPTER NINETEEN

Now that they were face to face, up close and personal, Jack finally understood why Madame De Vere commanded such high regard. The woman had gravitas, charisma, an undeniable presence, whatever you chose to call it. Jack was six-feet-three but she could meet him, eyeball to striking cobalt eyeball. Muscular but graceful, her ballerina's poise was barely diminished with age. Jack took the hand she proffered and, like so many men before him, he was captivated. He hoped to hell that he wouldn't end up having to arrest her.

Corrie watched the transformation with amusement. There was no doubt that Gloria had charm — oodles of it — and an amazing body. Even if she could spool back her own figure twenty years, Corrie thought ruefully, she still wouldn't look as good as Gloria did now. According to Cynthia Garwood, she was still flexible enough to wrap both legs behind her neck, although why anyone would want to was beyond Corrie.

'I do hope you don't mind having your lesson in our Grand Ballroom.' Gloria snapped her fingers at a hovering waiter in a spotless white jacket and white gloves. He brought three crystal flutes of champagne on a tray, then shimmered out. 'You'll rattle about like two peas in a colander I'm afraid, but the smaller studios are all booked well in advance.'

'We don't mind at all,' said Corrie, sipping her champagne, Bolly, if she wasn't much mistaken. 'It was good of you to take us at such short notice.'

'It's a pleasure. I expect you know that we are fortunate in having several high-ranking police officers among our members. Sir Barnaby, your dear commander and his wife, have been coming to us for some time and they now waltz beautifully together. And I'm sure I don't need to tell you that he regards the ability to dance as an important etiquette for senior policemen who aspire to climb the career ladder: there's the commissioner's Christmas Ball, Masonic ladies' night dances and so on. So I hope, Inspector Dawes, that I may soon add you and Corrie to my collection of accomplished movers. Now, before we begin, may I ask you both if you have any health problems?'

Jack looked deliberately puzzled. 'Why? Would it make a difference? We're only going to dance, after all.'

He wondered whether she had enquired about Whittington's state of health, whether he had told her about his weak heart, assuming he'd even known about it himself. But this was not the time to ask. He didn't want to put her on her guard by questioning her, although he had an uncanny feeling that despite her effusively warm welcome, she knew exactly why he was there but was supremely confident that whatever he was looking for, he wouldn't find it.

Gloria smiled and put a conspiratorial hand on his arm. 'My vocation in life, Jack, is to instil the delights of the ballroom into a mostly inept but paying public and at the same time try to counteract the diseases of affluence such as heart disease, cardiovascular disease, diabetes and obesity. If I can also introduce keen beginners like Corrie and yourself to the graceful elegance of the waltz and the fiery passion of the tango, so much the better. The reason for my caution is that regrettably I once introduced a gentleman to the slipped disc of the salsa and the ensuing litigation was punitive, which is why I find it necessary to enquire about the state of your health. And of course, you will be aware . . . ' she lowered her eyes sadly, ' . . . that poor Sebastian Whittington died recently of heart failure. He was one of our most enthusiastic dance disciples and such a lovely man. When I think of the vigorous quicksteps and sambas we put him through . . . ' she clasped her hands and raised her eyes to the ceiling. 'I pray the lessons did not contribute to his demise in any way. He never mentioned a weak heart, you see.' She cheered up and beamed at them. 'Now, are we both fit?'

'I'm very fit, thank you.' Jack had promised to keep an open mind about Gloria but if she *was* implicated in Whittington's death, it was smart of her to forestall Jack's enquiries by mentioning it first. And she'd fired a warning shot across his bows by name-dropping the senior police officers who were members and friends of hers.

'I'm fit too,' added Corrie, if you ignored a dodgy wrist from repetitive whisking, fallen arches from standing for hours on end and a floating kneecap caused by Cynthia Garwood whacking it with a lacrosse stick when they were twelve.

'Excellent. And have you ever danced before?'

'I tried Morris dancing with sticks when I was ten,' said Jack.

'And how did you get on?'

'I broke my glasses and chipped two of my front teeth.'

'Ah.' She concealed a smile. 'Well, let's start with something gentle, then. Would you like to change your shoes?' She strode to the far end of the ballroom and began speaking quietly on her wireless intercom.

Jack and Corrie sat on pristine velvet chairs to put on their dancing shoes. No beer stains and chewing gum here, thought Corrie, remembering some of the nightclubs of her youth where your feet actually stuck to the carpet. Jack laced up his perniciously expensive, shiny black patent ballroom shoes with the non-skid suede soles that he'd bought at Corrie's insistence from a dancewear specialist. Honestly, they must have seen him coming — he should have nicked them for extortion. He wondered if he could claim it on expenses.

Corrie had dug out a pair of flat pumps from the back of the wardrobe. Dancers on TV may leap about on killer heels but she was not about to risk the humiliation of falling on her bottom. And even if she did, she wouldn't suffer the ignominy of showing her knickers because she had prudently dressed in sturdy khaki-coloured corduroy trousers and a baggy grey cardigan for ease of movement.

'Right, shall we make a start then?' said Gloria briskly, like a vicar opening a whist drive. She fitted on a wireless headset and turned up the volume. 'Would you like to step on to the dance floor and take up your hold? The aim is to keep your diaphragms together at all times.' She pressed a discreet remote control and the lilting cadences of a modern waltz slowly filled the elegant ballroom. 'Now, Jack, step forward on your right, to the side with your left, then close your feet. Corrie, you do the opposite, only backwards. And . . . one . . . two . . . three.'

It was then that the problem became apparent. With Jack at six-feet-three and Corrie barely five feet, when he took her in his arms, her diaphragm was somewhere below his belt and the top of her head beneath his chin.

'Hmm,' said Gloria, circling them like a hungry shark. 'Just as I thought. A significant disparity in contact points. No matter. I've called up reinforcements.' The automatic door swished open to admit Lucien De Vere in flared Latin trousers and a tight-fitting, open-mesh shirt, the zip tastefully open to only half way down his chest. On his arm was a beautiful French girl, at least six feet tall, with long dark hair and an exquisite, heart-shaped face. Gloria beckoned them over, said something in French, then beamed affectionately. 'This is my talented son, Lucien, and the gorgeous Célestine, one of our most competent assistants. I think, to begin with, we shall progress much faster with partners of appropriate height, don't you?'

Flashing the smile that regularly buckled the knees of ladies throughout Kings Richington, Lucien took Corrie's hand and kissed it, his smouldering eyes never leaving hers. '*Enchanté, Madame.*' The French accent was especially exaggerated and sexy. 'Tonight, I take you to 'eaven and we dance on a cloud.'

Corrie was mortified. Why oh why hadn't she worn some make-up and her posh frock with the flared skirt that hid her bum and fat thighs?

Smoothly, Lucien took her in his arms and held her close, their diaphragms perfectly and breathtakingly aligned. They were so close Corrie could feel his heart beating and she felt certain he could hear her panting. Pound for pound, she was on the stocky side of welterweight and on an average day her figure resembled a badly stuffed Queen Anne armchair, but when Lucien swept her around the floor, she felt as though she weighed nothing at all. Soon they had reached the far end of the ballroom, twirling and gliding to the haunting music. Under his expert tuition, she slipped effortlessly into *whisks* and *chasses*, *lock steps* and *weaves*. When he whispered huskily, '*Enfin, chére Madame*, the *wing*,' she almost believed she was about to fly.

Back down the shallow end, Célestine moved shyly into Jack's arms, positioned his right hand on her back and took a firm grip of his left. Then she began to steer him around the floor, sticking to basic change steps and counting 'un . . . deux . . . trois' in his ear. For such a delicate-looking girl, she was surprisingly strong and when, after a few tentative steps, she changed up a gear, Jack found himself being carried helplessly along in a maelstrom of exhilaration and terror. It was a surreal experience that he could only liken to one of the more challenging rides at Alton Towers but without a safety harness. Since it would be churlish to struggle, he decided to try and tread water for a bit until he got the hang of it.

'Célestine, dear.' Standing on the touchline, Gloria's voice boomed out through the loudspeakers as they whizzed past. 'I think Jack has his sea legs now. Try a few double reverse spins, just for variation.'

Please don't, prayed Jack, fearing he would be sucked into the vortex that was forming between their rapidly rotating legs.

'Close your right foot firmly to your left and spin on the balls of your feet,' ordered Célestine, and meekly Jack obeyed. Then it happened. The inside edges of his new shiny shoes, now warm and tacky, stuck resolutely to each other. It was like having his shoelaces tied together. But for Célestine's steadying arms, he would have fallen flat on his face, taking her down with him. Instead he stood there, rooted to the spot and pitched forward at an angle of forty-five degrees.

'Jack, what on earth are you doing?' hissed Corrie, waltzing effortlessly past in Lucien's arms.

'It's these shoes,' he hissed back, bouncing, feet together, towards the nearest chair. 'I think I'll wait until the patent runs out.'

'Might this be a good time to take a break, ladies and gentlemen?' Gloria spoke in rapid French to Lucien who switched on his intercom to summon refreshments.

'That was wonderful, Gloria,' gasped Corrie, mopping her brow. 'Lucien really is the most amazing teacher.'

Jack had collapsed gratefully on to a chair and was silently vowing he would never dance again as long as he lived. It was bloody dangerous — worse than riot control. At least then you had a couple of burly coppers either side to hold you up.

'I wonder,' said Corrie, picking up her bag, 'if I might use the ladies' room?'

'Of course.' Gloria said something in French to Célestine who led Corrie back through the automatic doors and indicated a room opposite.

Once inside the expensively decorated rest room filled with guest towels, complimentary lotions and fresh flowers, Corrie pretended to wash her hands. After a few moments, she poked her head cautiously around the door. Célestine had gone back into the ballroom. Corrie nipped out smartly and sprinted back down the stairs. Jack said they had come to snoop around and that's what she intended to do, if only to convince him, once and for all, that Gloria wasn't a criminal and he needed to stop wasting valuable time and target his resources elsewhere. It was no good expecting him to make a move; he was still waiting for the room to stop spinning.

She made straight for a door they had passed on the way up marked *Strictly Private. Management Only*. It was a room she had not been shown on her initial tour with Gloria and she thought it might just be a good place to start if she was to find the proof she needed. She tried the door. Locked. Well, it would be, wouldn't it? Doors usually were locked if the room contained confidential things, like clients' personal information, for instance. After all, identity fraud was rife. On closer inspection, the lock turned out to be the kind you can sometimes prise open with a credit card. She'd had a front door like it once and had become quite adept at breaking in, since she was always forgetting her key. It was worth a try. Looking cautiously around for the uniformed guards, Corrie found her credit card and slid it into the lock between the door and the frame as far as it would go, then wiggled it until it was almost touching the door handle. Then bending the card in the opposite direction, she pushed it in the rest of the way, forced the lock back and leaned hard on the door. Click. It opened. So much for expensive, security-protected premises that could be cracked by a five-foot, short-sighted caterer. She slipped quickly inside, closed the door firmly behind her and switched on the light.

The first thing that struck her, and quite forcibly, was the huge bank of CCTV monitors virtually covering one wall. Some were live with views of the foyer, the corridors, the Grand Ballroom and the smaller studios where she could see people stumbling unsteadily around the floor with their partners. At the far end, the screens showed the gym and health club facilities and the bars. Quite a few of the monitors in the middle were blank, switched off presumably, because the rooms they covered were not currently in use. From here, in what was effectively the security engine room,

Corrie reckoned it must be possible for the guards to watch what was going on in every part of the building and most of the outside areas as well. The monitors were linked to a main computer and control panel, which, according to the labels, also worked the intruder alarms, the recording facilities and the panic buttons that were set into the dado at intervals along the corridors and inside every room, including the kitchens. It was an impressive system that Corrie reckoned must have cost a small fortune to install and required a good deal of power to run.

The remainder of the room was furnished as a typical office. Overhead, rows of shelving were filled with trophies and framed certificates, evidence of the first-class credentials and qualifications of the staff that De Vere's employed. A large workstation had been fitted into one corner with another laptop and a printer. The desk was strewn with various papers, orders and invoices, presumably awaiting input to the accounts system. Corrie had some really good software on her own laptop at home that made the financial aspect of her business a lot simpler to manage. She rummaged among the papers. It was the usual thing: wine receipts, her own 'Coriander's Cuisine' invoices for snacks, bills for heating, lighting etcetera. Blimey! Gloria's council tax made the lottery jackpot look like Bob Cratchit's take-home pay. But there was nothing at all out of the ordinary as far as she could see. She went through the drawers, everything perfectly normal and legal as you would expect.

One drawer contained boxes of the very ornate business cards that the staff gave out to their clients in the hope of being requested by name on their next visit. Most, Corrie observed, bore just the first name and the De Vere logo but some had a bluebell entwined, like the one Mrs Mackay had found in Sebastian Whittington's pocket and later given to her brother, Nat. That was odd. Why were some of them different? At first, she thought it was only the girls' cards that had bluebells but closer examination showed that cards with names like Alain and Pierre also had them. Corrie shrugged. Probably just a mistake by the printer.

Beside the desk, there was a case of Armagnac and some glasses. Corrie knew of Gloria's partiality and assumed they were there to sustain her when she was working at the computer. And why not? It must be flipping hard work running a business like this and Gloria was the hands-on kind of woman who'd want to keep a personal eye on the accounts. Corrie would have liked to have a look at what was on that laptop, particularly the size of De Vere's turnover and what profit she made on the snacks Corrie provided, but realistically, there wasn't time. The main thing was that it all appeared kosher as she had believed all along that it would. On the other hand, Jack would say it was the obvious place to hide anything that you didn't want people to access easily. This included the database of members that he was so keen to lay hands on so he could question them.

Corrie was about to leave, having found nothing remotely useful to support Jack's conviction or her own, when she noticed the dividing partition. It separated off the far end of the room and was decorated like the walls, making it unobtrusive unless you were purposely nosing around. She glanced briefly at the monitor that covered the corridor outside to make sure the security guard wasn't coming back, then she went across and poked her head around the screen. It concealed nothing more sinister than a rail of evening dresses. Some were decorated with feathers, others with sequins and rhinestones but all were blue, different shades, but unquestionably blue. They were gorgeous, the kind of gowns usually worn in a West End stage musical by the leading lady. There must have been twenty or thirty, each one, Corrie estimated, worth a small fortune. They obviously belonged to Gloria as Corrie couldn't imagine such expensive dresses on any of the other girls. Presumably she wore them for her soirées with important dignitaries. What a strange place to keep them, thought Corrie. Why aren't they in a wardrobe in the penthouse? She looked at them for several moments, wondering what it was about the dresses that didn't add up in her brain.

It was frustrating. She knew something wasn't quite as it should be, but she didn't know what. No matter, it probably wasn't important. Maybe it would come to her later.

A couple of expensively tailored suede jackets were hanging from a coat hook and caught Corrie's attention. She went through the pockets. Nothing much in the first one — some change, a handkerchief, a posh pen — but in the second one she pulled out a couple of cards and peered at them. One was membership of the Hermaphrodite Club but it had no name on it. She'd heard of the place, of course, but she and Jack had never been there to eat. It was well out of town and beyond their price range but the food was supposed to be superb. According to the card, they had live entertainment every evening, singers mostly. What if the criminal activities Jack suspected went on there and not at De Vere's at all?

She recognized the name on the other card immediately. It belonged to the Harley Street cosmetic surgeon from Dubai who had been at the Whittingtons' anniversary party. She'd heard from Mrs Mackay that he'd done a few nips and tucks for Annabelle and had botoxed a good many of the wealthy but desiccated matrons in Kings Richington. He'd even done some hair transplant work on Sebastian which, ironically, was something of a waste, since he'd finished up minus his head. But it was the reverse of the card that was most interesting. Here, the surgeon described, in two words, what was apparently his main specialism. Well, well, thought Corrie, as a number of bizarre and wild possibilities populated her lurid imagination. Surprising what you can learn, just from a business card.

There was a sudden noise outside, voices and laughter. A glance at the screens showed people coming down the stairs. Others were leaving the studios and heading for the bar and at the top of the landing, Wayne lumbered solidly towards the ladies' room, no doubt having been sent to look for her. Better get back to the ballroom before he found her. She stuffed the cards hastily in her bag then listened at the door until it was quiet. Cautiously, she let herself out, pulling the door firmly shut behind her. Then she scurried back up the stairs and nipped into the ballroom behind Wayne's immense, ape-like back.

'You've been a long time,' whispered Jack, with the warning look he gave her when he suspected she'd been up to something.

'Are you all right, dear?' called Gloria, in ringing, 'Edith Evans' tones. 'I was hoping to make some inroads into the quickstep, tonight.'

'I'm so sorry to keep everybody waiting,' Corrie twittered. 'I had a little lingerie trouble.' She lowered her voice. 'You see, I'm wearing one of those all-in-one body shapers, such a boon when you have a fuller figure. Anyway, when I put my head between my legs to undo the fiddly poppers, my glasses fell off into the loo and by the time I'd sorted everything out . . . ' she tailed off, lamely.

'No matter, dear,' gushed Gloria, only slightly fazed by the revelation. She clapped her hands to summon the others. 'Come along, everybody. Let's get to grips with a *fishtail* or two.'

At the end of their lesson, Gloria invited them to have a complimentary drink in one of the bars and to take full advantage of any of the other amenities they fancied. Then she thanked them effusively for their custom which she clearly didn't need, bid them farewell with a kiss on either cheek, and swept away to her penthouse. Lucien hooked Corrie's arm through his and escorted her down the stairs to the Cuban Rum-Bar, telling her all the while what a joy it had been to hold her in his arms and how he hoped she would return to him very soon. He would be utterly bereft until then. He kissed her hand and departed. Jack, wincing, finally let go Célestine's supporting arm and hobbled painfully to the bar. In all his years as a constable on the beat, his feet had never hurt as much as they did now. And people

195

actually *paid* for dancing lessons? No money had changed hands so he supposed he'd be invoiced later and it would no doubt be prohibitive. He wondered if he could put it on the overtime budget.

* * *

Safely back home, Jack was carefully peeling off his socks prior to soaking his blistered feet in the bowl of salt water Corrie had provided.

'I'm going to take those blasted dance shoes back to the shop and demand a refund,' he grumbled, 'I'll quote the Health and Safety Regulations. They're bloody lethal, sticking together like that. I could have twisted something.'

'Yes, darling.' Corrie popped a home-made cheese football in his mouth and patted him on the head like comforting a distressed pooch. She sighed. 'Isn't Lucien De Vere simply drop-dead gorgeous? And so talented too. Did you see the way he danced me around the floor? Light as a lemon soufflé.' She began twirling around the kitchen. 'He has thigh muscles like Aberdeen Angus topside. I could feel them rippling through his trousers. You know, Jack, I never realized how romantic ballroom dancing could be until he took me in his arms, and as for that sexy French accent! Rumour has it, he can take his pick of the women in Kings Richington any time he likes.'

'Lucky Lucien,' growled Jack. 'I thought we went there to look for clues.'

'We did, dear.' She stopped twirling. 'Tell me, did you notice anything unusual about the place?' she asked.

'No, but then I'm not sensitive like you. I only see the evidence in front of me and, disappointingly, there wasn't much. Certainly no chance of having a proper snoop with those uniformed heavies prowling everywhere. I really need a warrant to search properly. Maybe after we nab the blackmailer on Saturday, Garwood will let me submit one. Depending on who we arrest, of course.' He munched his cheese football, thoughtfully. 'She's very attractive, that Célestine. Do you think she fancied me?'

'Only if she's into ancestor worship, darling. Her father's probably younger than you. More to the point, did she give you her card?'

'Yes. She wants me to ask for her next time I book a lesson.'

'Does she, indeed? Show it to me.' Corrie held out her hand.

Jack reached for his jacket and felt in the pockets which bulged and chinked rather oddly.

'What's that you've stuffed in your pocket? It'll ruin the line of your suit.'

'Oh nothing,' said Jack, hastily. 'Just some loose chain and a bunch of keys.' He pulled out Célestine's business card, handed it over, then hung the jacket behind him, on the back of the chair.

Corrie peered at the card. 'Hm. No bluebell.'

'What do you mean?' Cautiously, Jack immersed his feet in the bowl of water and yelped as the salt reached his broken blisters.

'There's no bluebell entwined around her name. When I looked around Gloria's private office tonight, one of the things I noticed was a pile of business cards. Some had bluebells on them and some didn't. Curious that, don't you think?'

'When you did *what*?' Jack leapt to his feet, narrowly avoiding upsetting the bowl but successfully sloshing water all over the kitchen floor. 'I knew you were up to something when you were missing for such a long time. Lingerie trouble, indeed. You know, Corrie, when it comes to sticking your neck out, you could give a giraffe lessons. Supposing you'd been caught?'

'Well, I wasn't, was I? One of us had to do some investigating and you were no use, sitting there with your shoes glued together. Besides, you lack my inherent stealth and treachery, vital qualities for the successful snooper. Anyway, once I was in there, I found some quite interesting things.'

'I'm surprised the door wasn't locked.'

Corrie looked sheepish. 'It was.'

'How did you get in, then?'

'I used my credit card.'

'Corrie, that's illegal! I should arrest you, by rights.'

'Don't be silly, sweetheart. Who'd cook your supper? Now calm down and I'll tell you what I found in Gloria's inner sanctum.'

Corrie described with her usual detailed precision the massive wall of security monitors, the master computer that controlled them and even the case of Armagnac and the rail of beautiful blue gowns.

'As I said, it was interesting, even a bit puzzling, but not incriminating. Mind you, I bet there's some stuff on that laptop that would make fascinating reading. Like lists of members and how much they pay for my food. Maybe even details of what facilities they can access for their membership fees. Unfortunately, I didn't have time to look.'

'Thank goodness for that,' said Jack. 'At least you haven't added hacking and breaching the Data Protection Act to your list of felonies.' He had a sudden, alarming thought. 'Corrie, you didn't pinch anything, did you? I mean, you didn't take anything away that you thought might be useful?'

Corrie crossed her fingers behind her back. 'No, course not. Like you said, anything removed without a warrant wouldn't be admissible as evidence.' She hesitated. 'Why? You didn't nick anything, did you?'

'Of course I didn't! The very idea.' Jack uncrossed his fingers to dry his injured feet and put his socks back on. Then he stuffed his dance shoes back in their bag and zipped it up hastily, before Corrie saw what else was in there.

CHAPTER TWENTY

Seven-thirty on a dark Thursday morning and the rain was horizontal. Clenching his teeth against the chatter that tends to follow the collision of an icy gale with sodden trousers, DI Jack Dawes squelched across the car park towards the station. It was only when he'd climbed out of the car that he realized his raincoat wasn't on the back seat as usual; he'd left it at Madame De Vere's Académie the previous evening. He could remember handing it to that bullet-headed security gorilla when they arrived but he'd forgotten to collect it when he left, being somewhat preoccupied with his blistered feet. He hurried up the steps and across to the desk sergeant.

'Bill, could you get these to forensics for me, please?' He handed over a number of miscellaneous items, each in a plastic bag and labelled with a name. 'I want to know if they can match any of the fingerprints to those dabs they found on the note I sent them on Monday. Quick as you like, Bill. Thanks.' Then he strode down the corridor to the warmth of the incident room, where he hoped there'd be hot coffee waiting.

'So how did the dancing go last night, guv?' asked Bugsy, innocently. Jack looked around at the room full of grinning faces. 'How the bloody hell did you lot find out?'

'Your missus phoned about half an hour ago. Apparently De Vere's security geezer had been in touch to say he thinks you left your raincoat behind last night.' Bugsy looked down at Jack's dripping trousers. 'It appears he was right. Anyway, Mrs Dawes said not to worry, she'd be delivering some snacks there tomorrow evening, around five-thirty, and she'd pick it up then. Oh, and she hoped your blisters weren't too sore.' There were surreptitious sniggers around the room.

'What are the chances we'll see you on TV demonstrating the pasodoble, sir?' shouted someone.

'About as likely as a Frank Sinatra comeback,' Jack shouted back.

'Gather round everyone and bring that coffee pot over here. I'll get you up to speed with what I observed in Madame De Vere's esteemed Académie de Danse last night — off the record and unofficially. Then we'll do a recap of what we know so far about the three murders. And don't forget, some of this information is classified until I say otherwise so don't share it with anyone outside this room — and I'm afraid that includes Mr Garwood for the time being. OK?'

Pinkney whipped out his note book. He found these updates invaluable. At Hendon, they'd recommended at least daily reviews of progress in a murder case so that everyone in the team had the full picture as new information came on stream. The instructor called the meetings WAWAs — Where Are We At — which smacked too much of cheesy American consultant-speak for Pinkney, but he agreed the concept was sound.

'So what did you make of the old girl, Jack? Now that you've actually been there and met her?' Bugsy was sitting on the edge of a desk, squeezing several sachets of ketchup into a bacon, egg and sausage bap the size of a small dinner plate. 'D'you still reckon she's running something corrupt and deadly in that posers' palace of hers? I suppose your dancing lesson was our only way in as Garwood won't sanction a warrant application. Nice move, guv.'

'Yes, and I hope you all appreciate the sacrifice.' There were cheers. 'Unfortunately, I didn't see anything that takes us any further forward, Bugsy, but I'm hoping forensics will come up with something useful. My wife had a brief look round, too . . . ' (he omitted to mention the illegal entry) ' . . . and she noticed a few little inconsistencies but nothing significant and certainly nothing criminal. The place is bristling with uniformed guards and CCTV cameras, and a massive wall of monitors covers every inch of the place, day and night. You certainly can't fault their security arrangements. It would be impossible for anything dodgy to happen without somebody spotting it. At the same time, I can't help wondering why such an intensive surveillance is necessary if it's all legitimate. Mrs Dawes's view is that Madame De Vere would never allow anything unlawful to take place in her highly respectable Académie, if only because of all the senior police officers and members of the judiciary coming and going, and she's got a valid point.'

'So does that mean we don't pursue the De Vere connection any longer, sir?' asked someone at the back.

Jack hesitated, then: 'Before we abandon it entirely, let's separate what can we prove from what we only suspect and assess the weight of any evidence. Pinkney, you start.'

Pinkney began to read from his copious notes. 'We know Sebastian Whittington was a member of De Vere's club and went there regularly, both on his own and with his wife, and paid large sums to the club each month. We checked his bank statement. He died of heart failure sometime between twelve midnight and one a.m. on the Sunday following the Whittingtons' anniversary dinner party. Before his death, he'd been bound and sustained significant injuries to his genitals consistent with deliberate abuse. After he was dead, someone chopped him up to prevent identification and unlawfully disposed of the various parts. Those are all corroborated facts. In addition, the housekeeper, Mrs Mackay, has told us she found his bloodstained pants concealed among the rubbish and a card belonging to Sadie, one of De Vere's dance teachers, hidden in his jacket pocket.'

'I reckon he went to De Vere's that night, after the anniversary nosh,' continued Malone, 'but instead of dancing the foxtrot, he played some kinky sado games that went too far and the pain stopped his heart. Someone at De Vere's, maybe this Sadie, took dirty photos and is now using them to blackmail Mrs Whittington. We've got one of the demands with dabs on it and Mrs W told us it had been accompanied by a photo of her husband being tortured, but unfortunately she destroyed it.'

'We can't prove much of that, Sergeant,' said Jack. 'For a start, Whittington could have gone anywhere in the minicab that picked him up after the anniversary dinner. All we know for sure is that he didn't go where he told his wife he was going, which was to his chambers. A lucky Soho dominatrix might have recognized a rich and famous QC requesting her special services and thought it was her birthday. Being resourceful, she got her pimp to take photos of him while they were "at it" thinking she'd make use of them to blackmail him later. When he suddenly snuffed it in mid-punishment, she panicked, thinking she'd get the blame, and her pimp chopped him up and dumped him in the Thames. Afterwards, she decided she could still use the photos to blackmail his posh and very rich wife and pops along to the florist to send the demand in a bouquet of roses.'

'Why flowers, sir?' asked PC Molesworth, an attractive and very keen young officer sitting conspicuously close to Pinkney.

'Well, she could hardly jog up to the house and stick it through the letter box, could she, Julie? Much too risky. And if you put a letter in the post, you can never be sure if or when it will get there or even whether it might end up being delivered to someone else by mistake. Using a high-class florist to deliver it was quite a smart move. But there's no hard evidence to connect any of this skulduggery to De Vere's.'

'What about Fiddler, sir?' asked Pinkney. 'We know he was a licensed PI who carried an unlicensed gun. Mrs Mackay was his sister, and she hired him on behalf of Mrs Whittington to investigate the blackmail, having given him Sadie's card as a possible starting point.'

'Right,' agreed Bugsy. 'So he goes to De Vere's the next day to find her — we've got the dated pictures on his phone — and he asks some very awkward questions. They realize he's on to their racket so they chuck him out and get one of their security gorillas to follow him. He traps him down the dark alley and throttles him, then he sticks him in the nearest wheelie bin and legs it.'

'No proof of that, either,' said Jack. 'Apart from some very blurred images that could easily have been taken elsewhere. Forensics haven't been able to match them conclusively to the shots of the foyer on De Vere's website, so we've no evidence that Fiddler ever went to the club. And as you say, he had a gun. How do we know, just for the sake of argument, that he wasn't cornered in the alley by the pimp of the afore-mentioned Soho dominatrix? Fiddler, with his underworld contacts, might easily have traced them and sussed their little game. But instead of turning the blackmailers in, he demanded a cut of their proceeds. The pimp threatens him, Fiddler pulls the gun, the pimp overpowers him and chokes him. As we know, those sort of blokes don't mess about. Then the pimp nicks his gun in case it might come in handy and dumps his body in the nearest convenient receptacle, the hotel bin.'

'But aren't we sure the same gun was used to shoot Laidlaw?' asked someone.

'Again, no proof. It could have been a different gun entirely. And what's your motive? As a political incompe-tent, Laidlaw was Olympic standard, but you don't shoot a man just for that. Otherwise, Westminster would be littered with corpses.'

'Well, I reckon Laidlaw's murder is connected with the roses that were delivered to Jennifer Laidlaw and ordered by the same woman who's blackmailing Mrs Whittington,' said Bugsy. 'Mrs Jiggle-Tits looked guilty as hell when I asked her about them.'

'Fair enough, but where's your link to De Vere's?'

'Mrs Laidlaw has been seen drinking there?' offered Pinkney.

'So have Cynthia Garwood, Sir Barnaby's wife, Lady Henley-Ffoulkes and probably even a duchess or two for all we know, but you surely don't think they're implicated, too?'

'No, course not, sir.' He looked baffled. 'So you think we're completely wrong about De Vere's being key to all this?'

'On the contrary, I think we're completely right.'

'But, sir, you just said — '

'I've been playing devil's advocate, Pinkney, arguing like any good brief will, if we arrest Madame De Vere without rock-solid evidence. And trust me, Gloria can afford an extremely good brief. I believe Whittington did go to De Vere's that night after his anniversary party. He was much too arrogant to use a common prostitute and I think he had a regular arrangement with someone there, hence the bloodstained boxers hidden in the rubbish. And like PC Molesworth, I don't believe your average tart would have either the cash or the imagination to send a prohibitively expensive bouquet of roses with a blackmail demand. That smacks of someone with panache and audacity. As for Fiddler, I've seen De Vere's foyer and I'm sure the pics on his phone were taken there, probably under some kind of duress, hence the poor focus. I'm equally sure he went straight there last Thursday morning and was later strangled as a result of poking his nose into something that was way out of his league. And I agree with Bugsy, Jennifer Laidlaw is being blackmailed too. We don't know yet what dirt they've got on her, but when her husband found out, he believed he knew who the blackmailer was. He went to De Vere's to have a showdown, maybe threatening to expose what he saw as blatant law-breaking, condoned by the very people who had persistently treated him with undisguised contempt. Whereupon, he was shot at point-blank range with Fiddler's gun and his body was kept somewhere cool, maybe an outhouse or a wine cellar, until the killer could safely dispose of it in a suitable place, i.e. the brigadier's conveniently placed skip, and then torch Laidlaw's car in the woods. But as I've just demonstrated, a good brief, even a mediocre one, would tear all this to pieces in minutes, always supposing we had a suspect in custody, which we haven't. So what we need to do now is set about proving the unsubstantiated parts of our case so we can make it stick when we trap our killer.'

He drained his coffee mug and held it out for a refill. 'To this end, PC Molesworth has volunteered to spend next Saturday morning in the ladies' public convenience in the High Street, keeping obbo on a chain store carrier bag in the sanitary bin of the second cubicle. It will have been placed there by Mrs Whittington and it will contain torn up pages from the *Kings Richington Herald*. The rest of us, plus mob-handed uniform back-up, will be strategically positioned at intervals along the street waiting for Julie's radio signal as soon as the bait has been taken. Sergeant Malone has appro-priately named the exercise "Operation Sweet Pee". And no heroics, Julie. Don't try to arrest the woman on your own. Remember, there's still a gun out there somewhere and this could end up being a job for ARU.'

They shuffled out, chattering eagerly, looking forward to some real action after days of intensive but inconclusive enquiries.

'Nothing like a bit of clear thinking,' grumbled Bugsy. 'And that was nothing like a bit of clear thinking.' He scratched his head. 'Why did they choose a sanitary bin for the drop, guv?'

'My guess is that the blackmailer will be watching from a safe distance for Annabelle Whittington to go in and come out again to make sure she isn't being tailed. There could be a short interval between Mrs Whittington leaving the cash and the blackmailer collecting it, long enough for an ordinary member of the public to pop into the cubicle and use the loo before the blackmailer can get there. A sanitary bin isn't the kind of receptacle that any normal person would rummage about in, is it?'

Bugsy wrinkled his nose. 'No, definitely not, guv.'

* * *

'Don't take off your coat,' said Corrie, as Jack walked through the door that evening. 'I'm taking you out to dinner.'

'Do we have to?' he protested, loosening his tie. 'I'm absolutely bushed. I'd rather put my feet up while you cook me one of your tasty little pasta suppers with a bottle or two of chianti and some of that crusty, Italian ciabatta with melted provolone.' He could taste it already.

'Not tonight, darling. We're going to eat at the Hermaphrodite Club. I've booked a table.'

'What?' he groaned. 'But you've always said it's phenomenally expensive there. And you know what you're like when we dine out. You always tot up the cost of the ingredients on your napkin then spend all evening complaining about the colossal profit that restaurants make, never mind the mark-up on the wine. And if we drive, one of us won't be able to drink. Why don't we just stay here?'

Corrie put on her best coat. 'Because I don't feel like cooking and I haven't taken you out for a meal since our anniversary. Besides, I want to sample the food. A good caterer should always keep up to date with modern trends, check out what the opposition is doing. On top of which, I think it could be interesting.'

'Why?'

'I don't know yet. Come on, that sounds like the taxi.'

* * *

From the outside, The Hermaphrodite Club looked like it could be one of those murky, squalid little joints, frequented by tarts and dirty old men in raincoats, but inside, it was actually a subtle blend of boho chic and Sloanie boozer.

'Queer name for a restaurant,' commented Jack as they went in.

Corrie surreptitiously flashed her stolen membership card at the doorman, then handed her only good coat over to the cloakroom boy, hoping he'd put it on a proper hanger.

'What does "hermaphrodite" mean, anyway?' asked Jack.

'It's an organism with fully functioning male and female reproductive organs — like a snail, for example. It derives from Hermaphroditus, the son of Hermes and Aphrodite in Greek mythology, who was fused with a nymph, resulting in one individual with the genitalia of both sexes.'

'Blimey, poor devil. He couldn't have known whether he was coming or . . . well, coming. Don't tell me any more of your gruesome Greek mythology stuff; it'll put me off my food.'

The handsome young waiter regarded Corrie with vague surprise, raised his eyebrows at Jack then showed them to a booth in the corner. He took their order for drinks, handed them a menu then sauntered away. Jack decided that they'd been put in a private booth either because they still looked young enough to want to be alone or so old they might keel over suddenly and ruin the appetites of the other diners. Sipping his drink, Jack ignored the menu. Corrie always told him what he was going to eat, anyway. Instead, his attention drifted to a large, colourful poster propped against the piano. Jacinthe Des Bois, the singer for that evening, was described as the new Edith Piaf. Not so much a 'little sparrow' as a beautiful Parisian nightingale, gushed the blurb.

'She looks a bit of all right,' said Jack, pointing. 'I wonder if she can sing as well.'

Corrie looked and sighed. The young woman in the poster was certainly beautiful with an enviably slim, hourglass figure and a thick mane of burnished auburn hair which fell seductively over one eye to her bare shoulders. 'I doubt if she needs to be able to sing with a face and figure like that. Are we ready to order? I think we'll have the warm scallops and chorizo salad followed by the rack of lamb with garlic mash and pan-fried cabbage.'

'If you say so, dear,' said Jack, who never argued when it came to food.

They were halfway through dessert, a very superior treacle tart made, Corrie noted, with almond pastry, when the pianist climbed on to the tiny stage and began to play the opening bars of "La Vie en Rose". Towards the end of the introduction, Jacinthe Des Bois slowly undulated from between the curtains and began to warble in a deep, throbbing contralto. She wore a low-cut, off-the-shoulder gown, encrusted with blue sequins and twinkling crystals. It showed off her white shoulders and firm breasts to perfection. The floor-length skirt was split to the thigh, revealing toned and shapely legs in subtle, fishnet tights. She was simply stunning, even more so than the poster promised.

Jack, who had been commenting on the surprisingly good food, stopped in mid-sentence, a spoonful of tart halfway to his lips. His first thought was to wonder what this amazing woman was doing performing in what was effectively a second-rate night club. If she wanted to, she could fill theatres, star in films, marry a millionaire. There were young women, so-called international celebrities, who were winning Oscars and making a fortune and, in his view, they weren't half as remarkable and talented as this one. And she moved so gracefully, like a dancer. Jack watched, utterly spellbound.

'I say,' he breathed, after the first song. 'Isn't she just gorgeous? Why have we never come here before?'

Corrie was entertained for a bit and was genuinely impressed, but lacking a man's susceptibility to sudden surges of mind-numbing testosterone, she soon became bored and began observing the effect the singer was having on the other customers. She peered around the corner of the booth. Well, well. There was a familiar face. Watching Jacinthe with the same rapt adulation that was currently consuming Jack was the dear old bishop, bless him. Not in his clerical garb, obviously, and not looking particularly pious like the last time she saw him, which was when he was saying grace at the Whittingtons' anniversary dinner. She recognized quite a few of the other men, drooling and grinning idiotically, having served them quite frequently at the elegant Kings Richington functions she catered. All were there without their wives and when she spotted the row of beautiful young women sitting on stools at the bar, she understood why.

Clearly one of the perks of being a member of the Hermaphrodite Club was access to an escort for the evening, should you feel so inclined. But these ladies weren't tarts, thought Corrie. Not in the time-honoured sense. The function they performed may be the same but they were elegant, sophisticated and utterly gorgeous, wearing designer gowns and with immaculate but subtle make-up. There was nothing at all vulgar and obvious about their manner, nor did they show the slightest inclination to solicit custom, chatting quietly among themselves without any apparent interest in the men around them. Any contact appeared to be initiated by a gentleman asking the waiter to provide a glass of champagne for his chosen companion who would then saunter across to share it at the man's table. Nothing changes, thought Corrie. Not where men are concerned. No wonder they called it the oldest profession in the world.

But she was surprised to see the man sitting in the neighbouring booth on her right. It was another guest from the fateful Whittingtons' anniversary party. Jacinthe was coming to the end of her act and was belting out "Non, Je Ne Regrette Rien" with considerable gusto. Like Piaf, she certainly had a powerful pair of lungs for a small woman, thought Corrie, and her French accent was faultless. She tugged at Jack's sleeve and pointed at the booth. 'Look over there, darling. What do you suppose he's doing here?'

His attention dragged reluctantly away from the eye candy, Jack glanced briefly to where Corrie was pointing and muttered, 'It's that cosmetic surgeon from Dubai, isn't it? He's wasting his time if he's come to drum up some business. None of the women here need a face lift. They're all stunning.'

'Mmm,' said Corrie, pensively. 'But that's only a side line. What he really specializes in is . . . ' At this point, Jacinthe finished her performance and bowed deeply, her long auburn locks all but brushing the floor. The audience went wild. Together with most of the other men, Jack leapt to his feet shouting 'Encore! Bravo!' and clapping madly. And thus preoccupied, he dismissed as unimportant the two words that might have given him the clue to the killer.

CHAPTER TWENTY-ONE

It was 5.30 p.m. on Friday evening and an early dusk had fallen when Corrie pulled up outside the De Vere Académie kitchens. She threw open the back doors of her van and, assisted by the kitchen staff, she began to unload trays of her finest, most expensive snacks which sold so well at the weekend. After they'd finished, she drove around to the front of the building and parked the van in the car park where it looked totally humiliated amongst the plethora of Rolls Royces and Bentleys. Even as she locked it, she doubted any idiot would try to nick her van in preference to the Porsche parked on one side or the Ferrari on the other. She climbed the steps and pushed through the revolving door, conscious she was still wearing her 'Coriander's Cuisine' overall, liberally dusted with flour. All the better, she thought. The camouflage made her look inconspicuous and harmless, essential for what she was about to do.

'Good evening, Mrs Dawes.' It was the bull-necked Wayne, standing like the un-jolliest of green giants, massive legs akimbo and powerfully bicepped arms folded resolutely across his overdeveloped chest. 'I expect you've come to collect Detective Inspector Dawes' raincoat. It's in the cloakroom. Wait here and I'll fetch it for you.'

On this occasion, he was guarding the entrance alone. His twin gorilla, the other half of the belligerent bookends, had taken the night off to moonlight as a bouncer and was even now chucking drunks out of the Bat & Bullet down the rough end of Kings Richington High Street. Wayne turned to go and collect the coat just as half a dozen regulars in dinner jackets and evening gowns pushed through the door, braying and guffawing noisily. Like many of De Vere's members, they used the club as an interim venue to have a civilized drink and a snack before going on to the theatre or the opera and, after that, to a restaurant in the city for a late supper. The ladies' mink coats and the men's fat cigars indicated their ostentatious affluence and equally ostentatious disregard for convention regarding smoking and the fur trade. It also indicated their demand for Wayne's immediate attention if he was to get his usual, generous tip. He hesitated. This was Corrie's opportunity.

'Don't worry, Wayne,' she whispered. 'You see to your important clients. I know where the cloakroom is. I'll fetch Jack's raincoat myself then I'll be off. OK?'

Wayne looked momentarily doubtful. No one, apart from bona fide members, was supposed to wander about the building without a security escort. On the other hand, this was Madame De Vere's trusted caterer. She and her police detective husband had been having a lesson and drinking in the bar only a couple of nights ago. He guessed it would be all right. He nodded his agreement and hurried to welcome his regulars.

Wading through the deep pile carpet, Corrie made her way down the Académie's lengthy corridor to the main cloakroom to fetch Jack's raincoat. The girl in charge of the coats was busy texting her boyfriend on her mobile, her thumb flying feverishly over the key board. She fetched the raincoat and handed it over, barely pausing to look at Corrie or the coat, but remembering to hold out her free hand for a tip. Corrie ignored it and walked quickly away in the direction of the exit. Halfway down the corridor, she glanced back over her shoulder. The girl was still furiously bleeping away on the keys, oblivious to everything else around her. Good. Corrie did a quick retake, doubled back on herself and made for the door marked *Strictly Private. Management Only*. She knocked first in case someone was in there. If so, she'd feign a blonde moment, prattle inanely and pretend she was lost. No sound. She tried the door. Locked like before. She whipped out her credit card and did the business with the lock which, if anything, gave way more easily than last time. Once inside, she closed the door firmly behind her, hung Jack's raincoat on a convenient hook and sat down in front of the laptop. With Wayne working on his own on a busy Friday evening, she should have plenty of time before he came to do any routine checks on the monitors which she assumed must be part of his job.

* * *

It was 6.00 p.m. Chief Superintendent Garwood's knuckles drummed his desk top in a gesture of nervous anticipation. A rap at the door. At last. DI Dawes. A pause as he moved the blotter fractionally to dead centre, then he eased down his silver-buttoned tunic to immaculate smoothness. For some reason, he always felt Dawes had him at a disadvantage. While the man couldn't be accused of insubordination or dumb insolence, he had a quiet air of superior intelligence that made Garwood uncomfortable. It irritated him that the inspector was always cool and calm, impeccably dressed and enjoyed total loyalty and respect from his team while apparently having no aspirations beyond the rank of DI. This made him something of a political liability in Garwood's book.

Right now, Dawes was planning something radical; Garwood was certain of it, from the way everything went quiet whenever he entered the incident room. He needed to know what it was, so he could put a stop to it before it ruined his own chances of promotion for good. He paused for a suitably defining interval, then he called out in what he liked to think was an authoritative voice.

'Come.'

213

'You wanted to see me, sir?' Jack closed the door behind him.

'Yes, Jack. Sit down.' He indicated the seat opposite, the legs of which were at least nine inches shorter than his own throne-like chair, so he could look down on whoever he was interrogating. It made him feel better. He took off his glasses and held them to the light so he could better examine the total lack of smears on the pristine lenses. Then he adjusted his gaze to a spot somewhere above the inspector's head to avoid having to look him in the eye. 'The commander and I are becoming increasingly anxious about the time it's taking you to get a result on these murders.' His smile flickered on and off like a faulty street lamp. 'How are your investigations proceeding? Is there the slightest chance of an arrest soon, before we are pilloried even further by the press?'

Jack smiled enigmatically, which always annoyed Garwood. 'I think I can safely say that I shall have some important news for you tomorrow, sir. We are expecting a breakthrough very soon.'

'Yes, but what kind of breakthrough?' snapped Garwood irritably. 'I sincerely hope it doesn't involve further harassment of Sir Barnaby's friends, Inspector. I believe I made myself perfectly clear when I told you I wanted the investigations conducted separately and exactly according to the book.'

Garwood's voice droned on and on about discretion, treating important members of Sir Barnaby's social circle with the utmost consideration and ensuring their names did not appear in the press. Jack sat to attention in his chair, his face rapt, while his mind was running through the logistics of tomorrow's Operation Sweet Pee. He switched his ears back on. Garwood was still droning.

' . . . and on no account are you to manipulate flimsy evidence in order to fit up a convenient suspect, namely Madame De Vere.'

'I would never jeopardize the integrity of any honest member of the public, sir.' Jack attempted to look hurt by the accusation, knowing that Garwood would have a seizure if he knew Annabelle Whittington had agreed to act as a decoy and bait the trap with phoney cash. In the interests of the Chief Superintendent's health, the only responsible course of action was not to tell him anything about the blackmail or the proposed ensnarement until it was all over and they had the felon safely in custody.

' . . . make no mistake about it, I will not tolerate any deviation from my orders . . . any excuses for disobedience . . . '

Jack clicked off the sound again. Hurry up, Garwood, I've got work to do. He hoped Annabelle Whittington wouldn't freak at the last minute. She wasn't the most robust decoy he'd ever used but it had to be her. Any attempt to substitute a police woman would be spotted immediately by the blackmailer. They were dealing with a sharp mind and an audacious modus operandi. He opened aural reception again.

' . . . not the sort of behaviour I expect from an officer under my command,' asserted Garwood, finally.

'Of course, you're absolutely right, sir,' said Jack, leaving a lingering hint of doubt in his voice that would worry the Chief Superintendent for the rest of the evening.

'Yes, well . . . ' Garwood blustered, shoving files unnecessarily around on his desk. He was still convinced Dawes was somehow putting one over on him. 'I shall expect a full debrief tomorrow. That'll be all, Inspector.'

'Sir.' Jack went back to the incident room where the team was rehearsing Operation Sweet Pee with PC Julie Molesworth. He was amused to overhear a solicitous DC Pinkney repeating to her Jack's own, earlier advice not to try to go it alone as 'there's still a gun out there somewhere'. Words that would come back to haunt them very soon.

* * *

Corrie fired up the computer, feeling a slight pang of guilt about sneaking around behind Gloria's back. Madame De

Vere was a good customer, one of her best, and had been simply charming to them when she and Jack had their dance lesson. But the whole purpose of doing this was to find some positive evidence that would prove to Jack he was mistaken about De Vere's. That was why she'd wanted to visit the Hermaphrodite Club. When she found the membership card in the jacket pocket, she'd half hoped that it might turn out to be the real source of the criminal activity, especially when she recognized many of the other customers. But it clearly wasn't. The food had been excellent, the lady escorts were beautiful and sophisticated and the cabaret had been enjoyable. Nothing dodgy about it at all that she could identify.

All right, she still had a few unresolved issues about the puzzling dimensions of the De Vere Académie, and there had definitely been something odd about those evening gowns. And why did only some of the business cards have bluebells on them? But these were trivial matters, just personal niggles; nothing compared to the murder and mayhem that Jack was investigating. But her intuition told her Jack was wrong and it had never failed her yet. Well, not often.

Corrie was good with computers. She'd completed several IT courses which enabled her to manage the financial side of her business and submit her tax return online and also keep accurate and accessible control of stock, products, supply and demand. A vast improvement on all the copious paperwork she used to keep. Now, as the laptop flashed into life, she flexed her fingers like a concert pianist and began tapping away in an attempt to gain access to what must almost certainly be the database at the heart of the De Vere empire.

She didn't get far. It was password protected. Well, of course it was! What else did she expect? It wanted an eight-character password and hacking wasn't something she was good at, but she wasn't about to give up now. She tried the obvious ones. B-A-L-L-R-O-O-M, then F-O-X-T-R-O-T-S. Seeing the cases of brandy, she tried Gloria's favourite tipple — A-R-M-A-G-N-A-C. No luck. She looked at her watch — 6.15 p.m. already and she was still feeding in possible passwords. She must speed it up before someone discovered her. Suddenly a screen message flashed up and told her she had only one chance left before the system closed down automatically and threw her out for good.

She paced the room, desperately looking for a clue. She must think laterally! What was Gloria likely to choose as her password? She wandered behind the partition, absently stroking the beautiful gowns, then it came to her, a sudden burst of inspiration. Corrie sat down at the keyboard again. This time it was shoot or bust. She typed in B-L-U-E-B-E-L-L. Holding her breath, she pressed 'enter' and bingo! The screen changed and she was in.

The first database was predictably comprehensive, a vast directory of members, their names, addresses and contact details, which was exactly what she expected. She gasped with surprise at some of the well-known names. Who'd have thought such famous people came here to this very building, probably drinking champagne and maybe even sampling her salmon and asparagus canapés? If only she'd been able to slip them her menu! She ran down the list. Well, I'm surprised they allowed *her* to join, she thought, recognizing a ubiquitous female television personality. Common as muck with a gorblimey accent and hair like Worzel Gummidge. But she must be earning a mint, the number of times she's on the box, and when you came right down to it, privilege was all about money, wasn't it?

She discovered that, like credit cards, there were different levels of membership, from 'standard' all the way up to 'platinum'. 'Standard' was expensive, 'gold' cost an absolute packet, but 'platinum' would have required mortgaging the house and the business just to pay for one year's subscription! The 'platinum' members also had bluebells next to their names, which was curious. That enigmatic flower, again; the emblem of Gloria's previously splendid career in the Lido nightclub on the Champs-Elysées. But what extra membership benefits could possibly justify such huge subscriptions? She trawled for Sebastian Whittington's entry to see if he had been a platinum member but the entry had been permanently deleted, just as the man had.

The screen began flashing up the existence of a smaller directory, linked to this main one. Curious, Corrie tapped a few keys and gained immediate access. What appeared on the screen made her gasp again but this time with shock. This database held highly confidential information about members' professions, income, backgrounds and relationships, especially anything even slightly unorthodox or illegal.

To start with, it was just the odd case of adultery or a harmless aberration, such as pinching knickers off someone's clothes line. It seemed that a surprisingly large number of respectable Kings Richington's residents had some extremely peculiar personal habits. Corrie frowned, completely baffled by most of them. Obviously, she'd led a very sheltered life. For example, why would anyone want to do that with a can of squirty cream and a sink plunger? Then the indiscretions became slightly more serious. She smiled despite herself when she read about the elderly magistrate, a regular dinner party customer of hers, who had apparently got very drunk and exposed himself in Boots while attempting, he said, to try on a condom for size.

Her smile soon faded, though, when these linked records moved on to display evidence of shop lifting, tax evasion, embezzlement, arson for the insurance money and drunk driving, all of which had gone undisclosed and unpunished. As Corrie scrolled down, the crimes became even more serious. She found details of drug abuse, wife beating, rape and activities that would have undoubtedly resulted in a prison sentence and signatures on the sex offenders' register had they been revealed to the authorities. In many cases, there were deeply personal but non-criminal particulars about members that would nevertheless ruin them professionally and socially if they became public.

Corrie took a deep breath, wishing she could have a bracing slug of Gloria's Armagnac. Why? she asked herself. Why would Gloria collect horrid, sleazy facts about her members and more to the point, how did she get them? It wasn't the type of information people would volunteer just to get a membership card to De Vere's. And in the case of the really grave offences, why hadn't she reported them to the police? On the other hand, some of the offenders *were* police. There was really only one plausible explanation for holding such damning information but Corrie still refused to believe it.

She pressed a combination of keys which on her laptop at home would have toggled her through to the next database. On this system, it activated the other computer that controlled the security monitors. The screens that had previously been blank suddenly came alive. She moved across to the other seat to see what rooms the monitors covered and her problem with the dimensions of the building — the Tardis in reverse — was immediately resolved. There was an extra wing built on to the west end of the building. Obviously, the structure was visible from the outside, but there was no internal access to it. No doors or windows, just a long wall, blanking it off. This meant the inside of De Vere's Académie seemed smaller than the outside of the building indicated.

Why waste all that space by bricking it up? Corrie wondered. Of course, there was one other possibility. The area contained in the west wing may be accessible from the outside. Then she remembered. On the occasions that she'd delivered her snacks to the kitchens, she'd vaguely noticed a big, barnlike door, solid and impenetrable with an iron bar across it. She'd only noticed it because it was completely out of keeping with the rest of the modern decor. At the time, she had simply assumed it to be a storage facility. Maybe somewhere to keep the mountain of rubbish and bottles that the club must generate until they were collected. It wasn't the kind of establishment that would display a row of industrial wheelie bins, not even out of sight around the back. Or maybe they just kept surplus deliveries of wine in there. They'd be perfectly safe; it would be almost impossible to break that door down unless you ram-raided it. But now she could see from the screens that the space inside was much too large to be just a storeroom.

Corrie studied the control panel of keys linked to the bank of screens that covered the rooms in the west wing. It was quite a simple system and well signposted. She zoomed in on one of them, obviously bristling with cameras with views from every angle. It looked like a five-star hotel suite. There was a king size four-poster draped with silk curtains, an en suite bathroom with a huge whirlpool bath, and, in the softly lit lounge, Regency-type furnishings provided an atmosphere of bygone elegance with every conceivable luxury for a pleasant evening, right down to the bottle of champagne, chilling in an ice bucket. A sophisticated, inconspicuous sound system presumably provided soothing music if you fancied it. There was no one in the room but the bed was turned back, ready for guests to use it.

Corrie was amazed. She hadn't realized the Académie provided hotel facilities. It certainly wasn't advertised as such. Maybe that's what platinum membership got you — access to a suite for the night if you'd had too much to drink and decided to stay over with your wife, or even someone else's wife, come to that. She wondered if they served grapefruit and continental breakfasts in the morning. If they did, she might tender for the contract. She toggled down the middle bank of monitors. The rooms were all much the same, very plush and opulent. Only the colour schemes varied. Warm shades of pink, red and magenta often with rich gold and silver wall-hangings to balance the lack of windows. The central control panel showed that there were intruder alarms concealed in the dado rail that ran around the walls in every room. That seemed a bit paranoid. Why would guests need those, she wondered?

Finally, she reached the bottom screen and merely glanced at it, expecting more of the same, then she sat up, suddenly alert, and zoomed in closer. This room was very different. No warm lighting in this one or soft furnishings. The entrance was through a black, oak door with Gothic arch mouldings and an iron security grill. It was flanked by replica flaming torches lit by electric bulbs; then down two stone steps, guarded on each side by hounds from hell with slavering stone jaws. Like the set for an old Hammer Horror movie, all kinds of bizarre costumes rustled and swung on hangers. On the wall were whips, canes, a canvas strait-jacket, handcuffs, ropes, leather straps and heavy black iron rings, chained to the bare bricks. It was equipped to look like a medieval dungeon and a very convincing one.

Dear God, there was worse. Corrie zoomed in on a table where a collection of instruments was laid out. Thumb screws, iron collars, metal masks and a spiked, hinged implement that she decided was definitely not intended for cracking stubborn walnuts at Christmas. And instead of the comfortable, four-poster beds that occupied the other rooms, there was a reproduction rack with straps to bind the wrists and ankles of the unfortunate victim to be tortured. Horror of horrors, it was stained with blood.

Corrie had a pretty tough disposition but waves of nausea began to wash over her as she was finally forced to face the truth. Jack's intuition about De Vere's had been right all along, and hers had been totally wrong. The posh rooms were not hotel suites — they were tarts' bedrooms where Gloria's girls entertained their clients. They may be classically trained dancers, qualified and competent, but they were also prostitutes. Very high-class and expensive, but prostitutes nevertheless. No wonder the subscriptions were so exorbitant. 'Platinum' obviously bought sexual services to suit all tastes, including young men as well as young women. The bluebell on the business cards was a subtle way for the punter to identify which assistants merely taught dancing and which were available for extra business.

This ghastly dungeon must be where Sebastian breathed his last, cruelly tortured until his heart stopped. The blood on the rack might even be his. Corrie had to swallow hard, several times, to prevent throwing up. But why the blackmail? Wasn't Gloria making enough money from her exclusive, aristocratic brothel? Was it really necessary to inflict misery as well? Doreen's brother, Nat, either by luck or, for once, effective investigative skills, must have discovered what Gloria was up to and she'd had him killed before he could talk. She may even have done it personally; the pathologist's report said a woman could have strangled him. Then she took his gun and used it to shoot Martin Laidlaw. Maybe he was being blackmailed too, or even Jennifer over her drunkenness and infidelity, and her husband had been murdered, trying to put a stop to it. This was the evidence Jack had been seeking.

She searched around desperately for a CD or even a floppy that she could use to copy some of the information. What an idiot she was not to have brought one with her. There was a printer attached to the laptop on the office desk. A printout of the list of platinum members, their 'extra services' and their recorded transgressions for the purposes of blackmail would be better than nothing and should be enough to allow Jack to get a warrant and raid the place. She switched on the printer and it began to click and hum into action. Then she began to select the files that would incriminate Gloria beyond all doubt.

Out of the corner of her eye, Corrie spotted some movement on one of the far monitors. There was a man and a young woman in the lavish, magenta bedroom. She watched them for a few moments, just long enough to confirm her suspicions, then switched it off hastily. She wasn't here to observe that kind of behaviour, she was here to get proof of it. Had Corrie kept one eye on the monitor that covered the corridor outside, she would have seen someone approaching the security room, someone who had spotted the light under the door. But so engrossed was she in capturing the evidence that would convict Gloria and her accomplices of triple murder and blackmail, that she didn't hear the door open quietly behind her.

It was precisely 6.45 p.m. when a hand silently lifted down the *De Vere Professional Ballroom Trophy* from the shelf above and brought it down with a sickening crack on the back of Corrie's head. Bleeding profusely, she slumped unconscious to the floor, still holding the cordless mouse. For a brief moment, her attacker raised the trophy again with a view to finishing the job — then, for a variety of reasons, decided against it.

High-heeled, diamante-trimmed Latin sandals stepped delicately over Corrie's prostrate body and scarlet-tipped fingers took the mouse from her hand. Having poured a large Armagnac and knocked it back in one, Corrie's assailant sat down at the laptop and, with shaking hands, proceeded to copy all the files to an external memory stick, then delete everything from the hard disk. And for good measure, being unsure how much information the police could retrieve from a wiped disk, the attacker picked up the trophy and smashed the laptop to smithereens. Finally, the Bluebell killer hurried up the stairs to the sanctuary of the penthouse.

CHAPTER TWENTY-TWO

The call from 'uniform' came through at 6.45 p.m. — the same time that Corrie had been bludgeoned unconscious. Blithely unaware that his wife was still at De Vere's Académie, let alone in danger, Jack took the call in the incident room.

'Jack? We've just had a visit from Debbie, the Laidlaws' nanny. And she brought her boyfriend, Graham.'

'But I thought she'd been shipped off to be an au pair in Kazakhstan or somewhere similar,' said Jack, surprised.

'Apparently, she didn't go. After Martin Laidlaw was killed, Mrs Laidlaw took the little boy to live with her parents, told Debbie she wasn't needed any more and tried to persuade her to take a job abroad. Debbie decided against it and moved in with her boyfriend, Graham. He runs a very reputable car repair business in the city.'

'Is that right?' said Jack, wondering what was coming.

'The nanny came in to tell us that Jennifer Laidlaw had been involved in a car accident the Saturday night that Smelly Nellie was killed in that hit-and-run. It seems she told Debbie she'd killed a cat then swerved and hit a tree. She didn't want her husband to find out because he was always going on about what a bad driver she was, so she asked Debbie to take the car away and get her boyfriend to repair it privately, money no object. Debbie wasn't entirely happy about it and thought the real reason she wanted it kept quiet was because Mrs Laidlaw was probably drunk at the time. But she didn't associate it with the hit-and-run accident because the Old Richington Road where they found Smelly Nellie wasn't the road Jennifer Laidlaw would have used to drive home from the Whittingtons' house on the river. It would have taken her out of town, in the opposite direction entirely. So Debbie took photographs of the damage on her phone, just in case, but she didn't report it because she knew she'd lose her job. Then after Mr Laidlaw was killed, she felt she should speak out, if only for Timothy's sake. Graham says when he saw the damage, he reckoned Mrs Laidlaw had hit something rather bigger than a cat and there was quite a lot of blood. Unfortunately, he doesn't have the damaged parts that he replaced because, at the time, there was no reason to retain them.'

'Could you hang on a minute, mate?' Jack turned and spoke to Pinkney. 'When you interviewed Jennifer Laidlaw, did she say anything about an accident with a cat on her way home from the Whittingtons' anniversary party?'

'No, sir. She said she drove straight home and went to bed with a bad migraine.'

Jack face was grim. He called to Malone, 'Bugsy, I think we may have discovered the nature of the dirt that the black-mailer has on Mrs Laidlaw.' He frowned. But where was she going that Saturday night and who was she meeting? A lover? He went back to the phone. 'Thanks for letting me know. I imagine you'll be asking Mrs Laidlaw a few pointed questions about that Saturday night.'

'My lads are picking her up right now *and* impounding her bloomin' great Range Rover Cosworth. There's bound to be a speck of Nellie's blood still on it somewhere, and if there is forensics will find it.'

'Make sure you nail her. She deserves to have the book thrown at her if she hit that poor old lady and just left her there, lying in her own blood. Cheers, mate.' Jack was about to put down the phone.

'Hang on a minute, Jack, there's something else. Something that will really blow you away. Forensics say they've matched those dabs on your blackmail note with the fingerprints they found on one of the items you gave them yesterday. You'll never believe who they belong to!'

As the uniform inspector said the name, two words flashed a brief subliminal message from that intuitive part of Jack's brain that usually lay dormant. Two words on the Dubai surgeon's card that Corrie had shouted to him in the Hermaphrodite Club and that until now he believed his mind hadn't properly absorbed. For a few seconds, he stared into space. Then he gave his forehead a wallop with his palm.

'My God, I've been bloody stupid. I knew I'd missed something.' And in that fleeting nanosecond, everything became crystal clear. The clues had been there all along, staring him in the face; the sporty girl who sent the blackmail flowers, Big Ron's view that a small woman could easily have strangled Fiddler, the glamorous blonde in an old car outside the brigadier's house, Jennifer Laidlaw's lover and finally, the gorgeous, red-haired singer in the Hermaphrodite Club.

He put down the phone and turned to Pinkney. 'How good is your French, Detective Constable?'

'Pretty good, sir. I did a student exchange when I was at uni. Worked in a bistro for a few weeks.'

'What does "Jacinthe Des Bois" mean in English?'

Frowning, Pinkney racked his brains. His face lit up as it came to him. 'Translated literally, sir, "hyacinth of the woods" but in every day parlance it would be "bluebell".'

Jack hurled his pencil in the air with a whoop of triumph then leapt to his feet. 'Come on — move yourselves. We're going to make an arrest. Malone, Pinkney, you're with me. The rest of you follow with full uniform back-up. Blues and twos and mob-handed — I don't care if they hear us coming. It's more important that we get there fast. I've wasted too much time already.'

Bugsy and Pinkney were on their feet and at his side in a flash. 'Where are we going, guv?'

'Where do you think? The De Vere Académie de Danse, of course. We're going to pick up Lucien De Vere.'

'Lucien? Are you sure, sir? I thought we were after a woman.'

'We are — in a way. I'll explain as we go, but trust me, Lucien De Vere is our killer. Let's get him.'

* * *

The smell of burning oil from Malone's clapped-out Volvo grew stronger as he roared up Kings Richington Hill. His car had been the nearest in the car park and Jack knew instinctively that time was running out so they had flung themselves into it and made off, wheels spinning. The traffic lights changed to red and Malone screeched to a halt with Jack grunting his impatience. As soon as the junction was clear, he ordered Bugsy to jump the lights. Behind them, a convoy of police cars, sirens wailing and blue lights flashing, did the same. Those genteel residents of Kings Richington who were out for a quiet evening stroll observed this offensive and, deafened by the racket, they shook their heads and asked each other what had become of their once peaceful town.

* * *

'Mother, I need your help. It's urgent!' While Corrie lay unconscious and undiscovered in the security room, Lucien De Vere burst into the drawing room of Gloria's penthouse apartment where she was enjoying a light supper of langoustines with a glass of Chablis.

'Lucien, my darling, you look terrible. And is that lipstick smeared all over your mouth?' Shocked at her son's dishevelled appearance, as if he had changed in a hurry, Gloria pushed her plate away. 'Whatever's happened?'

'I have to get away, Mother. Leave the country.' Sweating profusely, he ran trembling fingers through his tousled hair.

He had hastily pulled on a pair of jeans and an old polo neck shirt, the first garments that came to hand.

Gloria was alarmed. Lucien never looked anything but immaculate nor did he easily lose his self-control. She made him sit down beside her and took his hand. 'Calm down and tell me what you have done, Lucien.'

'Mother, I really don't have time for this!'

'Tell me.'

He looked down at their joined hands. 'Everything was fine until Sebastian Whittington died of a heart attack in the dungeon. Things got out of control after that.'

Gloria sighed. 'I know. Poor Sadie was so upset. But we had no choice than to do what we did. I know it was awful for you, having to dismember him like that, but if we hadn't concealed his identity and disposed of his body, it would have ruined us. We had to protect the business, the boys and girls who work for us. Thank goodness it was you who went to fetch him that night, after the dinner party. If he had used a taxi, the police would have traced it straight to us. As it is, we may have broken the law, but morally I don't feel we did anything wrong. And even if the police suspect something — and I'm quite sure that was why Detective Inspector Dawes came here for that ridiculous dance lesson — they can't prove a thing. You were so careful, weren't you, darling? Besides, my friend Sir Barnaby won't allow any intrusion or harassment by the police, so why are you so worried? We're in the clear.'

'No, we aren't, Mother!' Lucien pulled his hand away, leapt up and began to pace the room. 'You don't understand. The security cameras we had installed in the bedrooms and the dungeon to protect the staff — I used them to record what those disgusting men were doing; paying obscene sums to abuse beautiful young women — and men — half their age. Then I used the pictures to get more money out of them.'

Gloria's hand flew to her mouth. 'Oh Lucien, not blackmail.'

'Well, why not?' He became defiant. 'They were cheating on their wives. Some of them, in positions of authority, had committed crimes for which they had never been caught or punished. They had used their status to squirm their way out. I made them pay, that's all.'

'But how did you get all this private information?' Gloria was shocked and horrified.

Lucien snorted. 'You're such an innocent, Mother. You'd be amazed what such men — and their wives — will let slip when they're in bed, high on coke, or they've had too much to drink at a wine-tasting. My friend at the wine warehouse was a constant source of useful information. You see, they're all so arrogant, so supremely confident of their immunity from justice that they almost enjoy boasting of the crimes they've got away with.'

'But why blackmail, Lucien? You didn't need money. I made sure you didn't want for anything.'

'Exactly, Mother. *You* made sure. I've always had to ask you. Come to you, cap in hand, like I did when I was small and wanted my pocket money. I'm a man now and I work just as hard as anybody here.'

'Of course you do, darling. I had no idea you felt like that. But why must you flee the country? If you stop this wickedness now, maybe it will be all right. The people who've been paying you money won't be in a hurry to complain to the police, will they? And even if they do, I realize blackmail is a serious crime but if we hire good lawyers, they may be able to plead mitigation, negotiate a fine or a suspended sentence. Of course, it will mean the end of our business. They'll close us down once it becomes public knowledge, but — '

Lucien exploded. 'Mother, it isn't as simple as that. I have to go! I need to get away, now!'

'All right, but first tell me why.'

He fidgeted impatiently. 'Do you remember Fiddler, that shabby little private eye who came here bragging that he knew we were running a racket and you had him thrown out?'

'Yes, but when he mentioned blackmail, I thought he was bluffing, just chancing his arm. I didn't believe for a moment that he was telling the truth. I intended to get one of our friends in the police to warn him off. As it turned out, I didn't need to because one of his underworld enemies put a stop to him.'

'Mother, the reason he came here was because he'd been hired by Sebastian Whittington's widow.'

Gloria gasped. 'You haven't been blackmailing Annabelle Whittington?'

'I took photos of Sebastian on the rack. I said if she didn't pay up, I'd send them to the press. Then I found out that Fiddler's sister was the Whittingtons' housekeeper and I didn't like what he'd found out, even if he did guess most of it. So I went to his office that night, waited for him to come out, and I cornered the little rat in the hotel alley.'

Gloria's voice was almost inaudible. 'Oh Lucien, you didn't kill him. Tell me you didn't kill him.'

'I had to, Mother. He pulled a gun on me. We grappled and I took it away from him. Then I strangled him to stop him talking. It was easy. I just kept squeezing until his eyes bulged and he stopped breathing. He was only a grubby little crook, after all. I was very careful; I wore the driving gloves you gave me with my Porsche and I made sure there were no witnesses.'

'And if there had been . . . would you have killed them, too?'

'I had to do it, Mother. It was the only way. You must see that. Then I dumped him in the bin and came home. Nobody knew it was me.'

Gloria felt numb, as if all the life had ebbed from her. 'The gun, Lucien. Is it the one that was used to shoot that MP, Martin Laidlaw?'

He pulled it from his pocket then and showed her. 'That's right. I'd been shagging his pathetic drunk of a wife for a few months, hoping to get some dirt on him, but then she told me she'd been the driver in that hit-and-run. You remember. It was the one where that filthy old hag of a bag lady got the chop, the one who used to hang about outside our kitchens, begging for scraps. Well, that was even better, so I sent Jennifer a blackmail note. The stupid cow must have told Laidlaw because he came after me. He cornered me in our wine cellar, waving the note and swinging punches. He said he knew about my affair with his wife, how I'd been feeding her coke and trying to get money out of her. He said he didn't care if it all came out about her drink-driving accident, a spell in jail would do her good. He was going to drag me down to the police station by the scruff of my neck and tell them everything. He was a big man — strong. So I shot him with Fiddler's gun. You should have seen the look of surprise on his face as he went down.' Lucien leered unpleasantly, remembering. 'Afterwards, I poured a couple of bottles of claret over the blood stains so nobody would notice. Then I destroyed the note and hid him in the cellar behind some cases of wine until the following night, when the coast would be clear. I waited until dark, then I put him in the boot of his car that I'd hidden in one of the outhouses, drove out of town and dumped the body in a convenient skip in Richington Parva. Afterwards, I realized I'd have to get rid of his car as well, so I took it to the woods and torched it. No forensics, you see? Am I clever, Mother, or what?'

Gloria still couldn't believe what she was hearing. This was Lucien, the child she had loved and nurtured for thirty-three years. 'Suppose someone saw you put Mr Laidlaw's body in the skip and they have already reported it to the police?'

Lucien laughed. A mirthless, sneering laugh. 'Don't worry, Mother. The thick gendarmes will never identify me from any description. Not in a million years. And dressed as I was, it was pathetically easy to thumb a lift home without being recognized.'

'Lucien, didn't you feel any remorse at all about extorting money from Jennifer Laidlaw instead of giving her up to the police? She was responsible for the drunken slaughter of an innocent human being.'

Lucien looked puzzled. 'No. Why should I? The bag lady was only a dirty old vagrant, after all. No loss to anybody.' He became agitated, constantly looking at his Rolex. 'Mother, please. I can't wait any longer; I must get away. You see, I caught that Detective Inspector's wife, the one who does the catering, snooping about in my security room. She must have broken in, somehow, and hacked into our computer records. I knocked her out and destroyed the laptop, but when she comes round, she'll tell the police everything. I thought about killing her, but if you kill a copper's wife, they'll never stop looking for you. You have to help me escape to my father in Paris. He's rich and powerful, isn't he? He'll protect me, help me get away to Dubai or Bangkok. I have friends there. The police will never find me. Our life here in England is finished now. It was finished the night Whittington died in the dungeon. Quick, Mother. I've already taken some money from the safe. Just give me my father's address.'

Gloria took a deep breath. 'Lucien, I know little of your father; only that he was a short, fat, ugly *charcutier* who stank of sweat and garlic. He was one of my anonymous regulars when I had to leave the Bluebell Girls and turn to prostitution in order to support someone who depended on me. I don't know your father's name or where he lives.'

A look of hatred and disgust suffused Lucien's handsome features. 'I don't believe you. You're lying. I can't be the son of a common pork butcher.'

'Oh but you are, Lucien. And as well as his lack of stature, you have inherited his corrupt nature and ruthless cruelty.'

White with temper, he drew back his fist and struck her full in the face. Then he heard the police sirens and ran to the window. Police cars were pouring into the car park with scores of officers spilling out and running towards the front entrance. Terrified, he pocketed the gun, ran out of the penthouse apartment and half-scrambled, half-fell down the back stairs, two at a time.

* * *

Corrie came round very slowly, having been unconscious for some minutes. She sat up and put a cautious hand to the back of her throbbing head. Ouch! She felt a big lump and her fingers came away with blood on them. For a few minutes, she sat where she was on the floor and tried to remember what had happened. Then she spotted the trashed laptop and it all came back to her, the brothel bedrooms, the dungeon, the instruments of torture and the database of information — perfect ammunition for blackmail. Whoever did this meant business and now they knew she could testify about what was going on, she wondered why they hadn't simply bashed her head in. She needed to get out fast before they came back and finished her off. She looked around for a phone to ring the police but there was none. Of course. All the staff used wireless intercoms and mobiles. She remembered seeing Gloria use hers to summon Lucien the night of their dance lesson. She struggled to her feet, seeing bright lights spinning before her eyes, and tottered cautiously to the door. She opened it a crack and peered out. Nobody there. She staggered out, reeling, and stumbled unsteadily down the corridor. If she could just make it past Wayne and out to her van, her mobile phone was in the glove compartment. She would ring the station and get Jack to come and rescue her. Then she heard the sirens. Thank goodness. He was coming. Jack was coming.

* * *

The police cars roared into the Académie car park, narrowly missing the security guard's Alsatian, now barking hysterically and straining on its leash. As they jumped out, ready for action, Jack clapped a hand to his brow and his heart began to hammer. 'I don't believe it! Look over there.'

They looked and saw a van with 'Coriander's Cuisine' emblazoned on the side, cringing sulkily between a Porsche and a Ferrari.

'That's your missus's van, isn't it, guv? She said she was coming to drop off some snacks and collect your raincoat around half past five. Why is she still here?'

Jack's stomach screwed into a tight ball. 'God only knows.'

The uniform back-up team ignored the revolving door and crashed through the adjacent disabled entrance into the foyer, batons drawn and shouting warnings to anyone inclined to run away. Wayne stood stock still, his mouth gaping open, then he shouldered Jack out of the way and lunged for the intruder alarm. Like lightning, PC Julie Molesworth was on him, hooking his legs from under him and grinding his face into the expensive carpet with all the finesse of a vindictive prop forward. Then she straddled him, yanked his arms behind his back and snapped on the handcuffs. Two more officers blocked the entrance to prevent anyone coming in or out and several more ran around to cover the back and side entrances. The rest of the team, enforcers at the ready, awaited Jack's order to raid the rooms in the building.

* * *

Corrie stumbled the last few yards to the foyer just as Jack and the team were about to advance. She smiled weakly, tottered forward and collapsed in Jack's arms. He held her very tightly for some moments, then he exploded.

'What the hell are you doing here? You're supposed to be at home making custard tarts. How many times have I told you not to interfere? One of these days, you'll get yourself killed!'

'Easy, guv,' cautioned Bugsy. 'Looks like she nearly did.' He pointed to the blood still oozing from the wound on Corrie's head and congealing into a matted lump in her hair.

Dazed, Corrie looked blearily from one to the other. 'Could you keep the noise down, please? I've got a terrible headache.'

'Did you see who hit you?' asked Jack, trying to stay calm.

She managed a scornful look. 'Course not. I was bashed from behind, wasn't I? I didn't see a thing.'

'Can you remember anything at all, Mrs Dawes?' asked Pinkney gently. 'A sound or a smell even?'

'Leave off, son,' said Bugsy, impatiently. 'I doubt if the bloke farted before he struck.'

Corrie thought hard. 'Actually, you're right, Jonathan, I did smell something. Perfume. It was very exotic perfume . . . expensive.'

'So it was a woman, then?' said Pinkney, confused.

'Can you remember which perfume it was?' asked Jack, his meticulous interrogation skills kicking in.

She lost her cool then. ''Course I bloody can't! I've just been welted over the head, haven't I? You're lucky I can still remember the really important stuff.' She pulled him close to make sure he was paying proper attention. 'Jack, you were right all along. This place is a posh knocking shop. There are bedrooms in the west wing that you can't get to from inside. That's where they entertain their "clients". And there's a dungeon. Oh Jack, it's ghastly. It must be where they tortured poor Sebastian to death. There are cameras in all the rooms . . . and microphones. They film the clients while they're "at it" and somehow they find out all their personal secrets — then they blackmail them for huge sums of money. The evidence was all there on the computer, only whoever hit me must have smashed it because it's all in bits now. Look for the room with *Strictly Private. Management Only* on the door. Incidentally, your raincoat's still in there. I hung it on a hook.' She took a huge, shuddering breath. 'Oh Jack, Gloria's running a criminal organization, just like you suspected. You have to stop her, you have to . . . sorry, darling, I'm going to faint now.' And never one to say anything she didn't mean, Corrie passed out in Jack's arms.

Gently, Jack handed her over to PC Molesworth. 'Can you look after Mrs Dawes until I come back, please Julie? I think she may be concussed so she'll need an ambulance.' Then, grimly, he gave the uniform officers the OK and they swarmed into the Académie, shouting and hammering down doors.

* * *

Shortly after Lucien fled down the back staircase, the MIT pounded up the stairs at the front. When they reached Gloria's penthouse apartment, Pinkney stretched out a hand to hammer on the door but Malone elbowed him aside.

'Out of the way, lad. This is no time for public school manners.' Bugsy stood back and aimed one hefty boot at the door. It splintered and burst open. Jack rushed in first, looking quickly around for De Vere but saw only Gloria, holding a cold flannel to her broken and bleeding nose.

'Ah. Inspector Dawes,' she said, wearily. 'I've been expecting you.'

'Where is he, Mrs De Vere?'

She pointed. 'He went down the back stairs a few minutes ago.'

'I'll get him, sir.' Glad of a chance to show what he could do at last, Pinkney dashed off in hot pursuit.

Gloria looked up at Jack, totally defeated. 'I think I should warn you, Inspector, Lucien has a gun.'

'Bloody hell!' Bugsy took off after Pinkney. 'Come back, son. The bastard's tooled up. Wait for the cavalry. Wait for armed back-up.' But Pinkney was already out of earshot.

Jack pulled out his radio and summoned the Armed Response Vehicle with ambulances on standby. Then he turned to Gloria. 'It was him, wasn't it? Your son is responsible for the blackmail and the murders.'

Tears were streaming down her face, partly from her broken nose but mostly from her abject misery. 'I'm afraid so, Inspector. He confessed everything to me before he ran away, like the self-seeking, deceitful coward that I fear I have brought him up to be.'

Jack motioned to the uniformed PC guarding the door. 'Get some medical attention for Mrs De Vere's injuries. Then she'll be coming down to the station to answer charges along with her son.' He shook his head briefly as the constable pulled out handcuffs. Then he turned on his heel and went after Pinkney and Malone.

* * *

Pinkney's feet hammered the pavement as he gained on De Vere. Some distance behind, Malone tried to catch up with him but he was dropping back with every laboured step. A stitch in his side almost made him cry out but he gritted his teeth and forced his legs to keep going. Feeble attempts to shout to Pinkney to stop were carried away on the wind and he wasn't answering his radio. Jack had jumped into a patrol car and roared off in pursuit with an escort of uniformed officers but even in cars, they were a good way behind and darkness was closing in. Unsure which direction De Vere had taken, the patrol fanned out, covering all possible routes and remaining in constant radio contact.

Lucien was fit but Pinkney was faster, having played wing three-quarter for his university's first fifteen. He kept gaining on his quarry until in desperation and with lungs about to burst, De Vere jinked to the right up a rough track leading to an industrial estate. He hoped to shake off his pursuer or maybe find somewhere to hide. If only he could have got to his Porsche. They would never have caught him in that. But it was parked around the front and police were teeming all over the car park. If his stupid, lying whore of a mother hadn't detained him, he would have had a head start by now.

When Pinkney realized De Vere had blundered down a dead end, he was elated. Now he'd got the bastard! At the end of the track, behind a row of recycling containers, there was a ten-foot wall which ran alongside the Kings Richington bypass. De Vere would never climb over that. Pinkney whipped out his handcuffs, ready to take him. The wind blew the trees back and forth across the light of the single lamp so that the figure, standing at bay against the wall, came and went in sodium glimpses. As Pinkney closed in, he could see the gun in De Vere's hand, and realized the inspector had been right. This was the gun that De Vere had taken from Fiddler's body after he choked him to death and then used to shoot Laidlaw. The man was a murderer and blackmailer and Pinkney knew it was his duty to arrest him. He called out.

'Come along, now, Mr De Vere. There's no point in resisting. Armed officers will be here at any moment and if you don't give up the gun, they'll shoot you. Just hand it over now.' Bravely, foolishly, Pinkney began to walk towards him, holding out his hand to take the weapon.

Lucien cast frantically about him for a means of escape. His only hope was to scale the wall behind him, but this dim-witted plod was getting closer, crowding in on him so he couldn't think properly.

'Come along, sir,' Pinkney said again. 'Don't be stupid. You can't escape. Where could you go? Where would you hide? Drop the gun.'

The idiot gendarme was just a couple of metres away, now. Wild eyed and panic-stricken, Lucien De Vere raised the gun and fired off two crazy, frenzied shots. Detective Constable Jonathan Pinkney, age 22 and barely a month in the job, took both bullets in the chest. He keeled over backwards, his face registering surprise and disbelief as he watched the blood well up and soak his best shirt. Fleetingly, he recalled what Sergeant Malone always said about never wearing anything to a murder scene that you wouldn't want to see covered in blood. He almost smiled, then he felt himself sliding into a black void from which he doubted he would return.

Terrified, Lucien dropped the gun and scrambled up on to the recycling bins, ranged in a row, some metres from the wall. They weren't tall enough for him to see over it but he knew the main road out of Kings Richington was on the other side. He could hear traffic. Heavy traffic. Maybe he could thumb a lift to London or the coast, but first he had to get over that damnable wall. If he tried to escape back down the track, he'd run straight into the arms of the police. Mentally, he measured the distance he needed to jump and was sure he could make it. This would have to be the *grand jeté* of his life, but it had to be a better option than waiting for the firearms cowboys to come and shoot him down, and they wouldn't hesitate now that he had killed one of their own.

He took several steadying breaths, then began his run, leaping nimbly from one container to the next until he reached the last one nearest the wall. Using the built-up momentum, he launched himself forward into a long, horizontal leap, right leg straight out in front and left leg extended backwards, achieving the *grand écart en l'air* — full leg splits in mid-air. He sailed effortlessly over the wall like a young stag.

The road on the other side was a dual-carriageway, a regular route for large goods vehicles. When Lucien hit the nearside lane, he tucked his head into his knees and rolled — straight under the wheels of a giant, six-axle tanker carrying fuel from the refinery to local petrol stations. The driver, ever vigilant for careless pedestrians, was totally unprepared for a man apparently flying over a ten-foot wall. He hit the brakes instinctively but it was useless. Screaming, Lucien was flipped from wheel to wheel like the ball in a deadly pinball machine. He didn't stop screaming until the last set of giant tyres had flattened his head into a gory pulp of blood and brains and spread it over the tarmac, like a crushed watermelon.

* * *

Malone staggered down the track, wheezing and gasping and holding his sides. He'd heard the shots and was terrified of what he'd find. His worst fears were confirmed when he saw Pinkney lying in a sea of blood.

'Oh sweet Jesus, no. Not the lad.' He dropped heavily to his knees beside Pinkney's motionless body and felt desperately for a pulse. He thought he'd found one but it was very weak. 'Pinkney, can you hear me, son?' He tore off his jacket, rolled it into a ball and pressed it hard against Pinkney's chest to try to staunch the terrifying flow of blood. With his free hand, he whipped out his radio.

'Officer down! Officer down! Pinkney's been shot. Get an ambulance here, NOW!' He gave a hurried location then put his mouth close to Pinkney's ear. 'Hang on, son, hang on.

The ambulance is on its way. That's right, keep breathing. You're going to be all right. The medics will patch you up and you'll be back at work next week. You wait and see.' Bugsy choked on the last words and had to gulp several times. He'd been a lapsed Catholic for most of his life and didn't have much time for God, but he was willing to pray if that's what it took to keep the lad alive. Where was the bloody ambulance!

After what seemed like hours, but was barely minutes, the ARV and several car loads of uniformed officers roared around the corner and screeched to a halt at the access to the track. Jack leapt out of the first car, sprinted straight to Bugsy and knelt beside him. Still leaning hard on his make-shift pressure dressing, Bugsy spoke quietly, his voice hoarse and cracked.

'He's bad, Jack. Real bad. The poor little sod's taken two slugs in the chest. I've never seen so much blood. I don't think he's going to make it.'

The paramedics arrived then, piling out of the ambulance and running hard towards them, their medical bags at the ready. They shooed a reluctant Malone away and in seconds they had stopped the bleeding, put an oxygen mask over Pinkney's face and set up a drip. Then they lifted him gently on to a trolley, adjusted the strap around his motionless, red-blanketed body and wheeled him away to the ambulance. Malone tried to go with him, even climbed into the ambulance, but the paramedics sent him away. He shouted after them as they closed the doors. 'You look after him, do you hear? Don't you let him die or you'll have me to answer to!'

On the other side of the wall, traffic police were already in the process of closing the dual-carriageway for at least the next 24 hours, while they carried out a full investigation into the fatal accident. A breakdown lorry had been summoned to remove the fuel tanker, now jack-knifed across both lanes; its driver, white and trembling with a blanket around him, was being led towards a waiting ambulance. Backed up behind the long queue of stationary traffic, a Fire Service pump waited patiently to undertake the task of hosing the road, once the police and the ambulance men had scraped up the bloody mess that was once Lucien De Vere.

Shocked by the appalling turn of events and helpless as to how to comfort a desolate Bugsy, Jack silently put an arm around his shoulders. Bugsy had to swallow hard before he could speak.

'It should have been me, Jack.' His normally cheerful moon-face was white and drawn. 'Pinkney's young and bright, just starting out. I'm a useless old sod. Past it. Couldn't run fast enough. It should have been me who faced that murdering little bastard. If Pinkney dies, I'm going to put in me papers. Hand back me badge. I couldn't face the job any more. The lad was my responsibility . . . still learning. I should have protected him.'

'He was my responsibility too, Bugsy. I'm as much to blame for this. Pinkney was so very keen to impress us both. To show us he was good at his job. We forgot to make it clear that it didn't mean risking his life.' Jack looked at Malone's ashen face. 'Let's go and find you something to eat, Bugsy, you're white as a sheet.'

Bugsy shook his head. 'No thanks, Jack. Just for once in me life, I'm not hungry.'

CHAPTER TWENTY-THREE

'This has become a very high profile case, Jack.' Chief Superintendent Garwood strode delightedly around his office, too excited to sit at his desk. It was 9.00 a.m. on Saturday morning, a time when Garwood rarely put in an appearance unless he thought it would improve his career prospects. 'Sir Barnaby and I are going to be in the spotlight. Three murders, a hit-and-run, demanding money with menaces and a bawdy house . . . all cleared up in less than three weeks. And the chief perpetrator got himself killed trying to escape justice, thus averting a lengthy court case at the expense of the hard-pressed tax payer.' He did another circuit of his desk, almost skipping with joy. 'Nor, I'm happy to say, did we need to deploy ARU and then have to deal with the inevitable accusations of trigger-happy firearms officers from the bleeding-hearts brigade.'

Garwood almost felt like purring. How marvellous to have some good news at last. This superb result would cut the ground from under the feet of those Kings Richington residents who continually complained of police inefficiency, extravagance and idleness. He would set up a press conference once the rest of the suspects had been tried, found guilty and sentenced; then he would take great pleasure in wiping the cynical smiles off the faces of sneering newspaper reporters. He perched on the edge of his desk and smirked, gleefully.

'The Vice Unit is having a field day, turning over that disgusting brothel. They're taking it apart, brick by brick. Some of the staff scattered during the raid but they've pulled in ten of them for questioning. Mostly kitchen staff and cleaners, I believe. Of course, it's a pity we weren't able to get our hands on the computer data with details of the prostitutes and their clients because now we can't prove conclusively who was involved in the illegal activities and who was there simply for an innocent drink in the bar or a bona fide dancing lesson. CPS can't afford to get it wrong, not with the calibre of person we're dealing with. But no matter, you can't win them all.'

Jack didn't think Garwood's expression looked particularly rueful and he reckoned he knew why. He had no doubt there were many smug, sanctimonious citizens in Kings Richington who would be breathing a secret sigh of relief at the loss of the information, and nobody from the Académie was going to grass, for obvious reasons. Garwood's elation flowed unabated.

'Didn't I tell you all along that the De Vere woman was up to no good, Jack? Can't think why you didn't get on to it sooner, once I'd tipped you off. It was quite obvious to me that there was something illegal going on in that flashy club, as I told Sir Barnaby.' He gave Jack's shoulder a man-to-man squeeze. 'Never mind, Inspector, you got there in the end. And Sir Barnaby has been congratulated by the Assistant to the Deputy Assistant Commissioner himself. Of course, Sir Barnaby explained to him that the only reason he'd become a member of the club was to infiltrate the organization at a high level and root out the corruption.' He rubbed his hands together. 'The Home Office statistics showing our clear-up rate will be exemplary this quarter. Oh yes, Jack, I think we can consider this a very satisfactory outcome to a nasty, pernicious business, don't you?'

Jack's face was grim. 'It wasn't very satisfactory for DC Pinkney, sir.'

Garwood blustered and cleared his throat. 'Hrm. Yes. Bad business, that. How is young Pinkney?'

'In the intensive care unit on a life support machine, sir. He's still unconscious.'

Garwood spotted the one flaw in his eagerly anticipated rise to the next rung of the ladder. Top brass didn't like men under your command getting themselves killed, even if they were only constables. 'Surprised you didn't keep him in check, Jack. Inexperienced officer, overzealous and all that. He'll pull through, won't he?'

'They don't know, yet. He's on the critical list. It could go either way.'

'Yes, well, bad luck, eh? Keep me informed. Let me know if I can do anything.' His mind was working fast, preparing a contingency plan. Taking DC Pinkney into MIT as a fast-track graduate had been one of Garwood's experimental recruitment ideas to demonstrate his flair for leadership and innovation. If the lad survived, he'd play him up as a hero, put him forward for a commendation. Say that he recognized senior officer material when he saw it. If he died, he'd imply Inspector Dawes failed to give his DC clear orders and neglected his duty of care, despite the rigorous regime of safety training that he, Garwood, always insisted upon. It was a typical Garwood ploy to ensure he would be seen in a good light whatever happened.

'Thank you, sir,' said Jack, curtly. 'Is it all right if I go home and look after my wife, now?' He had left Corrie at home in bed, playing the old soldier with a bandage around her head while gobbling all the orange creams from the huge box of chocolates he'd bought her. 'She was viciously assaulted by Lucien De Vere and sustained concussion and a nasty gash to her head while she was making a bona fide delivery to the kitchens.' He decided it would be more diplomatic if he didn't mention that she'd actually broken into a locked security room in order to lift protected data from the computers.

Garwood nodded vigorously. 'Yes, by all means, Jack. Give her my best wishes for a speedy recovery. I shall be sending her some flowers from Sir Barnaby and myself. Just sorry she was caught up in all the flak.' He looked momentarily perplexed. 'It was a queer business, De Vere going about dressed up as a woman. The man must have been unhinged. Caused, no doubt, by being exposed to all that ballet dancing when he was a child. Can't be good for a boy, can it? OK, carry on, Inspector.'

'Sir.' Jack turned abruptly and made for the door, before he was tempted to end his career prematurely by punching Garwood on the nose. The Chief Superintendent immediately picked up the phone to dial Sir Barnaby on the hotline so that they could congratulate each other all over again. At some point, he might have to warn him of the possible demise of a DC but it wasn't top of his list of priorities.

* * *

Saturday 10.00 a.m. Sergeant Malone had been at Pinkney's bedside all night, sneaking out to hide in the loo when the doctors and nurses came to monitor him, then sneaking back again after they'd gone. They'd tried to send him home several times but he wouldn't go. Pinkney had been taken straight to the operating theatre and had been in there for hours while they dug out the bullets and repaired the damage. He looked terrible — pallid and drained of life.

'He's lost a lot of blood but he's young and strong,' the theatre sister had said. 'Don't give up hope yet, Sergeant.'

Occasionally, Bugsy would fall into an uneasy doze only to wake suddenly if he imagined Pinkney had moved, even slightly. The lad had so many tubes and wires coming out of him, Bugsy feared he'd never survive it. He was in a half doze when he sensed rather than saw Pinkney open his eyes.

Thank God! The surge of relief that engulfed him almost took his breath away.

'Take it easy, son. I'll fetch the doctor. You just lie still.'

Pinkney managed a tepid smile and tried to speak. Bugsy leaned over and put his ear close.

'Did we get him, Sarge?' Pinkney whispered.

'Oh yes, son. We got him. Good and proper . . . thanks to you. The guv'nor's putting you forward for a commendation . . . ' Pinkney smiled weakly, closed his eyes and drifted away again. ' . . . but don't you ever do that to me again,' muttered Bugsy under his breath. He pressed the emergency button to summon the doctor. Suddenly, he felt hungry. He wondered if the hospital canteen did sausage sandwiches.

* * *

They interviewed Gloria De Vere late on Saturday afternoon. Bugsy would have liked to lean on her sooner, before she had time to get her story straight, but decency decreed that she should be allowed a little time to absorb the shock of losing her son, even if he was an evil little sod.

They sat on opposite sides of the table in the austere interview room where scores of villains had been interrogated over the years. It was a small, forbidding room; windowless and soundproofed, in order to enhance the quality of the tape recording. The atmosphere was heavy with stale sweat and unwashed socks, most probably Bugsy's who hadn't been home for nearly thirty-six hours. Now, he leaned across the table and switched on the recording machine.

'This interview is being recorded,' intoned Jack. 'My name is Detective Inspector Dawes. Officers also present in the room are Detective Sergeant Malone and PC Garsmold,' an acknowledgement of the uniform PC standing, silent and motionless, by the door, his arms across his chest like a cigar store Indian.

Gloria had declined the services of the duty solicitor. Despite the many eminent lawyers who had so recently been members of her club and professed themselves her good friends, none had come forward with an offer of legal representation. Bad news travelled fast in Kings Richington. Now she sat, quietly sipping the coffee Bugsy had brought her. No longer the vibrant, charismatic entrepreneuse of the dance who had so impressed Jack when they first met, now she looked her age, her face grey and gaunt with surgical tape across her broken nose. Her shoulders drooped beneath the pain she was suffering. Not much similarity to Fonteyn now, thought Bugsy. More like Queen Victoria with a bad period, but he was unmoved.

'I must caution you in accordance with the Police and Criminal Evidence Act 1984. You do not have to say anything but it may harm your defence if you do not mention when questioned something which you later rely on in court. Anything you do say may be given in evidence. Do you understand?'

She nodded.

'For the tape, please,' insisted Malone.

'Yes, I understand, Sergeant. Thank you.' She lifted her head and looked at Jack. 'Before you begin, Inspector, will you tell me this? Did Lucien suffer before he died?'

A heart beat hesitation. 'No,' lied Jack.

'He was squashed flat by a forty-ton petrol tanker.' Malone was not inclined to go easy on her. The little bugger she called a son had nearly killed a good police officer.

'And the young policeman he shot,' she asked, as if reading Bugsy's mind. 'Is he going to be all right?'

'We don't know yet,' growled Bugsy. 'He's still on the critical list.' Pinkney had been declared stable, thankfully, but Bugsy wasn't about to make her feel better by telling her.

'I'm so sorry . . . I really am.'

He ignored her contrition and glared at her. 'You know you don't have to say anything, but let me tell you how we see it. First, you should be aware that our Vice Unit has closed down your alleged "dancing club" and will be pressing a number of charges under, among other things, the 1751

Disorderly Houses Act. It's in your best interests to tell us the truth, everything you know.'

Gloria sighed sadly at Jack, the pallor of her face emphasizing the dark, bruise-like rings around her eyes. 'I suppose I knew it could only ever be a may-fly dance, Inspector. A fleeting taste of superficial respectability and wealth. I never expected it to last. But neither did I expect it to end like this.'

'Were you aware of the extra "services" the young men and women in your establishment were providing?' asked Jack.

'Of course I was, Mr Dawes. It was a case of supply and demand and, believe me, there was a great deal of demand from the allegedly decent, upright citizens of Kings Richington. At first, I resisted the subtle approaches from highly respected VIPs hinting that they would be prepared to pay for "extra private lessons" but some — not all — of our girls and boys indicated that they would be willing to comply. There was never any question of compulsion or coercion and, I can assure you, none of them was under age. I'd never allow that.' Gloria looked exhausted, as if she hadn't slept. She took another sip of coffee.

'Although my staff were well paid, many of them simply needed extra money to send home to elderly parents in Paris or to pay a child's school fees. In the end, I succumbed to the growing pressure to expand our range of services and we adapted the Académie to accommodate members' various predilections, which included the addition of a dungeon. You'd be surprised how much demand there was for those kind of activities.'

'No, we wouldn't, madam,' growled Bugsy. 'We have to deal with all kinds of filth in this job.'

'But I swear to you, Inspector Dawes, I knew nothing of Lucien's wicked blackmail or I should have put a stop to him. When he suggested security cameras in all the rooms, I sincerely believed they were for the protection of our staff, not a means of extorting money. The security room was always kept locked. Nobody but Lucien was allowed in there on pain of dismissal. It was in that room, using the computers, that Lucien did our accounts. I don't even know how to work a computer but he was a very astute businessman.' She paused momentarily to compose herself. 'I always knew he had a cruel, ruthless streak from the way he treated his girl-friends. He inherited it from his father. But I never believed him capable of murder. I can hardly believe it now, even though he admitted it to me. I think the worst part was that he told me as if he'd done something to be proud of, boasted of his cleverness, and I was in no state to argue. There was almost a gleam in his eyes when he described to me, quite dispassionately, how he had squeezed the life out of Fiddler and then shot Martin Laidlaw in the head. He even took a macabre pleasure in showing me the gun. His only regret was that he'd been found out.'

'Tell me about Sebastian Whittington,' said Jack.

'That wasn't murder, Inspector. That was a terrible and tragic accident. Sebastian was a regular, late-night user of our dungeon facilities.'

'With Sadie,' said Malone.

'Yes, Sadie was his favourite. She won't be punished for his death, will she? It really wasn't her fault.'

'How did it happen?'

'Sadie told me some time ago that she was becoming increasingly anxious about Sebastian because at every session, he wanted her to go further, inflict more pain, until he sustained significant injuries. He had a "safe word", of course, like all our BDSM clients. It was "bluebell" but he would never say it, although she begged him. On that last night, she had gone as far as she was prepared to and was about to tell him she wanted to stop when the poor man had a heart attack and died. Right there on the rack. Sadie panicked and called Lucien on her intercom. By the time he got there, she was hysterical. She was very fond of Sebastian. Lucien told her to go home and he would deal with it.'

'And he dealt with it by hacking off Whittington's head, hands and genitals and dumping his body in the Thames,' said Malone. 'Why didn't he call for an ambulance? It's what most decent people would have done.'

'I think you already know the answer to that, Sergeant. He was hoping it would take some time for the body to be identified. Maybe it never would be if the river carried it away. And the dismembered parts should have been set in concrete and lost for ever. If you had discovered Sebastian had been to the Académie the night he disappeared and had sustained injuries consistent with sexual activity, our very lucrative business would have been finished.'

'And you went along with that?' asked Jack. 'You were happy that Whittington's widow and children might never have known the truth about what happened to him?'

She sighed again. 'No, of course I wasn't happy. But the poor man was dead. Nothing we did was going to harm him after that. And I'm not sure his widow wanted to know the truth, did she? Try to understand my quandary, Inspector. A number of people depended on me for their living and that of their families. It would have been irresponsible of me to jeopardize all that for a dead man.'

'You do realize,' barked Malone, leaning towards her and shoving his face threateningly into hers, 'that failure to report a death, complicity in the dismemberment and unlawful disposal of a body and conspiracy to pervert the course of justice are serious criminal offences punishable by imprisonment — never mind running a bloody knocking shop! I think you should reconsider your decision about having a solicitor present, madam.' Bugsy reckoned he could nail her with a few more charges once he'd had time to think about it.

Jack put a restraining hand on his sergeant's arm. 'Were you aware that your son used to dress as a woman?'

It was obvious from her shocked expression that she was not. She swallowed and took a steadying breath. 'No, Inspector. I had no idea Lucien wore women's clothes. I never saw him like that and neither, to my knowledge, did anyone else in the organization. I had always believed him to be completely conventional, sexually. He had a number of girlfriends including Jennifer Laidlaw, so he told me. I knew nothing of any cross-dressing.' However, now that she did know about it, it explained the feminine underwear she had found in his drawer which he claimed had been left behind by one of his mistresses. And why sometimes his lips were very red, as if he had been wearing lipstick, and he had sometimes smelled of exotic perfume rather than manly aftershave. Gloria lowered her head and stared into her empty coffee mug. 'He kept that part of his private life very secret.'

'Even from his mother?'

She was silent for a very long time and now appeared to be staring straight through them to the far wall. Jack wondered from her ashen appearance if she was feeling ill and he would have to suspend the interview and get the police surgeon to look at her. A door slammed somewhere outside and a phone rang in the next room. Footsteps clattered up the corridor and voices chattered and laughed as they passed the door. Then silence again. Jack waited. The recording machine whirred softly. Bugsy raised his eyebrows, suggesting a break but Jack shook his head. A break could give her a chance to change her story. Finally, she spoke:

'I think it's time I told you, Inspector, that Lucien wasn't my son, even though it was I who brought him up. But I never told him I wasn't his real mother, not even at the end.'

Jack was taken completely by surprise. He thought he had the whole case sewn up, worked out every detail of it, but he hadn't foreseen this. 'I'm sorry, Mrs De Vere, I don't understand. If you're not his mother, then who is?'

'It's a long story, Mr Dawes.'

'Take your time. None of us is going anywhere.'

She took a deep breath. 'Helena Devereux, the bag lady you knew as Smelly Nellie, was . . . my sister. And I can't begin to describe the grief and misery I felt when she was killed, especially as I was unable to express it openly.'

Blimey, thought Jack. That explained why Gloria had taken financial responsibility for what was to be a very expensive funeral. But it didn't explain why one sister had been living in luxury while the other had been living rough.

Gloria continued her story, anxious now to get everything into the open. 'We were both born "Devereux" and we were, indeed, descended from Robert Devereux, second Earl of Essex. But I shortened my surname to De Vere when I became a dancer. I thought it sounded more artistic and would be easier to pronounce than "Devereux". In 1958, after Helena had "come out" as one of the last debutantes, the family moved to Paris so that I could study the ballet. I was twelve and Helena was just over seventeen. Six years later, our parents were killed in a car crash. But although we were grown up and Nell was older than me, it became my job to look after her. Nowadays, she would be described as having "learning difficulties" or diagnosed as suffering from some kind of "syndrome". In those days, she was just dismissed as "simple" or "half-witted" or even worse — "retarded". Despite that, Helena was very beautiful and she had a naive, delicate charm that made her very attractive to men. Although I had trained for the ballet, I had grown too tall and muscular to get work so I joined the Bluebell Girls and we managed very well, with Helena looking after our flat while I went out and earned the money. However, her condition became much worse and she needed more care, so I had to give up dancing.'

Gloria paused, clearly uncomfortable with what she was about to tell them. 'I loved my sister very much, Inspector, so in order to keep us and spend more time with her, I became a prostitute. At first I worked the streets of Paris at night while she slept, then, as I became more successful, I had a number of regular clients who came to our flat. One of them was a coarse, uncouth butcher, a bestial little man who could be both vicious and cruel. One day, I was late returning home from the hypermarket and he arrived early for his regular session. Helena let him in and, excited by her nubile figure and child-like innocence, he raped her. Brutally and violently. She became pregnant as a result and Lucien was born.'

The effort of reliving her harrowing past was etched on Gloria's face. 'Helena was so traumatized by the experience, her already fragile mind couldn't cope and she responded by making herself as dirty and unattractive as possible. And being too terrified to stay indoors in case the man came back, she wandered the streets, pushing an empty pram with her imaginary "baby" in it while I brought up her real baby. Try as I might, I couldn't persuade her to live indoors and to compel her distressed her even further. She would have nothing at all to do with Lucien and stayed right away from him, so I was never obliged to explain.'

Jack had always wondered what it was that had pushed such a lovely young woman into neglect and vagrancy. Now he knew and was full of pity for her and the tragic ending to a tragic life.

Gloria continued. 'Now I had three mouths to feed and I was fortunate enough to get a job as a ballet teacher. It paid reasonably well and I could take Lucien with me, which is how he came to love the ballet.

'Then, a few years ago, I had an unbelievable piece of luck. One of the clients from my days as a prostitute, a kind man but solitary with no relatives or friends, died and left me a great deal of money. I used it to move back to England and set us up in the De Vere Académie de Danse. Nell still insisted on living rough so I just kept a close eye on her, allowed her to eat in our kitchens and provided shelter outdoors in bad weather. Lucien despised her. He would chase her away if he caught her hanging about outside. He said she lowered the tone of the Académie and was bad for business. And then, at the end, he confessed to me that he knew who had killed her, but he was so indifferent to the death of an innocent human being that he had used the knowledge to extort money rather than seek justice. How could I possibly tell him she was his mother after that?'

Jack was speechless for a while. Unbelievably, so was Bugsy.

She smiled bleakly. 'Shall I be let out for Lucien's funeral, Inspector? I want him to be buried in his favourite Italian suit.'

You'll be lucky, thought Bugsy. They could put what's left of him in the top pocket, wrapped in his poncey silk handkerchief.

'I'm sure that can be arranged,' said Jack. 'Now, I think we need to take a written statement from you, Mrs De Vere.' Jack stood up, removed the tape from the machine and handed it to PC Garsmold. 'It's all there on tape. Get it typed up and Mrs De Vere will sign it.'

'What will happen to me, Inspector?' Her voice was toneless.

'I really don't know. That's for the Crown Prosecution Service and then the court to decide. There will be the charges as outlined by Sergeant Malone but if your defence lawyer can prove you had nothing to do with blackmail or murder, the court may be more lenient. You may even get a suspended sentence and a hefty fine.'

She shrugged. 'I don't think I care any longer, Inspector. The two people I loved most in the world are dead, my sister and her son, both crushed to death in road accidents.' The irony of this made her bow her head and sniff back tears, it doesn't really matter what happens to me now, does it?'

CHAPTER TWENTY-FOUR

'Are you sure you're well enough to go back to work tomorrow?' It was Sunday morning, just over a week since Corrie had been bashed on the head. Jack had cooked breakfast: the full works including mushrooms, black pudding and hash browns — his favourite. He dished it all up on one of Corrie's large, catering platters then carried it upstairs on a tray, so they could share it in bed. 'The doctor said that was a hell of a wallop you took. You could still get delayed concussion, you know.'

'Nonsense, I'm fine. Yum.' Corrie harpooned a sausage on her fork, dipped one end in ketchup and the other in a fried egg. Then she bit pieces off, alternately. 'I'm catering a cocktail party for Sir Barnaby tomorrow evening.'

'Are the Garwoods going?'

'Naturally.'

Jack took two slices of buttered toast from the mound he'd made and sandwiched rashers of bacon and a fried egg between them. 'In that case,' he mumbled, yolk running down his chin, 'it will be an evening of self-congratulation and a rehearsal for their anticipated promotion celebrations.'

'All the usual upper-class crowd are going. Annabelle Whittington hasn't been invited, though. Cynthia says Sir

Barnaby has cut off all communications with Annabelle with indecent haste since her deceased husband's hobby was made public. She says it was only a week ago that he was all over her, holding her hand and smirking in an overfamiliar manner that you don't expect from a Grand Master. She reckons Annabelle was the reason he'd started leaving his vest off and using dandruff shampoo.' Corrie smiled to herself. 'He could have had an entirely different reason, of course.'

Jack grinned. 'If he's short of guests, he could invite Gloria De Vere and Jennifer Laidlaw. They're both out on bail at the moment.'

'I hardly think so, do you?'

'I daresay we shall see a number of Kings Richington's finest taking a hasty step backwards now that MIT has exposed the corruption in their midst.'

'The worm in their golden apple,' mused Corrie, fancifully. 'Speaking of worms, what about the hypocrites who had committed crimes and got away with it? Were the forensic boffins able to recover any of the names I saw on Lucien's laptop?'

'No, unfortunately. He did a thorough job with that dancing trophy. The computer was totally demolished. Mind you, there were a few twitching sphincters amongst top brass when they found out De Vere had copied the hard disk on to a memory stick before he made a run for it. They found it in his pocket when they scraped him off the bypass. It was squashed flat, though, like him.'

'What a poisonous little swine Lucien De Vere turned out to be,' observed Corrie, pinching the last sausage.

'That's not what you said when you were dancing with him,' observed Jack, wryly. '"Drop-dead gorgeous", was what you said. "Thigh muscles like an Aberdeen Angus".'

'I didn't know then that he killed people, did I? And anyway, what about you at the Hermaphrodite Club? Standing up and cheering with your tongue hanging out.'

'I was just pretending so as not to blow my cover. I knew Jacinthe Des Bois was De Vere in drag all along. He didn't fool me for a moment.'

'You fibber!' squealed Corrie, incensed. 'You didn't know anything of the sort. "What an absolutely stunner!" you said. "A real corker!" You fancied her . . . I mean, him . . . like mad. Never mind all those "ladies" in expensive gowns, sitting along the bar, waiting to be picked up.'

'Nonsense. I knew they were all men the minute I walked in. I'm just an incredibly good actor, that's all.'

'Just as well,' said Corrie, 'because you're a lousy dancer. Incidentally, d'you remember those evening dresses of Gloria's, the ones on the rail in the security room? I said there was something odd about them that didn't add up. I've realized what it was.'

'They were too short for her.'

'That's right. She's over six feet tall and they were made for someone about five-foot-two or three. They were Lucien's weren't they? That man really did have the sulphurous breath of the devil about him.'

'That bang on the head seems to have knocked some sense into you.'

She grinned impishly. 'It can't have. I'm still here, looking after you, aren't I?'

'You won't do it again, though, will you? Seriously, Corrie. You have to promise me you won't interfere, ever again.'

'How's Jonathan coming along?' Corrie changed the subject seamlessly.

'Sitting up and taking notice, apparently. He'll be allowed visitors soon. Bugsy and I have been told to go later in the week, when he's stronger.'

'I'm really glad he's going to be all right. I'll come with you and take him some tasty nibbles. I expect his appetite needs reviving.'

* * *

'I feel a bit sorry for Gloria.' Corrie was setting out a variety of mouth-watering appetisers on the overbed table across the foot of Pinkney's hospital bed. Jack and Bugsy pulled up chairs on either side. Up the head end, heavily bandaged and still tethered to a drip, the patient had been instructed not to move in case he started bleeding again. Pinkney looked pretty good for someone who had only recently lost several pints of blood and had two bullets excavated from his chest. He was delighted to see the food because he was starving. He'd eaten very little in hospital as they only gave him tiny portions of easily digestible stuff, like poached fish and milk pudding, both of which he hated. The smell of the savouries was making his stomach rumble.

'I don't feel sorry for her.' Bugsy passed one of Corrie's lamb samosas to Jack then wolfed down four himself. 'If she'd kept a closer eye on that slimy little sod she called a son, she'd have found out what he was up to before he started killing people.'

'I agree, Bugsy,' said Corrie, 'but the worst crime *she* committed was allowing her Dance Académie to be used as a brothel. That and tacit agreement to the gruesome disposal of Sebastian in order to keep it a secret. What do you think will happen to her, Jack? After all, you could argue that the men involved — the "platinum" members with "extra services" bluebells against their name — are no less guilty than Gloria. And there were plenty of them, all rich, distinguished and self-righteous. Don't forget, I saw the membership list and the kind of services they bought, before Lucien wrecked the laptop.' She tapped her forehead. 'I have information stored in this brain that could bring down dynasties. It's just a shame I have such a lousy memory.'

'It depends how far a jury is prepared to permit the criminal law to control and punish the acts of consenting adults.' Jack helped himself to one of Corrie's smoked salmon blinis which, like the rest of the food, were still out of the hungry patient's reach. Pinkney was starting to feel like Tantalus, hanging from a tree with sustenance just out of reach and cursed with unending hunger. Every time Tantalus tried to get it, the food would recede out of his reach for eternity. In

Pinkney's case, this meant by way of Sergeant Malone. He coughed painfully and joined in the debate, so they would remember he was there.

'I think you'll find the law is rather contradictory with regard to this kind of thing, Mrs Dawes. In the UK, prostitution itself is actually legal, but most of the activities that surround it, like soliciting, operating a brothel or pimping, are illegal, making it virtually impossible to engage in prostitution without breaking any laws.' He sank back on to his pillows, exhausted from the effort.

Corrie nodded. 'When you come right down to it, Jonathan, exchanging participation in sexual activities for money or other goods has always been legal. It's what our grandmothers did when they got married. Nowadays, it's arguably less complicated to charge for your sexual skills than your cooking skills. You need certificates and a licence for that.'

'Given the influence and clout of Gloria's customers,' said Bugsy through a mouthful of chocolate cheesecake, 'I reckon they'll want the whole case wrapped up fast and with least fuss and publicity. They won't want her on the stand, grassing like a lawnmower, and that just might be to her advantage. CPS will probably struggle to make all of the mud stick and the men involved will slide into the background like sh . . . er . . . manure off a shiny shovel.'

'I understand now why Gloria didn't publish her photograph on the website,' wheezed Pinkney. 'There was just a chance one of her old "clients" in France might have recognized her from her prostitute days. Granted, it was a long time ago but these things happen, don't they? Look at the school reunion sites and the disasters they've sometimes caused. But what finally put you on to Lucien De Vere, sir? We all thought we were looking for a woman.'

'It was when forensics matched the dabs on the blackmail note to the fingerprints on one of the items I took from De Vere's Académie, the night Corrie and I had a lesson there. It was a champagne glass, the one that Lucien De Vere drank from. And I knew his would be the only prints on it because the waiter who served it wore white gloves. On the face of it, it seemed impossible because the florist had said the person who ordered the bouquets of roses and put the note in the envelope was an attractive woman.'

'Given how crafty the little sod had been, that was a bit careless of him, wasn't it, guv? Leaving his prints on the blackmail note.'

'Not really. He knew we didn't have his fingerprints on record and he didn't imagine for a single moment that Annabelle Whittington would hand the note over to the police. He believed she would be sufficiently disgusted to destroy it immediately, which is exactly what she did with the first note and the picture of Sebastian on the rack.'

'You cheat, Jack!' accused Corrie, suddenly realizing what he'd done. 'You said you hadn't pinched anything from De Vere's.'

'So did you,' countered Jack. 'But I won't arrest you this time, because the items you nicked gave me the answer.' He explained to Pinkney. 'Mrs Dawes broke into a locked room and stole two cards from the pocket of Lucien De Vere's jacket, DC Pinkney. One was a membership card for the Hermaphrodite Club.'

'Right.' Pinkney perked up slightly. 'And hermaphrodite means dual gender so it was a gay club. Now I'm beginning to understand, sir.'

'The other was the business card of the Harley Street surgeon from Dubai who was at the Whittingtons' anniversary party. He was also in the audience at the Hermaphrodite Club, presumably admiring some of his handiwork. While everyone was cheering and clapping Lucien De Vere's drag act as Jacinthe Des Bois, my wife pointed out the surgeon and told me his main line of work. Two words that I thought I hadn't heard at the time, but when I got the fingerprint match they came back to me with resounding clarity. The two words were "gender reassignment". The Dubai surgeon specializes in sex-change operations.'

'Christ Almighty! Do you reckon De Vere was planning to have it all chopped off, guv? You know, the full monty, with any leftover bits stuffed inside?' asked Bugsy. He reached for a sausage roll and bit it in half, wincing.

'I doubt it. I think Lucien dressed as a woman initially because he was AC/DC. He batted for both sides. There's evidence that the surgeon did some cosmetic work on him during his "holidays" in Dubai to make him more convincing when he performed as Jacinthe Des Bois. When Pinkney helpfully translated that name as "bluebell", it finally confirmed my thinking. In the end, De Vere had become a kind of third sex, like the lady boys in Bangkok. He used his "dual gender" to conceal his identity when it suited him. He could change his appearance at will and made us think we were looking for a woman. It was almost as if he was playing some kind of deadly game with us.'

Bugsy sniffed. 'I can't believe Old Mother De Vere didn't know her little boy was doing a drag act. When we questioned her, she claimed he was straight as a die and she didn't know anything about his association with the plastic surgeon.'

'I don't think she did,' said Jack. 'And I believe Lucien was dressed as a woman when he bashed Corrie over the head. She could smell his perfume. It was a busy Friday evening and I think it pleased him to go about the Académie wearing an evening dress occasionally and enjoy the fact that nobody recognized him, not even Gloria. I suspect some of the randy old men even made a pass at him, which he would have found hugely amusing, laughing at them behind their backs.'

'Did nobody honestly realize he was a man?' asked Pinkney, finding it hard to believe.

'You didn't see him as Jacinthe Des Bois, Pinkney. He was very convincing,' said Jack, trying not to look at Corrie. 'He nearly fooled me at first.'

'I know what you mean,' said Bugsy. 'I saw some of 'em when I worked in Vice. These blokes aren't just sad old queens with false tits and camp voices. These are men who can turn themselves into beautiful, desirable women. Bloody frightening, I can tell you.'

'It all makes sense, now,' said Pinkney. 'De Vere was the sporty, dark-haired woman who sent the blackmail demands, the glamorous blonde the brigadier's wife saw, and he would have been the woman who went into the ladies' loo to pick up Annabelle Whittington's blackmail money if we hadn't put a stop to him.'

Jack nodded. 'He was also Jennifer Laidlaw's lover. She said he made her call him Jas. Short for Jacinthe, I suppose — his idea of a joke. And I reckon he didn't want her blurting out his real name to her husband while she was stoned, although it wouldn't have mattered because Laidlaw knew about their affair anyway.'

'Did he?' asked Corrie, surprised.

'Oh yes. The manager of the anonymous little hotel they used for their assignations used to be the manager of the local supermarket. The store was new when Laidlaw was first elected and the Laidlaws were invited to open it. Naturally, Jennifer Laidlaw forgot the manager instantly but he recognized her all right as soon as she turned up in his hotel giving a false name. Being a fellow socialist and a public-spirited sort of chap, he thought it his duty to tell Laidlaw.'

'Why the hell didn't Laidlaw do something about it?' asked Bugsy.

'Because by then, he didn't much care who Jennifer screwed but he thought Lucien De Vere, being manager of the most exclusive club in Kings Richington, might in some way be able to ease his acceptance by the rich, influential set, so he turned a blind eye. But, of course, when the blackmail started, Laidlaw knew exactly who was at the back of it and went after him.'

'I expect Lucien seduced Jennifer in the first place, hoping to get some dirt on a serving MP. I bet he couldn't believe his luck when she told him about the hit-and-run and how she'd actually killed someone. What a corrupt lot they really are,' said Corrie.

Bugsy snorted disgustedly. 'Jennifer bloody stupid Jiggle-Tits!'

'I take it you don't rate her intelligence very highly, Bugsy?' said Corrie.

'Well, put it this way, Mrs Dawes. If brains were taxable, she'd qualify for a rebate.'

'I agree. I hope Jennifer Laidlaw gets exactly what she deserves,' said Corrie.

'Which is, I trust, a fair trial,' replied Jack. 'But I'll be surprised if she goes to jail, not with her team of slick lawyers. They sprung her out on bail and she's been released into her parents' cognizance. I've no doubt their defence case will be a spectacular and expensive work of fiction.'

Pinkney looked disillusioned. 'I'd never have believed Mrs Laidlaw could kill someone and then leave the scene. She came across as a deeply sympathetic and caring person.'

'She is,' agreed Bugsy, 'as long as you don't mind getting run over. Did you know she's pregnant?'

'Blimey!' gasped Pinkney, then wished he hadn't, as a stab of pain pierced his chest. 'Is it De Vere's?'

Jack nodded. 'Almost certainly, but she's telling everyone it's Laidlaw's. She claims her affair with De Vere was a temporary aberration because she felt lonely and neglected as Laidlaw was always away on constituency business. It meant nothing and she only ever loved her husband. I suppose DNA would settle the paternity issue but she'll never consent and now that both men are dead there doesn't seem much point in getting a court order in seven months' time. Her lawyers are playing her up as a poor, grief-stricken, pregnant widow with a seven-year-old child, and she has supportive parents who are looking forward to another grandchild, albeit a posthumous one. They don't care if Laidlaw wasn't the father-they never approved of him anyhow. If it goes to court, it'll be a typical jury tear-jerker.'

'It was when Gloria discovered that De Vere had chosen to blackmail Jiggle-Tits rather than shop her to the police that she decided to hand him over rather than help him,' said Bugsy. 'Helena was his mother, even though he didn't know it, and Gloria couldn't bear the little bugger's callous, insensitive attitude towards her death.'

'Funny,' said Corrie. 'I'd never have clocked him for a murderer. He seemed so genuine.'

'All bleedin' nutters seem genuine to start with, Mrs Dawes,' said Bugsy, wryly.

'I wonder why Lucien didn't kill me?' mused Corrie. 'He could have, quite easily, and he'd killed twice already so he wasn't squeamish about it.'

'No need,' replied Jack. 'You hadn't seen him and he believed he was about to flee the country to the protection of his rich father. He also knew you were the much-loved wife of a copper who wouldn't hesitate to track him down and tear his heart out. Safer to leave you alive.'

Corrie smiled at him affectionately.

'That last sausage roll looks tasty, Mrs Dawes,' whimpered Pinkney, his voice faint for lack of nourishment.

'I heard Doreen Mackay was jubilant when she found out her brother's killer was dead,' said Corrie. 'Can't blame her, I suppose.'

'Fiddler was just a toy-town bandit who got out of his league,' observed Bugsy, stuffing the last sausage roll in whole. 'He was no match for De Vere.'

The ward door was suddenly flung open and Doctor Veronica Hardacre strode towards them on sturdy brown legs, tightly encased in her customary 60 denier support hose. She nodded a greeting to his visitors, then astonishingly, she bent and kissed Pinkney on the cheek, moustache bristling. Big Ron had never been known to kiss anybody and nobody had ever dared to kiss her. Pinkney gagged slightly on a pungent waft of formaldehyde.

'Hello, Jonathan.' Her stentorian tones carried down the ward, causing nervous patients to jump and reach for their call buttons. 'How are you feeling? I've brought you some "grapes".' She opened her autopsy bag, took out a bottle of champagne and slid it stealthily down in the bed beside him, underneath the hospital counterpane. 'I've just been looking at your X-rays. One bullet lodged in your sternum out of harm's way and the other penetrated your thorax and settled just below your scapula. It clipped one or two of your more important organs en route but nothing terminal. Mind you, there was one point, when they were pumping in all those pints of blood that I thought I should have to make room for you in my mortuary. You're a very lucky young man.'

Pinkney thanked the doctor sincerely for the champagne but silently hoped he wouldn't get this lucky ever again.

'Of course,' she boomed. 'I can understand why you clung to life so tenaciously at the scene of the shooting. The alternative would have been to risk Sergeant Malone giving you mouth-to-mouth resuscitation. Too ghastly to even contemplate.' Ignoring Bugsy's feigned display of hurt, she turned to Jack. 'I can confirm, Detective Inspector Dawes, that the bullets plucked from DC Pinkney's chest were fired from the same gun that killed Laidlaw. But then you already knew that. Looks like you and your team have actually succeeded in solving a very intricate case.' She smiled mischievously. 'Don't let anyone call you a bunch of idle, useless tossers ever again.' She reverted to her customary severity: 'If you make a real effort, do you think you might get through the rest of the week without finding any more cadavers? I'm hoping to go on holiday next Sunday.'

'Somewhere nice?' ventured Corrie, politely.

'Cairo,' said Big Ron. 'I'm going to look at some of the lesser known Egyptian burial sites and their mummification processes.' Her heavy features lightened as they always did when she was talking about her favourite subject. 'The viscera were normally removed from the thoracic and abdominal cavities through an incision in the left flank, but in some instances, they were removed through the anus. Fascinating, don't you think?'

'Blinding,' muttered Malone. 'Like pulling tripe through a key hole.'

Doctor Hardacre gathered up her bag. 'Well, take care of yourself, Jonathan, and don't let this reprobate lead you astray.' As she passed Bugsy, she grabbed a generous handful of his midriff and squeezed. He yelped with pain. 'I think you may have lost some weight, Sergeant Malone.'

Bugsy winked at Pinkney. 'Good. Maybe I'll be able to run a bit faster in future.' He watched her stump off on walnut-coloured legs and tried to resist his enduring vision of two sizzling sausages, about to burst.

As Big Ron went out, she held the door open for PC Julie Molesworth who was on her way in, loaded down with flowers, magazines, a basket of fruit, chocolates and a huge, romantic get-well card. Staggering towards them, she spotted Pinkney and beamed, happy to see him sitting up. He beamed back.

'Come on, guv,' said Bugsy. 'Time we left. Mustn't overexcite the lad.' He winked. 'We'll leave that to PC Molesworth.'

'What a pretty girl,' said Corrie wistfully, sensing romance in the air.

'She may look like a delicate little flower,' said Jack, 'but you should have seen the way she kneed that big security guard in the goolies when we raided De Vere's.'

Bugsy wagged a finger at Pinkney. 'Not half. You'd better watch it, son. One twang of her bra strap and that could be you, bent double and gasping for breath.'

They turned to go and Malone permitted himself a theatrical smiting of palm to moon-like forehead. 'Well, blow me, Pinkney. It looks like we've eaten all that nice food that Mrs Dawes brought for you. What's the matter, son? Not hungry? Never mind, you'll soon get your appetite back.'

EPILOGUE

The photograph on the front page of the *Kings Richington Herald* showed Commander Sir Barnaby Featherstonehaugh of the Metropolitan Police in his best dress uniform. He was standing smartly to attention while smiling at the camera in what he believed was an authoritative but compassionate manner. He had taken over responsibility for the press conference from George Garwood on the basis that he felt the occasion demanded more gravitas than a mere Chief Superintendent could convey. He didn't want the public to feel that they'd been short changed, that the police weren't treating the recent crimes with sufficient sincerity. Such a shocking assault on the sensibilities of Kings Richington residents should not only be dealt with, it should be seen to be dealt with, and at a high level. Added to which, he was the senior officer and if there was any media kudos to be had, he was the one to have it.

* * *

'Jack, come and read this.' Corrie had spread the newspaper on the kitchen table and he came and glanced briefly over her shoulder. There was a formal statement below Sir Barnaby's picture and further down, a subheading that read: JUDGE SENTENCES BROTHEL 'MADAM' GLORIA DE VERE. The report covered the recent sentencing of Madame Gloria De Vere and lower down, that of Jennifer Laidlaw, widow of the late Martin Laidlaw, MP.

'I'm glad they didn't send Gloria to prison,' said Corrie. 'She was already a broken woman and jail would have finished the job.'

Jack nodded. 'Her lawyers got her acquitted of any involvement in the blackmail and murders. There was never really any doubt that Lucien had been solely responsible. Gloria pleaded guilty to complicity in concealing Whittington's death, unlawful disposal of his body and offences under the 1751 Disorderly Houses Act.'

'I wonder what she'll do now?' said Corrie.

'I heard she paid her fine, sold up and went back to Paris. Many of her girls who scattered during the raid are believed to have gone with her. They reckon she's planning to form them into a dance troupe.'

'Good for her. I hope she succeeds and is able to salvage a few crumbs of happiness from what's left of her life.' Corrie's sympathetic expression altered to one of animosity. 'I shouldn't have minded seeing Jennifer Laidlaw banged up, though. She's a lying, self-centred, unscrupulous drunk who slaughters innocent pedestrians.'

'Say what you mean, sweetheart. No point in being subtle.' Jack tended to agree, though. The woman had had more than a fair trial, thanks to her team of silver-tongued lawyers and a few funny handshakes Jack had observed outside the court. She had got off too lightly, in his opinion.

They had proof that she'd hit Helena Devereux because forensics had found traces of her blood on the Range Rover. But the CPS had gone easy on her, mainly because they couldn't prove she was over the limit at the time or that she had been speeding or driving dangerously. No witnesses had ever come forward, and tyre marks at the scene were inconclusive. And Annabelle Whittington, whose gracious life was now in ruins, said she couldn't remember how much champagne Jennifer Laidlaw had drunk at the dinner party and neither, strangely, could any of the other guests. The Kings Richington wise-monkey code of conduct had been invoked so no charges of vehicular manslaughter were ever brought.

At the trial, defence counsel claimed that the tragic accident had been caused by Helena Devereux suddenly lurching into the notoriously badly lit road, without warning, and on a murky, rainy night. Mrs Laidlaw had had no opportunity at all to take evasive action, despite the fact that she was travelling well below the speed limit for a built-up area. He also pointed out that the unfortunate victim was known to have learning difficulties and there were recorded incidents of her 'near misses' when crossing the road on many previous occasions. It was only a matter of time before some luckless driver accidentally ran her over.

The QC told the jury that Mrs Laidlaw admitted she had panicked when she realized the severity of what had occurred. She had been concerned for her husband's political career and what would happen to her little boy if she were to be unjustly blamed and sent to prison. This was why she had foolishly fled the scene without calling an ambulance and later undertaken repairs to her car without reporting it to the police. The barrister conceded that this was not a laudable reaction but it was an understandable one. He further stated that the defendant had been prostrate with remorse ever since and bitterly regretted her actions. Her attempt to conceal the accident had been an uncharacteristic error of judgement — an error which had been further exacerbated by the abrupt worsening of her migraine. A report from the Laidlaw's private family doctor confirmed that Jennifer was highly strung and suffered badly with her nerves. In his opinion, this could have caused her to act impulsively in a situation where she feared that the welfare of her loved ones might be threatened. Debbie, the nanny, when asked, confirmed cautiously that Mrs Laidlaw had seemed 'very upset' at the time. Jack pondered wryly that Lucien De Vere and Martin Laidlaw were the only witnesses who could have sworn unreservedly that Jennifer was a duplicitous, coldblooded cow who was lying through her teeth. But luckily for her, they were both dead.

In the end, a tearful Jennifer Laidlaw stood trembling and demure in the dock, face scrubbed clean of make-up and wearing a quiet grey suit to present an illusion of sobriety and humility. She pleaded guilty to failing to report an accident, leaving the scene and attempting to pervert the course of justice. In sentencing her, the judge said that while some blame must attach to the defendant, the prosecution had been unable to provide a shred of evidence to prove she had been driving carelessly, dangerously or under the influence of alcohol when the mentally challenged victim had stepped in front of her vehicle. In addition to the terrible burden of having terminated a life, however unintentionally, Mrs Laidlaw was now a grief-stricken widow who would have to live with the knowledge that her husband had been murdered by her lover while attempting to protect her from blackmail. These alone were severe and lasting punishments and he felt that nothing further would be gained by a custodial sentence. He must also take into account the welfare of her unborn child and her seven-year-old son.

And privately, outside of the court, he accepted the undertaking by her rich father with whom he played golf every Sunday, to 'take away that damn great car and keep her off the bloody streets!'.

A six-month suspended sentence, temporary loss of her licence and a £5,000 fine would mean nothing to Jennifer Laidlaw, thought Jack. She wouldn't even have to give up the booze.

'Have you read the commander's official statement?' asked Corrie.

Jack shook his head. 'It's just Barnaby blowing his own trumpet again.'

Corrie disagreed. 'It smacks more of damage limitation to me. Listen to this.' She read aloud the press release printed alongside the picture while Jack started to prepare welsh rarebit for their supper. One of his specialities.

The recent spate of serious crime in Kings Richington has rocked the local community. Police acted swiftly to apprehend the criminals and restore calm to this leafy suburb where, until now, incidents of homicide and prostitution were virtually unknown. The De Vere Académie de Danse, at the centre of the controversy, has now been closed and a full investigation is underway into the activities carried on there.

Metropolitan Police Commander Sir Barnaby Featherstonehaugh said: 'I am pleased to be able to report that the disturbing incidents of murder, extortion and organized vice in Kings Richington have been firmly stamped out by the police and the miscreants brought to justice. But I am not complacent. I want to do everything I can to ensure such offences cannot occur again.

'However, it is not enough for the police alone to fight crime. It is a task for the police and the community working together. If we are to achieve our aim of restoring Kings Richington to its former standing as a respectable town for decent people to live in, we need those people to do their part in making life impossible for criminals to infiltrate.

'In order for a criminal organization such as De Vere's Académie to prosper, support is required from the society in which it lives. Thus, it often seeks to corrupt some of its respected members, most commonly achieved through bribery or blackmail and the establishment of apparently symbiotic relationships with legitimate individuals. Judicial and police officers are especially targeted. Under these circumstances, criminals can operate with less fear of interference from law enforcement and may even demonstrate a semblance of affluence and respectability. It is imperative that we all recognize this insidious corrosion before it eats away at our cherished lifestyle. Lessons have been learned and, with your help, I shall toil tirelessly to keep our community safe.'

'The rest is a general moan about lack of sufficient officers and the funds to pay them,' said Corrie. 'I think it's quite good, on the whole. A bit pompous and self-justifying but those sort of statements usually are.'

'Barnaby is one of those people who hasn't got much to say but talks a lot.'

'Maybe. I think this time, though, he's firing a shot across the bows of the self-important stuffed-shirts who were happily taking full advantage of the available facilities in Gloria's Académie until all the scandal kicked off. Then they got the wind up and now they're denying all knowledge or responsibility.'

'It sounds to me like buck-passing. Barnaby is just trying to cover his arse,' said Jack, slicing bread for toast.

Corrie giggled. 'He should try harder.'

Jack stopped slicing and stared at her. 'How d'you mean?'

She hesitated. 'If I tell you something, do you swear not to repeat it to a living soul? Only I may have got it wrong. I do get things wrong — very occasionally.'

'Surely not, my little Wonder Woman,' said Jack. 'What is it that you may have got wrong on this occasion?'

'If you're going to be sarcastic, I shan't tell you.'

He grinned. 'Sorry. Carry on.'

'When I was in Lucien's security room, surrounded by all those monitors, I accidentally got them to work. Before he clobbered me, I mean.'

'I know. You told me. You said nothing was going on while you were looking at them. The rooms were all empty.'

She looked embarrassed. 'Well, actually, I fibbed a bit. One of the bedrooms was occupied.'

'Who was in there?' asked Jack. He put down the bread knife, his attention now drawn to something much more interesting than welsh rarebit. 'Was it anyone we know?'

'It might have been.'

'Well, come on. Who was it? What were they up to?'

'I'm not a voyeuse, Jack. If you remember, I was there at enormous personal risk to get vital evidence for your investigation. I didn't just sit there ogling the action. As soon as I realized what was happening, I switched it off.'

'Of course you did, sweetheart. So what were they doing?'

She stopped grating cheese and concentrated on remembering the more lurid bits. 'Well, there was this incredibly attractive young woman about twenty-five, very tall with masses of blonde hair and a voluptuous figure. French, most probably.'

'Was she naked?' asked Jack, trying not to dribble.

'No. She was wearing an old-fashioned nanny's outfit. You know, a sort of blue dress and frilly white apron, like Alice in Wonderland. But the skirt was very short, barely covering her knickers, and the bodice was so low cut, her breasts were nearly falling out. Stereotypical soft porn outfit. Sad, really.'

'Was she lying on the bed?' asked Jack, mopping his brow on a tea towel. 'You know, legs apart, all that stuff.'

'No. She was chasing a naked man around the bedroom.'

'Bloody hell! Who was it?'

'I couldn't say for sure.'

'Well, what did he look like?'

'It's hard to describe a naked man. They all look much the same without their clothes — sort of pasty and poorly finished.'

By this time, Jack's drooling curiosity had completely eclipsed his patience. 'You're doing this on purpose to wind me up! You must be able to describe some of him. You're always such a meticulous witness — you never miss a detail.'

'All right, I'll try. He was in his late fifties, I'd say. Dark hair going grey and thin on top. He had a fat paunch and man-boobs that wobbled up and down when he ran. Anyway, every time the girl caught him, she put him over her knee and spanked his bare bottom. It was white and pimply and it quivered, like smacking a huge jelly. The sound was on and I could hear him squealing like a piglet, each time she spanked him. "No, Nanny, stop it! Yes, harder! No, stop, Nanny!" He couldn't seem to make up his mind but he was obviously enjoying it enormously because he was . . . well, perky rather than passive, if you get my meaning. How undignified is that for a man of his rank and responsibility?'

Jack grinned from ear to ear. 'It wasn't really him, was it? I don't believe it.'

'Well, like I say, I couldn't swear to it. I didn't get a proper look, not full-face anyway. Bumshots aren't as conclusive as mugshots. But I'm ninety-nine per cent sure it was him because the girl was wearing a toy policeman's helmet and she was spanking him with a rolled up copy of the Metropolitan Police Annual Report.'

'That's absolutely priceless,' roared Jack, wiping away tears of laughter. He began to work out the logistics. 'You would have seen him on the monitor at around 6:30, wouldn't you? And we raided the place at seven. He must have got out by the skin of his teeth when he heard the sirens.' Jack capered about the kitchen, helpless with mirth. 'Every time I see him now, I shall have this mental picture of him hopping down the corridor to the fire escape with a smarting bum and one leg in his Y-fronts.'

He was still sniggering about the commander and his 'nanny', some minutes later. Optimistically, he put his hands around Corrie's waist. 'I don't suppose you feel like—'

'Certainly, not!' She whacked his fingers with a wooden spoon. 'And that welsh rarebit's going to burn if you don't take it out from under the grill.' She opened a bottle of Burgundy, poured two large glasses and glanced slyly at him, under her lashes. 'Maybe after supper. I'll keep my apron on.'

THE END

ALSO BY FRANCES LLOYD

FREE KINDLE BOOKS

Made in the USA
Columbia, SC
15 April 2020